The Snow Queen

MERCEDES LACKEY

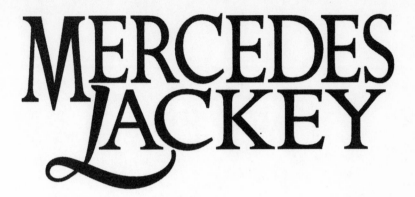

The Snow Queen

www.LUNA-Books.com

LUNA™

THE SNOW QUEEN

ISBN-13: 978-0-373-80265-4
ISBN-10:   0-373-80265-X

Copyright © 2008 by Mercedes Lackey

First hardcover printing: June 2008

Author Photo by Patti Perret

www.LUNA-Books.com

Printed in U.S.A.

Dedicated to the memory of

Alex the Grey

www.alexfoundation.org

Author Note

This has not been the best of years. It has not been the worst, either, but this year seems to have been fraught with things going wrong for everyone I know. Friends have lost family, lost jobs, lost health.

For me, this was the year of being nibbled to death by ducks. Every time we turned around, it seemed, something else went wrong. Illness seemed to haunt us. I lost not one, but *two* computers to lightning, the second not to the strike itself but to an EMP it generated…an EMP that also shorted *me* out for a few seconds. (I remember a bang…and then looking at a blank computer screen…and nothing in between.)

Soldiering on, the one thing I kept telling myself was that in all of this, I would get affirmations that people needed fantasy. When their lives were horrible, they always had a happily-ever-after to curl up with and make the world go away for a while. Heaven knows I certainly did. And I would hear that over and over from others—sitting in hospital waiting rooms or in hospital beds themselves, hiding in their bedrooms, finding a spot in the dorm where they could get away from roommates, in between job interviews...they would tell me they *read* to get away.

Dorothy L. Sayers used to say that mystery stories were the only moral fiction of the modern world—because in a mystery, you were guaranteed to see that the bad got punished, the good got rewarded and in the end all was made right.

I'd like to think that fantasy does the same thing. It reminds us that *this is how it should be,* and maybe if we all put our minds to it a little more, *this is how it will be.* The good will be rewarded. The bad will be punished. Sins will be forgiven.

And they will live happily ever after.

I hope you enjoy the Five Hundred Kingdoms novels.

1

"YOU'RE NOT LIKE ANY FAIRY GODMOTHER I EVER HEARD of," young Kay said, sullenly, his voice echoing in the enormous, and otherwise empty, throne room. He broke the silence and in doing so, created a reminder of how empty the room was. If Kay had taken the time to think—which he did not, because at the moment, the only thing he ever thought about was himself—he might have wondered why such a room existed here in the Palace of Ever-Winter at all. Aleksia did not hold audiences, nor have a Court. So far as he knew, there were only two living things in this palace: himself and her. So why would she need a huge throne room? Why would she need a throne room at all?

Such thoughts had not once crossed his self-involved mind; at least, not yet.

He did not shout; he was not the type to shout, and certainly there was no need in a room so quiet that even the faintest movement sounded as loud as a deliberate footfall. But his voice, midway between a tenor and a bass, was layered with frustration and anger, and had the distinct edge of a whine to it. It grated on Aleksia's nerves. *Kay* grated on Aleksia's nerves.

The throne room was austere magnificence itself, as was all of the

Palace. Walls that perfectly imitated snow were, in fact, the most pristine of white quartz. Floors that looked like clouded ice were marble. It was an enormous space, exactly like the interior of a pure-white egg. It was full of light, and when she was not keeping the temperature artificially low for the "benefit" of her "guests," it was warm and welcoming.

There were benches all around the circumference, also white, also of marble. Normally, they were softened with cushions of the palest blue velvet, but of course not when Kay was around. It was her intention to keep Kay as physically uncomfortable as possible while creating an illusion of comfort.

It was hard to ignore him; his presence itself would have shouted, even if he had not spoken at all. His black-velvet clothing and sable furs made an inky intrusion in the otherwise pure-white room—a very solid and substantial blot in the midst of light.

Black did not suit him, not even the lush black of velvet and fur that looked so soft it made the hand yearn to touch it; the lack of color, and the contrast of the very pure white of the surroundings, brought out the sallow tones of his skin, and made him look as if he had been sculpted out of raw piecrust. He was the one who insisted on wearing black, though. Presumably, he thought it made him look serious and to be reckoned with. He probably thought it made him look older. Most of her visitors did the same; it was as if there was a kind of unacknowledged uniform for the nonconformist.

She shifted a little, a very little, in her throne. The heavy, buttery silk of her gown, impregnated with warming spells, moved with her, sliding like cream over her arm. She did not immediately reply, letting the silence speak for her and make him uneasy.

Since Aleksia did not need to look at his expression to read his mood, she did not turn her attention away from the five-foot-tall mirror that she was watching with all the intensity of a hawk at a quivering bush hiding a rabbit.

The mirror was an incredible piece of work, both in terms of its craftsmanship and in what it was made of. This was a single flat sheet of ice nearly two inches thick, as clear as a pane of glass except when she wanted it to become reflective. It was held by a four-inch-thick, cloud-colored frame that was also made of ice, severe and plain, the surface so smooth that it seemed to deflect the curious finger. At the moment, the mirror was, indeed, reflecting something, but the reflection was not of herself, nor of Kay, but of another scene entirely. In the crystalline depths of the mirror, a tired-looking young girl was plodding through a forest.

She was, perhaps, sixteen or seventeen—a woman grown by most standards, though not by Aleksia's. She was blond and blue-eyed, with long golden plaits wrapped over her head like a kind of crown and just showing under the rabbit-fur cap. Her face was round, but not dumpy; she had a sweet expression, a pert nose and a mouth of the sort that made young men want to kiss it—full-lipped and soft and inviting. She was dressed as the more prosperous sort of village-dweller would dress, in a sturdy woolen dirndl in a cheerful red, that belled out around her ankles, a little white apron that had never seen the inside of a kitchen, a matching cloak in a darker red with a hood that could be pulled over the cap. On her feet were stout leather boots, also red, lined with rabbit fur, and mittens that matched her cap. Nothing more could be seen of her clothing beneath the cloak, but it could reasonably be assumed it was of equally good quality. She was burdened with a pack and used a polished wooden staff to help her along the path. And she looked entirely out of place there. It did not seem possible that such a person could be found in the middle of a forest; she belonged in a village square, buying embroidery yarn and gossiping with friends. Her cheeks should have been pink with exertion, but they were pale. Her eyes scanned the forest nervously, and her face showed her fear all too clearly.

The forest through which she was trudging was not the sort inclined to raise the spirits. "Gloomy" was probably the most flattering thing that could be said about it. There was no undergrowth, for the trees that crowded each other on either side of the dirt road blocked out the sun. Those trees were, for the most part, black pine, whose dark branches dripped water and occasionally sap, and dropped needles that carpeted the floor of the forest. Overhead, their branches formed a canopy so thick that not even a scrap of sky was visible. If there were birds, they were high up in the boughs and certainly not visible from the girl's point of view. There were no animals in sight, but one could easily imagine wolves or Bears lurking in the distance, suitably obscured by the closely crowded tree trunks. Even on the hottest of Summer days, this forest would be dank and chill. Now, in the Autumn, with sunset drawing near, it would be bitter under those trees. And it would be so damp that the cold would penetrate even the warmest of cloaks. Small wonder she was bundled up as she was.

There was no sound, though Aleksia could easily have it if she chose. Right now, though, she knew that all she would hear was oppressive silence, overlaid perhaps with the dripping of water onto a thick layer of dead needles, and the girl's soft footsteps, and perhaps the far-off call of a crow or some other bird of ill-omen. Hardly worth the trouble.

Kay, of course, could see none of this. All he saw was Aleksia staring into a mirror that cast no reflection. And ignoring him. He did not in the least appreciate being treated in this way. Aleksia caught his reflection off the ice. The corners of his mouth turned down farther, his eyes narrowed and a crease appeared between his brows. And then he spoiled it all, as his lower lip began to protrude in the start of a pout. For all that he allegedly wanted to be left alone, he hated being ignored. But then, Aleksia knew very well what was actually going on in her guest's mind.

"And you, of course, have such a *vast* experience of Fairy Godmothers," Aleksia finally answered him, in a voice that dripped with sarcasm the way that the trees in her mirror dripped moisture. Her voice rang crisp in the empty chamber—utterly calm, and maddening. At least, she hoped it was maddening. She shifted again, this time for the little pleasure of feeling the silk of her gown slip across her body.

Kay started at the sound of her voice, then glowered. He hated having his "authority" challenged even more than he disliked being ignored. Aleksia would have found it more amusing had she not played this same sort of scene over and over again with other guests in the past and would play it with still more in the future. Still. It was potentially as funny as watching an ill-tempered rabbit challenge a warhorse.

And that was a dangerous stance to take in the hall of one who could have sent him outside to be eaten by an ice-drake by merely snapping her fingers, but he was very young and utterly convinced of his own intelligence, knowledge and immortality. "I—" he began.

"Most of your sentences begin with *I,* and you might find it more profitable to find some other way to begin them," Aleksia continued, still not turning from the mirror. She wished that the next act of the drama she was watching would hurry up. She was regretting deciding to allow Kay to find her today—but this was the only mirror powerful enough to let her see all she needed to, from so far away, and she hated asking the Brownies to move it. "No one cares about *you.* You are an unlicked cub, a mere youth, barely out of childhood." She had been longing to say this for days; she might as well do so now. She began to warm to her subject and chose her words with care. "You have no experience worth hearing about, no store of wisdom from reading or studying with wiser men and your personality is repellant. There was but one person who loved you, and you persisted in thrusting her away. Instead, you wanted to be left alone to concentrate on your work. You were, in fact, injudicious enough to wish for just that out loud." She saw him start again, out of the corner of her eye. "So. I have given you that, on condition that you devote yourself to your work and make me wonders. There is a library here. There is a workshop. You only have but to say that you want something, and it appears. Go and make use of these resources, for which older and wiser men than you have pined and languished. And when you find something or make something you think *might* be worthy of my attention, you may bring it to me, provided I am not otherwise occupied, and provided you begin your sentence with some other word than *I*."

Reflected in the surface of the ice, Kay looked utterly, utterly shocked. No one had ever spoken to him like that before. He had been rather too much indulged and made much of by parents who thought he was clever; as a child, he'd had the best schooling and a mother and father who greeted every accomplishment as if he was the only boy in the universe to have achieved such things. And he was very clever, even Aleksia would admit that—but clever did not compensate for the level of self-absorption he had managed to achieve in seventeen years. When she had appeared before him on the night of the first frost—heralded by an out-of-season snowstorm—in her flying sleigh pulled by four snow-white reindeer, he had taken it as his due that such a creature should offer him her help. He had accepted her invitation, of course. There was never any doubt that would happen. He was too self-centered to consider that it could have been a trap.

And now he had been here for three weeks, seeing nothing and no one but Aleksia herself. She had made her servants and helpers invisible to him, so that he would be unaware how full the Palace really was, and so that he would be unable to talk to anyone. She had made herself unavailable to him as well, making it as clear as possible, without ever actually saying it, that she was far too important to cosset him.

And now, he found himself in the position of having everything he had asked for, and yet being subject to something he had never, in all his life, actually experienced before.

He was alone. There were no parents to praise him, no sweetheart to gaze at him with adoration, no rivals to triumph over or peers to boast to. There were not even any visible servants to question, look down upon or bully. It was just him and his own thoughts, and he was finding that an uncomfortable experience.

He was a prisoner in a cage made of gold and lined with silk, as isolated as any hermit-hunter snowed-in inside a mountain cabin. He took his meals alone, was attended but never contacted in any way, and only glimpsed her briefly, generally at a distance. Day by day, she watched him without his being aware of the fact, and saw it wear on him.

Today she had told the servants to allow him to find the throne room and her in it, rather than confusing his steps as they generally did. This was the result.

He *could* be redeemed—he would not be here, in the Palace of Ever-Winter, the home of the Ice Fairy, if he was not capable of redemption. The Tradition had made that part clear enough by building such an enormous store of magic about him that, if Aleksia had waited until Winter to fetch him, he would have found his initials written in frost on the windowpane, snowmen having taken on his features when he passed, and the cold having grown so bitter that wildlife would have been found frozen in place. Even so, things had gotten to the point that Ravens had taken to following him, which was a very ominous sign had he but known it. Presumably if Aleksia had done nothing, and no other wicked magician had discovered him and virtually eaten him alive for the sake of that power, he would have gone to the bad all by himself.

He was too self-centered and arrogant to have escaped that particular fate—and most likely, given his turn of mind, he would have become a Clockwork Artificer, one of those repellant individuals who tried to reduce everything to a matter of gears and levers, and tried to imprison life itself inside metal simulacrums. While not usually dangerous to the public at large the way, say, the average necromancer was, Clockwork Artificers could cause a great deal of unhappiness—and in their zeal to recreate life itself, sometimes resorted to murder.

Judging by the Ravens, Kay would have become one of that sort.

The only cure for this affliction was a shock, a great shock to the system. One that forced the youngster to confront himself, one that isolated him from the rest of the world immediately, rather than gradually. He had to lose those he still cared for, at least marginally, all at once. He had to learn that people meant something to him, before they ceased to.

"It's lonely here!" Kay complained, with a touch of shrillness, still not stirring from where he stood beside her throne. Well she certainly hoped it was! She would not have been doing her job otherwise.

She cast him a glance. Yes, definitely. He was unhappy, but not quite at the depth to which she wanted him to descend. Soon he would be profoundly unhappy, and he would understand just what it meant to get what you wish for, when what you wish for is to take yourself out of the ranks of humankind.

She looked back at the mirror to see shadows slipping through the tree trunks. Ah. There they are. It took two to make this dance, and Kay's little friend Gerda, the girl who loved him with all her heart, who was currently trudging toward the next episode in her own little drama, was the coconspirator in The Traditional Path that ended in a Clockwork Artificer. Her nature was as sweet as her face, her will as pliant as a grass-stem and her devotion to Kay unswerving, no matter how often he neglected her. She needed redemption almost as much as Kay did. Such women married their coldhearted beloveds, made every excuse for them, smoothed their paths to perdition, turned a blind eye to horrors and even, sometimes, participated in the horrors themselves on the assumption that the Beloved One knew best. Gerda required a spine, in short, and an outlook rather less myopic than the one she currently possessed. And this little quest she was on was about to give her one.

This had all been very carefully orchestrated, because if a Godmother didn't manipulate the participants in these dramas, The Tradition most certainly would. Everything had been planned to a nicety. Aleksia had called up a magical snowstorm in a very limited area around Kay's house. She had done so at an hour when she knew that Gerda would be in her little bedroom, probably looking out of her window, sighing at Kay's. When the snow began, Aleksia caused a gust of wind to drive a few hard snow pellets against Gerda's window to ensure that if she had not been looking out it before, she most certainly would be when Aleksia's flying sleigh came swooping out of the sky. It all worked, of course. As Kay studied the unseasonable snowflakes, Gerda was in place, watching from the window in plenty of time to see the sleigh land. Gerda saw Aleksia speaking to a dumbfounded Kay, saw her offer him her hand, saw her settle him in beside her, bundled in white furs, and saw the sleigh rocket off again.

Nor was that all. No Godmother worth her wand would leave things so half done. Aleksia had contacted one of the village Witches and made sure Gerda knew *who* had taken Kay, and in general, *where* he was.

Poor Gerda! Screwing up her courage to visit the Witch in the first place was only the beginning of her ordeal. She would never have believed it if she had been told the truth, that her childhood sweetheart was turning into a remote and arrogant elitist all by himself, so she had been told that the Snow Queen had done something to him as a child, made him coldhearted, so that she could whisk him off now. Gerda had also been told that she, and she alone, could melt Kay's heart and save him with her love—and being a young maiden of romantic nature, and wanting it to be true, she absolutely believed what she had been told.

Up until she had entered the forest, things had been relatively easy for her. Her sweet nature made people like her and want to help her. She had actually done very little walking up to this point; farmers had given her rides in carts, horsemen had taken her up behind them, peddlers had offered her space in their wagons. The trek into this forest, however, had been made without meeting anyone who could help, and at this point, she was footsore and very weary. Now she was about to find out that the quest was going to have a lot more hardship involved in it than a few blisters.

The shadows flitting through the woods, having ascertained that the girl was all alone, had surrounded her. Now they pounced—because they were robbers, and she was very tasty-looking prey.

The robbers materialized from among the tree trunks, crowing with glee at having caught such a pretty little prize. Gerda froze in abject fear; her mouth opened in a silent scream of terror and her face went as white as frost.

There. Nicely managed.

Aleksia dismissed the vision in the mirror with a thought and a simple wave of her hand, then turned to Kay. She schooled her face into an expressionless mask. She must seem as remote as a snow statue now. Mostly she was feeling a mixture of amusement and annoyance. Amusement, because Kay had no idea he was not unique, that he was treading a path already worn down by countless others. Annoyance, because, well, Kay was Kay.

"It is *lonely* here, because that is what you asked for," she said, crisply, thinking that she was going to be only too glad to have this over and done with. He was intelligent enough, or so she hoped, that she would not have to go through this speech more than once. "Or do you fail to remember?"

"Remember?" Kay's handsome brow furled. And he was a handsome young fellow, as blond and blue-eyed as Gerda. If his chiseled features habitually wore an expression as cold and forbidding as that on the marble bust of a religious fanatic—when he wasn't pouting like a spoiled child told there was no candy forthcoming—that didn't make the arrangement of his features less pleasing. If his natural complexion was too fair to wear black well, he was certainly handsome enough in other colors. And on the rare occasion that he smiled, his face was quite transformed, and showed exactly why Gerda had fallen in love. There was a heart in there. It just needed waking up. And if anyone *could* wake it, it would be Aleksia. This was not the first such guest she'd had in the Palace of Ever-Winter, and he would not be the last.

"Yes. Remember." Aleksia looked down at him from the lofty height of her "ice" throne—carved crystal made to look like spires and shards of ice that was cunningly provided with a spell that made it warm as a living thing when *she* sat on it, but as cold as what it looked like if anyone else dared set derriere to seat.

Kay had, of course, made the attempt, and been discomfited before he got much of a chance to make himself at home. She had watched, invisible, as he had given up after not too very long.

He was always cold, here. The very food was cold, or lukewarm at best. His bed was cold at night and did not warm up until his shivering body warmed it. The temperature in the rooms he roamed was always chill. His clothing was, unlike hers, just a trifle...thin; the fur trim did nothing but look soft, and the velvet was not thick enough to keep the chill away. Hers, when she must share the same space as he did, was warm and sometimes fur-lined; even her hands were kept warm—with a tiny touch of magic.

He, who had always thought that Winter brought perfection, who preferred Winter because it brought snowflakes, glass-smooth ponds and all ugliness covered with pure white, now was coming to find that he did not desire the cold nearly as much as he had thought.

He looked baffled; she sighed with feigned impatience. "The night when you and Gerda saw the falling star," she elaborated. "You both made wishes. *You* wished that you could go somewhere far from people, where you would not be bothered anymore, and where you could have time for your studies and inventions." She waved a hand at the implied expanse of the Palace beyond the throne room. "You wished that it would always be Winter, so that perfection could be preserved. You desired that you should be served invisibly, imperceptibly, so that nothing could intrude on your thoughts. Here you have all that. I fail to see why you are less than content." She made a shooing motion. "Go. Study. I brought you here so that you could create wonders. Leave me in peace until you have something to show me."

Long habit made it possible for her to repress her smile as Kay slouched out of the room. His shoulders were hunched, his hands balled into fists at his sides. He was angry but at the moment, he was not sure who to be angry with. *Himself?* He had gotten what he asked for. *Her?* She had given him what he asked for. As yet, he did not look any deeper than that. She hoped that he would, that he would see the fundamental wrongness of what he wanted, and why. Otherwise—well, something else would have to be done about him.

Any urge to smile faded once he was gone; she did not want to have to think about what would happen if she could not salvage him. She failed very rarely, but when she did fail, it meant she must act as an evil magician would—drain him of the magic building around him and place him somewhere that it could not build again. With some primitive tribe perhaps, but certainly in a land where he did not know the language and could not ever become a Clockwork Artificer. This would effectively ruin two lives, his and the girl's.

She shook her head to clear it of the melancholy thought. She had not lost yet. She was not even close to that point.

She surveyed her surroundings with a sigh. Other than the benches around the walls, the only two pieces of furniture were the clear crystal throne and the clear ice mirror. She would have used crystal there, too—except that she *was* the Ice Fairy. The Tradition made it so much easier to enchant things if they were made of ice.

Dear gods, she was tired to death of ice.

She left the throne room, moving silently as the kiss of snow through the long white corridors of her Palace. She, of course, could see the servants polishing, cleaning, making sure nothing marred the pristine white surfaces. The walls alternated smooth panels with carved ones, bas-reliefs of mountains, snow-covered forests, iced-over lakes, ice-caves. No humans appeared in these carvings, only the birds and animals of Winter. White Bears, foxes, deer, white Gyrfalcons, white Peregrines, snow-hares. She paused at the carving of her very own mountain and put her hand to the peak. The magic recognized her, and the entire panel slid aside. Scented warmth billowed out to embrace her as she stepped into her suite of rooms.

Here, at last, in her quarters, where no one was allowed to come but her Brownie servants, there was not one speck of white. It was all fire colors, the warmest of scarlets and browns and golds, like the red, beating heart of the Palace. The sweet scent of applewood wreathed around her. There was a huge hearth where there was always a fire burning, and standing beside windows that looked out over the trackless snow around her home were delicately nurtured plants in terracotta pots. She had, in effect, her own garden, complete with trees that reached to the lofty ceiling and gave the lie to the name Ever-Winter.

If she had not had that, she would have gone mad. Doubtless, nearly every other Ice Fairy had felt the same, since the trees and the warm private rooms had been here when she was first apprenticed—and it took a long time to grow potted trees that tall. Aleksia had changed very little except the color scheme; Veroushkha, the previous Godmother, had favored deep rose-pinks rather than scarlet and brown.

Aleksia moved forward into the embrace of her rooms, then waited while one of the maidservant Brownies unlaced her gown and slid it from her shoulders where it pooled around her feet. She shook her hair free of the crystal-topped pins, and the Brownie wrapped her in a soft, quilted-silk robe. She stood before her fire for a moment, then settled into a nest of cushions, to reflect on the odd turns of her life that had brought her here.

Aleksia was unique among the Godmothers; most of them were involved with reprimands and rewards in equal measure. Like all of them, she had been beset by a plague of magic when she had been apprenticed by Veroushka. In her case, had all the surrounding circumstances matched up, she would have been a Snow White. She had everything that was needed: she was pale as a Snow Maiden; her hair was as white as the moon; she had a sister as rosy as a flower in Summer. Their mother died in their infancy; their father remarried a Witch.

However, their new stepmother was as kind as anyone could have asked. When her own child died in infancy, she did not turn vile to the little girls. Instead, she cherished them the more. As they grew, she tried to find husbands for them that they would like—and both understood that, as they were princesses, the needs of the Kingdom came before their own. Both were prepared to wed dutifully.

But their Kingdom had a very good Godmother, who made sure to intervene at all the right times. She counseled Aleksia's stepmother when the baby died, spending long hours with her that Aleksia only now understood. She spent equally long hours with the nannies and governesses, so that Aleksia and Katya grew up as decent human beings rather than spoiled, pampered brats.

And it all paid off, although at first it certainly had not seemed that way when Katya was stricken with a terrible wasting illness. Everyone had despaired. Until a strange fellow appeared, claiming to be a doctor—and cured her.

She could still remember how she had been so suspicious of this fellow, who had looked nothing like any doctor she had ever seen. He had looked like a cross between a gentleman fallen on hard times and an utter vagabond. She had been sure he was a fraud.

He was nothing of the sort, of course. He was another of that massive tribe of wandering Princes, who scoured the Five Hundred Kingdoms hoping that something would happen to give them their own happy ending. He had, in the proper fashion, befriended a Salmon, who had advised him to undergo a quest to this very Palace, the Palace of Ever-Winter, and beg for one of the fruits of the trees of what was then Veroushka's chamber. Which he did. And, of course, the fruit was the magical cure for Katya's wasting disease.

The Prince, having no Kingdom of his own, was overjoyed to settle in theirs and become a son to their father and stepmother. Katya adored him. Prince Kobe was kind, clever, and if not handsome, was certainly not bad to look on. He loved music and books, preferring them to hunting and hawking, although he certainly knew one end of a blade from the other, and could fight very well if he needed to.

The trouble was, the music and books he adored were the same ones Aleksia loved. They both excelled at chess and games of strategy, while Katya found pleasure only in watching. Kobe went out of his way to be kind to Aleksia, and Aleksia found herself, all unwilling, watching her sister's happiness bitterly. She grew thin, and wretched, fighting the impetus to hate her sister and desire Prince Kobe. And everything was in place for Aleksia to become the despised jealous sister who murders her sibling and steals her husband.

She passed her hand over her eyes for a moment, still feeling the ache of that terrible jealousy. She had been poised equally between killing her sister and killing herself.

Until Veroushka showed up with another plan entirely, for now there was more than enough magic building up around Aleksia to fuel her spells for three or four times her own lifetime, what with not one, but *two* Traditional paths twined around her.

Veroushka proposed to apprentice Aleksia. Desperate for anything that would remove her from this intolerable situation—though she herself had not yet understood that she was being forced into it— Aleksia quickly agreed to go with her.

And it was here, in this Palace, that Aleksia learned what *really* steered the lives and fortunes of the people of the Five Hundred Kingdoms.

The Tradition, that implacable, faceless magical force that attempted to turn the lives of the people of the Five Hundred Kingdoms into time-worn paths dictated by myths and legends, tales and fables, was a force that the Godmothers in their turn did their best to manipulate and sometimes thwart. Take the well-known tale of the Cinder Girl. Not every girl with a vile stepmother and two equally repugnant stepsisters had an available Prince to rescue her from her life of drudgery, and not every available Prince was....suitable. Some were children, some were dotards, some were rakes and roués, some were...well, they would have preferred to save a beleaguered step*son* from a wicked stepmother. And yet, The Tradition would place incredible magical pressure on those whose lives outwardly conformed to a familiar story.

It was a Godmother's task to identify these poor souls, and somehow give them a life free of the further regard of The Tradition. Aleksia's own Godmother had managed to save her and her sister from attempted murder, by turning their tale from that of Snow White and Rose Red into that of the Wasting Princess. And once it became clear that Aleksia was going the way of the Jealous Sister, Veroushka came to the rescue, as Godmothers *had* to do when they could.

Because if they did not…sometimes things could go horribly, horribly wrong. Not only were there Traditional, tragic tales, there were also other dangers. With so much magic building up around the ones whose tales were thwarted by circumstance, they became prey for evil magicians and sorcerers, who would take them and drain the magic for their own use, thus not only killing the hapless victim, but giving themselves more fuel for further vile deeds. And sometimes the object of The Tradition's regard went to the bad. Or, as in what almost happened to Aleksia, The Tradition forced them into terrible deeds.

Not every tale has a happy ending, after all. Aleksia knew that only too well. She had been witness to some of the terrible endings, having come too late to be of any service. There were few Godmothers up here, and a great deal of territory to cover. She could not be everywhere. And there were places, dark places, even now, where the best she could do was confine the damage.

And so, most of the Godmothers had the pleasant task of rewarding and helping the deserving, or at least the innocent, as well as administering The Traditional rebukes and punishments to the Villains and preventing as many unhappy endings as they could. There were, of course, no end of Traditional tales about the unworthy getting their comeuppance, and no end of ways some of those people could be redeemed through trials. Or, if they could be caught in time, a few could be recruited into the ranks of the Wizards and Godmothers themselves.

Magic and the long, long study of tales and lore were the provenance of the Godmothers. They were aided in this by the wide ranks of the Witches and Wizards, the sorcerers and enchantresses, who served as their eyes and ears, and sometimes hands. Veroushka taught Aleksia much, gave her the tools to learn the rest and then—left.

And Aleksia, feeling as unready as any other who took up the mantle of Fairy Godmother, became the Ice Fairy of the Palace of Ever-Winter.

But of all of the Godmothers that Aleksia knew, only she was the Fairy Godmother in charge of—for lack of a better term—"Be careful what you wish for."

Maybe it was the remoteness of her location. The Palace of Ever-Winter was located high in the mountains, where the snow never melted, which made transportation a bit difficult and visits by those in need of Godmotherly help as much of a trial as the tribulations themselves. But there had been an Ice Fairy—sometimes called the Snow Queen—here at this place for as long as there had been Godmothers, and when Aleksia had been groomed for the position, it had not really seemed such an onerous one. In fact, since she had a rather solitary and slightly aloof nature, it had seemed ideal.

And possibly it was the nature of the position of Ice Fairy and the Palace she commanded itself. Certainly, no one was much inclined to attribute warmth and loving with names like those.... And The Tradition could work its will on Godmothers just as readily as on anyone else.

And Aleksia was by now very, very tired of it.

She was tired of playing the cold hostess to youths like Kay, who were obnoxious at the beginning of their tenancy and only became tolerable near the time when they were to leave. And at that point, of course, *she* had become the enemy, and they didn't care to offer her more than the briefest nod of grudging courtesy. She was tired of the isolation; the Brownies were good little folk, but there were times when all she wanted was to sit in a village tavern, have a nice bowl of soup and some fresh bread, and listen to ordinary gossip. She didn't visit her family anymore; that was just a disaster. People tiptoed around her, even her own twin, and acted as if they expected her to curse them with icicles if she were the least little bit provoked.

And besides, every time she went there, it seemed that there was yet another child. Now, Aleksia enjoyed children in moderation. They could be very amusing. But she preferred to be able to give them back to mothers or nursemaids in an hour or so, and in the Palace...well, there was no escaping the children, because Katya had gotten this notion that it would be a fine thing for all of the nobles to send their offspring to the Palace to provide playmates and schoolmates for her brood. They were *everywhere*.

And *they* looked at her as if they expected her to curse them with icicles.

She sighed and stared at her fire—and managed to refrain from making any wishes herself. Wishes were dangerous things, as Kay had proved. She was not going to wish for anything stronger than that one of the servants would bring her a snack. Presently, one of the Brownies brought her cakes and tea, and she took up the book that had been lying there. The cakes were sweet and nutty, dense and moist; the tea was one of her favorites, with the flavor of almonds. The book was utterly forgettable, very light verse, but it was something to read, at least.

From time to time, she looked up into a small mirror on a stand that held her plate of cakes and her cup. In it, she could see Kay laboring in his workshop. He seemed to be grinding lenses. She frowned.

"What's the cleverest lad in the world think he's doing now, Pieter?" she asked the Brownie who came to refresh her tea. The little fellow, who looked exactly like her sister's majordomo shrunk down to the size of a child, wrinkled his nose with amusement.

"He's making spectacles that will allow him to see us," Pieter replied, chuckling, as his bright brown eyes twinkled. "He seems to think we're spirits or something of the sort."

Aleksia sniffed. "He'd know better if he had paid half as much attention to his old nurse's stories as he did to taking things apart," she replied, and grimaced. "This is the *most* tedious stage of beating them into shape. Has he started trying to find a way to escape yet?"

"Not yet, Godmother. He's just starting to feel the edge of loneliness. It hasn't really dawned on him yet that it only gets worse with time." The Brownie offered honey for the tea; she tendered a nod of acceptance. "In my opinion?"

"Your opinions are invariably good ones, Pieter." She sipped the tea and felt the warmth penetrate into her chilled bones.

The corners of the Brownie's eyes crinkled as he smiled. Pieter had a wise face that would have looked very old indeed if it had not been for the perpetual hint of mischief about him. "It's time to give him a view. We're going to get a blizzard. Let him see it. I would say 'throw another log on the fire under him,' except that we really want the opposite effect." Pieter chuckled at his own cleverness.

Aleksia smiled. "The result is the same, a rise in discomfort. All right." She concentrated a moment, holding her hand palm-upwards, until a tiny spark of white light wafted up out of her hand, hovered there for a few moments, then evaporated. That was her way of getting the attention of the Palace.

The homes of all the Godmothers, whether they were Palaces like this one, fortified castles, lonely towers, or any other sort of dwelling, were living things. They responded to the needs of the Godmothers living there. Some of them were so good at it that entire rooms would grow before the Godmother herself realized she was going to need one. But some, like this one, needed prodding to wake them up.

Veroushka always assumed it was because of the Palace's immense age, but Aleksia had the feeling it had more to do with *where* it was. The

Palace slumbered like a hibernating Bear, and whenever she needed to communicate with it, she always got the sense that she was looking in on its dreams.

Presently, she sensed a difference in the room around her, and the mirror frosted over. Dim images that were certainly not Kay in his workshop moved behind the frost, pale figures that could have been human, or Elves, or spirits, or none of these things. She felt the sense of *waiting* all around her.

"I would like windows in the boy's rooms now, please," she said aloud. "Like mine, if you would, quite weather and leakproof. I don't need him getting ill from drafts."

She waited. The Palace generally took its time about these things.

Finally, the mirror cleared and showed her a view of one of Kay's two rooms. Now, instead of a blank, white wall, there stood an enormous glass-paned window, which looked down the mountain that the Palace stood on and across the valley to the unexplored peaks beyond. Everything was shrouded in a blanket of snow, of course, and it seemed waist-deep in most places. The mountains on the other side of the valley thrust their white peaks aggressively into the sky; the black storm clouds gathering just behind them provided a suitably ominous view should Kay return to his room before sunset.

"Thank you!" Aleksia said. Strictly speaking, it wasn't needful to thank the Palace, but she always did anyway.

The mirror cleared again, giving her a view of nothing more than her own reflected image.

"That looks like a bad storm," the Brownie observed. Aleksia nodded. Her own rooms faced east and south, rather than west and north. She disliked being able to see the storms approaching; the wait before clouds finally descended and let loose their burden of snow always seemed worse to her than the blizzard itself.

But there was no doubt this would have a profound impact on Kay. She could only hope that it would be for the better.

Because if it was for the worse...

She was going to wall him up in that workroom of his rather than be forced to listen to him whine and pout anymore. And she did not want to contemplate what she would have to do if he turned down any darker path.

ANNUKKA MAKELA SAT AT HER LOOM AND WOVE STEADILY,
the soft woolen threads of her own spinning forming solid, equally soft
fabric beneath her hands. The rhythm soothed her, as she passed the
shuttle through the warp threads, tamped them down with a double-
beat and passed the shuttle through again. Thread by thread, the fine
brown woolen cloth built up beneath her hands; thread by thread, the
subtle spell of warmth and protection she wove built with it. This was
simple magic, hearth-and-fireside magic. So far as Annukka was concerned, magic was no special gift, and most women of the Sammi could
do it, if they put their minds to it, if they took the time to learn how
to concentrate in just the right way. The lives of the Sammi were inter-
twined with small magics. For most women, such things could be as
natural as breathing, if they learned the tricks of it.

But most women didn't. In this, Annukka was special.

Annukka was not certain why; it seemed a logical thing, to her. If
you intended to keep your family safe, why not weave magic into their
clothing? Yes, it took a little more time, you couldn't just sit mindlessly
at your loom and let the monotonous back and forth of the shuttle in

your hand dull your mind. You had to think, to concentrate, to call up all the tales of narrow escapes and loved ones come safely home through peril. You almost had to speak to the power of magic the way you would make a prayer. To Annukka's mind, the effort was more than worth the reward, for what wife wouldn't want to protect her children or keep her husband safe?

But then…there was that edge of danger about magic. It didn't always answer in the way you thought it would. And there was always a cost to it, too. The whisper of power that Annukka put into threads she wove had to come from somewhere, and that somewhere was generally her. Weaving in this way meant she tired far sooner than she would have had she been weaving ordinary cloth. When the power did not come from her directly, she generally found herself being shoved into doing something that was always inconvenient, and sometimes a bit dangerous. So even though this was very minor magic in the making, there were repercussions.

Repercussions, Annukka thought to herself, as the sun warmed her back, as she listened to the birds in the eaves outside, as she took in the scent of wood smoke and the roasting fish that her neighbor was making for supper. *There are always repercussions to everything, magical or not. Most people just don't trouble themselves to see them.*

But weaving in this way meant that the cloak she would make from this fabric would not only keep the wearer warm no matter how killing the cold, it would deflect the mind of a pursuing hunter, so that the wearer would escape. There were wolves out there, and Bears, and uncanny things that were far, far worse than either. A cloak woven with magic would not come amiss.

This was women's magic, subtle and supple, and not like the magic of the Wonder-smiths, and the Warrior-Mages—magic that cut across the fabric of the world and pulled it into the shape that the man-magicians wanted. Women's magic worked with the elements, rather than against them, wove through the threads of everyday life as Annukka wove her spell through the threads of her fabric. It took far more time to master than the sort that the men generally used, so perhaps this was why so few troubled themselves to do so. It took putting part of your heart into it, too. You had to care, and care deeply, to use this magic. Emotion became part of will.

The last of the afternoon sun made the wooden walls of the room glow as if they had been gilded, and it warmed her as she sat before the loom. Outside the window, her bees droned in the borage planted along the cottage walls. It would be time to take the last collection of honey, soon, before she left the hives alone to store their over Winter supplies. Time for the last brewing of mead; Annukka smiled to think of the taste of that mead on a Winter night, sweet and sharp at once, and holding the memory of Summer in it. Time soon to collect nuts in the forest, herbs for Winter medicines and teas. Harvest was coming, and this cloak she was weaving would be needed to drive the cold Winter winds away.

There were no other sounds within these walls but those of her weaving. Annukka lived alone on the edge of the great forest of firs, above the Viridian River. It had not always been so. She had once had a beloved husband, but he had taken her to wife in his old age and had lived only long enough to see their son grow to a stripling. Mikka had built this house with his own two hands, long before he had married her, and there was not a finer house in all of the village. Her friends teased her that she had married him for this house—but no, she had married him for himself.

What a man he had been! His hair, once golden, still had gold threads among the silver, and his open, honest face had remained curiously unlined right up until the day he died. The only wrinkles were those around his bright blue eyes, and they deepened when he smiled. He had not been handsome; his jaw was too long, his nose too beaklike for that. But she would not have had him look any other way. She still missed him, his kindness, his strength of character, missed the feeling of his arms around her, sheltering her, missed the gentleness of his hands.

The house was very like the man, plain, sturdy, substantial, sheltering. The walls were of peeled logs, matched for size, fitted so closely together that they hardly needed any chinking, and the Winter winds never whistled between them as they did in other homes. The house boasted two floors and three rooms, which was one floor and one room more than most.

Two of those rooms were on the lower level, which had a wooden plank floor painstakingly smoothed until not even a thought of a splinter remained. One small room was the bedroom that Annukka had shared with her husband, and that now she slept in alone. The other held a big table that Mikka had also made, and two fine benches to sit at, as well as Annukka's loom, spinning wheel and three stools that were works of art. Here was the hearth where she did her cooking, built from stones brought up from the river, and the kitchen cupboard, stout enough to keep out a Bear, cunningly fitted together so tightly not even the most determined mouse could find a way inside. The second floor, reached by ladder, had been their son's as soon as he could climb unaided. It was empty now, and she used it to store fleeces and bundles of herbs.

The pot simmering over the fire this late-Autumn afternoon breathed forth a savory aroma, and the bread just pulled from the oven built into the side of the fireplace added its scent to that of the soup. But there was only one wooden bowl and one carved spoon laid out on the table, for her son Veikko had gone in the Spring to seek his Teacher.

Their people, the Sammi, did not have a King; they were one of the few lands that did not. Towns rarely housed more than a thousand people, and villages were much smaller. Half the population tended the migrating reindeer herds, which made it difficult to have a settled life. In Winter, the deer were always on the move, foraging for food as they traced paths through the trackless wilderness. Only in Summer could these folk settle, as their herds settled to graze on lush meadows and drop their calves.

Life moved at the pace of the land here, not the pace of man. As their fathers and their father's fathers had done, so did the people here. In Spring, the reindeer herds returned, to join the sheep and goats at their grazing, and with them, the herders. It was a slow life, but hardly a dull one. Those Bears, wolves and uncanny things found deer and man equally tasty; the storms of Winter could be unpredictable and equally deadly. In other lands, not one person in a hundred had to contend with the kinds of dangers that faced the Sammi every day.

And in other lands, a child would probably have been forced into the paths of his or her parents. But not here.

And Annukka would not have had things any other way. *Even if our ways have sent my son far from home.*

Tradition was not so important here as being good at what you did. Sometimes Annukka wondered if that had to do with need, or with the fact that there was no single ruler here and no ruling hierarchy. With no king, and no order of landowning nobility beneath him, there was no one to answer to except to one's own neighbors, who were not likely to take "because I said so" as an appropriate answer.

She smiled at that thought. *We are a stubborn people, we Sammi. A King would have a hard time with us.*

Whatever the cause was, when a child came of age, his or her runes were cast, and it was those runes that predicted the future for that child. Not what was to happen, but what he was to become.

There was, for instance, the rune of the Herder, which meant you would tend domestic animals of one sort or another. There was Hunter, of course, which was self-explanatory, and Home, which meant you would do well with all possible domestic skills. Those marked with Healing were very much sought after, as were those of the Forge. There was the Salmon for Fishing, the rare rune of Fellowship—which meant the skill to lead people. More common than Forge was Craft for the smaller handicrafts, and Wood for the hewers and shapers. Rarer than Fellowship was Singer, which covered not only the making of music, but the composing of it, and the ability to play one or many instruments. Last of all were two that were seldom seen in these parts, Warrior and Mage.

The boys and girls whose runes had been cast to follow the deer—the Herding rune with the Wanderer—took over the work of watching, tending, doctoring and milking them, under the direction of the adults. When the last of the frost left the fields, they were sown by those whose runes had marked them forever with the Plough.

For in the land of the Sammi, the man did not choose the occupation, the occupation chose the man. And at twelve, based on one's runes, the child took its first steps into the adult world.

Annukka smiled again to think of her son. Never had she seen a boy more confident than he was at that age. The runes had not surprised him; it was as if he had known from the time he was born what they would say, and he greeted the reading with a laugh and a nod.

She passed her hand over the cloth already woven, to make sure the weft was consistent, and felt the tiny tingle of the magic there.

It was possible to get mixed runes, of course; that was considered very, very lucky. All runestones had a blank side and an inscribed side, and it was theoretically possible for *all* of them to turn up inscribed, though Annukka had never, ever heard of *that* happening. Usually, not more than one or two showed their faces in a given reading. Three was highly unusual. Four, almost unheard of.

Annukka was a mixed-rune child, of Hearth, Craft and Mage, although the Wise Woman who had cast them only whispered that third into her parents' ears, and Annukka had not known, until the woman returned to teach her the Mage skills two years later, that she had been so marked. The Mage rune meant that she had the power, the ability, to do much more than the little domestic magics that all women could do. She had been schooled in some of the greater ones, magics that would permit her to do extraordinary things.

She had used them no more than once or twice a year in her youth—only when the need was very great indeed. Even now, she did not much use the magic except in small things like her weaving, as the Wise Woman had taught her; the use of it could attract some evil to the user, and by extension, to her people. And so she had never become even so much as a Wise Woman, much less one of the Wizardly kind.

Veikko had also gotten mixed runes, Warrior and Mage. Most boys at twelve would have practically turned themselves inside out to get such runes. He had been calm—so calm! Happy, yes, even content. But also calm and sure. But there were no teachers for either the path of the Warrior or that of the Magician in so small a village—oh, everyone could use weapons, but not with the skill that could be attained by one so rune-marked. And as for Magic—how was she to teach the hard path of the Magic? She only knew the earth-ways, not the Iron-ways. Accordingly, he had waited until he was a fairly skilled warrior by village standards, then went in search of a Warrior Magician to teach him. For that, too, was the way of the Sammi; if a teacher did not come to you, it was up to you to find the teacher. Perhaps so many generations of following the reindeer herds had made them more willing to go great distances in order to obtain a desired goal.

He had left behind not only his mother, but his sweetheart, Kaari—Kaari, the darling of the village, Kaari of the sweet voice and gentle hand, with hair like spun sunlight and the face of a flower. Their parting had been a reluctant one; Veikko would much rather that a teacher had come to him. Annukka loved the girl almost as much as her son did, and would gladly have had her living in the house as a daughter. But Kaari would not hear of it, refused to displace Annukka from the place she had held for so long. "When Veikko returns, we will have a house of our own," she said with quiet certainty. "I will never displace you, Mother Annukka. This will always be *your* place."

Truth to tell, that had pleased Annukka. She had not been looking forward to giving up her room and the big bed to Veikko and Kaari, of having to climb that ladder to the loft every night, nor to eventually having to lose the peace of her working to the wails of babies and the mischief of toddlers. She had made the offer twice more after Veikko left, and had been twice refused with the same gentle courtesy. That made it final by Sammi custom. And so Kaari remained in her father's house—though Annukka did not stint on gifts of her own making for the bride-chest. This cloak, for instance, was intended for Kaari, and besides protection, Annukka was weaving in a wealth of love.

She brushed her hand over the warp-threads and listened to the whisper, like the ghost of a harp-thrum. She gathered to herself the warmth of the sun on her back, the memory of this golden afternoon, and wove that, too, into her cloth.

The sun was westering, and even though the garden was warm and inviting—the earth giving up a scent of rich life, the herbs reminding her with their mingled aromas that she needed to be gathering and drying them—it was time to get more water for dinner, and that was Kaari's job.

It was laundry day as well—also Kaari's job. She liked laundry day; there was something infinitely satisfying about spreading the freshly washed things to dry, although she could do without carrying the baskets of wet clothing up from the edge of the river. Squinting a little against the later afternoon sun, Kaari arranged the wooden yoke over her shoulders, balanced the buckets on the hooks on either end of it and headed for the well at the center of the village. Her mother was too old to be burdened with this now, and her brothers were all at their own work, so that left her. Of course, for Kaari, every trip to the well took twice as long as it did for anyone except the most inveterate of gossips. Everyone had to stop and greet her, so that had to factor into the time she took. And even though it was the last thing she wanted to do on a day already overfilled with chores, she had to stop as well. It was, after all, the polite thing to do. And by now, her parents were more than used to it.

Virtually everything she did that brought her out of the house took more time because of this. And it was all because of her runes. Sometimes she thought that if she heard one more person tell her, "You must be the luckiest girl in the world," she was going to do something drastic. Scream, anyway. But of course, she never did, because she fundamentally had too sweet a temper. Having runes like hers—well, she suspected that you either had a sweet temper to begin with, or you got one in a hurry, because you had to.

Or else you went to the bad…and that did not bear thinking about.

When Kaari was born, her runes were read then and there, because there was a Wise Woman already in the village reading for several older children. It was unusual, but by no means unheard of, for an infant to be read, and since the woman was there, her parents must have thought, "What's the harm?" And at that time, the Wise Woman had pulled a strange face, for three runes had turned up instead of the usual one or two. Hearth, as expected. Also Craft.

But then came the third rune, one that her parents didn't recognize, the one that the Wise Woman pursed her lips over. She told them not to worry about it, and went on her way, with only a single, slightly odd, admonition.

"Don't spoil her."

Not that they were likely to do anything of the sort. She might have been the baby of the family, but it was a very large family, with many hands reaching for, and many mouths clamoring for, anything that happened to be desirable. Her brothers only considered another sister to be another nuisance. Her sisters already had enough of babysitting to regard the arrival of yet another child with resignation. Kaari had been destined to go through childhood wearing the hand-me-downs of four sisters, mended and re-dyed, turned and turned again, or cut down from much larger garments. Her toys were those her siblings had outgrown. She slept packed in the bed with all four of her older sisters, either too warm in the middle, or hanging on for dear life to her sliver of bed on the edge.

And yet, she had sailed through her childhood with no real difficulty. By nature sweet-tempered, by the gift of the gods a lovely child, the older she grew, the more everyone wanted her around and made a kind of pet out of her, even her siblings. If it was a lean season, people found ways of slipping her tidbits; if the season was bountiful, they still slipped her treats, but always the juiciest apple, the most succulent grape, the most perfect venison pasty. Older children took her with them on adventures or dressed her up like a kind of live doll; younger ones looked at her in awe. And no one thought twice about it.

Not until Kaari came of age and the same Wise Woman read her runes again, did she discover what that third one was. Because it turned up again.

Kaari could still see it, in her mind's eye, the little brown stone, flat, speckled with white, and the strange rune she could not read carved into it and filled with black paint. It had looked so harmless, and yet there was some feeling of portent about it, a heaviness in her chest, the sense that something was watching her.

"This rune," the woman had said, stirring the stone with her finger. "This rune is Heart."

Kaari and her parents had looked at her askance. None of them had ever heard of such a thing.

"You must have noticed how everyone loves Kaari," the woman had continued.

Kaari's mother and father had nodded. Of course they had, because by then, even the most sour-tempered old curmudgeon smiled to see her. On the very rare occasions when she got into naughtiness, it was always something mild, usually because she was the unknowing accomplice of an older child, and was immediately sorry for the results. Her peers made her the center of their games, and if it was work that was afoot, they made sure it went along with such singing and chatter that it seemed half play.

"And you've noticed she's not spoiled by all this." Again the old woman had stirred the rune. "That is the effect of Heart. It is a power that can bring people together. But it is a double-edged sword. It can cause quarrels, when everyone wants to be first in her eyes—and more quarrels will come in the future, when boys think about courting her in truth. The older she gets the more careful she will have to be. When everyone wants to love and be loved by a person with the Heart rune, that can spawn jealousy, envy, acrimony. As yet, it has not expressed itself too much in her life in that way. That will change before long. Trust me."

They had sent Kaari away then, and spent long hours that night talking. It had given Kaari an uncomfortable feeling, knowing that they were talking about her—all because of this Heart rune. Surely she could give it up! Surely this was something that she could decide to have nothing to do with!

A ridiculous notion, of course. The runes were only the expression of what you already were. Gradually, over time, she had learned herself what all this meant. For as she grew older, those innocent little flirtations over frogs became something a great deal more serious. When husbands said with enthusiasm how pretty she was growing, wives began to be troubled. When mothers complimented her, their own daughters wondered, even as they walked arm in arm with her, why their own mothers didn't find *them* as sweet-natured or as pretty or as clever. Everyone wanted to be her best friend, but having someone as a *best* friend means that someone else must be second-best.

Then things got even more complicated.

It is a sad thing to have a boy fall in love with you when you do not love him in turn. It is worse when someone else is already in love with that boy, or wants to be. Brothers can fall out over such a things, and sisters take sides. Mothers and fathers wonder why you cannot see all the good qualities in their sons. Slowly, Kaari had learned how to tell these boys that she could not be theirs in such a way as to make their heartbreak less—for heartbreak there would be; there was no getting around it. Slowly, she had learned how to shape things so that she became the ally of other girls in love. She learned, too, how to turn away the less-innocent advances of older—and often married!— men.

It was sad for her, too, for she realized by then that she could never be sure if someone loved her for herself, or because of her runes. She had to look on even the most handsome of boys with skepticism when they protested their love. Oh, yes, the Heart rune was the expression of her nature, and she *did* give her affections generously, but—

She frowned a little at that memory, and brushed her hair, worn loosely, like all the village maidens, out of her eyes as she sighed with reminiscence. Even now, when she was betrothed, she had to forcefully discourage protests of love, and sometimes more than mere protests. In fact, she often said that it was only because Annukka was going to be her mother-in-law, and everyone in the village suspected that kind of sorcerous power Annukka could wield if she chose to, that someone hadn't tried something…unfortunate. No one, however, wished to spend even a few hours as a frog—or, much more likely, find himself dressing up in a gown and apron and doing all of Annukka's household chores until Annukka decided that the offense had been paid for.

Fortunately, at this time of day, all the young men were off working. They would not return from the fields, river and forest—or be released from the tasks of an apprentice—until dusk. So Kaari was unlikely to encounter any of the most susceptible.

It was a difficult dance; sometimes all but impossible. Impossible not to create some heartbreak, impossible not to invoke some resentment. And so very, very hard to remain friends with everyone involved.

And then things became even more complicated—if that was possible—once she was betrothed. Kaari had always been the confidant of her playmates, now she found herself being confessed to and asked advice of, the holder of secrets she sometimes did not want to know. Everyone liked her; everyone trusted her; everyone wanted to know her opinion. She had long ago learned to keep a firm grip on anything she was told, but that became even more imperative when she was told secrets that could harm. People trusted her. She felt impelled to be worthy of that trust. The village did not have a priest, nor a Shaman; one had to go to White Birch for that. Young Kaari often found herself standing in bewildered stead for those worthies.

As a result, Kaari, while appearing to be the most pampered, was probably the least selfish person in the entire village. She had to be. Keeping other people's feelings more or less intact entailed an enormous amount of sacrifice. She found herself giving up every-thing—from time spent on others that she could have used for herself, to giving cherished possessions to soothe an emotional wound. For every pretty bead necklace of polished seeds and carved pendants she kept, she gave away ten; for every length of trim she wove, she gave four. And not just to girls, or at least, not directly. There were not a few young men in the village who had mended a quarrel with a sweetheart with some former possession of Kaari's.

There had only ever been two people around whom she had not needed to take such care—Veikko and his mother. He treated her no differently than he did any other girl when they were children, and teased her the same when they were older. His mother had made no more fuss over her than she did over any child other than her own son. As Kaari grew older, and had learned what Annukka *could* do if she chose, she began to understand that, because both of them were, or would be, magic wielders, they probably had some immunity to her own ability. Either that, or Annukka had cast a spell to protect them.

So when Veikko fell in love with her, she had known it was not the effect of her Heart rune, and it had been a distinct relief to feel herself falling for him. Only when Veikko had fallen in love with her had she felt truly free and at ease. Because—well—for almost too many other reasons to count.

Not least was the fact that all but the really lecherous regretfully had to decide that she was no longer accessible. And all the other single girls, with the exception of those who had been in love with Veikko themselves, heaved sighs of relief.

But just to be sure, after Veikko had declared himself and gotten her parents' consent, she had come creeping to Annukka to confess her power. Just in case.

Somewhat to her astonishment, Annukka had looked at her and said, "I know."

As she had gaped at her mother-in-law to be, Annukka had smiled and patted her on the head like a little girl. "Bless you, child, who do you think has been tending to all the little storms you stirred up that you couldn't fix yourself?"

Well, that made perfect sense, but—

"And who do you think Lyyli told when she read your runes the first time?" Annukka had continued. She had smiled to see Kaari's expression. "Oh, now, you didn't even know Lyyli's name, did you?"

"I never—" Kaari had stammered, "I thought—no one ever called her any name other than—"

"Than Wise Woman, yes, I know." Annukka had continued spinning, calmly, the drop spindle whirling hypnotically. "It's better that way. They call me the same in her village."

"You're a—in her village?"

"Close your mouth, child, or a bird will come feed you," Annukka had said kindly. "I act as Wise Woman for her village, she does the same for me. It's not considered…*appropriate* for the runes to be read by someone from the same village as the child. Too much pressure. Everyone wants his or her own child to be extraordinary, a Wonder-smith or an epic singer or some other sort of prodigy. To have to cast runes for the utterly ordinary, to cast runes for something the parents are not prepared to deal with, or worst of all, to cast runes that suggest trouble to come, is not something you wish to do for the people you live around. Every day they look at you, they are reminded of what you said." She sighed. "So Lyyli and I and those others with the Mage rune have an agreement. We all protect each other. And we alternate the other villages we go to, so that we never come to a village twice in a row. We each make sure that *someone* in a village knows about unusual runes that come up. Like yours. I have known about you from the time Lyyli first read your runes."

Kaari found herself nodding.

"You may rest assured that Veikko loves you for yourself alone and not because your wyrd compels him," Annukka had finished. "So now, shall we begin on filling your bride-chest? Nice, thick woolen blankets are always a good place to start."

No one could have asked for a better mother-in-law. How Kaari loved her!

Only halfway to the well now, Kaari stopped in a patch of sunshine and bent her head gravely for little Taina to put a rather withered crown of flowers on her. Yesterday, another child had beaten Taina to crowning Kaari, and she had promised Taina that today she could be the one.

Taina blushed and giggled and ran off shyly. Kaari nodded to the child's mother, who was spreading linen shirts on the hedge to dry in the sun, and went on her way again. No one liked doing laundry alone, but—as with most things—anytime that Kaari planned to do a chore that could be done communally, most of the village women and girls showed up at the same time. In this case—by unspoken consent— laundry day for the entire village was the day that Kaari chose. And by common, unspoken, practical consent, laundry day was the day the men picked to fish in farther waters. The chatter down by the river earlier had frightened all the fish away for the next day at least.

The flowers that the child had used were asters—Autumn flowers— and even wilting, they had a crisp, clean scent to them. Harvest would be soon, and then Winter. She hoped Veikko would be home by then, or at least, would persuade his teacher to Winter over here.

As she smiled and nodded to everyone in greeting, her thoughts were otherwise occupied. For some reason today, she had fallen to thinking about and speculating about her own runes rather than someone else's. She often had to wonder what someone absolutely without morals or conscience would do if *she* had the Heart rune; it actually made her rather ill to contemplate it for very long. If the person was petty-minded, she would simply take advantage of everything and everyone, allowing herself to be treated as something special and showered with gifts. Not only could that be done, and with the greatest of ease, but anyone so exploited would actually think himself lucky that she used him so. And if she was clever and evil…

Please, I would rather not see that sort of thing. With such charisma it would be possible to become—

A tyrant? Certainly, but one with a difference. A beloved tyrant, who walked over the backs of his people while they praised him for doing so. Or the sort of woman who ruins men or nations simply because she can.

Whereas someone with ethics and morals—

Allowed herself to look silly wearing a little girl's wilting flower-crown in order to make the child happy.

She finally made it to the well, and it was only there that her "power," if such it could be called, made her life just a little easier. She never had to draw up the heavy buckets of water herself; there were always a half-dozen volunteers to do so for her. And, of course, she would gently tease whoever volunteered until he had filled the buckets of *all* the women there. That was only fair. More of Kaari's balancing act at work.

Of course, she had to linger while the others got their buckets filled. That was only fair. If people actually *wanted* her company, who was she to be stingy with it, especially when she was being done a favor? She smiled at tall Ihanelma as he pulled up bucket after bucket of water, and she wrinkled her nose at him playfully. He laughed and puffed out his chest.

"Do you think that trader, the one with the amber jewelry and colored ribbons, will come by pig-killing time?" asked Suvi-Marja anxiously. "I so want red ribbons to go with the bands on my new overgown."

Kaari did not smile, although she wanted to. Suvi-Marja wanted more than red ribbons. She was hoping her sweetheart would buy her an amber necklace to match her honey-colored hair. She didn't so much want the jewel for itself as she wanted it as a token that he was serious about courting her. A fellow didn't go to the expense of a necklace unless he intended something more than just a Summer frolic. A flower-crown was a sweet gesture, a ribbon betokened a bit of interest, but a necklace—now, that was an investment. Kaari made a mental note to be sure and drop enough hints that Essa would manage to understand what it was he needed to do. He was a fine fellow, big and strong and rugged of features, but a few sticks short of a roaring fire. His notion of courting *her* had consisted of standing at the back of a crowd and making calf-eyes at her. Thank heavens, he was being more forward with Suvi-Marja. Well, after she had pushed him into it a bit. It hadn't taken much, just enough to get him over his initial shyness.

"The trader has managed to come every year so far," Kaari reminded her, as a breeze came up that made all their aprons flap like wings and brought with it the smell of drying hay. "You know he cannot resist Annukka's sausage. He will be here in good time." She smiled now. "I am going to weave the tablet-bands for my Winter dress tonight, and I *know* that the room will be full of my clumsy brothers, who are very loud, will step on my yarn, and probably will make me miscount at least three times. If you are going to weave, too, I should like very much to join you."

Suvi-Marja flushed with pleasure. "Oh, what a good notion!" And being good-hearted, she looked around the others at the well; most actually were older women who would be at their own hearths tonight, but Rikka and Ulla, two of their friends, were looking wistfully at her. "Let us all get together tonight!"

"I have mittens to make," Rikka said happily.

Ulla shrugged. "Mother has warped the loom and you know she never makes sure she has enough yarn when she starts something. I can always spin."

"Done, then. After sunset?" Suvi-Marja smiled. And Kaari smiled, too. This was a painless exercise of her talent for once. Suvi-Marja was always too shy to think of inviting the other girls over. She had been something of an awkward little girl, plain of face, her hair being her one great beauty, and she had not much improved as she grew into woman-hood, although she could cook as if her hands were enchanted, and her weaving and knitting were flawless. It was very clear what *her* runes had been—a double dose of Hearth. To have won Essa was, for her, a great triumph. Essa, bless his soul, would have been won over by a stone if it could cook and doted on him as much as Suvi-Marja did. His job as village woodcutter meant he would always have food on the table, and his skill with a carving knife meant that even in old age he would be able to make a living. So even if his thoughts tended to wander like a sheep without a shepherd, he was a good man, and would make a fine husband.

"We can talk about our sweethearts," Rikka whispered, making them all giggle, and Suvi-Marja blush as red as the ribbons she wanted to buy.

"Oh, but that is hardly fair!" protested Ulla with a grin. "Yours total more than all of ours put together!" And she was right, for Rikka was a great flirt, and had swiftly gathered up all those disappointed when Veikko had pledged his troth to Kaari. Rikka really *was* the village beauty, and if Kaari had not had the wyrd she did, no one would ever have noticed her when Rikka was about.

"Then we can tell ghost stories and roast nuts," Suvi-Marja said firmly. "But I do not want to tell fortunes. I do *not* want to know what is to come for me."

"Oh, pish." Rikka laughed. But for once, Ulla did not take her side; instead, the usually playful girl shook her head.

"Not tonight, for fortunes," the tall, angular girl said, looking dis-quieted. "Even at the best of times, so my mother says, such things can bring *unwanted attention.* And now—"

Kaari looked at her sharply. "What do you mean, *now?*" she demanded.

Ulla shook her head again. "I will tell you tonight," she said only. "You know that my father got a letter from his cousin yesterday. It might be that this is a misheard tale. But I would as soon not tell it in the open, where any—*thing*—can hear."

And with that, she shouldered her buckets and headed briskly up the path leading to her father's house, leaving the other three to stare at her retreating back. And by the looks on the faces of her friends, Kaari was not the only one to return home in a troubled state of mind.

3

OF ALL THE GODMOTHERS THAT SHE KNEW, ALEKSIA WAS the most adept with mirror-magic. Why that should be, she was not entirely sure. It might have been because of the nature of ice, so close to glass in its transparency and fragility, and most especially, in its reflective qualities. It might have been that it was not *she* who was so adept, per se, but that the position of Ice Fairy, perforce remote from everything, carried with it the compensating ability with mirrors, so that a friend and colleague was never more than a reflective surface away.

"And how are things on top of the mountain?" asked Godmother Elena as she faded into view. "Quiet, I hope?" The glimpse of wall behind Elena told Aleksia that her fellow Godmother was in her own study, rather than in her workroom of the Order of the Champions of Glass Mountain. Elena spent roughly half her time there; she and her husband, who was the Preceptor of the Order, had agreed to that arrangement. It seemed to suit them. Aleksia rather thought that such an arrangement would suit *her* as well. It meant that Elena was able to travel at least twice a year, and got a real change not only of scenery, but of a way of life. She would meet new people as new young Champions presented themselves. She would be living in a place *full* of faces she did not know so well—here she was more familiar with their faces than the one that looked back at her in the mirror.

Elena was possibly the closest thing to a friend that Aleksia had among the Godmothers, even though they had never actually met in person. Elena shared a bit of the Ice Fairy's sardonic sense of humor, and was one of the few sympathetic about Aleksia's rather onerous position among the Godmothers. Perhaps that was because Elena had a history of dealing with the same sorts of miscreants—one of whom had eventually married her. Those Godmothers who only had to reward the good and fend off evil simply didn't understand how tedious it was to be regarded with hostility by the very people you were helping. Elena's own Champion and husband had begun his acquaintance with her as one of her "problems." In fact, she'd turned him into a donkey for a while. Aleksia didn't often get to do things like that, much though she wished to at times; it was difficult enough to keep her reindeer in good condition up here, and they were cold-hardy in the extreme. It would have been very nice to turn the brats like Kay into beasts of burden rather than have them running about in her Palace.

Aleksia rolled her eyes and described her latest charge. Elena shook her head, a single blond tendril escaping from her upswept hair to bounce against her cheek. "I ought to talk to some of the others around Led Belarus, and see about getting you some congenial company. Perhaps a Snow Maiden, or someone of that sort. There must be some intelligent creatures that would find all that cold to be attractive. You are too much alone, Aleksia. I know you have your Brownies but—"

"But they hardly stay more than a month before another takes his place. And my three faithfuls—" she paused "—I would not for the world say anything against them, but I can generally recite everything I expect them to say, and I do not doubt that they can do the same for me."

The wood on the fire today was cedar, and Aleksia was mirror-watching from her cushions. There was a terrible blizzard outside, and she had felt disinclined to get out of her bedgown. Instead, she had wrapped herself in a dressing gown of quilted silk lined with rabbit fur, tucked her toes into slippers that matched, and was enjoying a very late breakfast of battered sausage and tea while the wind raged at her windows and it looked as if there was nothing out there but a solid white wall.

The idea that Elena had suggested was appealing, provided the poor guest didn't perish of boredom. "I would not for the world want to replace any of the Brownies, but it would be nice to see someone new, not a servant, and someone that I didn't have to discipline," Aleksia said, with a melancholy sigh. "If it is at all possible—if you could find some compatible beings that could do their own work from here, I should love to play permanent host. You are very lucky to have the Order about you: Sometimes the lack of peers to talk with is very wearing. Especially once I am snowed in. I know I shouldn't complain but—"

Elena sniffed. "You have every right to complain. You hardly ever come down from the Palace, and none of us ever get up there. How often do you see someone not in a mirror? I would be lonely, too! It's not as if you are close enough you can easily come down for a wedding or a christening. Mind, I would love to see you in person. The Champions—" Elena rolled her eyes "—they are all very *hearty* sorts. I have no one to discuss gowns and hair with, even the women want to talk of nothing but armor and weapons! Not that this is bad—it is just not something I care to debate for hours at a time. And I have not yet found a way to translate across the leagues instantly, or I swear, we would be having tea once a week."

"Nor have I…" She pursed her lips thoughtfully. "But it does occur to me that I might research stepping through a suitably enchanted mirror. The Elven-kind must do *something* of the sort, the way they can simply appear and disappear at will."

Elena laughed, and shook her head ruefully. "I am no inventive magician, really, to research this sort of thing. I will leave that to you— but—" she bit her lip "—I am glad that you contacted me, and brought this up yourself. It is good to know that you actually have not been able to invent such a thing yet. There are some troubling rumors I wish to apprise you of. All is not well in the North."

Something about the expression in Elena's eyes put Aleksia on the alert. "I trust you are going to enlighten me."

"Well, unless you actually are turning to the bad, and you *have* found a way to walk through mirrors and are hiding this from me, the fact that I am speaking to you and that I know you are in your Palace, means that whatever is going on, it is not *your* doing." Elena's lips thinned. "Someone is causing…problems…in the vicinity of the Sammi. And she is using the name of the Snow Queen."

Suddenly the sausages were no longer so appealing. Aleksia set them aside to listen very closely to everything Elena had to say.

When Elena was finished and the mirror was back to reflecting nothing more interesting than her own face, Aleksia found herself in a very disquieted state. It was not greatly surprising that she should have heard nothing of this. To most people, everything out of their imme- diate geographic sphere was vaguely "over there" and concatenated into a single whole in their minds. Granted, a Godmother's sphere did tend to be much larger than even the average monarch's—but there *were* five hundred Kingdoms, and a great many places which, like the land of the Sammi, were not strictly Kingdoms at all, and there was a lot of distance between the Palace of Ever-Winter and the land of the reindeer- herders. The very nature of this mountainous country magnified the dis- tances; the eagle might fly from here to there at will, but people had to find pathways through and over the mountains. So to Elena's mind, rumors of something that might herald trouble seemed to be centered on an area very near the Palace of Ever-Winter, when in fact, it was not at all surprising Aleksia had heard nothing.

She got up from her nest and allowed her attendant to help her into a gown, not paying much attention to it, until the Brownie was doing up her back-laces. Only then did she notice that her little servant had intuited that she was *not* going to want to see Kay in person today; this was not one of her Ice Fairy gowns, not a magnificent silk creation. In fact, when she was Princess Aleksia, her stepmother would probably have been horrified to see her in something so plain—it was a very simple, tight-sleeved gown of gray wool, without a single ornament. But the wool was not just from any sheep—it was from special flocks that lived only in the mountains, and grew fleeces softer than those of newborn lambs. Yarn spun from this wool could be made so fine that a lace shawl knitted from it could pass through a woman's wedding ring. It made her look businesslike, even a bit severe; when she spoke to her various contacts via the mirror, they would know this was no light matter.

She continued to plan what she would do as her attendant put her hair up in braids and wrapped it about her head, crownlike.

That someone up to mischief would have the audacity to use the title of the Snow Queen…that made her angry and just a trifle alarmed. As the blizzard outside subsided, she made out a list of who might know something about these rumors. And it was going to take some organization on her part.

She spent the rest of the afternoon until well after the sun had set and the moon was rising over the snowfields in front of her mirror, reaching out to those Witches and Sorceresses she knew who lived near the Sammi. Speaking with someone via mirror who was not expecting you to contact her was not just a matter of casting the spell and seeing them. Alas, no. She had to work a rather complicated bit of magic that would leave a message on whatever reflective surface was nearest them. It was simple—it had to be—just that she needed to speak with them. Then she had to wait for *them* to go to their own mirrors and initiate the contact. And, of course, none of this would happen in a controlled manner. At one point she had a conversation going in three different mirrors at once, resorting in desperation to her little hand-mirror that she used to see the back of her head when she was checking a complicated hairdo on the rare occasions when she made an appearance in public.

None of those she contacted had heard any of the rumors that Elena had reported. All of them promised to probe their own sources of information. And that was the best she could hope for at this point. The thing was, the land of the Sammi was rather—unregulated. There were not many Witches and Sorceresses of the sort that made regular reports to the Godmothers. Truth to be told, the few who actually knew anything about Godmothers tended to think of them as...irrelevant to the condition of the Sammi. And it was very true that in the land of the Sammi, the creatures of legend, godlets and powerful nature spirits tended to interact with humans much more than they did in the more "civilized" parts of the world. It was a wild land, and everything in it was primitive and more than a bit unpredictable.

That much she knew already; that evening was spent in her nest with books the Brownies brought from her library, and a great deal of hot tea. She learned that most magic workers among the Sammi were Wise Women and Shamans, who often were aware of Godmothers only vaguely, if at all. From a travel book by a Godmother, she proved what she had vaguely known already—that part of the world was full of demigods and nature spirits that were laws unto themselves and rather disdainful of the Godmothers.

That gave her a moment's pause. If it was one of them causing mischief, well…Aleksia would probably be able to tell right away if she could handle the situation herself.

Tread cautiously here, Aleksia.

Still, there were demigods, and there were demigods. A god of Winter would be able to squash her like a melting snowball, but a god of a single glacier did not even rate a level of concern. If she could not deal with the troublemaker on her own, well, quick delving into more books assured her that it had been proven before that not even a demigod could stand up to the combined power of two Godmothers and a Fae. Elena would certainly help, and she had more than enough contacts among the Fae to call in a true *Fairy* Godmother. The Fae had created the mortal Godmothers in the first place, because, Aleksia presumed, they had grown tired of the constant meddling in human affairs that steering The Tradition required.

With a goblet of hot mulled wine in hand, she went over all she had done that day. Finally, she concluded that there was nothing more to do at the moment, and with a resigned nod, she dismissed it from her mind. In the absence of information, the only thing she could do was allow her agents to gather it for her. It wasn't as if she didn't have quite enough to keep her busy at the moment.

She put her wine down, and passed her hand over the surface of the mirror to look in on Gerda.

The girl was braiding up another girl's hair, in some small room heaped with a magpie's treasure-trove of pirated goods. A bed was almost hidden under a riot of colored pillows, a truckle bed only partly shoved beneath it. Gaudy necklaces were festooned from a tarnished and blotchy mirror, and the dressing table was awash with silk ribbons, more jewelry, paints and powders, perfumes and kerchiefs. The owner of this room got whatever she wanted, and it seemed that what she wanted was Gerda to wait on her.

Though Gerda looked desperately unhappy, she did not look ill-used. *Ah, good. She seems to be holding her own.* As Aleksia had known would happen, because she had nudged things in that direction with her own subtle magic, nothing had happened to her other than being robbed, imprisoned and frightened. The Chief of the band Aleksia had chosen had a daughter about Gerda's age, and as Aleksia had made sure would happen, the daughter had taken one look at Gerda and claimed her as her own particular servant.

No one dared to molest the young woman after that; the robber girl had been schooled in violence since she could crawl and had no compunction about enforcing her demands with whatever weapon came to hand. In particular, she was masterful with knives, and every man in her father's band knew she could beat him to a pulp, then slice him up into ribbons if she chose. They already looked to her as her father's heir, and while it was barely possible that one of them might challenge her, it was more likely that such a man would be beaten and become her right hand and partner.

Aleksia had plans for *her* in good time, but she was not quite old enough yet. It amused her, though, to think of this wild girl righting all the wrongs of her father's band and more as a Champion—yes, and turning the entire band from robbers into freedom fighters. There was a tyrant ruling over the Kingdom of Svenska—one of those things that Aleksia had not been able to prevent; it was not yet time for him to be deposed, but that time was coming soon, and Valeri the Robber Girl would be just the woman to do the job.

That was at least three years away. First, Valeri had to do a bit of traveling and discover the truth for herself. Then it would be a matter of waiting until her father came to the end of all Robber Chiefs and she was called home. Yes, three years away, at the least. Perhaps as much as five.

So now the Robber Girl was acting as she always had: deep down, fundamentally kind, but selfish, helping herself to what she wanted. At the moment she was wearing Gerda's fine clothing; Gerda had been carelessly given some of the Robber Girl's leathers and furs—which were actually going to stand her in much better stead on the road ahead than her original clothing would have. Gerda needed to win Valeri's sympathy and to harden a little more under privation. In another week or so, it would be time for the next step.

So Gerda was sorted. As for Kay...

She passed her hand over the mirror and looked for him. He was not in his workshop, nor the library. Finally, she found him at the window in his bedroom, staring out at the snow, an expression of bleak loneliness on his face. On the windowseat beside him was a half-finished drawing, not of some clockwork mechanism, but of a girl's face. It wasn't very well done in comparison to his clockwork plans; in fact it was hardly recognizable. But the hair gave it away as Gerda.

Well, things were coming along nicely there, as well.

Time to look over the rest of her charges.

This took a bit more effort. Concentrating hard, she called up the image of the energies of The Tradition, silently telling her mirror to overlay them on a map. It looked rather like a many-colored fog-bank over the landscape rendered in extreme miniature, and she saw a problem almost immediately.

And just in time; a huge surge of Traditional power showed her where the trouble spot was, and she followed the train into the deep forest outside the tiny village of Gottsbergen in the Kingdom of Svenska. She made the mirror backtrack in time a little—it could look into the past, but unfortunately not move forward into the future. She watched as a cruel woman in Svenska sent her stepchildren out into the forest after nuts—it was, of course, just a little too early for nuts, but they didn't know that. They were already far too deep into the woods to be anything but lost. This could go badly very quickly. With that much Traditional power building so quickly around them, they were a far-too-tempting target for the Tyrant, or to be more precise, the Tyrant's pet magician. He would not even have to do anything, just allow them to die...or be killed. They could last for several days in the woods, getting hungrier, colder, with the power building all around them.

She firmed her jaw, feeling a flush, not quite of anger, but of something close to it. *This* was why she had become a Godmother. Not for the sulky Kays. For innocents like these. And she put everything else out of her mind but the need to save them.

Using her second mirror, while she kept an eye on the children in the first, Aleksia searched for someone who could help. A Witch, a Sorceress, one of the creatures of the Faean, like a Giant or a Unicorn, even a Wise Beast—

But the woods were singularly empty. Blast it. Blast the Tyrant and his pet magician all to perdition! Between his purely mortal evil and his magician's ability to track rivals for the pleasure of eliminating them and to hunt out the arcane beasties and other races for pleasure and profit, if there was anyone about, he, she or it was in hiding. For all practical purposes, there was no one nearby. She would have to work some magic at a distance. She could use the very magic boiling about these children to fuel it. But first—first, she made sure there was nothing about that could harm them in the time it would take her to search for a way to get them help. She set an "aversion" spell about them, that would make anything carnivorous avoid them. Crude, but effective.

Sure now that they were safe for the short term, she set about finding a solution that would make The Tradition "happy." In the second mirror, she searched for what she needed, and after a moment, found it in the Kingdom of Daneland. Just over the border was another, quieter eddy of Traditional power building up, where a lonely cottage stood, owned by a woodcutter and his wife. As the babes searched the underbrush fruitlessly for hazelnuts, she siphoned off some of the magic around them and cast the All Paths Are One Path spell directly ahead of them, putting the terminus in Daneland, just at the gate of that little cottage. She made sure the magical route would bring them there just at sunset. Then she waited, watching, holding both ends of the All Paths spell in her mind, keeping it balanced and ready; if someone else stumbled on that path at either end, it could make things very complicated indeed. They were already complicated enough. She was juggling two spells at a great distance, and one of them was potentially dangerous.

When both of the children had finally put their feet on the magic path, she dismissed the aversion spell, then let go of the terminus at Svenska—with a sigh of relief, for more reasons than one. Among other things, now they were entirely in her power. Neither the Tyrant's magician, nor any other, could interfere with them until she chose to let them go. Now, all she had to do was watch. If anyone from that cottage accidentally left and got tangled up in her spell, no worries; it only went straight back to the cottage.

But no one did, and in the blue dusk, two tired children, crying because they were lost and hungry, stumbled out of her spell, out of the dark and ominous woods, right onto a lovely little soft path that ended in a cozy cottage. And the middle-aged, childless couple who had longed all these years for children of their own, heard them and came rushing out—reacting instinctively and without hesitation—to the sound of children in distress.

They could not understand each others' language, of course. That wouldn't matter. In a few weeks, the little ones would be prattling in Dansk, filling the lives of their adoptive parents with joy. They would have forgotten their stepmother, and as for their father, well, he would become something vaguely remembered in dreams.

And as for the wicked stepmother…

Another day, Aleksia decided. She wanted to think on an appropriate punishment, in case what her stupid husband came up with was not enough. Or in case she managed to feign innocence and convince him that she was not to blame.

Having her own child taken by gypsies might serve the purpose…

She would have to look into that. Then again…there might be a simpler way.

It was very difficult to deal directly with The Tradition. You could not exactly "communicate" with it, and trying to do anything by brute force was a little like a flea trying to shift a warhorse. But if the flea bit the horse in exactly the right place at the right time…

She spent a good hour putting together a subtle spell. It was nothing like a compulsion, more like—a suggestion.

She turned it loose and it settled around the countryside like a cobweb, *much* too subtle for the Tyrant's Wizard to detect. And if he did, he would not care about it. This had nothing to do with him, nor with the Tyrant.

But from this moment on, every storyteller, every woman reciting tales to put the little ones to sleep, every gaggle of girls about a fire, every twopenny musician singing for his supper would be telling tales of wicked stepmothers who got what they deserved. This was the flea biting the warhorse, for the more these tales were recited, spun and sung, the more The Tradition would be impelled to make them come true. And who, at the moment, was the wickedest stepmother in all of the Kingdom?

Aleksia smiled with a certain smug satisfaction.

With that crisis averted, Aleksia continued to look into the Kingdoms for which she was responsible, following the flows of the power generated by The Tradition. Everywhere that there was a situation that corresponded to a tale, a myth or a legend, The Tradition accrued power to force it down that Traditional Path to The Traditional Ending. Sometimes that was just fine; Godmothers didn't have to intervene. In fact, there was an Ella Cinders story waiting to be recreated in Eisenberg—wicked stepmother, nasty stepsisters, lovely young girl turned into a servant, all in the capitol of Konigsberg. The girl was the right age to be married to the Prince, the Prince had no particular sweethearts and the King and Queen were not at all averse to him wedding a commoner if his heart took him there. It just needed a little more time to percolate, as it were, and then all it would need was Aleksia's timely appearance and just enough adversity thrown in their path to make the happily ever after all the more satisfying. She smiled to herself as she contemplated the poor girl scrubbing pots at the hearth. She should have been sad, but somehow she was able to take pleasure in small things. The Tradition was truly working hard on this one—if she had been any sweeter, any more self-sacrificing, any better-tempered, she would have been sickening.

This, of course, was one of her rare ones.

The list of her usual headaches, however, went much longer.

There was a woman who was so much a shrew to her long-suffering husband that she was legendary to everyone around her. The Traditional force building around *her* was such that Aleksia judged it was time to let it take its course. But she made a mental note to keep an eye on the old man, lest her punishment overflow onto him.

What would be best? There were a number of things in the area that she could put into the shrew's way.

The neighbors, she decided, finally. She wove another subtle spell and set that in motion—the idea that it would be a fine trick to play on the nag, to put her in a position where her sharp tongue dug herself a deeper and deeper hole until she found herself in real trouble. The only one with any sympathy for her then would be her long-suffering husband, who, strangely enough, still loved her, despite being mocked, ridiculed and berated without end. Well, there was no accounting for taste. He would save her or he would leave her; in either case, he would no longer be subject to her abuse.

The Tyrant, however, was more troubling. With his punishment at least three years in the future, and with The Tradition moving now to keep him in his place, she considered that there ought to be something she could do to ease the situation of his people. At the moment, he was grinding them into poverty, and The Tradition wasn't helping. Tyrants did not get good weather and bountiful crops. Tyrants got late Springs and early Winters, too much rain or not enough, and when their peasantry could not produce bountiful crops, Tyrants took it out on them, adding torture and murder to the hardship of semistarvation.

This, of course, tended to produce Heroes and Champions, but it was dreadfully hard on the people themselves.

Tapping one finger on her lips as she considered the image of the Tyrant himself, seated rigidly on his throne, Aleksia wondered what she could do to ease their lot. Interestingly, this man was no usurper; he had come to this throne legitimately.

Well, after a fashion, anyway. The King had managed to die without an heir, and that was entirely due to the current Tyrant. Benevolent though the old king had been, he had also been weak. His nephew had had no difficulty whatsoever in persuading him to put off marriage, meanwhile ingratiating himself to the old man and all his advisors in order to be named Crown Prince over all the other claimants. A little judicious spending, a bribe here, the assurance of reward there, the creation of a small private army, and when the King died, the Crown Prince was virtually rushed onto the throne by the greedy and corrupt Court.

Then, when the new King proved to be something other than what had been expected, it was too late. Because the new King had known very well that a man who takes one bribe will take many, and a man who seeks his own preferment over the good of his country can be counted on to turn his coat whenever anyone offers him something he wants.

So…the problem before Aleksia was how to distract him. "Show me those upon whom he depends," she ordered the mirror.

There were the usual types. The Tyrant did not much care for fighting, but he was very smart about how he dealt with the need to go to battle. He had put a General in charge of his armies who lived for conquest and blood—but was not at all interested in the tedium of ruling.

Aleksia frowned. The General was a simple sadist. He knew what he wanted—free rein to allow his men to run roughshod over the populace. He got it often enough, whenever the Tyrant saw the need for an object-lesson. No hope there; there was nothing that anyone could offer the General that he did not already have.

The Tyrant's advisors were all very shrewd as well as suspicious, shrewd enough to know that none of them stood a chance of deposing their Master alone, suspicious enough not to trust any of the others to help with a palace coup. That was a pity; it would have been the ideal solution.

The Magician was content to enjoy the fruits of his Master's success. Like the General, he had what he wanted: a luxurious life, the freedom to pursue whatever line of research in magic that he fancied, regardless of how blackly evil it was, and a steady supply of victims upon whom to experiment. Like the General, he had no interest at all in ruling a country, and his ambitions all centered on success in the Dark Arts.

But then, as she let the viewpoint roam, the mirror showed her someone she had not expected.

Ensconced in a tower chamber was a fellow in elaborate robes of black and purple. Surrounding him were all the trappings of a Wizard, although Aleksia knew he could not be anything of the sort, since there was not one jot of Traditional power about him, nor any other sort of magic so far as she could tell. This intrigued her enough that she issued orders not to be disturbed and had the Brownies bring her dinner in her rooms.

Who are you, my little man? she asked him silently. The Tyrant's Magician did not seem to consider him a threat nor a rival. She had never heard even a rumor of this fellow, who, from the crockery piled outside his door, seldom left his tower.

She spent the rest of the afternoon and well into the evening watching him, and finally enough of what he did struck a chord with her that she realized she knew what he was.

An Alchemist.

But this was more than merely an Alchemist. He was clever enough not to call himself one, hence the Wizardly trappings, although the Magician visited him once, and it was obvious that although the Magician considered the Alchemist an inferior, he also respected the Alchemist's abilities.

Once again, the Tyrant had been clever enough to find someone who could be given everything that he wanted. Now, whether he was also clever enough not to waste his time in the search for the Philosopher's Stone—which was a metaphysical concept anyway and did nothing to transmute base metals to gold—or whether he really *did* realize it was a metaphysical concept, he was not involving himself with crucibles and alembics and furnaces. She watched him, instead, making very useful things such as poisons and antidotes—cures for the unfortunate diseases that men who indulged themselves in certain vices were prone to—and watched with extreme interest as the Tyrant appeared for what must have been his daily dose of a concoction of at least thirty common poisons. No wonder he didn't employ a taster! His Alchemist gave him immunity to anything but a truly exotic poison, and probably had the antidote handy for anything truly exotic. Exotic poisons tended to kill slowly, leaving plenty of time to administer an antidote. This was sheer brilliance.

Once the Tyrant was gone again, the Alchemist turned to another pursuit entirely. Aleksia watched as he secured the door, bolting it from the inside, pulled a velvet pall off of some object and settled himself into a comfortable chair in front of it. He imbibed some sort of concoction of his own...and went into a trance. His head fell back so that Aleksia could see that he was staring into an enormous crystal ball.

Now, as every Godmother knew, it was possible for perfectly ordinary people to have visions of the future, if they took the right sorts of potions. You had to be very disciplined—which this Alchemist clearly was—and you had to be good enough to know how to sort the hallucinations from the real visions. Usually these visions were not very accurate once you tried to look more than three months into the future, but for someone like the Tyrant, that would be enough.

"Well!" Aleksia said aloud, staring into her mirror with probably the same expression that the Alchemist was wearing as he stared into his crystal ball.

But it just so happened that anyone who did this sort of parlor trick could also be very easily deceived. And that gave Aleksia precisely the opportunity she was looking for.

After all, the great crystal was a form of glass. She could make him see whatever she wanted him to see. In his drugged state, he would be very suggestible, and his powers of discrimination would be set aside. Besides, he would have no reason to suppose that anyone else would be sending him visions. Why should there be? There was no reason to think that anyone could, or would, interfere. No one knew about him but his Master and the Magician, and neither wanted him deceived.

So it was that when he emerged from his drug-induced trance, it was to run straight to the Tyrant with the description of what he had seen— a conspiracy against the ruler, the meeting of the conspirators, all of whom were robed identically and masked. And just to make it all the more interesting, she had made the leader some sort of Magician, who had conjured up a demon that promised them success in their endeavor. The surroundings, as crafted by Aleksia's imagination, were opulent, but apparently subterranean. When anyone spoke, it was with the cultured tones of the upper classes. And they made reference to the King In Waiting. It was quite the fantastic creation, but very believable, especially to someone like the Tyrant. The Tradition would be working against him in that way, making him suspicious and looking for conspiracies; the fact that he couldn't find any would make him all the more certain that they existed.

Now the Tyrant would be actively searching for this conspiracy, powered by a Magician. His search would concentrate on those of the upper classes. He would not be able to tell if these were his own nobles or those in exile, for she had given no clues at all as to the location. He would only know that whoever was involved had wealth, as well as occult power. He would assume that somewhere along the line he had missed a potential heir.

This would drive him mad trying to ferret it out. And he would be so fixated on it he would leave his peasantry alone.

Aleksia made a mental note to keep sending more false visions whenever she managed to think of some new variation.

I should also make an attempt to put disturbing things in the palace from time to time. Perhaps an ornate dagger in the Tyrant's bedpost, or a burned rug and the smell of brimstone in his dressing room. These things would take some arranging, but they would be worth the doing. Anything that kept him nervous and alarmed. Perhaps she could leave a hint that the apocryphal conspirators knew about his immunity to poison. Brownies could slip in anywhere, and slip out again undetected; alone of the Elven-kind, they had no difficulties with cold iron. They could easily leave daggers and burned places anywhere they chose, and one of them might find it amusing to slip some concoction into the Tyrant's nightly draught to make him sick.

And this would have the effect of making Valeri's job so much easier when she and her band were ready and made the attempt to depose him. It was not wise to depend too much on The Tradition alone to take you where you wanted to go. It was always better to have so many hedges around what you wanted accomplished that The Traditional power flowed downhill in the channel you wanted like so much runoff water.

Aleksia dismissed the image in her mirror and looked up with the realization that she had been bending over it for hours. Her shoulders and neck were stiff and sore, and her eyes felt dry. One of her Brownies was at her side as she straightened, appearing, as they often did, without needing to be summoned.

"It is after midnight," the little woman said, as Aleksia massaged her own shoulder carefully. Rosemary, that was her name. "Young Kay moped about the dining room, pushed food about his plate and retired to his suite when you did not put in an appearance. It seems he has decided to experiment with getting drunk tonight." Rosemary grinned, with just a hint of malice. "He is going to have a head in the morning."

"Then one hopes he won't repeat the experiment." Aleksia smiled a little herself. If Kay was suffering from a hangover, he would not be a nuisance for some time tomorrow. "Rosemary, would you have any objections to other residents here? Not like Kay," she amended. "Pleasant ones. And hopefully permanent ones. Peers of mine."

"None at all, Godmother," the Brownie replied serenely. "The Palace can hold a small army, and if we need more help here, 'tis easy come by."

"Ah, good." That was a relief. There were times when Aleksia was not quite sure just what her privileges as a Godmother were, nor what they extended to. As a Princess of the Blood, she had taken such things as servants and where one put guests for granted. As a Godmother, who tended to both the highest and the lowest, she had learned that it was never wise to take anything for granted.

In fact, her first apprenticeship year had been very enlightening. She would not have considered herself spoiled—but her eyes had certainly been opened to just how much work went on behind the rooms frequented by the noble and wealthy. She had learned that magic was not always the answer to a problem. She knew now, for instance, that the Palace was so remote that her Brownies changed monthly. At first, she had thought there was a never-ending stream of them, but now she knew that the little folk, who were highly social, aside from her very particular three—Tuft, Pieter and her special maid, Moth—most simply found remaining for any length of time at the Palace of Ever-Winter too much of a hardship. Aleksia did her best to learn their names in the month or so they were with her, but if she forgot one, she merely apologized, since the Brownies themselves didn't take it amiss.

Of course, one benefit of this was that her menu, which could have gotten very tedious with the same cook, was instead changed with the tastes and training of the Brownie in charge. This month, there were a lot of lightly spiced fish dishes, an excellent change from the cook of the previous month, who favored stews and complicated soups and meat dishes with fancy sauces. And that had been a change from the month before that, when the menu had boasted very little meat, and many varied noodle and vegetable concoctions, some of which had been so highly spiced her eyes had watered.

"Well, Godmother Aleksia, I trust you are hungry? You have certainly been working hard enough to warrant something before you sleep." Rosemary had the expectant look of one who is prepared to honor any request, from a single teacake to an entire baked horse.

"Just some herb tea and one of those cheese biscuits," Aleksia replied. "If there are any left." Not that she would be denied; even if there hadn't been any, she had the feeling the Brownies would produce a batch just to satisfy her. "I still need to record all this in my Occurrence Book."

Without being asked, Rosemary brought the latest volume of the Book. Aleksia—as had her predecessor Veroushka—recorded all her projects, whether they succeeded or failed, as well as work in progress. There were eleven other volumes so far for Aleksia; the work of the previous Godmother had filled more than seventy. Aleksia found them very useful, especially in the first year or so of her tenure as the sole Godmother here. Whenever she had been at a loss for what to do in a given situation, even if she had not found an exact answer in those books, she had at least gotten some direction.

Sometimes, she actually sat down with a pen and ink and wrote it all out by hand, especially when the situation was vexing or puzzling. But tonight, she simply dictated what she wanted to say, and watched as the words formed of themselves on the page.

More magic, this of her own making. Each book was enchanted to respond to her voice when she began it; when she had filled it, she ended the enchantment. In part, that was so she was never tempted to go back and revise. A few projects had ended very badly indeed, and she felt the need of honesty there, for the sake of the Godmothers who would come after her, as well as her own sake. Living in isolation, answering to no one but herself, self-deception was an easy trap to fall into.

When she was done, she left the book on the desk and went to her bedroom. As she had expected, a hot pot of tea and a freshly split and buttered cheese biscuit waited for her. The aroma was both heady and comforting at the same time. Her silken nightrobe was laid out on the bed—if she wanted to be dressed, she could, of course, ring for someone, but as often as not, she simply disrobed herself. It wasn't as if most of the gowns of the Ice Fairy were complicated or difficult to get into or out of. Not like the corseted, laced, and ruffled court gowns of her birthplace. It took two servants to get a girl into the simplest of those, and three to get her out again. Sometimes Aleksia wondered how anyone managed to have children; by the time one was ready for bed, one was already exhausted.

But the gowns of the Ice Fairy were intended to mimic the sweeping, snow-covered slopes of her mountain; for the most part they were loose, flowing and draped, with trains and sleeves that trailed behind her on the floor, and generally a diadem of quartz crystals. Depending on where she was going, the gowns were either of velvet lined with ermine, or of Sammite with embroidery of tiny crystal beads. White, of course. Except when she was in disguise, she never wore colors.

Tonight, though, she didn't immediately go to her fireside chair, which was a lovely warm pouf of a thing, rather like a soft nest. Nor did she go to her collection of cushions on the other side of the fireplace. Instead, she went to the window and swept back the gold-and-scarlet curtains to look out at the view.

The moon shone brilliantly down on the white breast of the snow, and the stars gleamed in the blackness of the sky like the most perfect of diamonds on sable velvet. And she wondered, as she looked out at it, if she was becoming as cold and unfeeling as that landscape.

Because tonight, she had had three major tasks to deal with. The first had actually involved working against The Tradition to save the lives of those two tiny children. The Tradition had another end to their story—exhausted and in tears, they *should* have gone to sleep in each others' arms and died out there, to be covered by leaves. Gerda's plight in the hands of the robber band was a terrifying one for any young woman; when Aleksia had banished her image, Gerda's expression of fear and grief should have melted a stone. And as for the Tyrant—there she was juggling life and death on a massive scale. Any sensible person would have been shaking with trepidation.

Instead, she had been unmoved. All that had excited her had been the need to find a clever solution, to outwit The Tradition and win the game. She had not been afraid for the children, in tears of sympathy for Gerda, or angry at the Tyrant.

And now, she was only tired. Not triumphant, only satisfied, as having done a good day's work.

Was she slowly becoming as locked in ice, emotionally speaking, as that perpetually frozen landscape?

She shivered and dropped the curtain over the window.

Perhaps before she went to bed, it would be wise to try to find some way of looking in on the Sammi. Even if she could not contact one of the Shaman, or Wizards, perhaps she could watch him. It did not matter what kingdom you were in, people brought their magicians information.

Perhaps by seeing a Wizard who was involved with the lives of his people she could reconnect with real life herself.

The difficulty, of course, was to find someone in the first place. To watch, she needed to have a reflective surface, and Mages that were aware of mirror-magic kept such things covered or dulled. Still…

Wonder-smiths. The Sammi have magicians called Wonder-smiths. And no smith worthy of his forge is going to turn out dull blades.

So that would be what she would look for. The reflective surface of a weapon, in the possession of one who could make it more, much more, than just a weapon.

As it happened, she found exactly what she was looking for far sooner than she had expected.

4

THEY WERE BROTHERS, AND THEIR NAMES WERE ILMARI and Lemminkal. Lemminkal was the elder of the two, though neither was young. It was Ilmari who was the smith, and Aleksia first saw him in his forge, stripped to the waist, corded muscles giving lie to the gray in his hair and beard as he labored over a—

Scythe. Not an ax, not a sword, but that most humble of farmer's tools, putting as much effort and magic into it as she would have expected of a warrior's prized weapon. Which was interesting.

She learned their names and that they were brothers when the elder entered the forge to check on his brother's progress. There was only the briefest of exchanges; the elder brother, looking not particularly impressive in the simplest of woolen tunics and breeches, finished with a wise waggle of his head, and the comment, "That stream has been overfished, brother Ilmari," and took himself off.

Ilmari only grunted and went back to his work.

But then she chuckled when the purchaser of the scythe came to the forge; it was clear why Ilmari had taken such trouble over it.

"Greetings, Ilmari." The voice was pleasant, if a trifle high-pitched.

The owner of the voice was not exactly what Aleksia had expected from so breathy a tone. Instead of being petite and fluttery, the woman in question was exceedingly buxom, sturdy and had languid eyes that held a great deal of warmth in them. The full lips echoed that warmth with a half smile. But the hands that reached for the scythe were strong and no strangers to hard work.

"Ah!" she exclaimed, examining the implement with pleasure. "A masterwork, for certain. And the magic you bound to it?"

"As you asked. It will never cut flesh, it will never need sharpening until it is taken from the field, and whoever uses it will tire much slower. I could not make it so that the wielder never tired—"

"No more than you could make it so that it never, ever needed sharpening," the woman agreed, nodding. "That would be unnatural. But this will help my brother do a man's work until he gets a man's height, and he and I can keep the farm until he grows into our late father's place."

"There are many who would help you with that, Maari," Ilmari began, coaxingly, with a glint in his eye. "Many who would help you for the sake of a friendly—"

"Oh, and you mean yourself, Ilmari?" The young woman chuckled. "Nay, nay, Wonder-smith. You know nothing of farming and care less. You would trample half the corn instead of cutting it. Your shocks would come undone and the grain would rot on the ground before it dried. Stick to your forge, Ilmari. Stick to your runes, and my brother and I shall stick to ours. Now, tell me what I owe you for this."

"Three silver coins, or a bargain." Ilmari hesitated before setting the price, and little wonder; most people in a small village wouldn't see that much money in hard currency in the course of a year. And indeed, the girl bit her lip, and in her anxiety, betrayed her youth. Aleksia reckoned her no more than sixteen or seventeen.

"That's half my dower—" she said, as if to herself.

"But I would readily make you another bargain, Maari." The coaxing tone was back in the man's voice, and the gleam in his eyes told as clearly as speech just what sort of a bargain he would like to make. "For so good a friend and neighbor, things need not come to money between us—"

"And for the dear friend of my *father*, who has been like a father to me and my brother, and a respected *elder* of our village, I would have it no other way. Cheap at the price to keep my brother safe and the farm in our hands." Maari did not need to say anything more, and the man flushed a little. Properly, too, in Aleksia's estimation.

And yet, she had said it with such politeness that there was nothing the man could do but graciously take the three coins she told over into his hand, and accept her thanks and let her go.

Aleksia chuckled as he swore a little and kicked at the floor. Outfoxed! Well there it was, even a Wonder-smith and a magician could be tripped up by his own desires and find himself making a fool of himself in front of a clever girl.

She watched him as he crossly banked the fire, then pulled on a tunic, like his brother's—plain and somewhat the worse for wear, clearly in need of a woman's hand. So these were bachelor fellows, then? Not surprising that he was making a fool of himself over a girl a third of his age. Or perhaps not a third his age, but surely less than half. A man without a wife could delude himself into thinking there was no gray in his hair and beard, that he was the same fellow he'd been twenty or thirty years ago. A man with children about him that were the age of this young maiden had no such delusions. And besides, he would be far too busy keeping close watch on his own young maidens, eyeing old rakes and impetuous young bucks with equal disfavor, to have the leisure to go making a fool of himself in the first place.

Lemminkal came in again just as Ilmari finished shutting the forge for the night. He was trailed by a handsome fellow who was the right age for the departed maiden. Ilmari saluted them both with ill grace, and Lemminkal laughed.

"And what did I tell you, brother? That stream's been overfished. You should be casting your hook for a tasty big salmon, not chasing after the slim little minnows."

"Bah," Ilmari said, as the younger man chuckled. "And I suppose that's to leave the stream for your apprentice!"

"Not I!" The young man laughed. "Oh, no, I have the sweetest girl in the world waiting for me at home, and compared to her, your pretty caller is a candle to a star."

"Well I'd liefer have a candle than a star," Ilmari grumbled. "It's of more use."

The three men went out, and Aleksia searched for another reflective surface near them, so she could continue her observation.

She quickly realized that there were not many in the home of a pair of bachelors… No polished ornaments. No mirrors—not that she expected glass, so expensive and so fragile, in such a place. But no polished metal, either, no shiny pots, the housewife's pride.

No wonder Ilmari thinks he is still a handsome young dog. I doubt he has seen his reflection in years.

Finally, though, she did find a reflective surface—the water in a barrel somewhere near the fire. She got a most unedifying view of the ceiling of the place, but at least she could listen.

She had often wondered what Witches and Wizards and Godmothers talked about when they sat around their own fires of a night. She discovered that it was of very little use to her. The young man—Veikko—spoke of the doings of the village at some length, while the older men commented, Ilmari with a touch of good-natured mocking. At least, she thought it was good-natured. Lemminkal asked how Ilmari's commissions were coming, cautioning him that Winter was coming and his patrons would be ill-pleased if their tools and weapons did not leave with the last trader.

"Well enough, old woman," Ilmari said, his tone a trifle peevish. "I take but one extra bit of work, and you pester me as if you thought I was falling behind."

"Because you took it and put all else aside, with the hope of trading it for a Winter between the maid's thighs," Lemminkal said bluntly, while the young Veikko made a choking sound. "That may well keep *you* warm, but it does nothing to pay for our bread to be baked, nor for any of our Winter provisions. So unless you plan to learn how to bake and make cheese, I think I've a right to act like an old woman where the money is concerned!"

"Oh, give over!" Ilmari snapped. "Here!" There was the sound of coins being slapped down on the table. "She paid me in her dower money and there is an end to it! And I have but the ax to finish, and that will be done well before the last peddler leaves! And what was I to do? Tell her no, and let that half-grown boy cut himself to ribbons with a scythe he's too young to swing? The corn won't wait, but that ax can. I wouldn't have turned her away, if she'd been harelipped and cross-eyed and hadn't two coppers to clink together, Lemminkal. Though she'll never know what sort of bargain she got for her three silvers. Kings would pay for what I gave her."

There was silence for a moment. "I beg your pardon, brother," Lemminkal said, humbly. "Here I thought—"

"Oh, it was on my mind," Ilmari grumbled. "I'm a man after all, and she's a toothsome creature. But she would have none of my hinting, and told me how she could not give an honored *elder* of the village less than his due. Good luck! Talking about me as if I was her grandsire! Well, she's paid, and they'll get their harvest in, and in good time, and maybe a bit more."

"And what did you do for her, brother mine?" Lemminkal asked.

"I put her father's strength and skill into the scythe, that's what," Ilmari said with satisfaction. "After all, he's hardly using it in Tuonela. There's no harvesting nor planting across the river of death. And I put in it what she asked for, that the lad not feel he's weary until day's end and time to put the tools down."

"Hakkinnen was a champion in the field," Lemminkal mused. "They say in the village, he could get more harvested in a day than most men in two."

"And well if the boy can. He can hire himself out to some of the other farmers in exchange for woodcutting and other work. As he grows into that scythe, the magic will fade, as it should. Eventually, the skill and strength will be all his." Aleksia could hear the pride in the smith's voice. And no wonder; that was a tricky bit of magic. It was one thing to put magic into an object. It was quite another to get it to recognize when it wasn't needed anymore. "I learned my lesson with that damned hand-mill, brother. Never again will I make a thing that never fails, never fades. Bad enough that the hand-mill attracted the attention of half the black sorcerers in the North. Worse that it became a bone of contention that nearly destroyed a family. But worst of all—to keep it grinding what was asked of it nearly drained people to death!"

"That was a bad business," Lemminkal agreed. "But you were young."

Ilmari snorted. "And an idiot. Enough, I haven't had my supper, and neither have you. Who brought us what today?"

There was no talk then, as the three men fell on their food like starving wolves, and with little more than grunts of satisfaction. And then, it seemed, they were minded to go straight to sleep. She broke her spell with a shrug. Perhaps something would turn up another day.

The deer were hitched and waiting, and Aleksia was dressed in her most impressive of Snow Queen gowns. She watched the preparations out of her window, readying the strongest of the All Paths Are One spell in her mind. She would otherwise have a very long way to go. And if only this was to be a pleasure trip! But alas...

This was a christening. She would be the only Godmother there. There was no reason for any evil Witches, wicked queens, dark Sorceresses to turn up, either. No, the reason she was going was an entirely ordinary one.

She was going to intimidate the stuffing out of King Bjorn of Eisland's Court. And the King, too.

"All is in readiness, Godmother," said the Brownie Rosemary from behind her. And with a sigh, Aleksia went out into the bitter air that was held away from her by a spell, and with her driver's aid, stepped up and into her sleigh. As they drove out of her gates and over the pristine snowfields, she called up the spell she had ready. She had to wait until they were off the mountain and down among the trees for it to work, of course—you couldn't have the spell without a path for it to work on. And every Godmother as far away as Elena would know she was using it, too—it was very powerful magic—to twist space—and that sort of thing echoed and echoed again for anyone with the talent to recognize it.

Which, now that she came to think of it, meant that this false Snow Queen was not using Godmotherly magics much. Aleksia would *know* if she was. Elena would know. And that, of course, was how Elena knew that it wasn't Aleksia working mischief among the Sammi, for Aleksia hadn't used this magic for herself in a very long time. Not since she last visited her sister. As for using it to further or thwart The Tradition, every time she did *that* she wrote it down in her Commonplace Book, and any Godmother who cared to could have a copy of that just by telling her library to get it.

Aleksia chuckled wryly to herself as the sleigh entered the forest and she let the spell run free before her. *Trust, but verify.* She had no doubt Elena was doing just that. Well, good. Someone needed to. Godmothers rarely went to the bad, but it wasn't impossible, and Aleksia had very little peer supervision up here.

The journey was not instantaneous, so she had plenty of time to review everything she had done to get to the bottom of the mystery. If, indeed, there really was a mystery. She was beginning to doubt it. It was entirely possible that the Snow Queen had gotten the reputation as some sort of man-eating myth among the Sammi, and that what Elena had heard was nothing more than The Tradition putting force behind the myth. One day it *might* create a false Snow Queen—after enough people believed in the creature. But right now, it might well be only distorted echoes of her true deed coming back as some sort of hobgoblin tales.

Certainly there was no sign that the three Sammi magicians had heard anything about it, and they were the most likely to do so. It was clear from what she had seen and heard that people came to them from leagues and leagues around for the brothers to handle any magical difficulty, and Lemminkal was seizing on these pleas for help to further train his apprentice, Veikko. Already, since she had been eavesdropping on them, they had gotten rid of a troll, taken down a boar the size of a horse and gotten rid of a cursed talisman. If there *had* been a false Snow Queen out there stealing away young men, they would have heard about it by now. And they would have gone out to do something about it. Instead, they were doing what every other Sammi was doing at this moment—preparing for Winter.

She reluctantly concluded, as the sleigh came within sight of the King's Palace, that she was wasting her time watching and listening to them. Reluctantly, because she was enjoying being the secret member of their household. Listening to them gave her a sense of camaraderie, as if she really was there in person. She liked them all, and despite his flaws—and there were many—she very much liked Ilmari. He had a good heart, and a care to the people who depended on him and his brother for protection. She wished he was a little less boastful and a great deal less lecherous, but he really did not have any malice in him, and when he cared to be, he was witty, amusing and altogether good company.

Still, the illusion that she was part of their circle was just that, an illusion, and since they had proved of no use to her, it was time to give over her watch on them and turn her attention to other sources of information.

Just as she came to that conclusion, the sleigh arrived at the main entrance to the Palace. She descended from her sleigh, the personification of icy dignity, and was met by an honor guard of four of the King's personal bodyguards. They looked very festive in new red-wool uniforms, with the King's arms embroidered across their tabards.

As she passed through the crowd, people pulled away to give her room to pass, conversations chilled and people avoided her icy glare. It was as she had thought. The King was up to no good.

Now, when The Tradition forced something upon someone, it was not always full of magic and wonder, and it was not always good. Often enough it could be as vicious and sordid as an evil stepmother wanting to be rid of her husband's children so her own could take their place in his care and affections.

Now in this case, the King had wedded…imprudently. He had lusted over the daughter of one of his lesser nobles and she was important enough—or rather her family was—that marriage was the only way to have her. She adored him. He, once his lust had cooled, was weary of her. She had presented him with only this living daughter, and that only after much striving. So now the stage was set for tragedy on a Kingdom-wide scale if he could not rein in his lusts and at least—if he *must* take mistresses—take only those who would not also demand marriage.

Her mirror told her that there was one of those too-ambitious harpies waiting in the wings, hidden among the ladies-in-waiting for a chance to spring her honeyed trap and catch herself a King. And if she did...well, there were not many ways by which a King could be rid of an unwelcome spouse, particularly not when that spouse still loved him. All of those ways had consequences for the entire Kingdom. One of those was civil war.

Which was why Aleksia was here.

She waited impatiently through the ceremony, waited until The Traditional moment for the giving of gifts came, and stepped forward. Ruthlessly, she drew on her magic, creating an island of warmth and light about the Queen and the child, and sending waves of chill and little eddies of snowflakes everywhere else.

"Wisdom, I give this child," she said. "Beauty she will have in plenty from the blood of her mother and father, I need not add to that. But Wisdom I give her, and high Courage and Strength, so that she can be Queen *and* King to her people when the time comes. Intelligence she has in plenty, too, but I give her Craft and Cunning, so that she will know how to use whatever weapon comes to her hand to safeguard her country. And I give to her and her mother my personal protection." And she sent out another wave of cold.

There. Let the King hear that and dare to disinherit her....

He heard all right. And he understood. Stammering, he thanked her, terror in his eyes. Clearly, he must know that she knew what he was about. He was not stupid, this man, only ruled too much by his nether regions. The Queen thanked her with tears in her eyes and unfeigned gratitude. She must have scented something in the offing.

Aleksia accepted her embrace, but looked over her shoulder at the muster of her ladies, looking for one face among them.

There.

An exotic beauty, this one, by the standards of this Court. Here among the blond was a night-crow indeed, slim where they were sturdy, dark where they were light. And she paled when she saw Aleksia's eye on her, paled still further when she read Aleksia's message in her gaze.

Go. Go as far as you can. And do not come back.

The compulsion was set upon her, and Aleksia left, knowing that, before the day was out, the King's supposed love would be gone. Where, was of no concern to her.

And that was that. She sensed the powerful energies of The Tradition turning away, having now no more interest in this place.

She left as she had come, the epitome of chill perfection. Back to the Palace of Ever-Winter, a spoiled brat she needed to tame, and the knowledge that she was going to have to give up her pleasant evenings "with" the Sammi Mages. The King himself escorted her to her sleigh, and the look of terror in his eyes did not make up for the fact that she was not going to hear any more of Lemminkal's kantele playing, nor Ilmari's tales and jokes.

Duty. Bah.

5

"THEY SAY SHE IS CALLED THE SNOW QUEEN, AND SHE IS AS
cold as the snow itself." Ulla regarded them all solemnly. The young
women had the hearth of the cottage to themselves; Rikka's parents had
gone to bed, leaving them in sole possession of the main room of the
cottage. Kaari and Suvi-Marja were carefully manipulating the wooden
cards for their ornamental bands; since they were both weaving patterns
in red and the natural dark brown and white of sheep's wool, weaving
by firelight was not a problem. Rikka's needle continued to make the
intricate knots of her mittens, but Ulla's spindle was idle.

"It is the Snow Queen," Ulla began, after looking nervously over
her shoulder.

"But she is only a legend!" Rikka protested. "No one has ever seen
her. Not that I ever heard of anyway. And anyway, how could she possibly
be real? She must be over a thousand years old by now."

Kaari kept her hands moving steadily, but she felt a kind of chill on the
back of her neck, and suddenly the fire did not seem to be warming her.

"Father's cousin knows someone who saw her," Ulla said firmly.
"From a distance, a great distance, but he saw her, flying through the

sky in her white sleigh. But that is not the point. The point is that where once she merely remained in her Palace of Snow, content to keep it always Winter only where she dwelled, now that is changing." Ulla shuddered. "Now she is taking young men who attract her, taking them in the night, and they are never seen again. And now—now she is killing. Whole villages, it is said, stricken with a deadly cold that strikes the villagers without warning, freezing them where they stand."

Kaari concentrated very hard on the patterns she was weaving. She did not in the least like what she was hearing. Normally on such nights, she was able to listen as avidly as the others were, to take it in with a delicious shiver, to feel the danger, and yet know, in her heart of hearts, that it would never affect her.

Not tonight. She could not think why, but it felt as if there was some terrible thing out there in the darkness—looming over her, looking at her, and chuckling, coldly, as it slowly tightened its invisible grip about her.

She didn't want to hear any more. And yet she did not, could not, stop Ulla from continuing her stories. In the end, it was Rikka, not her, who asked for an end to it, who managed to turn the conversation into more cheerful topics, and who managed to make them all laugh.

Eventually, it grew late enough that Suvi-Marja's parents began coughing pointedly. Taking the hint, the three visitors rolled up their work, stowed it in the baskets they had brought with them, and affectionately took their leave of their friend.

All but Kaari, who felt a reluctance to venture out in the dark, chill night—a night so powerful, it verged on revulsion. Impulsively, she turned to Suvi-Marja, seeking an excuse.

But she didn't have to make up one. It was her friend that put one hand on her arm and looked at her entreatingly. "Can you stay the night?" she begged. "Oh, Kaari...I so want to ask your advice, and mayhap your help, and I did not want to do so around the others—"

She bowed her head and flushed "——You all have had so many sweet-hearts, and I have only had the one——"

Relief made her feel giddy. She often stayed the night with her friends, particularly when they did not have such enormous families as hers. Her mother would not take it amiss that she had done so tonight. "Suvi! Of course I will! But do not hold out too much hope of my being terribly wise, for wisdom you should ask your mother——"

Even in the dying firelight, Kaari could see her friend blushing. "Oh, I could never ask my mother these things. She thinks that Essa is nice enough, but that I could do much better... I cannot make her understand."

Whatever Suvi-Marja's mother did or did not understand, in that moment, Kaari understood her very well and what she was trying to say. Poor Suvi! She was not *ugly,* but she was not as pretty as most of her friends. All her life, she had been in the shadow of the others and had become resigned to that position. And now, there was a young man...and now, she was afraid and a little confused and very conflicted.

So she spent no small amount of time reassuring her. It *was* true that Essa was not a fabulous catch as a husband, if all you looked at was how prosperous he would be. But he was kind—in his own fashion, he was thoughtful—and he did care for Suvi. And if it was not wild, obsessive, passionate love, the sort of thing that they made songs about—the sort of things that they made songs about was not at all comfortable, nor safe, and Suvi *liked* comfort and safety.

So they talked for a very long time together by the light of the fire, with Kaari reassuring her friend. And by the time they slept, Suvi was smiling again and Kaari was only a little uneasy about the strange stories out of the North.

Perhaps I was a little overenthusiastic, Annukka thought, looking a bit ruefully, and yet with pardonable pride, at a smokehouse so full of pig and venison sausage that it could not have held another link. She closed the door on it all, sealing the door tightly with wax from her hives. She would not open it again for another three days, by which time the sausages would be cured and ready to hang in the rafters, where they would get a bit more smoke, which would do them no harm.

Now, every year, she sat up all night on the first full moon of Autumn, the first harvest moon, and sang for a full, rich harvest. But this year, something—she was not sure what, a feeling of unease perhaps, or just the small indications that the Winter would be hard, cold and long— had prompted her to put a little more emphasis in her song than usual. She absolutely would not interfere with the weather—be it sent by gods or the winds, it was not hers to meddle with. But there was no harm in singing for enough, even abundance, to carry the village through a bad Winter, if one was to come. If the weather was to be *that* bad, things would die in the cold anyway, and if a few more birds and fish and animals died now, beneath the hunters' hands, it was a quicker, easier death than starving to death or freezing in the night. It was a good balance. It was also a good balance to ask the crops to be abundant—if the Winter was a hard one, then an abundant crop now meant that there *would* be seed to plant when Spring came.

So she sat up and sang, for everyone with a Mage rune knew that the most powerful spells were sung, not spoken. There was something about music, and the way it was easy to get lost in it, the way it was easy to call up mental images of what you wanted, that made sung magic, for the Sammi at least, that much more powerful.

Now it seemed that her spells had been very effective indeed. The cellars were full of beets, onions, turnips and cabbage, dried blueberries, lingonberries and cloudberries, dried mushrooms, sacks of rye and barley flour, sacks of whole barley, stacks of dried cheese, waxed wheels of aging cheese, casks of dried and salted fish, potted birds and meat.

Hams and sausage hung from every ceiling. Cupboards were full of preserved pots of butter, lard, jam and honey. The entire village had been feasting for days on the traditional foods of Autumn, butchery-time—blood pancakes, blood dumplings, blood soup, fried cracklings, stews and soups rich with meat scraps, and dishes made with various organs that could not be preserved—for nothing, nothing went to waste, not even, or especially, in times of abundance. Fish had almost been leaping into the nets, and game flung itself in the way of the hunters. There were peddlers and traveling entertainers coming through at this time of year, and they generally tried to spend as much time as they could in the villages that had a reputation for generous hospitality. The Sammi did not have harvest fairs of the sort that Annukka had heard of; Autumn was too busy a time for that. But anyone that came through was more than welcome to partake of the ongoing feast of things that could not be stored for the Winter.

One such peddler, very, very fond of Annukka's sausages, had just been through. He had left with some of the first batch of the season stowed in his cart, and she was now the owner of a curious and very beautiful mother-of-pearl comb. That might have seemed a very uneven trade for a couple of strings of sausages, but he had confided in her that no one wanted it once they heard he had traded for it with one of the seal-people.

Now she had no particular aversion for the seal-people, although it was generally held to be bad luck for someone who made his living fishing to have anything of theirs. After all, they might want it back, and their way of getting it back might well be to drown you....

But the peddler, who she knew to be an honest fellow, had sworn he had come by it honorably. And it was a lovely piece, carved with swirling waves and fronds of kelp. She intended to give it to Kaari for her bride's-gift.

As she sealed up the door of the smokehouse, she smiled a little, thinking about that particular peddler. He was the one with the most beautiful pieces of amber, and sweet ambergris for making scents. Suvi-Marja had seen one particular necklace in his store, three big drops like huge drops of honey, suspended from a delicate chain of amber beads, and it was clear to anyone with eyes that she wanted the piece. Between the two of them, she and Kaari had managed to put it into Essa's thick skull that this would be a grand betrothal token for Suvi, and even more cleverly, managed to make him believe that *he* had thought of it.

I wonder if she has even taken it off to wash, Annukka thought with powerful amusement. Well, at least that was settled. She had known Essa since his birth, and never once had she known him to go back on a thing once he had decided to do it. That girl was as good as married this moment.

But the recollection of the peddler suddenly made her frown, because goods were not the only things that peddlers brought with them. They also brought news. And some of his stories were...disquieting.

There had always been tales of a strange, magical creature that some called the Winter Witch, some the Ice Fairy and others the Snow Queen. She was said to live up so far north—or else, in the mountains—that there was no other season but Winter there. That was not at all disturbing. There were all manner of things in that region that were magical in nature. If she were to concern herself with all of them, she would spend her time constructing defenses and never get anything done. This creature had been up there for generations, it seemed, and most of the stories were about people who had been stupidly or criminally foolish and had essentially gotten their comeuppance.

But these stories were different. The creature had suddenly turned malicious, and rather than sitting in her fortress or castle or ice-cave or whatever it was she lived in, she was extending her domain into places

she had never been known to walk before. There were stories now of
a Winter come so early that the snow caught apples not yet ripe on the
trees, and grapes were frozen on the vine. There were stories of a
killing kind of cold that swept down out of nowhere and froze birds and
animals in their place. And there were stories of young men just—
taken. For no apparent reason.

So far, none of those stories had been about anywhere too near
the Sammi "kingdom" of Karelia. But Annukka knew her tales, and
she knew that when bad things were on the move, they didn't stop
for borders.

She bent down to apply the wax she was warming to the crack where
the door met the frame. The rest of the smokehouse was tightly chinked
with moss and clay, so this would be the only place where smoke could get
out except the vent in the roof. It was taking extra care like this that made
her sausages so good. And there was nothing like sausage on a cold morning.

If the Sammi had an enemy, it was Winter. There was not enough in
the way of riches here for anyone to want to conquer their land; they
were in no way strategic; and the very nature of the people, so depen-
dant on the reindeer herds as they were, made them difficult to confine
and fight. Sammi warriors did not make stands. Sammi warriors faded
into the forest and the snow, struck from shadows, let the landscape
wear the enemy down. Not that they did not, individually, fight vali-
antly toe-to-toe with the best of them! But as an army, as a force—no.
When they organized, it was to divide the enemy, make him come to
ground of their choosing and fight him as ghosts in the night.

But they could not do that with Winter. Winter was implacable.
Winter's cold sought you out and tried to kill you and could not be
hidden from. The only defenses against Winter were food, shelter and
warmth. As the days grew shorter and the nights longer, there was
always that fear in the back of every mind: what if the sun faded and

never returned? What if the night and the cold were forever? What if this was the season when the battle ended and Winter won?

Annukka shivered and walked back to the house. She had another wheel of cheese to coat with wax before she put it down in the cellar.

No one spoke of this fear, although the oldest songs, the strong magic songs, did. Strong magic had to acknowledge fear in order to conquer it. But that was what all the celebration at MidWinter was about, at bottom. There was the long watch through the darkest night of the year, the hope of driving back the dark with fire, of driving back hardship and privation with feasting, the driving back of the cold with the warmth of fellowship. And in the dawn, when the sun truly did rise again, there was rejoicing and a relief that was the stronger for being unspoken. The people had survived; they would live until Spring.

Of course, people could—and did—die between MidWinter and Spring, but somehow it never seemed as terrible an omen—unless the year had been so bad that stores were scant to begin with. Even then, this village had a most fortunate location. There was good hunting and good fishing, even in the middle of Winter.

But this year, unless the Winter never ended, there would be no need to fear the coming of the snow, even if it began early.

She could not help the thought that followed, as she checked the pot of beeswax beside the fire to see if it had melted yet. *And what if Winter never ends?*

She banished that thought with another. *If there is some great and terrible Magic at work, then the Wonder-smiths, the Warrior-Mages, the Wise and the Shamans will band together and defeat it.* It might be difficult to get the Sammi to fight together, but it was not impossible.

That internal voice chuckled a little. *Difficult? No more difficult than teaching a cat to herd reindeer.*

"Stop that, you!" she said aloud, glad that there was no one about to hear her. Well, other than the cat, who jumped at the sound of her voice and looked guilty, then immediately turned the guilty look to one of nonchalance. "And *you* may stay out of the cheese!" she scolded, not sure what the cat was getting into before she made it jump, but knowing that the likeliest thing was the cheese it had been eyeing.

The cat put his tail in the air and sauntered away, very clearly conveying that he had no interest in the cheese, and she was incredibly rude to think so, and worse to *say* so. After all, someone might be listening. A cat had his dignity to think of. The nerve!

She was still laughing at the affronted cat when Kaari came flying up the path, face white, something wrapped in cloth in her hands. As she burst through the door, Annukka could see that she was sobbing.

"Mother—Mother!" she wailed. "It is Veikko!" She held out the bundle before Annukka could say anything, her hands shaking. The cloth fell away from it, and Annukka saw a little silver cup had been wrapped in it. "Before he left, we shared a loving-cup!" The girl sobbed. "He knew the spell—he said that it would keep me from worrying if he couldn't find a messenger to bring me letters, that as long as it was polished and shining, I would know he was safe. Last night it was fine, bright silver, not a speck of black. I looked at it just now—and look!"

Annukka, who knew very well what the Loving-Cup spell was, since she had taught it to her son, looked at the silver vessel in mute horror.

It was black from base to top, with only a thin silver line left near the bottom. Annukka knew exactly what this meant.

Veikko was in deadly danger.

Aleksia was back in the throne room, at the ice-mirror. Today, her gown was a sweeping creation of white velvet trimmed in white fox and lined with white mink, with a belt of plaques of silver holding faceted crystals, and a crown to match. Her hair was done up in a severe knot.

She was warm and comfortable, but looked chilly and utterly unapproachable. It would take a very brave man indeed to do so. The throne room was especially cold today, because she expected Kay at any moment.

Meanwhile Gerda's second trial, her captivity among the robbers, was coming to a turning point, and Aleksia needed to keep a very sharp eye on it indeed. She was not inclined to trust any of this to luck.

The robbers had learned that Gerda was not rich, that her parents were very far away indeed. Since they were all completely illiterate, to reach them and demand a ransom—even if one could be paid—one of their number would have to spend most of a month traveling to her city, and then, when he got there, somehow convince them that the girl he had was her. The rest of the band would have to trust him to bring back the money—and cows would be flying like swallows before *that* happened. And in his turn, he would have to keep from being captured; pigs would be joining the flying cattle if he managed it. The robbers themselves were not going to trust him with money for his journey out of their own stores, which meant that, to make that trip, he would be resorting to robbery, but doing so alone and out of the forest. The bandit in the forest and the robber in the city were two very different creatures. And neither functioned very well in the environment of the other.

Though illiterate, they weren't fools and had worked all of this out for themselves. That meant that anything they were going to get from Gerda in the way of material goods, they had already gotten.

Now this group of men were looking at Gerda in an entirely different fashion. There were, after all, only two women here, and the Chief's daughter was not to be touched, or even looked at impertinently. Not just because the Chief would gut the offender, but because Valeri would castrate him, *then* let her father gut him.

Now, it was true that Valeri had claimed Gerda for her own personal servant. It was also true that Valeri had lost interest in things after a while. The pet rabbit she had once that had escaped, the fawn she had raised that became venison roast when she wearied of trying to keep it in a pen, the various "ladylike" pursuits she had attempted and dropped when she was no good at them. The truth was, Valeri was more at home in breeches than skirts, happier with her hair chopped short than being braided and fussed over, more apt with a knife and a bow than a needle and a pan. She'd had a fancy to play lady and had seized on Gerda to be her lady's maid. But the men knew that, sooner or later, she would tire of the game and, they hoped, of Gerda.

And even if she didn't, the word of the Chief was law even to his daughter. If the men all banded together and demanded the girl, they would get her. They had not yet gotten to the point of banding together—each still hoped to get her for himself alone—but they would.

And soon.

Winter had already come to that forest, and there would be no more travelers coming through to be preyed upon. The band was snowed in; their hideout was part cave and part a stoutly built fortress of stone and massive logs. Aleksia was fairly sure that they didn't know who had built the place originally, and probably would never have dared to use it if they had known.

Trolls. Only trolls were big enough to have felled the trees these logs came from, and strong enough to move them here. Why they had built this place, Aleksia had no idea, nor why they had abandoned it. Perhaps a Hero had come along and tricked them into the sunlight. Perhaps they had just wandered off. They might come back today, tomorrow, a hundred years from now, or never.

This mattered not at all to the current situation. And it was very important this time that Aleksia hear what was going on. Her point of view was a huge old mirror, very dusty and tarnished, that had been shoved over against the wall of this, Valeri's room in the outer fortress. Her father,

Aleksia had learned, had claimed this room as her nursery long ago because it had a fireplace. She had kept it because she liked her privacy.

Aleksia could only hear and see through reflective surfaces, although it was surprising how many of those there were that people were not aware of. A drop of water in a forest, the shiny surface of a metal cup, even a bit of mica embedded in a rock wall—any and all of those were enough for her to see and hear through. So it didn't matter how tarnished and dusty this old mirror was, it still served.

"Give over," Valeri said, pushing Gerda's hands away from her head. "And hand me that knife. I'm tired of this."

Gerda picked up the scissors instead. "If you are going to have your hair chopped off, let me do it and make it tidy," she retorted. "You don't have to go about looking like a magpie's nest."

The Robber Girl snorted, but let Gerda cut her hair for her, long black tresses falling around her like Autumn leaves. When she was done, Gerda handed her a hand-mirror and she surveyed the result and grunted her approval. Her hawk-sharp face was suited to the shorter hair, Aleksia thought. Having it braided up made such a face, all angles and planes, look even more angular than it already was. "This business of being a lady gives me a pain," she announced. "It was fun to play at it, but it gives the men ideas. I don't want 'em thinking of me as somethin' they can pounce on."

"Like me, you mean," Gerda replied steadily.

There was silence in that cramped, cluttered room. Then Gerda bent over, picked up all the hair and tossed it into the fire without a word. Valeri took out her knife, cut the women's clothing she was wearing off herself, and pulled on her usual leather breeches, heavy woolen shirt and leather vest. With a look of contentment, she strapped on a belt with two heavier knives on it, as well as a whip. She crammed a wool hat on top of her newly shorn head. "*Now* I feel like meself," she said, with pleasure.

Then she stopped, and looked sharply at Gerda. "You noticed," she said. "'Bout the men, I mean."

Gerda raised her chin. "You'd have to be blind not to. And deaf. They're just waiting, like crows watching something dying—"

She caught herself and looked away. Aleksia smiled. This was going well....

Valeri put her hands on her hips. "Aye, and they think I dunno. That I dunno my rabbit ended up i' the stew an' my fawn ended up there, too. They think I just forget things an' don't care about 'em no more." She clenched her jaw. "Bet they're just waitin' for me to get tired of bein' a lady an' not needin' you."

Gerda nodded wordlessly.

Oh, very good, girls, Aleksia thought with approval.

"Well, I might get tired of things sometimes, but that don't mean I don't care about 'em." Valeri's eyes flashed. "An' what's more, I haven't forgotten about things since I was nine an' they ate my deer. *I* see when my things disappear. I just don't say anything. But I'll tell you what, missy. They ain't getting you."

And just like that, Gerda found herself with a rucksack in her hands, shoving things in that Valeri threw at her. Of course, half of those things were weapons, which Valeri then took back, muttering something about a rock being more use to someone like Gerda. But it certainly was not much more than an hour later that they had a tolerable pack put together, with a bedroll tied atop it and plenty of journey-bread in oiled paper inside the top. Gerda looked at it doubtfully, then back up at Valeri. "But how am I to get past the men out there?" she asked.

Valeri grinned. "You just leave that to me. You put on them things, and be ready when I come for you."

Gerda shook her head, but obeyed, pulling on the thick woolen breeches—though she settled her discarded skirt over them, Aleksia presumed for modesty's sake—the knitted wool shirt and the leather tunic. She put on two pairs of stockings to make the too-large felt boots Valeri had thrown at her fit, then crammed on the battered fur hat and sheepskin shepherd's coat. And just as she was swinging the pack onto her back, Valeri reappeared.

She put her finger to her lips, eyes sparkling with mischief, and beckoned. Gerda followed her out into a cavern that the bandits used as their main room. Aleksia flitted her point of view to the reflective surface of an overturned silver goblet.

There were snoring bodies everywhere.

Carefully, they picked their way through the sprawled bandits, Valeri leading Gerda deeper into the caverns. She stopped once to get a lantern and lit it with a candle left there for that purpose, then made her way to a hole in the wall only a little taller than a man. That allowed Aleksia to transfer her focus to the glass of the lantern.

They both plunged into the darkness.

Valeri's lamp cast just enough light to show that they were in a narrow tunnel, too rough and too small to have been carved out by the trolls. Likely, this was the original cave that the trolls had enlarged. With the lantern held out in front of them, Aleksia had a fine view of the tunnel. Well, a few feet of the tunnel, anyway.

The two young women were very quiet. Finally Gerda whispered, "Is it safe to talk?"

Valeri chortled. "Oh, aye. Them back there won't be waking up any time soon. I rolled out a keg of brandywine for 'em." Her laugh grew deeper. "Not the first time, neither. See, I'm the one thet brews it. Papa, he got no notion where it comes from, and he'll be all over 'em to find out which one of 'em does the brewing. They can say for true it ain't one of 'em, an' Papa never thinks of me. I been doin' that since one of the lads we ransomed showed me how. He figured he'd use it t' get into me breeches, but he got ransomed 'fore he could try."

There was a silence from Gerda that Aleksia could only imagine meant she was stunned by Valeri's bluntness. Not that Gerda could possibly be ignorant of sex—the town she lived in wasn't *that* large that a girl her age hadn't seen animals and possibly even servants fornicating. But in Gerda's class, you didn't talk about it.

Valeri continued on. "I found this passage when I was half this tall, and I been usin' it to come an' go when I wanted t' creep off somewhere where Papa and the men didn't know."

"But it's not secret—" Gerda protested. "All those lanterns—"

"This part ain't. It goes down t' the little lake where we get our water from. See?" She raised the lamp and light bounced back at her as they came out into a much larger chamber.

The steady drip of water from the ceiling echoed around the rocks. This was a sizable room and it was hard to tell just how deep the "lake" was. Valeri skirted along a ledge to the right so narrow that she and Gerda had to put their faces to the rock wall and edge along sideways. At the back of the cavern was another crack, this one very narrow and not at all visible from the other side. Gerda had to take off her pack to squeeze through it.

"Papa thinks when I disappear it's 'cause the men have gotten drunk an' I want some peace," Valeri continued when they were finally making their way down yet another rough tunnel. "I told him I come back here to think and get some quiet. So he don't come lookin' for me. I did just that just enough times that he figures that's what I always do."

"That's clever!" Gerda exclaimed. Again, Valeri chortled.

"You think that's clever, you just wait." It seemed that Gerda and Aleksia did not have long to wait, either. There was light at the end of this crack, and soon the two young women pushed through a screen of cedars into a tiny pocket valley.

And there, looking at both of them with great interest, was a tall, shaggy reindeer. When he saw Valeri, he snorted, and shambled over to them.

"I learnt my lesson," Valeri said, scratching around the base of the deer's antlers. "I got me another fawn, an' I kept this 'un safe." She pulled an old, withered apple out of a pocket and offered it to him. While he crunched it up, she blew out the lantern and pulled a sledge and an oiled canvas bag from out of another tangle of bushes. In moments, she had the deer harnessed and hitched to the sledge. The deer snorted happily.

"Well, get on!" Valeri said impatiently to Gerda, who hastily—if gingerly—settled herself onto the back half of the sledge. Valerie led the deer to a cleft in the rock walls surrounding them, pulled back yet more brush to reveal a stout and very tall gate, and opened it. Then, taking up the reins and jumping onto the front part of the sledge, she snapped the reins briskly on the deer's back. Without a moment of hesitation, he loped forward, starting the sledge over the snow with a jerk.

Aleksia moved her viewpoint to a shiny buckle on the deer's harness.

They made very good time. Valeri drove standing up, looking like a practiced sailor in a storm as the sledge bumped and skidded over the snow. Gerda clung to the sides of the sledge, white-faced.

It was at that moment that Aleksia heard Kay's footsteps outside the throne room. Satisfied that things were going well for now, she dismissed the mirror-vision, and turned to face him.

He looked miserable.

He had certainly lost weight, and if the reports her Brownies gave her were true, of how at meals he listlessly pushed things around the plate before finally swallowing a few bites with apparent difficulty, there was no question of why he had lost the weight. His eyes were darkly circled. More reports had reached her that he woke up in the night often, sweating, shaking, out of the grip of nightmares.

She simply looked at him, schooling her features into a mask of boredom. "Yes?" she said, finally, when the silence had stretched on too long. "You may speak."

He coughed. "Great Queen," he said, hoarsely. "I—uh—"

"You began with 'Great Queen' rather than 'I' and that is certainly an improvement," she said coldly. "I presume you have more to say?"

He went red, then white. "It—it's very lonely here—" He faltered. *Interesting.* All of the arrogance seemed to have leached right out of him!

"You should have thought of that before you accepted my invitation," she reminded him.

"It's—not—" He faltered again. "It's Gerda. It's—I'm worried about her—"

She tilted her head to the side. "Gerda? What a common name. Who is this wench?"

She could see him struggle. He wanted to lash out at her because she dismissed Gerda as common and insulted her by implication. But he had finally accepted the fact that she was, and always would be, more powerful than he was and that he was under her control. "Gerda…" he finally managed, "Gerda is a young lady who has…always been my friend. And I—am very fond of her."

Aleksia almost laughed, but her control was too good to let that slip. He had almost said that he loved Gerda.

She shrugged. "I am sure she will find someone else. You have important work to do. You should not be distracted by a mere girl."

Once again he went red, then white. "She wouldn't—I am worried about her!" He persisted. "Without me there, she might—"

"Might find someone with an equally shallow mind, who is only interested in settling down and raising fat babies." She shrugged. "You are destined for greater things as long as you concentrate on your work and not on silly girls."

She could see him struggling with all this. On the one hand, she was complimenting him. She clearly valued him, and for the thing he had once thought was the most important.

On the other hand, somehow over the past several days, Gerda had pushed everything else out of his mind. She knew that look in his eyes now. He was lovesick, obsessed. His nightmares were probably compounded of equal parts of terrible things happening to Gerda, and Gerda finding some other young man.

My, my. An interesting development.

"Go," she said, with a shrug. "If that is all that concerns you, put your fears to rest. The girl will be fine. Her parents will find her a husband, she will have a litter of brats and all will be well in her world. Meanwhile, you will be uncovering the secrets of the Universe. And in the end, it will be you who makes a difference, while she just adds another lot of round-faced children to be good, obedient subjects of your King."

She watched him struggling with his desire to retort, watched him conquer himself, and watched him walk away in defeat, shoulders slumped. It was all she could do to keep from jumping up and dancing.

She did retire to her own rooms for a bit—partly to make sure, should he brace himself up and return to confront her, that she would not be there, and partly because, despite her warm clothing, her hands and feet were cold and numb.

Her Brownies brought her pea soup and hot bread with butter melting on it. Peasant fare—the cook must have changed again. She sighed with satisfaction. It was a good change; peasant fare was tasty, hearty and very comforting. She felt strongly in the need of comfort.

Meanwhile, she watched the boy in her small mirror. And it was obvious that her deduction was correct. The boy was lovesick. Thoughts of Gerda clearly intruded on everything he did.

She could not have engineered a better outcome here if she had personally directed The Tradition into this path.

Actually, I wonder if I have....or rather, if all the Godmothers have. Is it becoming part of The Traditional Path for us to intervene?

She shook off the thought. If it was, well...the work would be going easier. And aside from the occasional moment like this one, it wasn't.

Pity.

Because if things would just go a *little* easier...she might be able to leave them for a bit. Go somewhere. Somewhere without ice and snow.

She made a face and put down the empty bowl with a sigh. Outside, the sun was westering. She wasn't sure how far Valeri was going to take Gerda, but there was not a chance that Valeri would be coming with her. She hadn't packed up her own things, after all. No, Valeri would take her out of immediate reach of the bandits and then leave her to find her own way. That should be just about now.

6

ALEKSIA RETURNED TO THE THRONE ROOM FEELING ALL the better for the meal and the chance to warm herself. She settled down to her mirror in a much better frame of mind than when she had left it.

The great mirror clouded for a bit as she reminded it of what it had last been reflecting, then the cloudiness resolved into the image she had expected, a look backward across the loping reindeer's back, the grin of Valeri as the sledge flew over the snow, and behind her, Gerda's white, strained face. Interestingly enough, they were out of the trees and tearing along a long, flattish slope. From the look of things—yes, Gerda was within striking distance of the Palace of Ever-Winter. With help.

Just as Aleksia recognized that fact, Valeri brought the sledge to a halt.

"And here is where I leave you!" she said cheerfully. She waved her hand in the general—and correct—direction of Aleksia's Palace. "What you want is over that way. Not sure how far, but it's there all right."

"You aren't coming with me?" Gerda faltered, getting carefully up from the sledge. From the way she winced, it hadn't been an easy ride.

"Of course not! I've got the band to help look after! And when I do leave—" Valeri's face took on a look of speculation. "When I do, it'll be t'see the world. No offense, but not t'go rescue some little girl's boy. So! Best of luck and off you go!"

And Valeri did not even pause to see Gerda sling the pack over her back. With a yell and a slap of the reins, she was off again, turning the sledge back along the track they had made, the reindeer's head high as he loped along. And Valeri did not look back.

Poor Gerda…standing there all alone in a vast expanse of white, she looked very small, and very lost.

And there was no way, no way at all, she was going to get across the mountains on her own two feet. No matter how brave she had been so far, no matter how earnest she was, she was still a town girl. She simply did not know how to survive out there.

She was going to need help.

And now was the time for her Godmother to arrange for some overt aid.

Aleksia redirected the mirror for a moment, into the depths of an ice-cave. And there, as she expected, was what she was looking for. It did not at all surprise her to see Urho, the Great White Bear, looking back at her.

My scrying told me you might be needing me, said the slow, heavy voice in her mind.

Urho was one of the Wise Beasts, the sort that could speak and reason like humans. He was a frequent visitor to the Palace, and although she could not exactly call him good company, his stories were interesting, and he actually enjoyed breaking up the monotony of Winter with the occasional task for her. His usual tasks—for he was something of a Mage himself—were to see to it that the more inimical of creatures were reported, and if possible, kept far from her door, and to come to the aid of travelers wise enough to see him for what he was or innocent enough to trust him.

"I have a peasant cook now," she said, and with amusement saw his eyes light up. "Oh, yes, Urho. All your favorites, I do think. And down below your cave, where the snowline meets the treeline, just above the cairn of thirty stones beside the trout stream, there is a young lady. She is all alone, rather ill-equipped and marching with great determination to rescue her lover from wicked me."

What, another one? Urho rumbled with laughter. *So, so, so. I should hurry, if I am to intercept her before nightfall.*

"Thank you, old friend. I will see you in a few days."

Look in on us between now and then. I will find shiny places.

"I will," she promised, and the mirror clouded over.

She took a long, deep breath. Well, that was sorted. Kay was in love with Gerda after all, with emotions all the more potent for having been suppressed all this time. Gerda had grown a spine, not sitting down in the snow and weeping until someone found her and took pity on her, but marching over inhospitable territory with every intention of getting there by herself. The difficult part of all of this was over.

Of course, she was not going to count this over until the lovers were reunited and on their way home together. Many a Godmother had been tripped up by being too confident of the happy ending.

She rubbed her hands together to warm them. No matter how hard she tried, she was never quite able to keep herself completely warm here. She was about to get up when the glass clouded again.

She blinked to see her mirror-servant appear in the depths of it. He hardly ever used *this* mirror. He hated it, actually. Despite appearing as nothing but a disembodied head, he swore the mirror made shivers run down his spine.

"Jalmari," she said, looking at the blue-shadowed apparition, closely. "Have you…done something to your hair?"

The head somehow removed its hood, though there were no visible hands. What was revealed was a bizarre—at least to Aleksia's eyes—mound of white hair with tight rolls over each ear and some sort of tail with a black ribbon tying it back.

"What in the name of all that is holy is *that?*" she asked, astonished.

Jalmari stared back at her. "It is the highest of fashion in the Frankish Court."

"It looks like something died on your head," she replied, too astonished by the sight to be anything except blunt.

Jalmari sniffed. "Well, since you need me so seldom, *I* have been taking the opportunity to educate myself in the ways of some of the other Kingdoms. No one would take me seriously in Frankovia if I didn't wear my hair this way."

"No one will take you seriously here if you do," she muttered, amused. "So to what do I owe the favor of an appearance?"

Jalmari became intensely focused, so much so that his absurd hair vanished, leaving him with his normal curly black locks. "You wished to find information about your imitator, Godmother Aleksia," he replied. "Well—this is what I have found—"

Look for magical trouble among the Sammi, centered on ice and snow. Hardly useful, since it was what she already knew, except that Jalmari had at least given her a small area to search in. *My own searches lead me here, and no farther. This probably means that the players in this Traditional path have not moved yet. So look for powerful magic, Godmother. This has clouds of great danger about it.*

Outside of being able, like Aleksia herself, to see and hear anything in a place with a mirror in it, Jalmari's one powerful ability was to see directly the magic that The Tradition gathered about its instruments and pawns. Something about this particular river valley and village was aswirl with that magic. So Aleksia was looking through every reflective surface she could find in order to—

"—but Mother Annuka," said a tearful voice, as the vague shapes in her mirror coalesced into two women of the Sammi, standing outside the doorway of one of their log houses. It must be harvest season by the look of things. The leaves of the trees above their heads were gold, and the sky was a crisp and chilly blue. One of the women was a stunningly beautiful girl, a maiden by the fact that she wore her hair uncovered and loose, with a studded headband of ribbon confining it, while the other wore a square felt hat with bands of card-woven decoration, or perhaps embroidery, around the hem. Both were dressed the same: in a woolen, high-necked dress with more fanciful bands decorating it at the neck, along the arms and at the hem, and aprons also decorated with embellished bands. The dresses were so short that, in many lands, they would be considered scandalous, which only made sense for someone who spent all Winter traipsing about in the snow. A dress that ended below the ankle would only end up soaked and sodden, heavy and ruined besides. In towns where roads were trodden down and paths swiftly cut, you could wear a long dress. Out here, where a "village" might consist of three huts, you adapted. So beneath the dresses, both wore woolen breeches, finished at the bottoms with yet *more* colorful bands, tucked into felt boots. In the deepest Winter, those boots might be sheepskin or reindeer hide rather than felt. The older woman's costume was black, the younger, a golden brown, and the style marked them as the Sammi, people who herded reindeer in the most northern regions of Karelia.

So...why was the mirror showing her these two? There had to be a reason. When she was seeking like this, the mirror never showed her anything without a good reason.

"—Mother Annukka," the girl repeated, only a step from tears, her face a virtual mask of fear, "this is scarcely the time for music!"

The older woman was holding a lovely wooden kantele, a harp used mostly by the Sammi, and she gave the girl a sharp glance. Her eyes were a very piercing blue, and Aleksia found herself wishing that she actually knew this woman. Her face had a look of strength, bravery and wisdom about it. "Have you ever seen any true *sorcery*, Kaari?"

The girl shook her head, and wiped her eyes. "No, only things like casting the runes, and the little household magics. You are the only Sorceress I know. Everything else I only know from tales."

"The greater Magies that I know all work through music," the one called Annukka said, tuning the kantele with practiced fingers, one ear cocked to the sound as she plucked the strings too softly for Aleksia to hear. "Shaman use the spirit-drums, Wise Women and Wonder-smiths the *kantele*. So be still and learn."

Annukka's fingers moved deftly over the strings, and she began singing. Her voice was low, and very strong, though not loud; pleasant, but by no means the level of a great musician or a bard. Yet there was power, great power, behind it. Even through the mirror, Aleksia could feel it. "*Oh, Road that leads out from my door,*" she sang, "*Who led my son to seek his fate. Now I command you to tell me where his wyrd has led e'er 'tis too late.*"

Now the girl probably could not tell this—and surely thought the woman was daft for singing to a road—but the power behind the song took even Aleksia aback. This was a Wise Woman indeed! For those with the eyes to see it, power flowed around her, golden as honey, as if she was immersed in a swirling river of light.

The dust of the road stirred, the fallen leaves moved as if twirled by an errant breeze. Leaves and dust began to fall into a pattern; Aleksia felt the hair on her neck prickle, and the girl stepped back a pace, her mouth forming into a little *O* of surprise. Then there was a kind of grinding noise, and a face gradually formed out of the dust, the bared earth, with the leaves settling into its hair and lips.

The blank eyes were two stones, the ruts of the road forming a suggestion of nose, cheekbones, eyelids and eyebrows. The lips moved, and words formed, somehow, sighing into the air with the sound of rocks grinding against each other.

Veikko took me northward, it is true. The Road groaned. *He followed me into the forest. He spoke with many people who could not help him find a Master, until at last, he came to the home of the Warrior-Mage Lemminkal Heikkinen. There he was accepted as the Master's apprentice. But they left there some time ago, and they did not go by road or track. I have not seen him. I cannot find him. Perhaps the sun has seen them, but I have not.*

There was a final groan as of the earth settling; the breeze sprang up and scattered the leaves; and then—there was no face, no face at all. There were two stones near one another, but they didn't look like eyes anymore, and the ruts were merely ruts. Aleksia shook her head, marveling. It not only took great power to bring the inanimate to life, it also took great passion. This woman, living unnoticed in a tiny Sammi village—how was it that Aleksia had never known of her?

And—Lemminkal Heikkinen? Surely there could not be two Mages with that name—

And she wasn't done yet, it seemed....

"*Now hear me, bright and golden sun,*" Annuka sang, turning her face to the sky. "*You who sees where pathless travelers go. Where is my son out wandering? He is in danger! I must know!*"

The sun did not form a face—but another voice, like the distant roaring of flames, did come out of the sky above them. *Veikko and his Master were told of a terrible creature in the North, where only the reindeer herdsmen are. They call it the Icehart, and they say its breath can slay entire clans in a moment. They went in search of it, to test Veikko. But I have not seen this creature myself, and I have not seen them since they passed under the snow clouds. Perhaps the Moon has seen them.*

Veikko! So it *was* the magicians she had watched for so long! It seemed she had given up too soon. Aleksia pursed her lips. The Icehart? That was something entirely new to her....

And it certainly sounded like something this imposter would think up.

But Annukka was already turning to the west. The sun was only just up over the trees and the moon had not yet set. The determined set of her chin told Aleksia that the woman had not even begun to run out of magical strength. And indeed, the magic of The Tradition was so thick around her it could practically be cut with an ax.

"Oh moon, who shines down through the dark upon the trackless snowfields white—where is my son? I cannot tell! You must have graced him with your light!"

The pale ghost of a day-moon seemed to shiver as it touched the horizon, and a silver voice whispered out of the western sky. *The Warrior-Mage and his apprentice followed on the track of the Icehart, which only travels by night. They traced it through three villages where it had slain every man, woman and child with its icy breath. But then they fell under a shadow of sorcery, and I saw them no more. Perhaps the North Wind can say where they are, but I cannot.*

Then the moon, as if hurrying to get out of sight before Annukka could ask it more questions, dropped below the horizon, leaving the sun in sole possession of the sky.

Annukka did not even pause for breath, but swept her fingers across the strings, and cried out, *"Oh, North Wind, child of ice and air, who cannot be kept out or stayed—where is my son? Oh, hear me now! He can't be found! I am afraid!"*

For a moment there was nothing. And then—

Leaves dropped off the trees around the two women as if their stems had been cut, and the falling leaves swiftly turned white with a rime of frost as they fell, and the air itself thickened and whitened with ice-fog. The women's skirts were plastered to their legs, as a wind carried the leaves in a swirl around them. Although probably Annukka wasn't paying attention, Aleksia counted nine full circuits around the two, before the ice-fog settled before them, and formed into a vague and puffy face that changed from moment to moment.

I saw your son and his Master, the North Wind said, in a voice like the howl of a blizzard heard from leagues away. *They followed the Icehart until it led them to its Mistress. She is called the Snow Queen and she lives in the Palace of Ever-Winter, on the side of the Mountain. She took them captive and into her Palace. And there they remain.*

Before the stunned women could reply, the North Wind swirled itself up and away through the cloudless sky, leaving the frost melting behind it.

And Aleksia was jumping to her feet, fists balled at her sides, her temper flaring and overriding every bit of calm she had ever learned in her life.

"You wretched, ill-begotten *liar!*" she screamed at the mirror. "Wait until I get my hands on you!"

Aleksia was employing every technique she knew to cool her temper. She had tried counting, tried willpower and now she was out, on the slopes of the mountain called Varovaara, pushing herself to exhaustion in a trek around what passed for a garden up here—ice and snow sculpted into fanciful shapes, immaculately groomed paths and feeding stations for wild birds. Her breath puffed out in little clouds, her feet were getting numb and still she wanted very much to hurt something. She was going to summon the North Wind herself, but before she did so, she knew she had to get herself under control. Rare indeed was the magic that benefited from being performed in a rage; most of the time, control was needed. The icy air did nothing to cool her temper, a glance upwards at the sun through the thin screening of ice-clouds only made her angrier. The Road, the Sun and the Moon had all told the truth. The

North Wind had *lied*. How had it dared? She wanted, very badly, to summon it now, to hurl something at it, to indulge in a fit of temper completely unbecoming of a Godmother. It had said she was a murderer of dozens of people! If this was the kind of rumor that had reached Godmother Elena's ears—well, no wonder her fellow Godmother had looked at her sideways for a moment!

And at the moment, she had no other target for her ire than the North Wind. Oh, how she would like to strangle the creature! Not that she could—you couldn't strangle a wind—but she *wanted* to!

She continued to circle the garden until at last sheer weariness, and nothing else, wore down her anger. By then her feet were sore, her hands were half-frozen and it took several moments of concentration to invoke a heat spell to thaw herself out, and that by itself was an indication of how unprepared she had been to work any magic at all. Only when she was sure she was steady did she take a strong stance in the center of the garden, clear her mind, and *summon*.

She didn't chant her summons aloud, nor did she sing it. She didn't have to; she was a Godmother, after all. *By ice and by fire, I summon a liar!* she called fiercely in her mind, concentrating on the North Wind, for she knew it as only a Great Mage or a Godmother could; knew its true name and incorporated that into her image of what she sought, knew that right now, in its own mind, it was not identified by anything it knew of itself more strongly than that word. *Liar.*

The world became very still, the potentials of magic swirled all around her, then exploded outward. There was the sound of shattering ice crystals, thousands of them. A flash of blue-green light, like that seen from the inside of ice-caves. A whiff of the sharp, wet scent that comes just before snow starts to fall.

And it was there.

It brought with it none of the theatrical freezing of leaves and swirling of eddies of ice-fog. Not now, and not with her. It *knew* that it was in very, very deep trouble. And although it was one of the four named winds, it also knew that a powerful enough set of human magicians, or even a single Great Mage, could hurt it, or even imprison it. The Sammi were well known for imprisoning and releasing Winds—though only the most powerful and terrible of Sammi magicians would dare to imprison one of the named winds—so it stood to reason that a God-mother could do the same.

After all, once, long ago, a great and evil Witch of the Sammi had imprisoned the Sun...and had kept all four of the Winds in chains.

So the North Wind huddled on the ground in a spreading pool of ice-fog at Aleksia's feet, looking rather like a ghost, although a good bit more fantastic. In form, it looked like a skeletally thin, long-nosed man. Its hair and its beard were spines of ice, and its "clothing" did not move at all, being basically only the North Wind's imperfect mimicry of clothing. It had an extremely long and pointed nose, with, as the final touch, an icicle permanently clinging to the end of it. And just now, it looked utterly miserable and quite afraid.

"Do you know who I am?" Aleksia asked, not loudly, but with great intensity and just a little magic behind the words.

The North Wind shivered, cowered and wailed—a sound like a hundred lost souls. Ice crystals formed at the corners of its eyes and tinkled down its cheeks to fall with little ticking sounds into a pile in the snow. *You are the Snow Queen, the Godmother Aleksia!* It wept. *Do not harm me! Do not chain me!*

Well that was a satisfactory reaction. "Perhaps I should *melt* you instead," Aleksia replied threateningly, allowing one hand to glow with a heat spell.

The North Wind wailed again. *I am sorry! I am sorry! I lied to the mortal women!*

"Yes, you did. Did you think I would never find out about it?" Aleksia's voice dropped to a dangerous purr. "You *lied,* and about a God-mother! You placed the deaths of dozens of mortals at *my* doorstep. I will be blamed for this, and mortals will come here looking for revenge. It was not enough that you lied, but you compounded the lie by bringing trouble down on my head! I am *not* amused!"

She did not go further and say what she wanted to—that she had now been marked as a murderer of dozens of innocent people—because the North Wind was not mortal and did not much care what mortals lived or died. In fact, the North Wind was personally responsible for many, many deaths every year, most of them, by any standard, innocent. Murder was a way of life to it; whatever this Icehart creature was, it didn't care how long the Icehart continued to kill. It cared only that she was angry, and it was only interested in somehow wiggling out of the situation it found itself in,

Don't hurt me! It cried pitifully. It shivered uncontrollably as she glared down at it.

"Then tell me why you lied!" she snapped. The creature cried harder, more ice-crystals ticking onto the pile. Its shivering increased, and it shrank in on itself.

I—I—I cannot!

"You *will,*" she countered viciously, scowling down on it and allowing the heat spell to flare up in her right hand. There was a lot of satisfac-tion in this, truth to be told. It gratified her to have the thing so petri-fied of her. "Tell me who put those words in your mouth! You will—or you will pay! I can make your life far more of a misery than the one you are protecting can!" Of course, these were hollow threats. It wasn't as if a Godmother was allowed to torture anyone—or anything. But the North Wind didn't know that.

I dare not!

Aleksia growled, and held up her hand, glowing with heat and light.

With a cry of despair, the North Wind hid its face in its hands. Aleksia extended her hand toward it—

Loviatar.

She paused. This must be a name, but it was not one that she knew. "What?" she replied. The North Wind whimpered in abject defeat. She had won her bluff, and now she had a name.

Loviatar, it repeated, its glance flitting about now as if it expected this person to materialize at the first hint of the name. *She is a Witch.*

"I gathered as much," Aleksia said dryly, as the Wind hid its face in its hands. "More detail, if you please."

The North Wind peeked up at her cautiously through its fingers. *She is beautiful. Very beautiful. And very angry—almost all the time. She will be furious with me when she finds out.*

"Angrier than me?" she asked, narrowing her eyes dangerously. She noted with further satisfaction that the Wind grew a bit more transparent at that.

The North Wind shivered.

She lives to create pain, chaos and confusion, the North Wind said, from behind gritted teeth. *She especially hates men, Mages most of all. She has been destroying as many as she could, sending them to the Underworld on impossible quests, setting monsters on them. Lemminkal and his brother, Ilmari, decided that he should take the young apprentice into the wilderness to train him further, for he had gotten beyond the mere monster-slaying and fiend-binding they could do near their home. They are great Heroes, are the Heikkinen brothers, and their fame has spread far into the North. The Witch Loviatar saw a chance to slay them, and corrupt the young Hero, and she took it. She has taken the boy. I do not know what has happened to the men. I only know that she has the boy in her thrall.*

"And why compel you to lie to those women?" Aleksia asked, with perhaps more venom in her tone than she intended, for the North Wind shrunk back in fear. "And why lay the blame on me?" That was one thing that sorely puzzled her. There seemed no reason for the lie.

Do not punish me! I had no choice! She was going to bind me in a cave forever with chains of fire, as my brothers and I were bound once before! She can do it! She has great power!

Aleksia frowned. "I still do not see why she chose to lay all of this at my feet. It makes no sense——"

She was more or less speaking her thoughts aloud, but the Wind answered her anyway.

I do not know! I do not know! How can I fathom the mind of a mortal, and a woman at that?

Well Aleksia had some ideas, now that she knew a little more of the shape of this situation. Certainly Veikko's mother and sweetheart would tell others what had supposedly happened to the boy, and they would tell others, and soon it would be spread far and wide, as she had foreseen. Such a tale would not be kept quiet for very long; that was the nature of such things.

And then the Heroes would come to the Palace of Ever-Winter, looking to defeat her. Such was the nature of Heroes. The Tradition itself would aid and abet them, even though Aleksia was actually the innocent victim here.

Now it was one thing for Aleksia to take the occasional young man off and teach him much-needed lessons. They always came back. They were usually much the better for it, or at the least, sadder, but much, much wiser. *Real* Heroes understood instinctively that she was doing much good, even if they were not already aware that the Snow Queen was a Godmother. That was the way of The Tradition, too; that young men who deserved it got their comeuppance. There were many Elder Princes who returned, chastened, to the family fold when a Godmother, or The Tradition itself, tempered by the hand of a Godmother, got done with them. No lesson of that sort came without some pain.

It was quite another thing for her to imprison or slay two great Sammi Heroes and their apprentice, to kill whole villages in the night with ice-magic. The other Godmothers would call her to account; Heroes would come to destroy her. And even if they knew she was a Godmother, would assume she had gone to the bad and come to take her. And yes, she was powerful, but there was only so much she could do to defend herself without hurting those who were acting in good conscience. And, yes, it was possible that she would hurt or kill someone in trying to protect herself. Even if she did not, she would be weeks, months, perhaps even years, in proving that this was not her doing. While she was defending herself and clearing her name, she would *not* be doing her job. And then, how many young girls, twisted by the insistent pressure of The Tradition, unable to fit the path it wanted for the good, would themselves go to the bad? How many would wind up in the hands of evil magicians to be drained and die? How many young men would turn cruel and hard and become monsters? How many innocents would go unrescued?

And Ilmari, Lemminkal and Veikko—if only she had not given up her watching! She felt guilt and anger and an upsurge of grief at the thought that they might be dead. And that, too, was her fault. She would be called to account for it, one way or another.

The thought made her shiver inside. But not visibly. The last thing she wanted to do was to betray any signs of weakness to this creature. She must keep the upper hand here.

This Witch Loviatar was not all-seeing. She had not guessed that Aleksia had already found her out. Aleksia glared at the North Wind, but behind that glare, her mind was working quickly. The Tradition preferred that evildoers be overconfident, when they were not so paranoid and self-protective that they were inclined to slay someone on mere suspicion that he might be an enemy. It *appeared* that this Witch was of the former sort. *I must keep things in that path,* was the one clear thought in her mind. And that meant dealing with the North Wind in such a way that Loviatar would not detect her, nor anticipate that she was coming, nor plan against her meddling.

This was a very great risk. The North Wind was not a mere human, and certainly was not one of the lesser elementals. But—

"*She* will punish you, even if I do not," she told the North Wind, her voice silky with menace. She rather thought that her deception would hold up, since the North Wind had never dealt with her before. It did not know what she would—or could—not do. It had no idea of her power, and what was more, it was used to dealing with something that was completely evil. "You know this, or you would not be so afraid. And you know that if you see her, she will have that out of your mind—you cannot possibly conceal such thing from one such as her."

The North Wind wailed; she had thought it was afraid before, but now it was nearly mindless with fear. *I must hide from her! Hide!* It made as if to flee, but Aleksia still had its magical "leash," the summoning, and she metaphorically jerked it back to her side. It flattened itself against the ground and tried to blend in with the snow at her feet. Whatever, whoever this Witch was, she must be terrible and powerful to frighten the North Wind like this. Not for the first time, she wondered if it was a demigod. If so, she would need some help in being rid of it.

Then again, there were two Heroes and an apprentice out there. If she had not killed the Heroes outright, there could very well be some help here for her. She must definitely research this in the archives. If there had ever been a similar situation, she needed to find it, and figure out how to make The Tradition work for her.

Meanwhile, given that the North Wind was so terrified of her and the Witch, that it would do anything, she was going to take full advantage of the situation. "If you run, she will chase you. If you hide, she will find you." She smiled nastily. "*I* would."

By now, the poor North Wind was shaking so hard that all the icicles of his hair and beard were rattling together like glass reeds in the wind, and the one on his nose broke off with a metallic "chink." *What will I do? What will I do?* It clawed desperately at her hem with translucent blue hands. Under any other circumstances she would have felt sorry for it. But it had brought this situation on itself. *You must save me, Godmother! It is your duty! You must save me!*

"Save someone who betrayed me?" She widened her eyes as if in astonishment, and chuckled dryly. "So you think you are dealing with some soft creature like a Godmother of the South? I am the *Snow* Queen, as cold as ice and as hard as the rock of my mountain! Don't you know I have no pity in me?"

Please! I beg of you! Have mercy! The poor thing was really reduced to a pitiable state now. She had rarely in all her life seen anything so consumed with fear and desperation. She hooded her eyes as it wept copious amounts of ice crystals. So demoralized was it that it even forgot to maintain its ice-fog. Now it was just a translucent blue caricature of a man, with comical hair and beard, emaciated and helpless.

Finally, before it was reduced to babbling, she spoke again. "Very well. I will save you—"

Now it was all over the hem of her dress again, kissing the cloth, blubbering its thanks. *Have I ever had any creature abase itself so much to me?* She couldn't remember. *This is remarkable.* She would have to research the archives to see if any other Snow Queen had had such an experience.

Truly, this was a reasonable revenge for what it had done to her; she enjoyed it for a moment, then cut it short with an upraised finger and a single command. *"Silence!"*

It went as still as a windless day, ironic since it was a wind. It even stopped moving altogether, looking now like a grotesque ice-sculpture clinging to the hem of her gown.

She became incongruously aware of how wet and sodden her gown was, with the chill and wet almost all the way up to her knees now. Small wonder the Sammi women wore the dresses and breeches that they did.

"You must give me a piece of yourself," she said, flatly. "You must give me a piece of your memory, the memory of my summoning you here, of you telling me about Loviatar, and of my agreeing to help you. You will lose that piece forever."

It hesitated, for to a creature like the North Wind, only imperfectly tied to the world and unable to have possessions as such, its memories were everything. Even bad ones. Its memories were the map to tell it what to do should something like this arise in the future. But it hesitated only for a moment. Then it bowed its head to her. *I give my consent.*

"Let go of my dress." When it had released her hem as if the thing burned it, she called up her warming spell and infused it into the velvet. The gown steamed for a moment, drying quickly in the arid air of the heights. With a sigh of satisfaction, she wrapped her magics around herself again like a cloak of power, and prepared another summoning, although this one was not so much a summoning as an *invitation.* One did not *summon* a god, even if it was a very small god. That sort of arrogant behavior rather well got one in trouble very quickly. And she must phrase her invitation in a very different pattern—the chant of the Skald and not the rhyme of the Bard.

Harbinger of storm and battle, black-winged, bright-eyed secret keeper, will you grace me with your presence, swift all-seeing Memory-holder?

She knew that the North Wind could hear her; his eyes widened as he realized what she had meant. It was not possible for him to become more deferential, but he certainly became quieter. They waited. Presently, a distant, mocking sound echoed across the snowfields and a black speck appeared in the sky. The speck grew larger and showed itself to be a bird. A great, black bird.

A Raven. But no ordinary Raven, as she and the North Wind both knew. This was a very special bird, one of a pair—they did not "belong" to the being that they aided, but they served as his eyes and ears on all of the world that gave him worship and regard.

Aleksia stretched out her arm as the Raven approached, and it landed heavily, talons biting into the fur and velvet of her gown and coat. "Greetings, Munin," she said, bowing her head to him. "I thank you for your attendance."

Quork, said the Raven derisively, then made a chuckling sound as it looked down on the trembling North Wind. There was no doubt that Munin was amused to see the North Wind in this state. Then again, in the past, the Wind had probably tossed the Raven all over the sky just for the malicious amusement of it. Small gods were not powerless, but their powers were very narrow; it was unlikely that Munin had any means of retaliation against insult by the Wind—until now.

"Indeed." Again, she bowed her head. "I crave a boon and grant you a gift with one and the same act. We give to you a piece of memory, this creature and I. This is a piece, not for keeping, but for your own devouring. Not for the One-eyed, but for you. Not for sharing, but for consuming. You will, however, need to extract it with great care. No one must be able to tell that the North Wind's memory was tampered with. I know that you, and only you, have the skill to do this. Do you consent to this?"

She had just offered the Raven called Memory something that he

rarely got—for it was his duty, his function, to serve as the repository
for the memories of the One-eyed Father-God of the Skandians. It was
his duty to whisper those memories into the One-eyed's ear when they
were needed, as it was the duty of his brother Raven to read the thoughts
of mortals and immortals and whisper those into the One-eyed's other
ear. And yet, Munin yearned to consume those memories; they were,
for him, the same as the flesh of the fallen for the lesser Ravens of the
earth. Only rarely was he granted such a treat. And this! It was the
memory of a creature not mortal at all! Such a feast as he had not been
presented with in—surely a hundred years.

Ravens are by their nature, greedy, even demigods in the shape of a
Raven. So The Tradition arranged things; the outward appearance
dictated the inner self. And having been offered such a thing, he could
not resist it. *Quork! Qwa, qwa, qwa!* he assented, head and shoulders
bobbing with eagerness.

"Then go, feast, and work with skill upon this creature's mind." She
held her arm out and he bounced from it to the North Wind's shoulder.
"You may take the memory from the moment he left the Wise Woman
Annuka and her daughter-to-be until the moment you and I both leave
him. Only this much, and no more—but you will find it flavorful with
fear, I think, and with the echoes of magic."

Inside, she was feeling as alive and excited as she had ever been. This
was all new ground she was breaking here, using her knowledge of the
creatures of the North and all that they stood for. Rarely did a Godmother ever get to forge whole new paths, even small ones! It was as
hard now to keep her icy demeanor as it had been when she was livid
with anger.

Gahhh! said Munin with relish, regarded the North Wind with a
shining black eye, then quick as a thought, stabbed his huge black beak
into the North Wind's head. The saberlike, ebony beak plunged fully,

encountering no resistance; the Wind's eyes went glassy blank as the Raven worked his will within the Wind's mind.

She turned her back on them both, knowing that the North Wind was safe now. And in the scale of things, both Munin and the Wind owed her, although the Wind would not remember. It didn't matter if the Wind remembered. The Tradition would. She made her way quickly back into her Palace; she had used a great deal of energy calling on Munin, and had been forced to sacrifice her own spells of warmth to do so—that was the cost of forging new ground, the magical power did not come from Traditional magic, but from her own. Swiftly as she moved, she was still growing chilled by the time she reached the little door to the garden, an entryway that could scarcely be seen at all unless you were looking for it, barely more than a rectangular crack in the otherwise seamless white walls of the Palace.

The wave of warmth struck her in the face, forcing her into involuntary relaxation. She felt very weary all at once, as if she had been running for a dozen miles. Then, with a chuckle at herself, she realized that, besides working personal magic, she had certainly been walking for a mile or more out in the heavy snow, if not running. Oh, she was going to ache...and a hot bath was probably in order once she knew that she had done everything that she could, for now.

Once safely inside, she went to the great window that looked out into the garden, rendering the outside reflective so that not even the keen eye of an elemental could see her there. She watched the Raven feasting, making the same motions as a mortal bird would, as if it was tearing out bits of carrion, tossing its head back and gulping the morsel down. Eventually, it finished its invisible meal, shook itself hard and took a good, contented look around. It lumbered clumsily into the sky. Then she watched it fly away, slowly, heading upwards into the ice-clouds. By that time she had noted at least two of the Brownies appear, look at her thoughtfully, then slip away again. As the Raven vanished into the hazy blue of the sky, one returned.

As the Brownie put a fire-warmed shawl about her shoulders she watched the North Wind slowly come to himself, look about as if surprised to find himself here, then shrug. In the blink of an eye he was gone, whirling away into the ice-clouds, going North and east. Whether or not he was going to report to the Witch Loviatar was irrelevant for now. The Wise Woman Annukka and the Maiden Kaari could not get within her purview for some time yet. By then, Aleksia would have more of a plan in place and some idea of what she needed to do to keep them safe as well as deal with this Loviatar.

Even if the Witch found that scrap of memory, the only thing that linked Aleksia to the North Wind, the fragment of him awakening to find himself at the Palace of Ever-Winter, by the time he reached the Witch, the Wind would have constructed a perfectly good reason *why* he was there for himself. That was the way that memory worked. If you did not have a way to make something make sense, you would construct it for yourself. Memory was odd that way. That was why it was so unreliable.

With a shiver, she turned away from the window. Time to think, to plan.

And definitely time to call Godmother Elena.

GOOD NEWS KEEPS COMPANY WITH THE TURTLE, BAD NEWS WITH the hare. That was the old saying, and before the day was out, Annukka had cause to think that it had never been more true. She and Kaari had gone into her house, thinking to do no more than to put up the kantele safely and go to find some help. And by the time they came out again, scant moments after entering, the carrion crows were already gathering.

Somehow, everyone they met seemed to know immediately that Veikko and his teacher were in terrible danger. *Someone must have been watching us,* was all that she could think. She should have known better, really. Given what Kaari was, it was inevitable that there was someone watching her, hoping to get her attention, most of the time.

Now that Annukka thought about it, she could have slapped herself for being so precipitate. Kaari had come to *her* in tears, which meant that she had run out of her own house in tears. Kaari in tears was bound to attract attention, the way that meat attracted Ravens. Someone had to have followed her, hoping to help, seen she was going to Annukka and—

Well, everyone would want to know why Kaari ran to Annukka, now wouldn't they? So watchers stayed, and the moment Annukka began working magic, something she did so rarely that hardly anyone in the village could say they had seen her do so, you could not have dragged a watcher away with a cart horse.

Bah.

And, of course, what the Road, the Sun, the Moon and the North Wind had to say was audible to just about anyone. The watcher must have torn away with wings on her feet, with news that juicy.

But more discouraging, there was not one of their friends and neighbors, *not one,* who seemed to be of the opinion that Veikko was anything other than doomed.

By the time the third woman came up to commiserate to Annukka and Kaari on the death of son and sweetheart and offer a shoulder and a lot of unwanted advice, even Kaari's sweet temper was stretched to the breaking point. And when they reached the center of the village to find *everyone* assembled there, waiting for them silently, they were both very near to the boil.

Silence descended over the crowd as they both stopped and stared, Kaari with growing anger, Annukka with growing impatience. Awkwardly, Alto Vaara, the headman of the village, cleared his throat, clasping his hands together as if that would help him muster his thoughts better.

"Annukka," he said, sweat starting to stand out on his red face. "Kaari—we are very sorry—that is—"

"Veikko has been taken by this *creature* we have been hearing rumors of," Annukka said briskly. "I intend to find and free him. While I appreciate your sympathy I had rather not declare him buried just yet, and I would much more appreciate some help with finding and bringing him back."

There was even more awkward shuffling. Finally Alto coughed. "Annukka, you are asking a very great deal of us, you know, and, this is harvest season. Winter will be here soon, and really, you must be sensible—"

"I *am* being sensible!" she snapped. "If I were not being sensible, I would not have come in search of help from my neighbors, I would have saddled a reindeer and ridden off alone! Now—" she looked around "— who is coming with me? I don't know one end of a sword from another, and we will certainly need some help from a hunter or a herdsman, someone who knows how to travel in the Winter."

It was the turn of the younger unmarried men to look away and shuffle their feet. While every single one of them had rushed forward to comfort Kaari on her presumed loss and to offer himself in the place of Veikko, there clearly wasn't one of them willing to help bring him back.

She raised a scornful eyebrow, and layered her voice with enough contempt to cut with an ax. "What, no one? No one at all? No one is willing to come with two mere women into this danger? Was my son the only *man* in this village?"

That stung. More than one of them looked indignant, and yet—and yet—not one of them was prepared to step forward even after that insult. Finally Janne found his voice. "Veikko was the only one with the Warrior rune!" he protested, looking shamefaced and angry at the same time. She heard the resentment in his voice that she should ask this of the men of her own village. Resentment that she would dare to compare them to her son, as if they were now somewhat lesser because they did not share his runes. "If he couldn't fight his way out of this, how are we to—"

"Oh? Well, then *I* will have to learn one end of a sword from the other!" Kaari burst out. "For I am surely going! And if you will not, it would be well for all of you if you do not seek maidens from other villages after this, for I will surely let it be known that the young men of *this* place were such cowards that they allowed two women to undertake this journey without so much as lifting a finger to help!"

"Kaari, be sensible," pleaded Janne, who had been one of her foremost suitors before she was betrothed to Veikko. "You should mourn Veikko, that's only right and proper. But go after him to die with him? That's madness. You mourn him over Winter, and in the Spring, you'll see, you'll want—"

"Even if Veikko is dead, which is by no means certain, and even if I chose to take another man someday, I'll want no coward," Kaari retorted coldly. She raked the crowd with a scorn-filled glance and Annukka noted how many of them flinched and avoided her eyes. Most of them, in fact.

And those that didn't looked—well, oddly pleased with themselves and angry and annoyed, all at the same time. It was a mix of people with that expression, too—several of the girls Kaari's age, several of the young men and a couple of the older ones.

Now under any other circumstances, she would have gone to work, cajoling, wheedling, browbeating if she had to, in order to get more people to come with them. But something inside her hesitated, and she paused to listen to it.

They are frightened.

Well, who wouldn't be?

The useless sort of frightened.

Ah.

That inner voice was right, absolutely right. Even if she convinced one or more of them to come with her, they would be more hindrance than help. At the first sign of trouble they would freeze, or run or—

Or if this Snow Queen is powerful enough, they might go over to her side. Why not? By going over to her side, they can bargain to be rid of Veikko and to get Kaari at the same time. And, oh, she hated to think that of her own people, but…people were people and temptation was temptation, and it was not wise to put people under the burden of a temptation that they simply could not resist.

She clamped her lips shut at that point, grasped Kaari by the elbow, and pulled her away, back up the path to her home. No one followed. Not even Kaari's own mother.

The two of them kept silent until they were back inside Annukka's house. Then it was Kaari who had an outburst—not of words, but of angry, frustrated tears.

"Not one of them!" she sobbed, her anger so hot Annukka could have toasted cheese on it. "Not one! *Why?* When have we ever done anything other than do them all favors, over and over and over?"

Now, Annukka could have shared her thoughts with the girl, but...

That would accomplish nothing other than to make her angrier. She might then rush out with accusations, and that would only make things worse.

She tightened her lips, grimly.

"This is what we are going to do," she said, finally. "First, you are going to get my reindeer from the herdsman. While you do that, I will pack. You and I are the same size. You can share my clothing, and I have plenty. I never got rid of the things I wore before I was married and they will suit you well enough." She sighed. "I had always hoped to have a daughter, you see...."

Kaari blinked and stared at her, but she went ruthlessly on. "By not going home and packing up yourself, we will make people think that we are not planning to leave until later, and they will not think to try and stop us tonight."

Kaari's eyes widened. "They would dare?" She gasped.

"Oh, certainly," Annukka replied. "Especially now that they know for certain that I can work greater magic and am a Wise Woman. You are the treasure of the village, and I am the one that can keep them safe against the dark, and do you think they would let us go without a struggle? Hardly." She shook her head. "They are frightened now. Something that was only rumor and legend has come to life and taken one of us, and they are very, very eager to make sure it doesn't coming knocking on their doors."

"But——"

"People are people, and often enough they act like frightened sheep, child." Annukka set her jaw. "So, you get the deer, I will pack. I wish there was snow, now—we could have carried more on a sledge. Perhaps we can barter for one when we get farther North. Get all four deer, mind. Now go."

The truth was, she had no further idea than that, yet—but in order to be free to act on any ideas she might have, she and Kaari would have to be out of the village. She had no doubt at all that eventually the others would work themselves up to doing whatever they thought needful to keep the two of them from leaving.

And...she smiled grimly...she was going to have just a little revenge. After she had packed up everything that she and Kaari could carry, she would work a little spell on her house and outbuildings. *Nothing* would be able to break into them once she was gone. Even if the Winter was long and hard, and people were growing hungry, she would see to it that they got not one bit of good out of the things she had stored there....

Well, one exception. She was not going to punish the children for the faults of their parents. She would make a small addition to the spell. A starving child would be allowed to pass her guardian, go in and eat its fill. But it would not be permitted to take anything out.

Be sensible, indeed. Well you can tell the Spirit Bear I shall leave to be sensible, and we will see how far that gets you.

They left by moonlight. They waited until the knocking at the door had stopped, until the village had settled. Annukka, taking advantage of the need to wait, had put some very careful crafting into her house-guardian. It wouldn't exactly hurt anyone, but it couldn't *be* hurt, either.

And it almost certainly would frighten anyone that encountered it out of his or her wits.

Kaari did not go home after fetching Annukka's reindeer, despite her mother asking her to. She simply refused to see her own mother, hiding in Annukka's bedroom until her mother went away.

After that, Annukka closed the door of her house, pulled in the latchstring and refused to answer knocks herself. Eventually people stopped trying to make them come out and "be sensible."

Perhaps they thought they were clever, lurking outside silently for some time, waiting. They forgot that she was a Wise Woman. The irony of the situation was not lost on Annukka; they didn't want her to leave because she was a Wise Woman, but when it came to practical things, like being able to tell when there were people lying in wait outside her house, it never occurred to them that she would not be caught that way.

On the other hand, that just wasn't something she'd ever done before. It seemed her lifelong habit of being circumspect in the use of magic was reaping unexpected benefits.

She considered setting a spell to keep the villagers sleeping while she and Kaari slipped away, but decided against it. It was a dreadful waste of magic, for one thing, and for another, what if something happened to the village while they were all spellbound? It was easier to muffle the reindeer's hooves in sacks of bran, lead them out of the village silently and only mount up after they were well away. The moon was rising late anyway and was nearly at the full. They would get the benefit of its light right up until the dawn.

Not many people rode reindeer; they were amenable to pulling sleighs and sledges, but not many of them cared to be ridden. Now, as a Wise Woman, Annukka had only ever been able to coax a few of her beasts into allowing a saddle on their backs. Strangely enough, they objected less to a pack than to a rider. Some of the villagers had thought it odd that through all these years she had persisted in trying to find deer that would allow themselves to be ridden. She had never done so with an eye to slipping away one dark night; mostly, she supposed, it had been a matter of seeing if it could be done at all.

Now, of course, she was very glad that she had.

Reindeer, deer in general, were easier to move at night than horses. With the moon up, the only thing they objected to was the bags on their feet, and she couldn't blame them for that. And once she and Kaari felt safe enough to stop and take the bags off, they moved out at an easy amble that would cover a surprising amount of ground without the danger of stumbling and breaking a leg.

There was some awkwardness with Kaari getting herself up into the saddle; riding anything was fairly unusual for the Sammi. Annukka knew that before the night was out, they would both be in pain from this. Reindeer were not *comfortable* animals to ride; their gaits were all jolting, and their spines prominent. And riding in general used entirely different muscles than walking. Still, better a bit of discomfort than the alternative of being a virtual prisoner in her own home.

She thought she might catch Kaari looking back, and having second thoughts about this. Instead, Kaari seemed impatient to put as many leagues between herself and the village as possible.

"No regrets?" she finally asked, as the deer followed the main road, the same one that Veikko had taken, under the silvery moonlight.

They were riding side-by-side here, for the road was just wide enough to do so. Kaari did not turn her head to look at Annukka, but her voice was steady. "Yes," she replied. "But I would have more if we did not do this."

That was enough for Annukka.

* * *

Aleksia bit her lip in vexation. Like the villagers, she had assumed that Annukka and Kaari would wait at least a few days, if not longer, in order to try and persuade at least one of the stalwart young men to come along with them. Now she looked for them in the glass, only to discover that her viewpoint was from a bit of harness-brass on a moving reindeer, ambling through the night.

This was unfortunate. She needed more time—time to try to find out what Loviatar had done with Ilmari, Lemminkal and Veikko; time to discover where the Witch Loviatar had her stronghold; and possibly to discover what the Icehart was. If Godmothers were manipulators by nature, she was going to have to be a master manipulator now, and that wouldn't be possible if the two women rushed into things and upset them.

And there was still one piece of unfinished business on her plate.

While she decided what to do about Annukka and Kaari, she checked her glass for Gerda.

Instead of an image, she heard the Bear's voice in her mind.

We are sleeping in a cave, Godmother, very near your Palace. I trust you are ready for us.

She had to chuckle at the amused tone of his mental voice. *If her lad pines any more for her, he is going to wither away into a shadow. That is assuming he doesn't starve to death first. My cook is outraged.*

Since they were in an ice-cave, there were plenty of reflective surfaces to carry her magic, but the image, of course, was of blackness.

We must salvage the temper of your cook, by all means. Tomorrow, then?

He was a good friend, was the Bear. *I am not quite sure...*

Then we will wander in circles until you are ready. I think you should send them home in one of your sleighs. She is of no use in a wilderness.

Aleksia had to shake her head. *All the braver, then, for setting out into one. Thank you, Bear.*

The Bear chuckled, and the mirror slowly filled with white mist before clearing again.

All right. The women were on the road going north and would not depart from it for a while. Now, what was on or near that road that she might be able to use?

"Mother Annukka, if I have to ride another step——" Kaari ended her sentence with a groan of real pain. The sunrise had been glorious, the woods to either side of the road were a riot of golds and scarlet, punctuated by the greens of the great fir trees. Neither woman had been able to appreciate the view.

As Annukka had anticipated, they were both in pain. Riding stretched and exercised muscles that were used in no other ways, and no matter how sturdy one was, no matter how used to doing hard labor, one would still be sore from riding.

"There is a stream down there." Annukka pointed to a place where the road was cut by a foaming brook. It was shallow enough to ford, but more than deep enough to support fish. "We can stop there, rest and eat."

"And sleep?" Kaari begged.

"Taking it in turns." She cursed herself now for not thinking of getting a dog. But in the village she hadn't needed one, neither as a guard nor as part of a sled-dog team, for she had always had a riding reindeer or reindeer trained to harness. If she had "kidnapped" one on the way out, not only would that be wrong, it would only have run home again. But she surely wished for one now. If they'd had a dog, they could both have slept. The half-wolf sled dogs of the Sammi were loyal, as vigilant as their wild cousins and could be counted on in a fight.

But then again, the deer would have been understandably skittish around a dog like that, for it would remind them too much of wolves. That was one reason why those who had dog teams did not usually bother with reindeer. Trappers and hunters used dogs, mostly, and herders used the deer.

Bah, my mind is wandering.

First things first. Get down the hill and get a camp set up. Not just any camp, either, a relatively hidden camp.

Dismounting was a bit of an ordeal, actually. Kaari tried to be stoic, but a whimper escaped her, and as they went about the chores, they were both hobbling stiffly. Annukka's thigh muscles screamed at her as she moved; she knew that Kaari could not be in a much better state, her youth notwithstanding. The only good thing about the pain was that it took both their minds off their worry about Veikko. They watered the deer at the stream, which poured over its rocks with great enthusiasm, then tethered the deer in a thicket that would hide them enough that they would look like a wild group, but still give them enough browse within reach that they would be contented there. Then they found another spot, close to the deer but just out of reach of the tethers, where they could tuck their bedrolls under a bush and be invisible from the road. The nearness of the stream was both an advantage and a disadvantage. Any sounds someone might make sneaking up on them would be covered—but so would any noises that *they* might make. Annukka was not going to chance a fire; the sun would warm them enough while they slept the morning through. At the moment, she was most concerned about others traveling on the road. There could be bandits very easily, and not everyone that traveled openly was going to be safe.

"No tea?" Kaari said wistfully as Annukka laid out some cold food for both of them, barley bread, dried blueberries and water. "Willowbark tea would be welcome right now."

"Here—" She handed Kaari some strips of willowbark to chew. "It's bitter but it will do the same thing."

Kaari made a face, but took the bark—really the inner bark of the tree, that carried the pain-killing properties—and began chewing it. Annukka chewed her own bitter-tasting bark until there was nothing more to taste, then spit the wad of pulp out. "Do you want to sit up first, or shall I?" Kaari asked, doing the same.

Well the answer obviously was, *I would like you to,* but Kaari was not at all used to riding, ever, and at least Annukka had some practice in it, so she was probably the least sore of the two of them. "I will take first watch," she said, and tried not to sigh as Kaari wrapped herself up in blankets and rolled under the bush. A moment later, the sound of her even breathing told Annukka that despite frantic worry over Veikko, anger at the villagers and fear of what was ahead of them, exhaustion and pain had taken their toll, and she had succumbed to both.

Now the question for Annukka was, what should *their* course be?

Go straight to the last place I know Veikko was, I suppose. I can get the Moon to show me, I expect.

She could, if she wanted to draw attention to herself by working a Great Magic.

Drat.

There was always a price to be paid for doing magic, and in this case, the price would be exposing herself and Kaari to possible discovery by the Snow Queen. That was not an option. Not now. She rubbed her aching thighs as she considered other courses of action.

If she didn't ask the Moon to show her—well, she needed to be clever, then. She knew that Veikko and his Master had gone looking for the Icehart. She could go to the village where Lemminkal lived, and do the simplest thing, which was to find where Veikko and Lemminkal had gone from there and keep listening for tales of the Icehart. Find the Icehart, and the Snow Queen was probably not far away.

That, at least, would not draw as much attention. One definite advantage they had was that the Snow Queen would probably not expect two women to come after the men.

So far, the loving-cup still retained that sliver of silver, which meant that Veikko was not dead. While that remained, there was hope. And until she and Kaari could find out exactly what had happened to Veikko and his Master, all either of them could do was to hang on to hope.

Meanwhile, although they had gotten away with as much as she could manage, they were still not as prepared as she liked for this journey. Food, at least, they had in plenty, all things that were light—dried fish and meat, dried cheese, dried fruit, barley. The only fresh food she had packed were things that they would eat before they spoiled. They did have all of her herbal medicines, all of the things she used for healing. They had bedrolls. They did not have a tent. They had her bird bow, arrows, knives. They did not have bigger bows. They had Winter clothing, and thank heavens, she had finished the cloak for Kaari. They had a fire-starter and a cooking pot and an ax. They did not have a big enough ax to actually cut anything large, and she would have to use her cooking-knife to butcher things. They did not have fishing gear—and probably there were a great many other things that one needed for camping that they simply did not have. They were going to have to trade for things along the way...fortunately that, for a Wise Woman, was not an issue.

She slipped out from under cover of the brush to gather the long, flexible stems of dried sweetgrass, keeping a careful eye on the road as she did so, and ducked back under the concealment as soon as she had enough. Once there, she deftly began weaving it into tiny charms. The fragrant dried grasses mingled their scent with the Autumnal tang of fallen leaves. The sun was warm on her back now, and if it had not been for the ache in her legs, and the circumstances that brought them here, she could have been supremely content.

And, on the other hand, with Veikko in peril, she could have been frantic. But a Wise Woman learns how to put her own woes aside when the need calls.

With each charm she wove, she softly sang a spell as she worked, binding the magic into the weaving. A little goat for luck, a six-pointed star for health, a four-armed cross with the seed-heads at the end of each arm for prosperity, a forge hammer for protection—she refused to make love-charms unless she knew the person asking for them, but these four symbols were always in demand. Once, her husband had spent long Winter hours carving little trifles for her to put such spells on; she hadn't had the heart to tell him that they weren't as effective when she didn't make them herself, so she had compromised by weaving grass cords to string them on and wove the spells into those.

When she had a dozen, the sun was halfway up the sky; she woke Kaari, and told her to wake her when it had reached the zenith. By then she was so tired, she could scarcely keep her eyes open.

And it seemed as if she had barely closed them when Kaari was shaking her awake again. As she moved, it also seemed as if every muscle stretched and strained by that long night ride had stiffened, and now she hurt twice as much as she had when she had gone to sleep. But she wasn't going to set a bad example to Kaari by complaining; instead, she built a very tiny fire with almost no smoke; they made willow-bark tea to share and toasted some cheese and barley bread. Then they packed, harnessed the deer and resumed the journey.

Now that it was light and they could see, the deer quickened their pace to the ground-eating lope they used when migrating. They had eaten well while the humans slept; now they were ready to move. They were very different in temper and nature from the horses that some folk like the traders used, but the traders only traveled in the snowless months. Annukka was just glad now that she had spent as much time on having them for riding as she had.

But until she and Kaari were more used to it, Annukka had no intention of spending an entire day in the saddle. She planned to stop about sunset; if they were lucky, there would be a village where she could barter for supplies, or if there was a Wise Woman in residence, actually get some help. Ideally, it would be better if they could overnight as much as possible among other people and within four walls. That way, they could save their supplies for when they were in the wilderness with no other choice but to camp. She regretted now that her own small travels had never taken her in this direction. She knew nothing of the lay of the land, nor who was living out this way. She only knew that Veikko had stayed on the road the whole way to finding his Master because he had told her so in letters. And that was another thing she needed to barter for—a map.

Some things, however, were possible. You could tell if there was a village nearby by looking for smoke rising above the trees. Even in Summer, there would be cookfires, baking ovens, pottery kilns. As sunset neared, she scanned the horizon for such signs, and perhaps she spent a little too much of her attention on the horizon and not enough on her surroundings—

Because Kaari gasped, she pulled her attention back to the road and saw a half-dozen rough-looking men blocking their way.

Fear sharpened her vision; they were ragged, dirty, with hair and beards tangled and greasy. Their ill-fitting clothing was stained and torn in places. They were, however, well-armed.

She heard a laugh behind her, and knew without looking that there were at least that many more to the rear.

The reindeer snorted in alarm, and stood there quivering, threatening to bolt. Annukka could feel hers trembling under her legs.

"I would keep a tight hold on those beasts of yours, woman," said one. Neither young nor old, his blond beard roughly trimmed to just below his chin; his eyes were cold and appraising. "Our arrows can fly faster than they can run."

Annukka drew herself up. "You are bold, to risk the curses of a Wise Woman," she said, trying to put menace into her voice, hoping she could bluff her way out of this situation.

But the man shrugged. "Mummery and trickery," he replied with indifference. "I believe in nothing I cannot see with my own eyes. If you were so Wise, why didn't you know we were here before we surrounded you?" He turned to his men. "Take them," he ordered. "Try not to harm the deer—trained ones are rare. And don't touch the women. I'll be having the pretty one for myself. We'll see how useful the old hag is before we decide what to do with her."

"Offer no resistance," she had hissed to Kaari, before the men converged on them and seized the halters of the deer. She need not have bothered. Kaari was frozen in her saddle. They were in a tremendous hurry to get off the road, it seemed, for they did not try to pull the two women from their mounts, but instead, loped off in a body with the reindeer in their midst. Annukka feigned the same terror that Kaari was showing, but only so that she could memorize the way back to the road—which turned out to be absurdly easy, as the robbers fled south until they struck a watercourse, then followed it all the way to their camp, leaving a trail a child could follow.

The robbers had not been in these parts for long. They had only a rough camp, fires and bedrolls, some stockpiles of weapons. No tents, nothing near enough to weather out the Winter, which meant they had only two recourses when the weather turned. They could find a steading and take it, or they could find a cave and make it Winter-proof. Either was possible, the former was a risk, the latter took labor.

Annukka rather thought they would try the former. Somehow she couldn't see this lot doing anything that required work. They hadn't even set up latrines or a proper cooking area.

She and Kaari were roughly pulled from their saddles, the deer were stripped of tack and packs, and everything was gone through as the leader took possession of Kaari. Annukka wondered if he would rape her there and then, and from her expression, so did Kaari, but instead, he merely hauled her over to a rough seat made of a log, pulled her beside him and began alternately drinking and pawing her. Annukka was tied by the hands to a tree while the rest of the robbers went through their things.

"What's this trash?" one snarled, looking through her bags of herbs. He was about to throw it aside, when another stopped him with a whisper and a glance in Annukka's direction. She narrowed her eyes at him, and he whispered something more. The herbs were set roughly aside. There was some hilarity as they tried on her clothing and Kaari's, none of which fit, and which also was set aside with the herbs. There was fighting over the bedrolls and more fighting over the weapons and anger when they got down to the bottom of the packs and found not even a single copper coin.

"Make dinner, old woman!" the leader shouted, one hand up Kaari's shirt. Kaari was a stone, but Annukka assessed the situation and judged that she was in no danger of rape from the leader, at least. He was too drunk to perform at the point, if she was any judge.

Hmmm.

She held up her tied hands mutely, and with a snarl, the same man that had tied her up now cut her loose. It was clear at that point that none of the robbers intended to lift a finger as long as she was around to do their work for them. So she gathered together everything that looked like a foodstuff or a cooking implement, then she hauled wood and water to the camp. She did her best to leave her own stores intact, although she did use some herbs and juniper berries for flavoring—not because she liked these bastards, but because she wanted to disguise the taste of the meat she found that was starting to turn. If what she was planning didn't work, maybe she could give them all the flux with this stuff.

She started stew with that bad meat, some turnips and carrots they must have stolen from some farmer, thickened it with rye flour that could only have come from the same source. It still smelled just a bit wrong as it cooked, but they all sniffed appreciatively when their tasks took them near the pot. She supposed that since they themselves smelled so rancid, they probably couldn't tell there was anything wrong with the stew. She wasn't worried about Kaari; as petrified as the young woman was, she wouldn't be able to eat a bite.

She mixed up flatbread to bake on a griddle improvised from a shield no one seemed to want. She kept her eyes and ears open.

This was not a band that had been together for very long. Even robbers could develop camaraderie and a kind of family feeling; this lot showed none of that. And more telling, there was a great deal of grumbling going on over how the leader had handled the division of the latest spoils. Kaari had excited lust and avarice in equal portions, and the fact that the leader had taken her for himself and clearly had no intention of sharing her had made no few of these men very angry indeed. They were even angrier when they realized that the women had carried nothing of any great value with them, meaning that Kaari was the only "prize" to be had. Add to that, there were some who, unlike the leader, were clearly not happy that he had risked the wrath—and curses—of a Wise Woman, and you had the situation where, after the sun had set and the food was ready, the men did not gather together to eat in company, but rather sat apart, in twos and threes or by themselves, glaring at their leader who sat with a terrified Kaari, her clothing pulled all about as he pawed at her breasts and fumbled at her thighs.

Meanwhile, Annukka had not been idle.

Into the wood of the fire she built, into the food she prepared, she sang spells. Dissension, rebellion, discontent and rancor. Jealousy, envy, greed and anger. She built on the unhappiness that was already there, fed it and nurtured it. With every cheerful crackle of the flames, with every whiff of smoke, waft of cooking meat, her spells seeped into them. By the time she came around to serve the men, the pot of resentment was seething and ready to boil.

She brought the food around first to the chief and Kaari. "I like not the look of your men, warrior," she said, handing him a bowl of stew and the best piece of the flatbread.

He pulled his hand out from under Kaari's shirt and aimed a cuff at Annukka's head; she evaded it. "Mind your tongue, hag," he spat. "What have my men to do with you or you with them?"

"Only that, without you, who would protect us, my apprentice and I?" she whined. "They look at her with greed in their eyes and at you with envy. Have a care for daggers in the dark—"

This time, the blow he aimed did connect. Kaari gasped and made as if to run to her, but the man grabbed her and pulled her roughly back beside him. "Mind your place, slut," he growled, and commenced eating his stew. He offered Kaari none, which was just as well, seeing what was in it.

Annukka had rolled with the blow and made a great show of getting slowly to her feet as if he had hurt her greatly, when in fact she had gotten worse blows from her reindeer butting or kicking her. She hobbled away to serve the rest of the men.

As she brought them their portions, she made sure that they heard her muttering curses against him under her breath, but interspersed with those curses were little suggestions only they could hear, things that were not meant to register with them consciously.

"You would be a better, a fairer leader than he is. You are smarter, tougher, more

cunning. You would never risk the curses of a Wise Woman. You would get her on your side and she would work her magic to bring you wealth and more women. And you would have the wench all to yourself. You should have her, you should be the leader. You deserve it. What has he done that he should get it all? He's not as good a fighter, his luck is bad and he keeps all the best things for himself.

Their minds drank in her words, they ate her spells, and when they were all served she brought around the beer and wine in whatever containers she could find. But she had also worked a greater magic on the drink, making it a hundred times more potent than it had been. And with every flagon, mug and helmet full, she whispered into their minds.

You should challenge him. You should challenge him. You should challenge him. . . .

And on the third round—they did.

She was not sure what started it, for her back was to them at the time. It might well have been that the fool finally decided he was going to try to have Kaari in front of them all, rather than just fumbling with her. All it would have taken, as raw as their tempers were, was a flash of breast to set them off. All she knew for certain was that one man began shouting. And suddenly the entire encampment was a battlezone.

She had been ready and had planned to get to Kaari, but before she could turn around, Kaari was at her side.

"I th-thought I g-guessed what you were about," the young woman stammered, still white-faced, as they began to back slowly toward the cook-fire. There had been a man there guarding what she did, making sure she did not make off with a knife. Now he was gone, part of the melee, which was swirling around the erstwhile leader.

As soon as they reached the dying fire, she equipped them both with wicked long blades that she had been eyeing for some time. "Cut anyone who comes near us," Annukka said grimly. "Go for the throat. They will be too drunk to defend themselves, I think."

Kaari did not argue. Several hours of being mauled by a brute, with the promise of worse to come, was enough to make even the gentlest of girls prepared to take matters into her own hands.

With one hand she held the knife; with the other she tried to put her clothing into order. Annukka's attention was not on her, but on the fighting and on what she was doing about it.

She sang a song so old that she didn't know the exact meaning of the words, only that she had been told it was a song of battle-madness intended to make men fight against their enemies until they were cut to ribbons. And since every man here seemed to consider every other man his enemy...

With ax and sword and knife, with sticks of wood still ablaze from the fire and with their bare hands, they tore each other apart.

It didn't last very long; it couldn't, not when you had men who were gouging out eyes and hamstringing each other. The leader went down first, with the killing blow being any one of a dozen lethal strikes aimed at him. Then they turned on each other.

At that point, Kaari hid her face. Annukka, on the other hand, watched the melee like a carrion crow, and whenever it moved, leaving behind wounded in its wake, she darted in with her long knife to finish those left behind before they could even realized she was bending over them. This wasn't revenge; this was survival. There could be no one left standing at the end of this but herself and Kaari.

And so it was.

Although she was white-faced and nauseous, Kaari was made of sterner stuff than Annukka had guessed. The young woman helped Annukka harness the deer and the two women used them to drag the bodies far from the camp and leave them in a heap for predators and scavengers. There was enough there to keep anything that showed up busy for one night at least; once morning came, she and Kaari would be gone.

One fire burned high that night with all the garbage Annukka threw on it. The bandits' clothing, the little they had not actually had on their backs, was not worth trying to save, so rank it was. But Annukka went carefully through everything she found and by the time the camp was cleared up, she had found enough copper and silver coins to make a small pouch bulge, two decent bows and the arrows with them and a lot of other weapons. She looked at the swords, but discarded them; neither she nor Kaari knew how to use them properly. The knives, however, would be of plenty of use, and she intended to have them concealed all over her person.

There was a lot more in the way of food gained than they had lost, too. And, surprisingly, a tent. It looked as if some attempt had been made, then abandoned, to set it up. It made her snort with contempt, although it did not surprise her, to see that these fools had not been able to assemble a simple tent.

It was probably midnight by the time the camp was clear and the two of them had sorted out what was useful and what was not.

"Mother Annukka," Kaari finally said, swaying where she stood, "I c-cannot—"

Annukka barely had the strength to push a bedroll toward her with a foot. "We both must sleep, and trust to the wolves out there to eat the feast we have left them and let us be."

Kaari did not even have the ability to do more than nod, drop down on the blankets and fall asleep. Annukka only waited to be sure that the fire was banked before doing the same.

"ALEKSIA," ELENA SAID SLOWLY, GAZING WITH CONCERN OUT of the mirror, "I hope you are not taking on more than you can handle."

Aleksia chuckled dryly. "So do I. This is why I am telling you just what it is that I am doing, so that if something does happen to me, the rest of you will know that this Witch was good enough to remove me and be able to take steps."

"I had rather that didn't happen," Elena replied, with a frown.

"Only because you would probably have to become the Snow Queen, since you are the one best suited to the job, temperamentally speaking." Aleksia laughed at Elena's expression. "Oh, yes, and then where would that handsome Knight of yours be?"

"If that happens, I swear I will go to the Underworld and bring you back, you wench," Elena growled. Then her expression sharpened, and she peered closely at her fellow Godmother. "I just gave you an idea, didn't I?"

"Indeed you did! And a very good one!" Aleksia waved her hand at the mirror. "I promise, I will keep you informed every step of the way. Keep my book open in your library. Instead of writing down only what I *have* done, I will write what I intend to do as well, so that you have a good record. Now, I am going to go see what preparations I need to make to do this. It is going to take quite a bit of trickery on my part."

After checking on Kay—still moping—and Gerda—still being led in circles by the Bear, and getting some good, sound advice on standing up for herself in the process—and making sure that there was nothing *else* that needed her attention—evidently The Tradition had decided she had enough on her plate—Aleksia retired into her library.

The Snow Queens had been in residence here for a very, very long time, and had been the only Godmothers to cover an enormous amount of territory, and the library reflected that. As Aleksia contemplated the huge, circular room that was the true heart of the Palace of Ever-Winter, she was struck once again by the likelihood that the first of the Snow Queens had been a true Fae, a real Fairy Godmother and not a human at all.

This room was twice the size of the throne room, with no windows at all. Instead, the entire ceiling was a skylight that poured light into the room by day. And by night, hundreds of lamps provided light to anyone who prowled the shelves.

Hundreds. Because the room was easily ten floors tall, and it had floor-to-ceiling bookshelves. In order to have access to the books, there were beautifully crafted wooden walkways circling the room on every bookshelf level. There were roughly two levels per floor, and the sensation of standing down on the floor and looking up at all those books was of seeing all the knowledge of the world in one place.

While this was probably not true, it *was* true that there were treasures here that existed nowhere else, because this was the repository for all of the books and scrolls rescued from what could have been a terrible disaster hundreds of years ago.

It had happened that the Kings and Queens of a desert kingdom now no more had decided that the capital city would house the greatest library in all the world. Because their land had been rich in gold, their wishes were commands. Within the lifetime of the first King to make this command, it had become a scholar's pride to send a copy of his work there. By the lifetime of the tenth Queen, there were very few books in the literary world that were not preserved there.

Then, disaster. Despite clever negotiations, despite using her own beautiful body as a bargaining tool, her Kingdom was invaded. And the invaders, caring mostly only for warfare, did not care about learning. So when during a riot, someone set fire to the Great Library, nothing was done to save the books.

But fortunately for the world, the Godmothers *did* care. Not everything was saved, as Godmother after Godmother worked magic to pull the books from their doomed homes into her own, but most were, and those that were not, had copies elsewhere.

Eventually all those books, either the originals or copies, found their way here.

Here, where thirteen Godmothers and thirteen Fae—who also cherished learning—worked together to create the perfect home for them, protected from fire, water, worm and rot. And then they worked a further magic, so that any one of the Godmothers and great Wizards who needed to consult one of the books here had but to go to his own library and look for it. And there it would be—a copy, perfect in every detail. Thus, over time, they ensured that none of these books would ever be lost again. What was more, the library continued to grow, with new books added to it daily. This was not just the past being preserved; it was, insofar as possible, just what the Kings and Queens of that long-lost land intended.

The room had that special scent of a good library: old paper and parchment, a hint of dust, the smell of aged leather. Aleksia had an appreciation for it, although she was not the book lover that some people were. She had had one of those as a visitor once, and he had stood in speechless awe for a good hour, then broke down and wept with happiness. He had been a very easy visitor to care for; she scarcely saw him except at meals.

Needless to say, Kay was not permitted here. If he had known such a place existed, it might well have erased Gerda from his mind.

It would take someone who devoted himself or herself full-time for several lifetimes to learn all the books here. Fortunately, the library had such a person.

Well, "person" in the broadest sense of the term.

"Citrine?" she called.

From somewhere up near the top of the room there came a rustling sound. "Up here, Godmother!"

A moment later, something unfurled itself and descended through the air in a tight spiral.

The tiny dragon—tiny by draconic standards—landed next to Aleksia neatly and precisely. Citrine was a BookWyrm, one of a rare breed of dragon whose treasure consisted of books, rather than gold and gems. They tended to be small, but Citrine was exceptionally small, being only double Aleksia's height when she stood on all fours. She was a gorgeous little thing, golden yellow shading to deep gold on her extremities, and deep rose-gold eyes with a kindly look to them. She was, in fact, a dwarf. As such, she was easy prey for dragon-hunters.

But the Godmother who had been in residence four generations ago had been quick to offer the young dragon a home in the library and to officially designate it as Citrine's "hoard." Citrine had been in charge of the library ever since.

"I need to know how I can get into the Underworld and back out again," Aleksia said carefully.

Citrine cocked her head to one side, and regarded Aleksia thoughtfully. "I could be flippant and say that it is easy to get *into* the Underworld, but very hard to get out again...but more to the point, I think, would be to ask *which* Underworld. There are a very great many."

"The Sammi one," Aleksia replied, after a moment of mentally placing where the villages destroyed by the Icehart were.

"Tuonela, hmm? Give me a moment."

Citrine flew up to about the middle of the room, and landed on the railing, her long neck extending as she scanned the shelves. After some time, she selected one book, and then another and finally a third. She pushed herself off the railing and glided down to the floor again.

"Here you are!" Quickly she leafed through the first book and marked a page with a slip of paper, then did the same with the second and third books. She handed all three of them to Aleksia, who took them with a nod of thanks.

"Don't forget to bring them back, Godmother!" Citrine blinked owlishly, then bared her teeth in a draconic grin that Aleksia knew was friendly, but would probably look horrifying to an outsider. She nodded her head and flew back up to the top of the room where she had been when Aleksia entered—probably reading another of the new books that had arrived.

With a faint smile on her face, Aleksia took the books back to her study. She was not at all sure that Citrine knew her name. The BookWyrm was entirely focused on the books and what was in them. She might not recall what the information was, but if you told her what you were looking for, she could find the book it was in, and probably the page it was on.

With all that to remember, it was probably not surprising that Citrine could not remember the name of the Godmother-in-residence. That, after all, was irrelevant. Well, it was, right until the moment that the Godmother in question did something worth remembering and putting in a book. At that point, Citrine would know the Godmother's name and what she had done. She still would probably not *recognize* the Godmother if she saw her, but by all that was holy, Citrine would remember her name and in what book she had resided.

And truly, what did it matter what the name of the Godmother here and now was for what Citrine did? Godmothers came and Godmothers went, but Citrine would be here for several more centuries at least, growing slowly with the library, learning the books and what was in them, and serving as the living index to all of them.

No open flames were allowed anywhere in or near the library, but here in her study, she had a cozy fire and scented candles filling the air with the aroma of cinnamon. She settled down with her books, first to determine what languages they were in.

The Sammi were not ones for writing things down, depending mostly on their oral traditions. So all three books were in different languages, but—much to her pleasure—one was an account by one of the Great Wizards, one was a Godmother collecting the first-person accounts of Sammi Shaman and the last was of collected tales passed down in the oral tradition—which, to be fair, was a source much less reliable.

It pleased her even further to learn that all three were fundamentally alike.

So she had a good account. She also had evidence that The Tradition would also give her some protection if she stuck strictly to the guidelines these tales offered. She closed the last book to find one of the Brownies at her elbow, tugging at her sleeve.

"Godmother, you must eat," the little man said insistently. "You have not eaten for hours, and the cook is furious."

She looked down at the worried face with amusement; both at his concern and at the idea that the cook would be furious because she had not eaten. It wasn't as if the food would be wasted. She insisted on eating the same things as the staff, and the leftovers, if they were things that did not store overnight well, kept a very healthy flock of Ravens fed. But she was touched as well as amused.

"If you will say that I beg the cook's pardon, but I was deep in studies, I should very much like soup and bread if he would be so kind." She smiled at the little fellow. "You would help me immeasurably if you would return these books to the library. I shall go to the sitting room to wait for my soup."

"Don't go wandering off and forget you have food coming, God-mother!" the Brownie replied, insistently. She did her best to repress a laugh. Whoever he had been talking to had evidently impressed him with the need to keep an eye on her, which was rather funny. She might not be the kind of rounded and odalisque-like creature often depicted as a fertility goddess, but she was not going to pine away in half a day.

In fact, he lingered, books piled in his arms, until he was sure she had settled herself next to the fire in her sitting room.

Once safely there, she picked up her hand-mirror and waited for Godmother Elena to answer her call—which was almost instantly.

"If you must know, I am keeping track of you," Elena told her with a wry smile. "You worry me right now."

Aleksia felt her eyes widening. "Why?" she asked, astonished.

Elena sighed. "Because you have never personally had an adventure," the other Godmother said reluctantly.

"Excuse me?" That didn't precisely make sense. "I think I have had an adventurous enough life! After all, how many girls become Godmothers?"

"But you, personally, have never had an adventure," Elena repeated. "Think about this. Yes, you and your sister had adventures happen around you before you became a Godmother, and, yes, you *almost* became a jealous sister, and, yes, you were whisked off by Veroushka to become a Godmother, but you, personally, have never done anything that would risk your own life. You go out and make *other* peoples' lives adventurous, but what do you do? You rarely leave your Palace, and then it is generally to go only to a gathering of other Godmothers rather than to thwart someone evil. Now, well, I sense that you are about to leave your shelter and go and do things that will put you in personal danger."

Aleksia felt a surge of resentment. "You had adventures!"

Elena nodded vigorously. "Yes, I did, and I think I am all the better for it! But the one thing I did that was very, very stupid was that I did not keep the other Godmothers apprised of what I was doing. Of course, I was not aware that I could do that at the time, but you are. And I was just a little worried that in the excitement of being able to go and do things, you might forget—"

After listening to that astonishing speech, all Aleksia could do was laugh. Elena looked relieved.

"Prickly, I might be, Elena, but I also prize honesty. And I am very touched that you are worried about me. However—" she wiggled an admonishing finger at the the mirror "—you, of all people, should know me better than that. I am going *nowhere* without a mirror. And I am not too proud to ask for help if I need it. Now, this is what I have found out, and this is what I plan to do...."

She slowly outlined her ideas to Elena, who agreed that it seemed to be the best course of action. "And you can leave from your own Palace?"

"So it seems. Tuonela can be reached from anywhere. As they say, 'Death is universal.' There seems no great difficulty in getting in." The Brownie bustled up at that moment with a tray with a bowl of thick soup and a small loaf of bread, broken open and buttered already, still steaming from the oven. Aleksia's stomach growled, and she hoped Elena had not heard it.

"No indeed," Elena replied. "Traditionally, there never is. It is always leaving that is the difficult part. But you do have a sound strategy. Good luck, Aleksia."

"Thank you, Godmother Elena," Aleksia replied.

She had, very carefully, avoided the undeniable fact that if she did get in over her head, it was unlikely that anyone could reach her in time to be of any use.

Then again, so had Elena, who probably was just as aware of that as Aleksia was.

The way to almost every Underworld was through a cave, and there was a cave in the cellars of the Palace of Ever-Winter for just that purpose, at least, according to the notes of Godmother Riga, who had been the fourth back from Aleksia. All one had to do to enter a *particular* Underworld was to set up a spell that invoked that culture.

As familiar as Aleksia was with the Sammi, it was the work of no more than a half an hour to establish the cave-mouth in her cellar as sacred to the Sammi, to invoke a variant of the All Paths Are One Path spell, and to add the twist that linked this cave with the actual entrance to Tuonela, wherever *that* was.

She took a very deep breath before she entered the final fragments of the spell that would open the way. Carefully, she took inventory of herself. Her shroudlike, enveloping white gown should pass muster. She had spent hours whitening her skin and hair in a way that would not obviously be due to magic. Her hair was encircled with a wreath of dead flowers, and if anyone was to touch her, her skin would feel icy.

She was as ready as she was ever likely to be.

She stood before the cave, and sighed the last words of her carefully fashioned spell. *Passing from the world of men, shadow-bound, then back again.*

The ground trembled, and the cave-mouth glowed with blue light. She stepped into it.

She paused for a moment to take stock of her surroundings on the other side. This was a strange land, in perpetual shadow, with no discernable horizon. The air smelled of chill and damp, with a faint hint of mildew. The land was flat and unremarkable, covered with brittle, dead grass and leafless bushes. A pall of gray covered the sky, and there was neither sun nor moon.

Ahead of her was the river of Tuoni, and in the distance, something shimmering and white approached her. She took slow, very hesitant steps down toward the water, then stood on the shore with the cold water lapping at her bare feet. She pretended that she did not feel it, did not even notice it. This was the first test of her disguise, for this was one of the guardians of Tuonela, and on that river, in fact, heading toward her, was the most beautiful Swan that she had ever seen.

The Swan was taller than a man, and as it came closer, she could hear it singing. To the dead, this was but the background of their existence here, but it could be deadly to the living. A living person that listened too long to that beautiful, mournful dirge would be lost in it, forgetting everything else, forgetting all about life on Earth, desiring nothing more than to listen to that music forever. He would be trapped beside the river, lost in a dream of forgetfulness, until he died of hunger and thirst, or followed the Swan out into the middle of the river and drowned.

Aleksia had taken the precaution of stopping up her ears with wax. The song came to her muffled and imperfect, as the Swan approached, looking almost like a carving, gliding on the water with no sign that it was paddling itself along. Only when it neared her, did it deign to move its head to look at her, briefly. It saw nothing amiss—a spirit would not have stood there watching it; spirits did not hear the song the way that the still-living did; to them, it was lovely, but not enthralling.

Which was the point, really. No need to ensnare the dead. They could not leave.

After the Swan had passed, a faint splashing in the distance told Aleksia that the moment she was waiting for had arrived. Behind the

Swan, a small, black boat glimmered out of the mist shrouding the river, poled by someone who looked very like Aleksia...perhaps younger, and not quite so corpselike.

She was very beautiful, in a kind of empty-eyed way, was the Tuonin pikka, Death's Maiden. Like Aleksia, she wore a white, shroudlike gown of material far too flimsy to keep an ordinary mortal girl warm in this place. As she was a maiden, she wore her golden, floor-length hair unbound except for a silver-studded headband of white ribbon. Her blue eyes were curiously vacant, as if not only her thoughts, but her very soul was elsewhere.

She poled the boat with a mechanical grace; her vacant eyes were fixed on Aleksia. For *her* part, Aleksia remained where she was, maintaining a passive posture. She was supposed to be dead, her own ghost wandering for thirty days to get this far. And the dead were...

Boring.

Tuonela was the most boring form of the afterlife that she had ever heard of. The dead did nothing, wanted nothing, cared for nothing and carried out a shadow play of their previous lives, but without the passion, becoming more and more divorced even from that, until at last they moved into a state very like sleep. She wondered why any spirit would want to stay here. Well, it was better than the alternative of oblivion, she supposed.

When the Tuonin pikka's boat bumped upon the gravel of the bank, the girl waited passively for Aleksia to step aboard. After a moment, she did so. The maiden waited until she had seated herself on the single bench seat in the middle of the boat, then pushed off from the bank, heading for the farther shore.

Halfway across, in a colorless voice, the maiden finally spoke.

"Who are you?"

In an equally colorless voice, Aleksia replied, "I don't know." After all, what intelligent person truly knows who they are? She concentrated on that fact, that the wisest of men will freely admit that he does not truly know himself.

"Why are you here?"

She had to be very careful not to lie here. A direct lie would definitely be something that would set the maiden off. But a shading of the truth...

"I am looking for something." That was close enough.

"What do you seek?"

"Wisdom." That was *safe* enough. And true, entirely true.

To her intense relief, the maiden said nothing else, presumably satisfied with what she had been told. She continued to the farther bank, and the island of Tuoni itself.

Fog and mist gathered over the surface, hiding everything that was more than a few feet from the boat. The surface of the water was glass-smooth and utterly still. The only sound was that of the pole, rhythmically splashing. It was even colder out here on the river than it had been on the bank. The damp chill, now smelling a bit of waterweed, penetrated every fiber of Aleksia's gown. Her bare feet felt like little lumps of ice. And she was not yet anywhere near the end of her journey.

Finally, the keel of the boat grated against rock; the maiden expertly poled the boat parallel to the bank. Moving slowly and deliberately, as if she had all the time in the world, Aleksia stepped out of the boat, into ankle-deep, cold water. She did not even flinch. She did not pick up the skirt of her gown. She simply waded ashore as if this were all of no consequence. And she thought that out in the fog, she'd caught a flicker of movement of something very big, and very black. She thought she'd detected a hint of a fishy odor. But there was no way to tell for certain, and the maiden poled the boat away to the other side, to wait for her next passenger. She suppressed a shiver; she knew what that large black thing might well be—the giant pike-fish that was said to eat those that did not belong here. You could spend eternity in the belly of the fish if you could not convince the maiden that you, too, were a spirit.

Without seeming to look around, Aleksia meandered up the bank. At least the vegetation wasn't dead here, although it certainly was lifeless-looking. As she had been led to believe, Tuoni was essentially a duplicate of life on the living earth, an endless series of identical villages going deeper and deeper into the fog. Those who had died the most recently were nearest the river, and the marks of what they had died of were still visible on their bodies. It could have been gruesome, had their wounds not been bloodless and their bodies as pale and chill as the maiden's. It was said, by the sources that Aleksia had studied, that the longer a spirit remained her, the more of its death it forgot. Signs of wounds and injuries and illness vanished, severed limbs reattached and the spirit looked more and more as it remembered itself, in its prime of life. It would move away from the bank and deeper into the island, finding a home for itself, beginning a kind of passionless second life that was a mirror of its first. It would push the memories of that first life into the depths of its mind, unless it was asked. But then, if it was questioned too closely, or in the wrong way, all those memories would come rushing back, and with them, all the remembered pain and pleasure of living. Then it would turn on the questioner—and that could be fatal. Eventually, the spirit would come to a place where it would just lie down and sleep. It could be awakened, but if it was not, that was how it stayed—in a state of endless slumber.

Fortunately, questions were more common, here on the shore. The spirits wandered, looking for loved ones, looking for answers, looking for a purpose. She wandered among them, also looking. In her case, she was looking for the victims of the Icehart. They should be obvious enough; an entire village worth of people that had all died at once should stand out.

There was a strange feeling to this place. It was not despair; it was too dull for that. Apathy, perhaps. It seemed to permeate everything, lying over Aleksia's spirit like a gray pall.

It made it hard to move and hard to think. She had armored herself as best as possible against this very thing, and still the all-pervasive melancholy made it hard to move and think. And this was the second trap, this terrible lack of anything but ennui, this leaden weight on the soul that made it tempting, so tempting, just to lie right down and never move again.

This place did not need monsters to keep it free of the living. And it did not need guards to make it deadly. Not all traps were violent, or needed to be. This was why the spirits of the dead stopped moving, stopped thinking, and went to sleep.

Aleksia kept moving, staring at the faces of the dead, until she became inured to what she saw there, and to some of the terrible things they had died of. What was perhaps the most disturbing about them was how they went about perfectly ordinary tasks with the signs of terrible deaths on them, or wrapped in shrouds instead of clothing. They moved slowly, dreamlike, in and around the ghostly houses and buildings that were only half there, chopping wood, cooking, washing and yet, not really accomplishing anything.

And then, finally, she saw what she was looking for, the signs that these people had been victims of the Icehart. An entire village full of people, many of them, men, women, children and even infants in the arms of some of the women. All of them with ice-rimed faces and hair, skin frost-covered, and wearing, not shrouds, but ordinary clothing that was also ice-coated.

She drifted closer to them, letting the eddies of the crowds carry her toward them. Finally she was in among them, and paused, then stood completely still, her eyes on her feet. It was very cold among these people, as if they still exhaled the freezing breath of the thing that had killed them.

One of the men finally noticed her. He sat knotting a net, or seeming to anyway, although the net never got any bigger. Of course it didn't. Nothing ever changed here. Nothing ever would.

"Do I know you?" he asked, with a vague frown.

She took care not to show any interest. That would point her out as being different, and that would be bad. "Do you?" she replied dully. "I do not remember..." Not remembering was a safe answer.

"Are you from my village?" He looked around at the others like him. "We all seem to be here. I think something happened, although..." Now it was his turn to trail off his words as uncertainty washed over him.

Hmm, he might not even remember dying. "What village is that?" she asked as if she really did not care.

"Inari," he said promptly. "This is Inari. Although...it does not look like Inari." He faltered. "I do not remember Inari having this much fog."

"I am not from Inari," she replied quickly. "I do not think you could know me." She sidled away from him before he could ask many more questions, leaving him staring at the half-finished net in his hands.

She moved farther along, down something like a path, to the next village. The people here displayed similar signs of death by freezing. With luck, this was the second village that had been the Icehart's victim. This time, her quarry was a woman doing laundry, washing out shirts that showed no sign of dirt, spreading them to dry on gray-leaved bushes,

Once again, she waited until the woman herself asked, "Do I know you?" It seemed this village had been named Purmo. Again, the villagers had no idea what had killed them, or even that they were dead. It was enough to make anyone weep with the pathos of it, but Aleksia did not dare show any such signs of emotion.

The third time, although the village was obviously the third victim of the Icehart's power, it took several tries before she could find anyone to talk to her. These villagers were already forgetting who and what they had been; most of them ignored her as if she was a buzzing fly. Finally, one of the children spoke to her; its little face contorted into a mask of concentration as it tried to remember just where it was supposed to be. This was the village of Kolho, or rather, this was what the villagers thought *should* be Kolho.

Now she had the names of all three villages. Unfortunately, no one had seen what it was that had killed them. For that matter, most of them were not yet aware that they were dead.

She made her way back to the riverbank, slipping around the villages, avoiding the spirits as much as she could. Now was the time to run, and swiftly, before she was unmasked; she had gotten what she came for, but this was the hardest part of the quest.

Getting back. Because the things guarding Tuonela were not to keep things out, they were meant to keep things from escaping. Why should the guardians here be concerned about anything getting in? Whoever tried would only end up dead and remain here anyway.

Not always true…but true enough. Some of the great Heroes of Sammi legends had tried to come here and had died here. Of course, being great Heroes, according to the legends, they did not necessarily remain dead—but that was legend and not fact.

Now if *she* ran afoul of Tuonela's guardians…it would not be good.

She was going to have to deal with them and get past them without actually fighting them; the point was that she not be surprised, that she meet them on her terms and not theirs.

This would take some very careful maneuvering.

She went as far as the edge of the river before pausing. The moment she set so much as a toe into the water, the guardian would be alerted, but according to all three of the stories she had read, it was at the cave's mouth that she had to beware the most. Carefully, she looked around, made sure that there were no spirits nearby to catch her at what she was about to do, then took one of three tiny bundles that appeared to be a packet of leaves wrapped up in white thread out of her sleeve. She set the first down at the water's edge.

"Blood of my blood, my semblance be, Let them see you and not me."

A kind of pillar of smoke arose from where the packet had been. A moment later, it was not a pillar of smoke anymore. An identical twin to Aleksia stood there, regarding her thoughtfully, as she was regarding it. It *looked* uncannily intelligent—thank goodness it was not—it was nothing more than a mindless, soulless copy that would do exactly what she directed it to. But this was good, because she was about to be very, very cruel to it.

"Dip a toe into the water," she whispered to it, as she passed her hands across her own face, rendering herself invisible. "Then, when the spirits come to tear you apart, *run.*"

She withdrew a little way, and watched as the simulacrum obeyed her. As if the contact with the water had been a signal, spirits, eyes bright with anger, swarmed out of the fog to converge on the hapless duplicate. And, as directed, she ran.

She fled along the shoreline and was soon out of sight, with the uncannily silent mob in hot pursuit. The moment they were gone, Aleksia slipped into the water.

It was numbingly cold. The chill was somehow worse than being in a cold river up in the world of the living. The cold seemed to penetrate somehow, and the water itself made her clothing far heavier than it should have been. Such light garments should have floated weightlessly, but instead, they felt as if they were made of stone. She struggled as she swam, keeping her eyes fixed on the farther shore. Halfway over, she saw what she had hoped not to see; the huge Swan approached, gliding here and there through the mist, its neck outstretched as it peered among the reeds and then returned to the center of the river, and it looked as if it was searching for something.

Quickly, she took out the second of her packets, whispered her spell, and let it go, saying "Swim away! Swim *fast*."

The simulacrum obeyed, heading upriver, against the sluggish current. Since it was white against the gray of the water, it took the Swan a moment to spot it. By then, it had a substantial head start.

The Swan uttered an angry hiss, and paddled furiously after it, as Aleksia herself continued for the farther shore, swimming as hard as she could without making any splashing sounds.

She almost fainted with relief when she felt the gravel of the river's edge beneath her toes. She dragged herself out of the water, her limbs feeling like lead, and her teeth clenched to prevent chattering. It was all she could do to muster the energy to create a warming spell and dry her clothing, and for a very, very long time she simply sat on a stone in on the bank, chin on her knees, arms wrapped around her legs, getting her energy back. Because the final guardian was going to be the most difficult of all to pass.

And this was going to take very good coordination indeed. She had only one more of her decoys, and if she misjudged...

Walking silently, and very, very carefully, she moved up the bank to the cave-mouth. She examined the ground ahead of her minutely, not proceeding until she was satisfied it was safe to do so. Finally, as she drew nearer to the rock wall that marked the boundary of this place, she spotted what she was looking for, a curved row of white pebbles across the path.

She backed away, slowly and carefully, and waited. Had it heard her? Sensed her? Her heart pounded in her throat, and her mouth was dry as she waited for a sign that she had been detected.

Nothing.

She leaned down and placed the leaf bundle on the ground, and *thought* her spell at it. Once again, the pillar of smoke sprang up from it, and then turned into her duplicate. She gave it a tiny shove between the shoulder blades to start it moving toward the hole in the rock that would lead to safety.

The simulacrum crossed the row of white pebbles.

And the enormous jaws of the monster that was the last guardian of Tuonela snapped shut on it.

That row of pebbles had been the tops of its lower teeth! The upper teeth were the stalactites that appeared to protrude from the ceiling of the cave. When the jaws slammed shut, it became clear that the cave's entrance was nothing more than the monster's mouth and throat. And that anything walking into it would be devoured.

But Aleksia had been waiting for that moment, for the stories all said that it was much harder for the monster to get its mouth open than to slam it shut. She leapt for the snout, putting all her strength into her legs, a new burst of energy coursing through her, fueled by pure fear. Her left foot hit the creature's snout, her right landed between its piggy eyes, each the size of a feasting platter. Her left impacted the middle of its neck, and then she was through, into the real cave, running as hard and as fast as she could for the entrance, with terror and elation in equal parts singing in her veins.

She did not stop running until she was in the cellars of her own Palace again, dismissed the spell and stood there, barefoot, bedraggled and exhausted.

9

ALEKSIA STUMBLED UP TO HER ROOMS SHAKING WITH COLD and reaction. And yet, deep inside, there was a sense of elation. Elena was right; she had never yet "done" anything herself, and really being active made her feel like nothing else ever had. For the first time *ever,* she was a part of something. Instead of merely guiding the tale, she was in the middle of it. It was exciting and frightening all at once.

"Godmother!" her attendant exclaimed as soon as she entered the door. "You are going to catch your death of cold! Let's get you out of that—what *is* that thing? It looks like a shroud!" The little Brownie scowled at her as if she had committed some terrible faux pas. Perhaps in the Brownie's eyes, she had. This damp concoction was hardly the sort of thing a Godmother of the Snow Queen's stature should have been wearing.

"It is a shroud," Aleksia replied wearily. "I have been to Tuonela to speak with the dead. If they did not think I was one of them, they would have torn me to pieces."

The Brownie's eyes grew large and round. "You? Went yourself? Is that not the task of a seeker? Or a Hero or Champion at least? Should you not have sent Kay?"

She laughed weakly. "This is not Kay's tale, my friend. I might have asked if any of you were willing, but there are no Brownies in Tuonela. Therefore, it must be me, and I very much think that I am going to have to enter this tale further. The truth is, someone is masquerading as me, so I believe I am going to have to take a personal hand in this story."

The Brownie shook her head. "Better you than me, Godmother. Better you than me."

"Well, for now, I must tend to Kay's tale, and I need warmth and tea." She paused and realized just how empty she felt. "And food." She sent a moment of thought to her big mirror in the throne room, telling it to find Gerda for her. She would need to look in on the girl once she was feeling better.

With the Brownie's help, she pulled off the damp, cold and rather mildew-scented gown and once it was off, she realized at the same time that the Brownie wrinkled up her nose that it was not just the gown that smelled of mildew and algae.

"You're having a bath," her attendant said. She was not in the mood to argue. The mirror, and Gerda, could wait. It was not as if the girl was in any danger with the Bear there. At this point, Aleksia could probably tie the whole tale up once Kay was well and truly ready.

Without a moment of hesitation, she went straight through her bedroom to the bathroom, which, like the rest of her suite, was a haven of warmth. Tiled in golden marble, lighted by an oversized Mage-light in the center of the ceiling that also gave off a warm, golden glow, the chief feature was a huge bathtub carved of honey-colored, translucent stone. To be honest, her bathroom was one of her favorite places in the entire Palace. Whenever she felt overwhelmed and tense, a good long soak always made her feel better, and this above all was the place where the contrast between her old life as a Princess and her life as a God-mother was the greatest. Even as a Princess, hot baths were labor-intensive affairs that involved a great deal of hot water being carried to a hip-bath in pails; the water never stayed hot for long, and a hot soak was a great indulgence. Therein was the great contrast. Perhaps this was equally indulgent, but she sacrificed so much already by living up here, and what was the use of having magic if you couldn't have a steady supply of hot water whenever you wanted it?

It did not take the Brownie very long at all to draw the bath; within moments, Aleksia was able to sink up to her neck in glorious hot water, scented with jasmine and lily. The tub was of a unique design that allowed the bather to recline against a slanted back and put her head back so that her hair fell into a separate, deep basin for it to be washed. Aleksia's hair was not as long as some, only reaching halfway down her back, but this arrangement was as much practical as it was indulgent. Right now, her hair smelled of waterweeds, and the Brownie made disapproving noises over it. As Aleksia let the heat soak into her very bones, and nibbled at the batter-dipped sausages and bits of vegetables that had been brought to her, the Brownie poured more hot water over her long hair, soaped and washed it, then repeated the washing until she was satisfied it was finally clean.

"I cannot imagine what you were doing, Godmother," the Brownie said in a scolding voice. "Your hair was positively green." She worked snow-lily scent through it, combed it out and spread it over the back of the tub to dry, fanning it to speed the process. Aleksia closed her eyes with a sigh. She was full, warm and floating in scent, and there was no reason to move. All was well for the moment.

"I was swimming," Aleksia explained. "It was the only way to leave Tuonela once I was done with my business there."

"In *this* weather?" her attendant gasped.

"In Tuonela, it is not Winter." She cracked open an eye to see the Brownie's baffled expression. "Tuonela is the Sammi Underworld," she elaborated. "There is a river about it, a ferry takes you over if you are dead—or if the spirit thinks you are—but there is no way back save to swim the river."

"And a nasty river it must be." The Brownie sniffed. "You may be sure I am never going there."

"You are not likely to have to." Aleksia chuckled, and closed her eyes again. "As I said, there are no Brownies in Tuonela, only the spirits of the Sammi dead." She could easily have fallen asleep in the tub. She could certainly have stayed there until her fingers and toes were wrinkled and white and her dinner wore off.

But a gentle tugging on her scalp after a time told her that her hair was dry and her attendant was braiding it and pinning it up again, and when the Brownie was done, she stood up with a sigh of regret and accepted the huge, soft towel the little creature offered her. She felt heavy as she stepped out of the tub and out of the support of the water. When she was dry, she put on the white silk underthings and white velvet gown the Brownie presented to her.

But now she felt restored and ready to deal with whatever was about to be tossed in her lap.

Slipping on a pair of white, fur-lined, ankle-length slippers, she made her way to the throne room—and stopped in surprise. Kay was already there, gazing into the depths of her mirror with an expression of naked longing on his face.

Granted, she had "told" it to display Gerda. But he should not have been able to see her. Not unless—

Unless his feelings for her had gone from lovesickness to true love. If that happened to be the case, then Kay would be able to see whatever image of Gerda any magician or soothsayer called up.

He looked up at the sound of her footfall. "I am," he said, bitterly, "a fool."

She looked him straight in the eyes. There was something entirely new there. Humility. Humanity. She controlled her elation. "Yes," she agreed, "you are."

He mistook her meaning. "Look at her!" he said, gesturing to the mirror. "Look how good and brave she is! How gentle and kind! Even the wild beasts recognize it! I was blind not to see it, and now——" He choked and turned away. "Now I have lost her, through my own doing."

She felt like cheering, but it wouldn't do to let him know that. "You haven't lost her yet, my lad," she replied briskly. "Though it has certainly taken you long enough to realize what should have truly been precious to you. Not your own self-importance, nor how clever you thought you were, but the affections of those who cared for you, and that you should have cared for in return. We become truly great only when we work for others as well as ourselves. By your own light, you can only illuminate a small part of the world, but when your light is reflected and shared, it is magnified."

When he looked at her, puzzled, she sighed with impatience. *Bah. Another pretty speech wasted on the literal-minded.* "Never mind. You will figure it out soon enough. Come." She gestured imperiously to him. "You have passed your tests, it is time for Gerda to pass hers." As he stared at her, blank-faced, she repeated her order. *"Come."*

He scrambled to her side, and she snapped her fingers to dispel the illusion that the Palace was empty. He gasped to see the Brownies hurrying about their tasks down a hallway, and his cheeks flushed as she permitted him to feel warmth again. To his way of thinking, suddenly the cold and empty Palace had come to life, and it took him completely by surprise.

She lifted a finger; a bell sounded, and a Brownie came hurrying up with a pair of white fur cloaks, one for him, and one for her. She turned to the mirror as the Brownie was helping Kay into his, and spoke silently to the Bear. *"Leave her, old friend. I am coming with her sweetheart for her final test. But before you go, tell her that the Snow Queen makes a ride each day along where you are, and that her sweetheart might be with me. If she sees him, she is to seize and hold him and not let him go, no matter what she sees or hears, no matter what he tells her. We will see if she has gotten enough of a spine to weather that ordeal."*

The Bear chuckled. *It shall be as you wish, Godmother. I think you will be pleased.*

Aleksia dismissed the image in the mirror. Kay made a small sound of protest, but she seized his arm and proceeded at a fast walk—out the door, down the corridor, making a left toward her stables—pulling him with her whether he wished it or not. Her frail appearance was very deceptive; she had no trouble dragging him along.

"Where—are we—"

"Be quiet, boy," she replied. "From this moment, you are baggage. The important one is your Gerda now."

And at last she was able to do something she had longed to do for months. She sealed his lips with a gesture. Now, the only sounds that would come from him were the ones that she decided he would utter.

The sleigh and four white reindeer were waiting and ready at the outer door, under a hard, blue sky without a trace of cloud. Two of the Brownies, who were also waiting, seized Kay's arms and pitched him into the sleigh. Aleksia, they aided in more gently, then one jumped up onto the driver's seat and the other jumped on behind. A flick of the reins along the reindeers' backs and they were away, out of the white-walled courtyard, down the side of the mountain, the deer running effortlessly on top of the hard-packed snow, speeding along on singing silver runners at a pace fast enough to make Kay's eyes bulge. Either he didn't remember how this sleigh had been flying through the air when she fetched him in the first place, or else he had been so excited about getting what he wanted that he hadn't paid any attention at the time.

Probably the latter, as he had been an intensely self-absorbed brat. It was amazing what changes could be made in a relatively short period.

Gerda was easy to spot at a vast distance, a single speck of brown against the snow, and the driver slowed the deer to a trot as soon as he saw her. Aleksia knew that they would see the girl long before she could see them, white-on-white as they were. Poor child... Aleksia spared a moment of pity for her. Unlike Kay, she *knew* this was the climax of her story, felt it instinctively if not intellectually, and she had to be on fire with nerves. Everything she had done so far had led up to this point. She was like a runner before the starting shout of a race, knowing and feeling everything she had endured to get to this point, yet not knowing what the end of the race would be.

The Brownies were watching the girl with great interest. She didn't recognize either of them, although, as was the custom for these outings, both were dressed in outfits that The Tradition deemed peculiar to Dwarves or Gnomes—red, pointed hats, heavy brown coats belted at the waist, moleskin breeches, sturdy brown boots. The Tradition deemed that Brownies should not be seen outside of a dwelling, and that the Snow Queen was too haughty and imperious to be served by Brownies anyway—yet Dwarves and Gnomes absolutely loathed the snow and ice-fields around the Palace of Ever-Winter. Since most humans couldn't tell the difference between Brownies, Dwarves and Gnomes anyway, in public her Brownies dressed like Dwarves and The Tradition seemed satisfied.

These particular Brownies might never have served this duty for her before, but every Brownie in her service was taught what their responsibilities might entail, so they both knew the way this should go. Now the driver reined in the deer a little more, and the postilion up behind made sure that Kay was still spellbound by peering into his eyes and poking him a little. The nearer they drew to the girl, the slower they went, because if Gerda did as the Bear had told her to—

Just as they got close enough to her to see her expression, and Aleksia noted that her face was full of a mixture of fear and determination, she stepped out in front of the deer and flung up her hands. The driver hauled on the reins to stop the deer; since by that time they were hardly going faster than a walk, that was easy enough. Aleksia had to work hard to keep from smiling. All, so far, was going according to plan.

Gerda grabbed the reins of the lead deer and hung on to make sure they were going nowhere.

At this point, the girl in question sometimes made a brave speech; Gerda's mouth opened a little but nothing came out. Aleksia decided to give her a bit of prompting, just to get her going.

"How dare you!" Aleksia barked haughtily. "Don't you know who I am? I am the Snow Queen, the ruler of the Palace of Ever-Winter, before whom the mountains tremble! Leave go of my animals, miserable wench, and be on your way!"

"Not without Kay," Gerda replied, looking to where Kay sat beside Aleksia, held fast in her spell, looking straight ahead with no more expression or recognition than a statue. "You stole him from me. I'll have him back, now."

Aleksia allowed one brow to arch up significantly. "Oh? Really? Is he your servant? Your slave? You hardly look to be more than a wretched peasant, a mere chit of a worthless girl. But if he is your slave, I will buy him from you."

She nodded to the postilion, who fished a single gold coin from his pocket and dropped it contemptuously at Gerda's feet.

"Now, be off." Aleksia motioned to the driver, who, of course, knowing his duty, did nothing to drive away.

"He's not my slave, and you stole him away from those who love him!" Gerda said indignantly, her cheeks flaming. "I saw you!"

"What is all this stealing and taking back nonsense, then?" Aleksia scoffed. "If you saw him go with me, you know he came freely and of his own will."

"I know you have frozen his heart," the girl replied courageously, her cheeks bright red now, and her eyes wide and frightened-looking despite the determination in them. Poor thing, she was terrified. But that was the point of all of this. If this was to work, she would have to be the one keeping Kay's feet on the ground. She would have to stand up to him in a temper, when he didn't want to be bothered. She had to be made of very stern stuff. It would be just as frightening to have to stand up to the one she loved as it was to stand up to the evil Snow Queen. There would be times when she would have to remind herself of that. "I know he is not himself. Free him! Let him make his own choices!"

Aleksia laughed at her, putting a world of scorn and withering contempt into her voice—just as Kay would probably do in a temper. In fact, everything that she was doing now was to test her to see if her own self-worth was strong enough to stand up to the worst the one she loved could deliver. *It is so much harder to take a hint of scorn from the beloved than a verbal battering from an enemy....* Kay would always be more intelligent, more clever than Gerda was. She had to know, deep inside her, that what she offered was just as important and just as valuable as wit and intelligence. "Very well, child, if you want him so badly, see if you can take him!"

She sat back in the seat of her sleigh with an air of haughty and confident amusement. Gerda did not need a second invitation; she grabbed Kay by the collar of his fur cloak and hauled him out of the sleigh bodily.

No matter how many times she did this, Aleksia always found the moment when the girl tried to hold to her boy fascinating. Not that the boy ever varied his performance; he couldn't, since he was, for the first time since she had taken him away to her Palace, actually spellbound. No, it was how the girls reacted that was fascinating. This was where she showed what she was truly made of, and how she was going to face living with her young man in the future.

Kay seemed to wake from a trance, and his face went from stony to as haughty as Aleksia's. "Let go of me, peasant!" he spat, trying to brush off her clinging arms, then actually fighting to get her to loosen her hold. "Stupid, ignorant filth! Unhand me! Who do you think I am? I am Kay, chosen consort of the Snow Queen! You are—who? I never saw you before! You are nothing! You know nothing and do not care that you know nothing! What are you, compared to her? You are a sparrow in the presence of a Swan, a mouse in the shadow of an eagle! You can scarcely manage to raise your eyes above the mud at your feet, and she soars among the stars! I am meant to be with her, you stupid, silly little girl! Let me go!"

At this point, barraged with insults, some girls wept, some girls begged the boy to recognize them and one had just given up. That last one had infuriated Aleksia so much that she had very nearly given up on the two herself and stripped both of their incipient power. Only the fact that the boy had come to the same point as Kay kept her from doing just that.

Instead, she had put the boy into an enchanted sleep, then whirled the girl away in a snowstorm. After a truly terrifying "appearance" and a "curse," she had sent the girl on a full year of questing to find her boy again, until her clothing was in rags and the pair of iron shoes she had been given was worn thin. She had felt rather sorry for the boy actually—he had certainly managed to come up to the mark on his end—and had kept him asleep for that year before consigning him to the obliging trolls who had finished out the story for her.

Gerda was made of very stern stuff, thank goodness; she hung on for dear life, grimly, cheeks flushed, saying nothing.

Good for her. Time for the next test. She can handle him in a senseless rage. Let's see how she handles this.

Aleksia made an unobtrusive sign, and Kay went from raging to weeping, moaning, crying out in pain. "Gerda! Gerda, it hurts, it burns, let me go! Please, please let me go. This is killing me. If you love me, you will let me go! Please! I cannot bear this! I cannot. The pain, the pain is terrible, and if you love me, you must release me, I beg you!" His cries and moans were heartrending and sounded very genuine. They weren't, of course, but Gerda couldn't know that. Which was, after all, the whole point. There might well be a time in the future, perhaps when he was ill or hurt, or utterly despondent, when he might beg for her to leave him. And again, she would have to trust in herself to know that she must not.

Gerda hung on, still saying nothing, though tears streaked her own cheeks. Aleksia allowed this to go on a few moments more, and then set the next phase in motion. Now things were going to get interesting, for this would test what Gerda could face down in the way of physical trials. In a sense, Kay himself would no longer be "important" here; he would no longer be recognizable as himself.

Aleksia wrapped The Traditional power around both of them, power that grew with every moment that Gerda held fast. Now it was so strong that she could do things with it that utterly transcended the usual magics she could manage, and went from magic to the realm of the almost miraculous. With a shriek, Kay burst into flame.

He screamed at the top of his lungs, and so did Gerda. It looked exactly as though he had been doused in oil and set ablaze. Nothing of him was really recognizable in the fire, not even his voice. The flames weren't hurting him, though they were burning Gerda—or at least, she thought they were. The pain and the burns were illusory, but very convincing.

Aleksia smiled a little, with pardonable pride, and then concentrated on controlling the fire, which was a very tricky proposition. Veroushka had never managed that part of it, although the Godmother before her had, and advised this as being integral to the test. The fire had to be real; in fact, the snow all around the two of them was melting, and anyone near either of them would feel the heat. The reindeer moved uneasily away a pace or two. The fire had to hurt Gerda enough to make her feel she was burning, and yet, the pain had to be entirely in her own mind. And, of course, the fire could not touch Kay at all. It was a very tricky bit of magic to manipulate, in spite of all the power that was at her disposal. Aleksia didn't let this go on for very long, however. That would have been altogether too cruel. With a final shriek, the fires went out.

Before Gerda could even take a breath and realize that she was unhurt, Kay writhed bonelessly in her arms, shivered and then—

—he became a giant serpent, and it was Gerda's turn to be seized as he flung his coils around her. She went white, as she looked up at the flat, hideous head with its slitted yellow eyes, when she saw the huge fangs as long as her hand as the pale mouth opened and the noisome breath washed over her. She looked as if she was about to faint as Kay reared his head above hers, poised to strike.

She screamed in terror—and hung on.

At this point, if a girl fainted, Aleksia never considered it a flaw. There was such a thing as going beyond what a girl could bear, and as long as, when the girl woke up again, she tried to hold to her lover, the trial was still on.

But Gerda didn't faint. The serpent gave another angry hiss, feinted a strike and writhed in her arms again. Once again, Gerda found herself holding on to something that was changing even as she clung to it.

In a way, that might be the most terrifying part of the trial, really. The in-between forms, so strange and horrible, things that matched nothing, things that could become anything. And not knowing what you were going to be hanging on to when the monster that had been your lover settled into a form.

This time, she found herself holding on to a double handful of coarse mane. He became a stallion, kicking and fighting—though Aleksia was very careful to make sure that none of those kicks or bites actually connected, and that as long as Gerda maintained her grip, Kay would not actually break free.

Gerda hung on, teeth gritted, muscles straining, eyes blank as she concentrated.

Again Kay writhed, became amorphous, changed.

And now he was a hideous Troll in her arms, stinking to high heaven of rotting meat and foul breath, a thing that slobbered over her, laughed greedily and tried to kiss her. This thing wasn't trying to escape—oh, no. Now her fight was with herself, to keep from letting go of the awful thing. She averted her face and hung on.

Kay writhed again in her arms.

She found herself clinging to the ankles of an enormous eagle, that beat at her with his wings as its cruel talons opened and closed, and its shriek fit to split the eardrums as it tried to get away from her. She hung on.

No matter what form he took, no matter how he tried to escape, she hung on, battered, beaten, burned, frozen, threatened; it did not matter.

Until, at last, Kay lay in her arms again, exhausted, but himself. And Aleksia released the spell on him. *He* would have no memory of all of this; this was her trial, and not his. It was just as well, really.

Some Snow Queens of the past had not been as skilled in magic as others, and had elected to use mere illusions instead of transformations. Those were never quite as convincing, Aleksia had found. There was always some self-doubt in the girl's mind afterwards.

He blinked; saw who was holding him for the first time. So far as he knew, a moment before, he had been telling Aleksia that he was sure he had lost her forever. How not? For all he knew, he really *was* the Snow Queen's prisoner, and he would never see his childhood sweetheart again. He had no idea that Gerda had been looking for him all this time—all he had known was that he saw her charming a giant Bear somewhere. And there were stories about that, too...the Bear could easily have been a Prince in disguise or under a curse. He could have been on the verge of losing her forever. But now—here she was.

With him.

"Gerda?" He faltered. "Is it really you?" He reached up to touch her face as if he still couldn't believe she wasn't an illusion herself.

She looked up into his face, tears still on her cheeks, but her expression had been transformed by love. "It's me! Oh, Kay, do you know me at last? I have been searching so long for you!"

"Know you? Oh, my love—" He took her face in both his hands and covered it with kisses. "Why did I ever leave? Why couldn't I see what was right in front or me? My love, my only love!"

Aleksia chuckled with satisfaction and let her haughty expression drop. The Bear ambled forward at that point, making whuffling sounds of contentment. He truly enjoyed seeing the happy endings of tales, and she would never deny him that pleasure when she had a chance.

Silly cubs, he said affectionately. *Wouldn't you think, with all of the stories they are told, that they would manage to keep themselves out of trouble?*

"They can't help it, as often as not," she replied quietly. "When The Tradition decides for them, the best we can do is to make sure nothing horrible happens."

Hmm, true enough. He whuffled again. *I am glad I am not a human.*

She chuckled.

She motioned to the Bear, who nodded to her and took his cue, as she called up a halo of bright light around them both. Now it was time for her to change from the mantle of the Snow Queen to that of the

Fairy Godmother—and time for the Bear to become the Mystical Helper. He waited for the two lovers to pause for breath and made a coughing sound. They both looked up, startled, eyes widening at the sight of the smiling woman radiating light, and her ursine companion who was doing the same. The Brownies attending the sleigh were grinning broadly, and even the deer were watching with approval.

"You have passed all the trials I have set you," Aleksia said, another touch of magic giving her voice a ringing quality. "And your prize is that you have won each other and found yourselves." The Brownie driver handed her down from the sleigh, and she took off her own fur cloak and put it around Gerda's shoulders.

I lose more fur cloaks this way . . . She made a mental note to have another half-dozen sewn up for her.

She held out her hand, and the Brownie serving as postilion put a gold filigree casket the size of an apple and shaped like a heart into her hand. This, she handed to Gerda. Gerda opened it, and gasped at the fortune in sparkling gems that lay within; this would be more than enough to set the pair up with a fine home and workshop, where Kay could invent clever things to his heart's content. It would also ensure that he would not find himself seeking work only to discover that his cleverness was being used to fabricate terrible weapons. "For your steadfast heart, I bequeath to you the means to make your way in the world without sacrificing your integrity and ideals. Seek peace, help each other and never forget to aid those who are less fortunate than you, or your prosperity will melt like snow in the Summer."

Again she held out her hand, and this time the casket that the Brownie put into it was steel. "And for you, Kay, who has learned that there is nothing of value that surpasses the love another has for you, something very special. For as long as you remember this, and remember to love Gerda in return, this box will hold whatever it is you need most and cannot find on your own, be it silver and gold or a bit of clockwork, or the book that gives you the clue to solve a problem. But the moment you forget this, the moment you break her heart—" her face darkened "—this casket will fail you, and all you attempt will come to naught."

Kay took the box with a sober expression. "I will make no eternal vows, Godmother," he said with genuine humility, then grinned sheepishly. "I can be a single-minded and selfish bastard, as we both know. I only promise that I will try, I will try as hard as I ever have to solve some tangled problem."

"And I will remind him, no matter if he pushes me away," Gerda said, raising her chin and looking at Aleksia with determination.

She smiled. They would be fine. It was the ones who swore stupid things like "I will never fail her!" who ended up starting another tale. The Tradition seized on things like that the moment that the words left the lips.

And then they are my problem all over again.

"Then keep each other strong and sure," she told them firmly. "Remember that it can be vital to fix mistakes as soon as you know you have made them. And remember to be very, very careful of what you wish for, because sometimes the worst thing that can happen to you is to get it. My sleigh will take you home. You will find every provision you need on the way."

She stepped back; Kay handed Gerda in, then climbed up after her. The driver slapped the reins over the reindeers' backs, and the sleigh moved off, going faster and faster, until at last it lifted right up off the ground and into the air, where it soared off and became lost in the blue.

I do hope they send it back, the Bear chuckled.

She slapped his massive shoulder. "Silly goose. Come on, then, you know what happens now."

The Bear sighed with content. *I take you home, and then you feed me. I hope you have honey-and-oat cakes with berries in them.*

She laughed, and hoisted herself up onto his back. "If we don't, we soon will—as soon as my cook hears that you want them." He was as broad across the shoulder as a bed and she had no trouble settling herself down. As warm as he was, with a little magic to help, she did not even need her cloak. She patted his massive neck. "Right you are, my friend. Let's go."

Annukka hooked her rope around the ankles of yet another dead bandit, and patted the shoulder of her nervous reindeer. He moved off in the direction of the untidy line of corpses that Annukka had laid out where predators and scavengers could easily find and feast on them. This would virtually ensure that their spirits would wander about for a good long time before finding an entrance to Tuonela, and she hoped that every single moment would be sheer misery for them.

The encounter with the bandits had, curiously enough, left Annukka and Kaari better off than they had been. Aside from destroying her charms, they had done nothing to despoil what the two women had brought with them. So not only did they have their reindeer and the provisions that they had gotten from Annukka's stores, they were now in possession of things they had not been able to obtain before fleeing the village.

Weapons, chiefly, but also other items.

Annukka had insisted on Kaari going through the campsite, while she disposed of the bodies. There were three or four hide tents, all in poor repair, that with some work, Annukka would be able to piece into one tolerably good tent. That was probably the best find of all. But they also had weapons now, a bow apiece and plenty of arrows, a pair of long daggers and a hand-ax, which would be useful for chopping wood as well as being a weapon.

Kaari had been very thorough about picking out everything that could be used, although both of them had drawn the line at scavenging clothing. For one thing, it was all dirty and reeked of sweat and things best not contemplated. For another, most of it was so patched together that it was not worth the time to repair it.

But it looked as if most of the bandits' victims had been individual travelers and hunters, who had carried things more useful to the women than to the bandits. They had rope and cord, spare hide, a stout pry-bar, extra strapping and brass bits and tools to mend harness, proper packs instead of the sacks they had tied on the backs of their deer, and any number of small things that were likely to prove useful. Individually, the robbers had been a scurvy, ragtag lot, but being able to pick through *all* of their belongings had been fruitful. It was ironic to think that if they had been willing to share, they all could have been living much more comfortably than they were by hoarding their spoils.

Annukka had frankly expected to have to do most of the work of hauling the bodies off to a pile in the woods and picking through the camp, but to her surprise—and gratitude—after an uneasy night's sleep, and after all the useful things had been picked out, Kaari had mustered up enough spine and guts to help.

But now a difficult moment was coming. Annuka had been the one to rifle the body of the chief, and then had left him for last. When she returned with the deer, she found Kaari standing over the corpse, staring at it. Annukka watched her carefully, expecting an explosion of some sort—

And as Annukka had expected, after a moment, Kaari unleashed a barrage of vicious kicks on it, then seized a stout branch and beat the corpse's head until it was unrecognizable, then burst into tears.

Gently, Annukka led her away, comforted her wordlessly and let her cry herself out. *Poor child,* she thought, a lump in her throat. It was one thing to hear about robbers and bandits and the like around the home fire. You could exclaim in horror, feel all the sympathy in the world for their poor victims, but still, *you* were safe. Now—well, there it was. It wasn't someone else this time, it was Kaari. The worst that *could* happen had not happened to her, but it was the worst that *she* had ever experienced. Until this moment, the nastiest thing that a man had ever done to her had been when her father had spanked her as a child.

In a way, eventually, this would be very good for her. As Annukka knew, even in their own village, there were men who were less than good to their women. Now Kaari would have some idea of what they went through.

She held Kaari against her shoulder and rocked her a little, reflecting that she was holding up remarkably well. Then again, she hadn't been raped, only pawed and slobbered on. She did not say that, however. This was quite bad enough so far as poor Kaari was concerned.

Finally, when Kaari had cried herself out, she said dryly, "Imagine, when they get to Tuonela and have to say how they died. That two women tricked them and set them against each other. Everywhere they go, they will be met with laughter. Other men will make them do womanish chores. They shall spend the rest of eternity as the butt of other men's jests, and the objects of scorn for all."

Kaari sniffed once, and rubbed her eyes with the backs of her hands. "Do you think so?" she asked.

"I know so." Annukka patted her shoulder. "Now, you go finish loading the deer. I will dispose of this carrion. Then let us get out of here, before the scavengers come."

They left the campsite just before noon, and headed roughly back to the road. Annukka felt angry all over again when she thought how much time they had lost thanks to the attack. She begrudged every step taken in the wrong direction—and this was enough to make her blood boil if she thought about it for too long.

She kept that from Kaari, however. The girl had more than enough to think about for the moment, and there was no use in adding more misery to her current burdens.

They journeyed as far as they could that day, and made a much more comfortable and very well-hidden camp that night. Annukka took care to doctor Kaari's tea so that she fell asleep immediately and slept dreamlessly.

This was not just for Kaari's sake; Annukka wanted to do something that required that she not be interrupted.

As soon as Kaari was asleep, she took out her kantele, and gathered her magic around her. The encounter with the bandits had shaken her more than she wanted to admit in front of the girl. Kaari was relying on her to be strong and clever; after all, the girl had never even been out of their village except to occasionally go out with some of the nearer reindeer herds, as the youngsters did in Summer. All this was new—and now, it was terrifying. Yet without Kaari, this journey might well prove impossible. As Fall turned to Winter, they would have to watch out for each other. Wolves would be a danger later, as would uncanny things. Once the snow fell, not only would they have to keep watch at night, turn and turn about, but one of them would have to stay awake to make sure that the fire did not go out, or they would both die. One person might survive in the Winter wilderness alone, but only if that person was an experienced woodsman, which neither of them was. They absolutely needed each other.

Which meant that Kaari would need to discover courage and resources within herself that she did not know she had.

And it meant that Annukka was going to have to do what she was reluctant to do: use magic. There were a number of things that Annukka could do, magically, but they all carried with them varying degrees of danger. Every use of magic left a sign that other users of magic could read; out here, where there was no one else about, at least she would not be endangering anyone but herself and Kaari—but that also meant it would be easy for anyone looking for the magician to find them.

You could wrap yourself in protective magics, but that also left signs, and if you relied on those spells too much or assumed they were working, when something very dangerous came across you, something that could counter those magics, you could very well find yourself in deep trouble without warning.

What to do? *That* was the question. Whenever there was an option, Annukka preferred to do things that would work within the "natural order" of events. So what would fit that particular option?

Finally she thought she had a solution of sorts. So while Kaari slept, she played without singing. Words made the magic more immediate and powerful, increased the obvious "footprint" on the world, and that was the last thing she wanted.

Instead, she concentrated, as she did when she wove. She recalled every tale she had ever heard of lovers overcoming impossible odds to be with one another, of brave souls meeting every obstacle in their way to make a rescue. In her mind, she recited them as best she could, to the sound of her own fingers on the strings. She pictured the events of the stories in her mind. She added to that all the tales she knew of clever Heroes—not necessarily strong, nor great warriors, but those who were quick-witted and wise, who slipped by guards, made brilliant escapes and tricked their way out of trouble. That was who she wanted emulate; after all, she and Kaari were not fighters and there was no use trying to become fighters. It wasn't swordplay that was going to win the day this time.

And last of all, she called to mind all of the stories of Heroes finding help in unexpected places; it was heartening to realize just how many of those stories there were. And equally heartening to reflect on how often it was the smallest and the weakest who provided the most help.

We will be kind-hearted and generous, she promised the magic. *We will earn our good fortune. We will help everywhere it is needed. Not just now, but in the future.* That was how you earned those unexpected favors.

She looked down at Kaari's sweet, troubled face. *Let her see she is braver than she thinks. Keep her mind clear so that she can be clever. Let her keep her gentle heart,* she added. All of this would be for nothing if Kaari lost some of what made her so unique, so cherished. Gained wisdom and experience on top of that would only be good. Anything lost—

No. Unacceptable.

She played and concentrated until she could no longer keep her eyes open. And only then did she set the harp aside, and put her own head down.

But not before checking the silver cup.

The thin rim of untarnished metal remained. Veikko was still alive.

With that hope in her heart, she slept.

The next day, the track took them into deeper forest than any that Annukka had ever seen. Mostly fir, the trees spread thick boughs that interlaced with each other to the point where the land beneath the boughs was in a perpetual state of twilight. These were old, old trees here, not much taller than the ones she knew, but so big around that she and Kaari could not encircle their trunks with their arms outstretched. The trunks were bare of branches to well above their heads, with only the occasional shaft of light penetrating to make spots of brilliance on the forest floor. The ground was carpeted in needles so densely that it muffled all sounds completely. As they passed under the shadow of these forest giants, the very air changed. There was a scent of age, as if the carpet of needles that covered the forest floor and the track that they followed had been undisturbed for centuries. Birdcalls seemed very far away, quite as if they were coming from another world altogether, and there was not even a hint of a breeze to stir the branches.

It was cold, too. Not the Autumnal cold, the bite of frost, the hint that Winter was coming. This was the cold of long, long years, of things for whom the life of a human was the merest blink of an eye. It was not a damp chill, that was the strangest part. It made Annukka think of mountains, and dragons, and things for whom little, little human beings were of no consequence.

And there was the sense of being watched. The back of her neck prickled, and the hairs on her arms tried to stand erect.

"Do you feel it?" Kaari whispered, eyes darting from one side of the track to the other. There was nothing to be seen—just the huge trunks marching into the distance, the sparse undergrowth that struggled for the least little bit of sun that managed to penetrate the canopy of boughs. And yet…Annukka would be willing to swear that there were a dozen pairs of eyes on her at that moment. Not unfriendly, not hostile, but…eyes, nonetheless.

Annukka nodded. "I do not know what it could be, but something—"

She bit off what she was about to say, as the least little movement out of the corner of her eye warned her that they were about to find out just what was watching them.

The reindeer stopped dead in their tracks, trembling. Then *they* faded into view, appearing, one by one, among the trunks, stepping out to surround them.

Twenty of the most beautiful maidens that could have been imagined. They had faces that sculptors would ache to copy, complexions like rose petals, lips like strawberries, eyes as blue as the cloudless sky above, and bodies that would make a man faint with desire. Long, flaxen hair, like a waterfall of shining gold, fell unbound to their ankles. Annukka had never seen one woman to compare to them, much less twenty.

Despite the chill, they wore nothing more than simple, white linen shifts tied at the waist with ropes of woven vines to which a few scarlet leaves still clung. And it was those ropes around their waists that told Annukka what they were.

Forest spirits. Soulless creatures that were a dreadful danger to a man, creatures that every mother warned her sons about. Annukka had been no exception to this, and unlike some sons, Veikko had taken his mother at her word. He must have, or he would never have gotten to his teacher on the other side of this forest.

Annukka strained her mind to recall anything else about these spirits. Had she once heard a tale that they were cursed to be this way, because they had spurned the love of some missshapen forest god? She could not remember....

And strangely enough, it was not that these spirits were inimical to men, it was because, in their desire for a soul of their own, they would seduce men and kill them with loving. The need for a soul was a hunger in them that they could not control. They could not help themselves— and the men, unless warned, could not help themselves, either. They would succumb to the beauty and the embraces of these beings, sur- render themselves—and die in the arms of loveless love.

"Greetings, sisters," Annukka said, with a little bow of courtesy. "We wish to pass in peace." She waited, a little breathlessly, to hear their reply. Would they be allowed to pass? They could offer nothing to these spirits, but legend did not say what would happen if women encoun- tered them instead of men.

One stepped out from among them. "Well you might call us sister," she whispered, looking at them sideways. "You, too, have the blood of men upon your hands."

Annukka felt a deeper chill. Did this mean that the forest spirits would try to recruit the two human women to their ranks? Kaari gave a start, eyes widening. "Evil men," Annukka said firmly. "Men who would have caused us great harm, who had no compunction about slaying others. We were but the instruments of justice."

The one that had stepped forward turned back to whisper to the others, and revealed the secret of the forest spirits. Her back was hollow behind the hair, the sign of her soullessness. Kaari gasped involuntarily. The maiden turned back to her, that coldly beautiful face regarding the girl dispassionately. "Are we horrible to you?" she asked. "Are we so terrible? Are we monsters?"

"You—are—the soulless ones," Kaari managed. And that was all that she said, her hands, still clasping the reins of her mount, covered her mouth.

The leader nodded. "Yes, sister. You see us for what we are. Men have slain us for this, which we cannot help." The creature showed the faintest shadow of sorrow on her face. "And that makes what they do all the more terrible, for they slay us for doing what we must. We cannot stop ourselves, not for love, which we cannot feel, nor pity, which we cannot have. They call us monsters for this. They desire us, and hate us, and slay us for these things, and when we die, we die forever. There is nothing for us after death but....ending."

"So who, then, are the monsters?" asked another. "We are monstrous, but when *they* die, their souls journey on—where when we die, we are gone from every world. None mourn our passing, not even our sisters, for they cannot mourn."

"We wonder what hard-hearted creator was so unkind as to make us without souls," said another, in that heartbreakingly dispassionate tone. "Yes, unless we are slain, we are immortal, but what good is immortality without the ability to laugh, to love, to weep? Our lives are nothing but enduring, our death is a cipher. Any of us would trade all of our long, long lives for a day with a soul. Can you understand that, sister? Can anyone feel the sorrow for us, the pity for us, that we cannot?"

Annukka shook her head. The lives of these poor creatures were terrible indeed, and yet she could think of no way to remedy their lot. All the magic in the world could not create a soul in something that did not have one—

If this was the result of a curse, it was the worst such curse she had ever heard of, and the most tragic.

And then she heard Kaari begin to sob.

"You poor things!" the girl wept. "Oh, cruel the hand that made you! How I pity you, sorrow for you! If I had a way to share my soul with you, I would, I would!"

She buried her face in her hands as the forest spirits stirred and moved forward a pace. Her tears streamed down her cheeks, trickling between her fingers, and—

Annukka felt the powerful stirrings of magic—deep magic, *old* magic, magic much older than anything she knew. This was magic from the beginnings of the world, and it had been waiting for just this moment, just this selfless act on Kaari's part, just this person, just those words...just those tears.

As Kaari's tears dropped down from her face and her fingers, the magic flared, and they turned in midair to drops of crystalline ice that fell to the carpet of dead needles and lay there, glittering like diamonds. The forest maidens gasped with shock, then moved slowly forward. The magic swirled about them, so thick and powerful that Annukka could actually see it, currents and swirls full of golden light and brief sparks of white. They pressed in closely about Kaari, who continued to weep as if all her own sorrows were forgotten in theirs. As Kaari continued to weep, more and more forest spirits emerged from the trees, gathering up the crystalline drops as if they were the most precious objects in the universe, each taking only one. Then, one by one, they turned their backs to one another, gently placed the teardrop in the hollow, and stepped back.

And the hollow backs shimmered with power, and closed over. One by one, teardrops fell, were gathered, were placed, until there were no forest spirits left without a precious drop, and—

The magic dissipated, evaporated. There were no more forest spirits—only the lovely, lovely maidens who were slowly, gradually showing the spark of something new in their brilliant blue eyes.

Kaari choked off a sob and took her hands from her face, looking around at the army of beautiful girls surrounding their deer.

They were weeping. Each and every one of them had tears slowly forming in their eyes and spilling over to slip down their cheeks.

"What—" she said, bewildered.

The one that had spoken before tossed back her hair with a kind of happy sob. "Oh, most generous, most kind, most compassionate sister!" she exclaimed. "You, with a spirit so overflowing that you could share it, share your pity, you have, all on your own, given us all what we have never had, the seed of a soul!"

"I did?" Kaari replied, looking bewildered.

"You see!" the leader said, wiping away her tears and gesturing at the others. "We weep! We never could weep before! We weep for sorrow at those we slew in the past, we weep for joy that we can weep and feel sorrow! Oh, kind one, go in peace, and we shall guard your path through this forest and nothing, nothing shall harm you!"

"Yes," said another. "And in your name, for your sake, oh, tender-hearted savior, we will make safe the path for all travelers of goodwill. Let that be our expiation! We shall make it so that a child can traverse these woods, and never come to harm!"

"Let it be so!" cried the others—and with that, they faded back among the trees again, leaving the forest as empty-seeming as it had been before. But now—now it felt welcoming, like an old, old house that had sheltered many generations and will shelter many more to come.

Annukka felt more than a little numb with surprise. Kaari looked just as dumbfounded.

"What did I just do?" she asked, faintly.

"You—followed your instinct, dearling," Annukka managed. "You gave them something of yourself, your ability to feel compassion. Evidently that was enough for them."

"But—can they really grow souls?" Kaari asked doubtfully. "Is that even possible?"

"I have no idea." Annukka looked out at the forest, sensing the remains of magic there. "I don't know why they never had souls in the first place, to be honest." She paused for a moment. "But you know, if there is such a thing as a seed for a soul—compassion is a very, very good place to start."

Kaari wiped her eyes and smiled. "You know, Mother Annukka, I think you are right. And I wish them well."

And that is why you could give them what they needed, my dear. Annukka felt a rush of love for the girl. "And so do I," she replied, and took up the reins of her deer. "So let us take advantage of their new compassion and move as swiftly through this forest as we may. Veikko needs us."

Kaari bit her lip, took a deep breath, and touched her heel to her deer's side to move it forward. "Oh, yes, Mother Annukka. Oh, yes."

10

"WELL, WELL, WELL!" ALEKSIA EXCLAIMED, AS SHE WATCHED the forest spirits dispersing throughout the ancient woods. She was truly surprised for the first time in a very, very long time. The Brownie who stood silently next to her, also watching the strange events unfold, was equally baffled.

"How was that possible, Godmother?" the Brownie asked. "I thought they were cursed to be that way forever."

"Well, all curses must have some way of being lifted," Aleksia replied thoughtfully. "The Tradition requires it. Otherwise no one would ever have any hope at all. I sometimes think that The Tradition requires hope, that maybe it even feeds on hope somehow."

"Odd sort of thing to feed on if you ask me," the Brownie muttered dubiously, looking out of the corner of her eye at Aleksia. "A good lamb roast, or a nice meat pie, now, that's something a body can feed on."

Aleksia suppressed a smile. For creatures of magic, the Brownies could be very earthy and literal-minded. "If The Tradition were something we could bribe with a meat pie, our jobs would be a great deal easier!" she said, and was rewarded with a half smile from her small companion.

Well, this was becoming more and more intriguing; she had spun a deliberately vague spell that the two women should be delayed without coming to much harm—and this was the result of it. She had felt a bit guilty about the bandit attack, for the younger woman had gotten a terrible fright out of it, but this—this was extraordinary. For as long as she had known about them, the forest spirits had been soulless and dangerous. To her knowledge—though admittedly, her knowledge was limited—there had never been so much as a hint that this situation could ever be turned around. But now, *now* they had been saved, so to speak. What was more, they had gone from being a danger to being protectors, of the innocent at least. This was a major change in the world, something that went right outside The Tradition, at least as she understood it....

Although it was certainly true that stories of redemption were part of The Tradition, and always had been, this had her completely baffled. She sensed, though, that this involved something older and deeper than even The Tradition itself. Something that The Tradition had built off of—something so old and deep that, when invoked, it could effortlessly change The Traditional path that a story was set on and redirect it as easily as she could change her mind and redirect what the cook was preparing for her dinner.

"Well, I need to make another excursion," Aleksia said after a moment. "It will require an actual shape-change, and I may be gone for some time."

The Brownie gave her a penetrating look. "Something tells me you don't intend to just go looking for information this time."

"No. This is going to be far more involved than that." She considered her options for a moment, and realized that it was completely unfair for her to just arbitrarily decide that she was going to pick up and abandon the Palace—at least, not without some consultation with the other creatures involved in her work. "I should like you to be here,

Rosemary, as I consult with Godmother Elena. This could be quite dangerous for me, and I'd want every safeguard in place that I can manage. For that, I think, I will need the help of the Brownies, and I should ask you to represent them."

The Brownie looked startled, and sat up straighter. "Me?" she said, eyes going wide. "You want my opinion? You want me to tell you what I think that you should be doing?" Unconsciously she smoothed her spotless apron with her hands, as if she was reassuring herself that she was the same person she had been a moment ago.

"As a representative of the others, yes, please," Aleksia told her. "This will be something new for all of us. I am about to enter a tale myself, and that will mean—changes, certainly." That was an under-statement. Rosemary looked more than a bit alarmed. "What kind of changes will be involved and what it will mean for all of you here, I am not sure. Godmothers have become active parts of tales before—cer-tainly Godmother Elena has—but once you put yourself in the position for The Tradition to act upon you, you can lose some of your ability to act upon The Tradition." She smiled down into the Brownie's bright brown—and now worried—eyes. "But look on the bright side! While I am gone, there will be no Kays here to plague you!"

The Brownie took a deep, long breath, ignoring that last attempt at humor. "Then we need to take every precaution," she said with a decided nod. "We'll need to make sure that, if you get into trouble, we can help. As ever, Godmother, we are yours to command."

Aleksia found herself grinning. Not smiling—grinning. No matter what came of this excursion, one thing was absolutely true. Nothing was going to be the same for her after this. And she was going to do things, get right out into the world and be a part of something! "Let's go to the throne room then, and talk to Godmother Elena where you and whoever else wants to listen in can hear us. I would prefer it if you did all the speaking for the others, however, just to cut down on the possible chatter and confusion."

"Certainly, Godmother," Rosemary said with great dignity. She had quite the air of authority about her, which was one reason why Aleksia had decided to ask her to represent the others. For another, she was not one of Aleksia's three old friends among the Brownies. She knew what *they* would say—which was not to go. Rosemary, she thought, would be more impartial in her advice. And since she had been here, Rosemary had not been at all backward about taking charge of things. Aleksia had the feeling that Rosemary would take no nonsense from anyone, which was all to the good in this case. Some of the others were almost certain to be upset, and while Aleksia did want to hear what they had to say, she also was not going to be talked out of this.

Now that Kay was gone, the throne room was a much more welcoming place. The light from the dome had taken on a warmer tinge, like the rosy kiss of the first light of dawn on a faraway mountain peak. The benches had their cushions back again, and the air itself was warmer. And there was a faint scent of mint in the air. Other than the cushions, this was none of the Brownies' doing, nor Aleksia's—this was the Palace itself, responding to the change.

With a mental shake of the head, as she wondered just how much the Palace *could* do on its own at need, Aleksia took her seat on her throne and brought the ice-mirror to life with a flick of her hand. She felt both apprehensive at this moment, and excited. Her Palace was finally entirely her own again after getting rid of Kay. This was a time she usually savored—and instead, she was actually going to leave this place and head into what could very well be a great deal of physical danger for her. She would probably be facing the false Snow Queen herself. Godmothers were not trained in magical combat. She wondered, briefly, if too much isolation had made her a little mad....

Then again, it seemed to her that this was something that was absolutely necessary. Well, that was what getting other peoples' opinions was for, wasn't it?

After sending the message to Elena's mirror-slave that she wanted to speak to the Godmother, she called up the images of the two questing Sammi women. She found a good viewpoint from one of the harness-brasses. They were still under deep forest canopy, still beneath the shadows of the thick evergreen boughs, in a semidarkness that had gone from cold and threatening to—somehow...protective. Even through the veil of the mirror she could feel that. This was not the shadow that hides menace. This was the peace of twilight, that promised a restful night to come. The transformation was startling, but Aleksia did not spend time contemplating it. Instead, she sent the mirror searching, darting from reflection to reflection—a drop of water, a bird's eye, a glistening line of sap along a broken branch—until she found something high above the women, out of the shadows and up into the highest tops of the trees, so that she could see just where in the forest they were. It must have been another bird's eye—by the way the viewpoint glided and circled, and from the astonishing clarity of vision, she suspected it was a hawk of some sort. But the important thing was that she could see the edge of the forest from here. She estimated the distance by eye, allowing for the fact that their progress would be helped, not hindered, by the forest spirits. After a moment, she reckoned that they would reach it in a day or so.

She looked for another viewpoint, higher this time, and found another bird circling a dizzying distance about the earth. Here, the edge of the forest looked like the place where a thick, green carpet had been cut and laid on a bare wooden floor. Beyond that edge, looking across meadows and more normal patches of forest, she spotted the distant fires of the village that had been Veikko's destination, where his mentor, the Warrior-Mage Lemminkal, had lived. And beyond that...the start of the wide sweep of the glaciers, and the mountains that looked so very much like the ones where Aleksia's Palace stood. This was where the mystery began, where the Icehart had killed entire villages, the wilderness where three men, all of them warriors, all of them magicians— even if one of them was only half-trained—had vanished.

And she was planning to go into that. Maybe she was mad.

It would take the women some time to get that far, but Aleksia did not want to put further obstacles in their way at this point. They were drawing too near to the place where the Icehart was, and given what had happened with the forest spirits, Aleksia did not want to chance them encountering the Icehart until she knew exactly what it was and what it could do. The name suggested a lot of things, but of course, a name could be completely deceptive. That it was some creature of the false Snow Queen, she had no doubt at all. And that made a very dangerous creature for the women to approach without help.

She also made note of the dark clouds ahead; those were snow clouds, and heavily burdened ones; she also paid close attention to the leafless state of those few trees that were not pines and other evergreens. The women did not know that this lay ahead of them. When they emerged from the forest, they would move from Autumn to Winter. And if the false Snow Queen shared Aleksia's powers, that would mean she would be stronger as the Winter deepened.

She looked up at the sound of soft footsteps. Several of the other Brownies filed into the room, following Rosemary. Aleksia nodded a greeting to them, and turned her attention back to the mirror. Even as she surveyed the clouds, trying to judge how long it would be before the snows fell, the image clouded over, and was replaced with that of Godmother Elena. This was much sooner than she had dared hope; Elena must assume this was very important.

Elena raised an eyebrow, and smiled. "Rid of your brooding brat, are you? You have more patience than I do, my dear."

Aleksia laughed. "That tale is safely ended, and I hope there will not be another to follow it. The lovers are united and rewarded and I think both have thoroughly learned their lessons." Then she sobered. "However, it appears I must interfere more directly in the other tale of which I spoke to you. There is a false Snow Queen, and she is creating great deal of harm. I think that this calls for me to deal with her directly. And perhaps even confront her."

Elena nodded. "I had the feeling you might have to do just that." Although the mirror through which she was speaking was not large enough to show more than her head and shoulders, it was clear that she took this as a cue to settle back in her chair. She was prepared for a long discussion on this. "All right. Unfold this tale for me. Tell me how it goes so far."

This time Aleksia recounted every tiniest detail, even though she knew she had already told Elena some of this. Elena's very expressive face reflected interest, agreement and surprise in turn as Aleksia continued, although she did not once interrupt. Recounting all this served any number of purposes: it helped her to put her own thoughts in order, it reminded Elena of how all the events had tied together and it gave the Brownies a good summary.

"That is why I believe I am going to have to take a direct hand," Aleksia concluded. "These women are brave and resourceful, but the fact that this false Godmother probably has similar powers to mine leads me to believe they will meet with failure if they have to deal with her." She frowned a moment. "And ordinarily that would be tragic, but not insurmountable—except that the business with the forest spirits leads me to think that there is enough going on with them that we need to be very cautious about anything happening around them."

"I am in agreement with you." Elena's eyes were dark with thought. "There *is* something new going on here—or something old. I am not sure which. There was no reason for the forest spirits to converge on them like that, for instance. If they were men, yes. But those creatures tend to leave women alone, if my memory serves me correctly. Something is moving up there, some magic I am not familiar with, and it is interacting with The Tradition in ways I don't think we can predict. In order to react to this in time, you are going to have to enter the tale. But that does not mean you have to go on in there entirely without support behind you. I can watch you, and I can make sure there are others who do so as well."

"But the reason the Snow Queen—that is, my Tradition—is so effective is because of the mirror-magic," Aleksia objected. "We can see things that you would never catch. None of you are nearly as good at this as I am."

"You forget, there are more ways of watching than through the mirror-magic," Elena admonished. "Yes, it is the clearest and the strongest and no one is as good at it as you. But we have Fauna's apprentice, who can see through the eyes of birds and animals directly rather than through reflection, and Regina, who speaks to the Winds, and myself— since my mirror-slave is a rather dab hand at watching through reflections himself. I can and will speak to the Faerie, and ask them to speak to the Fae creatures of cold and snow for me."

Aleksia nodded, although she was extremely dubious about all of this. Not that the other Godmothers couldn't keep an eye on things, but that they would be able to interfere in time to do any good. That was part of the problem; she was a long way from the rest of them, and where she would be going was farther still. If Elena was right, and this did involve some ancient magic working along with The Tradition, it could be very dangerous to try to interfere. And by the time help got there, it could very well be too late to do anything but control the damage.

Still, there was no doubt in her mind that something had to be done, if only to muster help for the Sammi if this spun out of control, or if the false Snow Queen proved too strong, or simply to quickly find a replacement for herself if something happened to her. That was imperative. There *must* be a Snow Queen in the Palace of Ever-Winter.

"My next thought, now that I know in what direction the men went, was to try and hunt for them as unobtrusively as I could," Aleksia said, without commenting further. "I thought the best way to accomplish that would be to undergo a shape-shift. Or rather, several of them."

"A full shift?" Elena raised an eyebrow. "Have you ever done one?"

"Not since Veroushka left, but I was rather good at them then," Aleksia replied with pardonable pride, for shape-shifting was a very difficult magic to master. "She was an excellent teacher."

"Godmother Veroushka was as good at shifting as Godmother Aleksia is at mirror-magic," Rosemary put in quietly. "That was what she relied on as much as mirror-magic. And she was hardly ancient when she retired and left the position to Aleksia. She might be about somewhere, shifted, you know. Would be no bad thing to go hunting for her."

"You have a good point," Elena replied, craning her head to try and see who had spoken, since Rosemary was just out of sight of the mirror. The Brownie obligingly moved into sight, and Elena nodded her thanks. "I'll have someone get on to that. And do you know, I believe I will send our dragon Champions that way as well. It will take them a while to arrive, but if they go now, should something need dealing with, they will be that much closer to you than they are by staying here." She spoke to someone out of sight of her mirror, then turned back to Aleksia. "Winged form is what you'll take, I presume?"

"I thought I would change into several forms, in fact, and yes, several will be winged. Peregrine, Gyrfalcon and Owl, Swan, too, if I can find some open water, and possibly Gull. But the hunting birds can at least allow me to feed myself without resorting to magic." She was extremely reluctant to even consider using magic out there in the wilderness; if she did so, she would stand out like blood on snow. "And I will shift to Bear also. It will probably be the safest form to rest in."

"Just don't stay too long in those smaller forms," Elena cautioned. "Shift to the Bear or something else big enough to have a real brain once in a while, even if you can't cover as much territory that way."

Aleksia did not say what she was, with some wry amusement, thinking. That she knew, probably better than Elena, about the dangers of being shifted into something that couldn't actually sustain human thought for long. That was the great danger of shape-shifting. You could easily find yourself losing bits of yourself, going more and more into the mind of the animal and thinking less and less like a human, until one day you realized—though dimly—that you couldn't remember how to shift yourself back. And you might not care. Altogether too aware of that, Godmother Veroushka had actually insisted on having Aleksia experience that firsthand—having her shift into a house cat, and doing it during the Winter when no feline in her right mind would venture out into the snow.

The experience had been, from the perspective of the human apprentice, terrifying. From the perspective of the cat, it had been Tuesday. The human had been in horror at how close she had been to losing her "self." The cat had been relieved, for all those human thoughts and compunctions had interfered dreadfully with doing what she had wanted to do. The cat had not *wanted* to be a human again, despite the dim ghost of the human in the back of her mind screaming to be restored again. That was why Veroushka had insisted on doing the shift in company, for she was able to force the change on the cat.

There was no such difficulty when the animal form had a large enough brain to fit all of the humanness into it.

"I intend to rest as a Bear," Aleksia assured her. "I had considered a dragon, but that is rather too obvious a creature. A Bear can defend itself, forage if it must, and I have been a Bear before."

"Good." Elena looked profoundly relieved. "Well then, which first?"

"I need to get ahead of the women, so a Swan for swiftness and endurance." Swans migrated hundreds of leagues without needing to touch down for rest. They ate grass and waterweeds, so they did not have to hunt. For as long as she could find things for a Swan to eat, she could stay in that fairly unobtrusive form. "I know where the men were last, and tonight is a full moon, so I can fly all night. Once I have discovered some trace of them—and I hope that will not take long—I can see if I can find where this false Godmother is. After that, I will know better what to do, though it will probably involve joining forces with the Sammi."

"Well, what is sauce for the goose serves the gander, as they say," Elena replied thoughtfully. "As much magic as she must be using will surely blaze out in that wilderness. Just as you wish to avoid using magic as much as possible to avoid being detected, she will be easy to find once you are in the general area—"

"Exactly." Aleksia nodded. She turned to Rosemary. "Have you anything to add, my friend?"

The Brownies put their heads together for a moment. "Yes," Rosemary replied after the conference. "We don't like any of this, but it's not our business to meddle in the matters of Godmothers. You think you need to enter the story, well, then you probably do. We will do whatever we can to make it easy for you to do that." She turned to the mirror, and faced Elena. "But we want you, Godmother Elena, to find Godmother Veroushka and get her back here as quick as ever you can. For one thing, once you find and get her here, there will be another experienced Godmother with everything that the Palace can supply, if

Godmother Aleksia gets into trouble. This Palace is nearer to where she is going than any of you are. For another, begging your pardon, but this is a big territory for any Godmother to cover, and it shouldn't be left unattended for long. No disrespect meant. But we know our business, as we have been tending to Godmothers and the Palace since Palace and Godmothers were here, and there's plenty of pots that could boil over if they're not watched."

Aleksia looked at the Brownie in astonishment that turned into admiration. It was nice to see one that thought for herself and stood up for what she thought was right and proper.

And she had been rather nervous about leaving all those "unwatched pots" behind her, but could not think of any way she could be in two places at once.

"All right, Rosemary, we will make that our priority," Elena replied. "And while I am at it, I shall make a search among the Sorceresses to see if I can find one suitable to hold the Palace if we cannot find Veroushka. Will that suit you?"

"I had druther a real Godmother," the Brownie grumbled. "I've never been much impressed by all those airy-fairy magicking types as think that a big enough whallop will solve any problem. But a Sorceress would be better than no one. And maybe someone who knows how to fight with magic might be good if Godmother Elena gets into trouble."

Aleksia had to turn away from the Brownie to keep her from seeing the smile. The hand, for a moment in front of Elena's mouth, told her that the other Godmother had the same reaction, despite how serious the situation was.

Not that Aleksia was unhappy about getting Veroushka or a Sorceress here in her absence. Very much the contrary. It was a relief to know that someone would be here to handle trouble to her or a Godmotherly crisis.

"I believe we have come to the best plan that can be made, under the circumstances," Elena said, gravely, after taking her hand away from her mouth. "Aleksia, good fortune. There is no one else I would rather see dealing with this, and now I will leave you to get on with it."

Aleksia nodded gravely, and she and Elena dismissed their mirror-spells simultaneously.

Then she turned to Rosemary. "Can you think of anything else that might serve to help?" she asked. "And thank you for demanding that someone replace me here. I think that the request came better from you than from me."

Rosemary sniffed with self-deprecation. "'Tis your job to be the Godmother. 'Tis ours to think of this place, this Palace and the needs of the territory, regardless of who is Godmother here."

Aleksia nodded soberly. That summed things up pretty well, actually.

"As for what I think might help, I'd look to that great hulk of a Bear that's down in the kitchen, eating enough for twelve," the Brownie said promptly. "We can be putting a pack on him and sending him after you. He won't be as swift as you, but I've seen those Bears on the move, and they can do a fair pace when they're minded to it. Then once you come to earth, he can track you by scent. More to the point, he belongs there, so he won't be drawing any attention to himself. It might be he'll get to you about the time it's too hard or dangerous to hunt for yourself. And it wouldn't hurt to have him on your side."

Privately, Aleksia thought that the Bear was going to be of less use that way than help that Elena could send, but she kept that thought to herself. "Then that's what we'll do," she said.

Rosemary looked as satisfied as she was likely to. "Best get yourself going then, Godmother," was all she said, as the others turned to leave. "If things are chancy as you think, no point wasting time."

Aleksia had no intention of wasting time. "All right then. I'll want the white bird harness and the smallest pack on it. In the pack I'll want my lightest hand-mirror, a fire-starter and a flute, in case I need to use Sammi magic. And a little blank book linked to the library; I'm rather sure Citrine has something of the sort about."

"Nothing else?" Rosemary looked as if she, too, was thinking.

"The Swan can't carry more than that even though the Bear form can, and I'll have to cache it all somewhere if I become a bird of prey." It was not the best solution, but at least shape-shifted she would not need to worry much about shelter or food, and the one thing she felt she absolutely had to have was a mirror.

"I'll get it ready. Where do you want it?" the Brownie asked.

"The North Tower. And make sure my commonplace book is where any replacement can find it. That will tell her what I am watching, besides this situation." Aleksia was already heading in that direction before the Brownie finished speaking. Now that the decision was made, she felt a sense of urgency, and a Godmother swiftly learned to trust her instincts once she had settled into the job. Whatever this was all about, the tale needed her. Needed her now.

The North Tower hadn't been used for a very long time; not since Veroushka had been in residence, in fact. Aleksia's mentor had liked to shape-shift into a bird once every few days at the least; it had been her way of coping with the isolation of this place, Aleksia suspected, and her way of escaping the sense of being trapped in the Palace. Perhaps Aleksia had her own form of escape through her mirrors, and that was why she had not felt it so urgent to keep in practice shifting. The North Tower itself was nothing more than walls surrounding a spiral staircase that led to an enclosed and roofed platform with two enormous doors that opened up into thin air. When there was a guest here, the North Tower was kept locked; the last thing Aleksia wanted was for someone unwary to go exploring and fall from the top of it. Or jump...there had been guests who had been so despondent before the end of their tales that they might have done just that. No one in her right mind would go up there even to survey the countryside. The mirrors gave you a better view; there were mirrors set into the outside Palace walls facing every direction, and it was so cold and windy up here that unprotected flesh would freeze far too easily.

There was an addition to the otherwise bare room since Veroushka's departure: a full-length mirror. As might have been expected, Aleksia found it easier to do an initial shift from human to animal if she could see herself and use her own mirror-magic to help. Veroushka had shifted so often that her own body-memory made a mirror unnecessary.

She stood before the mirror still fully clothed. Unlike Veroushka, who expected to return to a warm Palace with everything she needed in it, and could thus drop her clothing and perform a simple shift without worrying about what she was wearing, Aleksia was going to have to do something a bit trickier, a combination of shape-shifting and transformation magic. Her gown was going to have to become her feathers—or her hair—or her fur. Since it was not actually a part of her, she would have less control over it than her own flesh.

So, as she stared into the mirror, it was her gown she concentrated primarily on first, with the briefest of nods to her own form. With her eyes narrowed in concentration, she carefully gathered some of the magic of the Palace itself. The gown shimmered, shivered, became misty and indistinct as she bent her will and the magic on it. Then, with a feeling as if a little whirlwind whipped her clothing around her before wafting away again, and a brief hum of power, the image that looked at her from the mirror changed.

The Aleksia that stood there was still recognizable as herself, but as a version of herself that was a strange hybrid of woman and bird. She nodded in satisfaction; she planned to become as big a Swan as could be credible. She had already lost her voice; the lengthened neck could not support it.

She beat the wings against the air experimentally; they felt strong and sturdy. They would serve as a weapon at need; anyone who had ever experienced the power in a goose or Swan's wings knew very well that a blow from one could knock a man unconscious if aimed correctly. And she was about to become the biggest Swan that had ever graced the sky, correspondingly strong. She was not proof against an arrow or a spear, of course, but she rather doubted that the false Snow Queen was going to use either against her in this form.

Once again she gathered the magic of her Palace around her, and with it, her will.

She stared fixedly into the mirror, while in her mind she summoned every memory of what it had felt like, as well as what it had looked like, when last she was a Swan. How her chest had thrust forward, her hips behind, and yet she had not felt overbalanced. The odd clumsiness of the webbed feet and the relatively short, bowed legs. How her neck had a kind of life of its own, her vision had been spread to either side rather than being focused in front, the feeling of having her nose and mouth merged into one and made hard, her tongue shrunk, and her sense of taste and smell dulled to almost nothing. She concentrated on all of these things, on what she saw before her and what she wanted to see. She held herself, poised like a diver, winding it all tighter and tighter, until it felt as if she must let it all go or explode.

She let it go.

There was a soundless burst of light just as Rosemary entered from the staircase, bundled in a warm fur coat and hat, harness in one hand. The Brownie shielded her eyes with her hands and exclaimed with indignation.

When they could both see again, it was not Aleksia that looked back at herself from the mirror, but an enormous Swan.

"You might have warned me," Rosemary said crossly, hands on her hips. "You really might have." She strode forward with the harness in her hands, and with a few brisk motions had buckled it on over Aleksia's feathers. Stretching her neck to limber it, Aleksia gave herself an enormous shake to settle the feathers and her harness. The white harness blended into the feathers—no one would see it unless they were closer than Aleksia would like. She swiveled her head on the long neck to check the lay of the equipment-pouch; it sat perfectly square.

Well that is one advantage of this form. I can see my own back.

She nodded at the doors. Rosemary walked toward them, unlatched them and flung them open. A wave of frigid air engulfed both of them. Insulated by some of the warmest feathers in the world, Aleksia scarcely noticed, but Rosemary shivered.

"Off you go then!" she exclaimed, then hesitated. Aleksia tilted her head to the side, waiting.

"Good luck and godspeed, Godmother," the Brownie said softly.

Aleksia bowed her head in thanks for the wish. Then she went to the very edge of the opening, spread her wings to their fullest, stretched out her neck and called to the wind to fill her pinions. And when she felt the strength of the wind in them, felt as light as one of her own feathers, she pushed off the tiniest bit—and lifted to the sky.

The Swan did not need a compass or a map to know where she was going. She felt direction in her bones; she read it in the sky, in the pattern of the land. Wings beating strong and sure against the cold air, blood pumping in her veins, listening to her instinct, she arrowed across the sky, watching the land unroll beneath her. The snow that had threatened in her mirror was far from here; with luck, by the time she reached its present location, it would be gone. For her now was the sky graced only by wispy tails too far above her to be worth noting, and the sun on her back.

Down from the mountains she came, out of the grip of always-Winter, down into the valleys where the first snows lay lightly on the firs and the meadows, down to the half-frozen lakes and the calls of the last geese that had not yet made up their minds to travel south. *Go!* she warned them with her mind, and they went, lifting off the lakes in skeins, heading into the south, to where warm waters lay, and grass still green, where there would be longer days and warmer sun, and goose-gossip and eventually, mate-choosing. All that she could feel in her bones, feel the Swan-instincts demand that she follow them and leave this place.

But the Swan was weak in her at the moment, and she had lost nothing of herself yet. As the geese fled south, she flew on. She stopped at sunset, landing on a half-frozen lake, filled her belly with watercress and sharp-edged sedge and the bitter, frost-seared grasses at the edge of the lake. When the moon rose, she beat her way across the lake, half-running, and half-flying, legs and wings pumping, until the wind filled her feathers again and she was up and away.

All night long she flew, until the moon began to descend, until she saw below her the trees that hid the forest spirits, and knew she had caught up with the two women. She passed over the forest in the last of the moonlight, and before it became too dark to see, followed the harsh scent of smoke to Ilmari's village and set down in a poultry yard, where a surprised little girl, sleepy-eyed, with a bucket full of grain to feed to her chickens, found her. Carefully, the child poured a tribute of the grain in front of Aleksia, who bowed her head in thanks, and nibbled it all up, hungrily. The child ran off and returned with her mother, who brought more grain, and a slice of bread warm from the baking. They whispered to each other as she ate, and she caught some of the conversation in their accented Sammi tongue, as they noted the harness, the little pack on her back, and recognized her for something out of the ordinary. Well, this was Ilmari's village. They should be used to wonders, or at least used to recognizing them when they saw them.

When she was done eating, she closed her eyes and concentrated for a moment, feeling magic moving in her blood and bones. She needed to find a way to thank them and "pay" for the gift of food, otherwise that would throw off the balance of things.

They were looking for something lost; *every* person always has something of value that has been lost and is looking for it. Finding such things took only a little, little magic, too small for her enemy to feel. It was what Annukka did back in her own village, what Ilmari had done without a doubt when he was still here.

She felt the thing they were looking for as a bright warm spot to her left. She opened her eyes and followed the pull of it, out of the yard, to the garden, and the dug-up area where turnips had probably been planted. She began to peck at the clods, loosening them and turning them over with her beak until a glint of metal told her she had found what she was looking for. She pecked at the clod with all the force of her long neck and stepped back, fanning her wings in triumph as it split open.

With an exclamation, the mother darted forward and pulled her silver ring out of the dirt. As she turned to Aleksia, tears of gratitude in her eyes, Aleksia bowed her head once, then turned away and set off again into the sky.

It was, as she had hoped, a cloudless sky. The storm she had seen threatening had passed, leaving trees laden with new snow and the ground softened and blanketed in white. But this was not a good thing. This snow was too early for this part of the Sammi country. Below her, she saw herdsmen struggling to bring the reindeer across the snow into safe pastures, saw birds caught unawares on lakes that should still have been open and now had rims of ice. The birds, she warned to leave. The herdsmen she could do nothing for. All she could do was to speed on, but the Swan felt the wrongness of it in her bones, and was outraged. Winter had come too early. The false Snow Queen stretched her hand out with cold greed.

By midday, she had reached the first of the stricken villages, and she descended to see what she could make of it.

It was quiet. Far too quiet. No dogs barked, no roosters crowed and nothing moved between the handful of houses and outbuildings.

She waddled ponderously through the snow to peer into the open doorways. Someone, possibly Ilmari, his brother Lemminkal, and young Veikko, had gathered the bodies of the dead humans and taken them away somewhere. Possibly they had been stored in one of the closed buildings until Spring and the thaw when they could be buried—possibly they had been burned on a common pyre. Aleksia debated transforming back to herself to investigate, but on reflection, decided against it. There was nothing she could do that had not been done, and she needed to be on her way.

But this village was a quiet horror in and of itself. It was utterly empty, without a sign of anything living at all. But dead? Oh, yes. A sled dog frozen at his tether, pigeons stiff and white in the eaves—she knew if she looked around she would find more such victims, chickens dead in the roost, deer in the paddocks, goats in the barn.

With a wrench, she launched herself back up into the clean sky.

Nightfall found her halfway between the first village and the second, and when she found herself tiring, found it becoming too dark to fly, she had to drop down again to skid across the surface of a frozen lake, scuttling into hiding in the shelter of frozen bushes. There she sat, eating grasses that were still green, though frozen stiff, until the moon came up. She was glad there was no one to see her as she slipped and slid clumsily across the ice until she could get herself airborne.

She passed over the second village without stopping, flying on through the night. Whatever was there, she could not help it now. And there would be no clues here as to what had happened to the missing men. When dawn broke, she reached the third village and set down in the midst of it.

She was starving; the frozen grasses had not been enough to sustain her, and since this village, like the others, had been destroyed without warning in the night, there was no way that she, in Swan form, could get at grain that had been locked up in homes and barns. But there was something she could do.

Reaching around with her beak, she picked open the single buckle that held her harness together, and carefully began working her way out of it. Once it was on a heap on the ground, she hunched herself down on the ground to preserve heat, tucked her head under her wing and began to concentrate.

The Bear form was easier; she had, over the years, spent some little time in it with the Bear, who enjoyed a bit of company now and again. It took a great deal less time to remember what being a Bear felt like, the weight of the limbs, the way the head hung low on the shoulders, the roll of the walk and the vividness of scents. This time, she was acutely circumspect; she cast all around herself for any hint of another magician before she hunted for magic power to augment her own.

She was not at all surprised to find Traditional magic swirling around her in little eddies and whirls. After all, she was part of this story now, and as such, she was going to attract it. The magic seemed—well— confused, however. As if it couldn't quite understand what she was doing here, nor why.

Good. That at least meant that, for a while, she wasn't going to get any pressure to conform to a particular story-path.

She gathered up all the rags and tags of the magic she could find, wove it into her own power, and again, concentrated on the new form she wanted until it felt as if she was going to snap under the burden. Then she let it go.

The Bear uncoiled herself from the sleeping position she had been in, stretched forequarters, then hindquarters, then gave herself a good shake. Raising her nose to the faint breeze, she went hunting for food.

She didn't have to hunt far; her nose told her that a nearby building was a chicken-roost, and a single blow of her powerful forepaw destroyed the door. Under any other circumstance, she would have felt guilty about such destruction of property, but there wasn't anyone left here alive to use those buildings anymore, and probably no one anywhere near to inherit them, either. This village was dead now. When Winter passed, people would be afraid to live here, afraid of ghosts, or that there might be a lingering curse on the place. The buildings would be destroyed, the frozen animals eaten, if not by herself, then by real Bears and other predators, and by wind and weather. There was nothing to feel guilt over.

Her heavy jaws made short work even of chickens frozen hard, and feathers were an irrelevant gustatory detail to a Bear. She ate them, feathers, beaks and scrawny legs, and all.

Appetite sated, she prowled the village, looking for signs that the men had been here. Signs there were, in plenty; the most notable was that the houses were open and lying empty, just as at the first village, all but one. That one, the stoutest in the village, was locked, barred, and the door sealed. She could smell nothing, which meant no other predator could, either. She guessed that the men had gathered up the bodies of all the villagers and sealed them in here, presumably as they had in the first village.

She paused for a moment to consider whether she should take her human form, and finally decided against it. If there was anything spying on her right now, nothing she had done so far was out of character for a real Bear. But she could do some things as the Bear that would make it easier for her in Swan form, and still look and act like a normal Bear while doing them.

She hunted through the village until she found the paddocks for the reindeer, and broke into the barn building, and then into the bins that held their Winter grain. There were only a few dead deer in the paddock; most of them had been out with the village herder. Probably this was who had brought the news of the Icehart out to Ilmari and Lemminkal. And naturally, he would not want to stay anywhere near; he must have taken the herds far, far south by now. If she had been in his place, that is what she would have done. With the herds of the whole village—even if it was a small one—he would be welcome wherever he chose to settle.

Poor herder! He would likely have nightmares for the rest of his life. And guilt, for having survived when his village did not.

Of course, other wildlife would be at the grain as soon as fear was overcome by hunger. She didn't begrudge sharing the grain with the creatures of woods and fields. With this unnatural Winter holding the countryside fast, life was going to be hard on the wild things.

With that accomplished, she stood in the middle of the building, swaying on her feet in a kind of daze until she came to herself and realized that she was exhausted. With a shake of her massive head, she considered her surroundings, decided that it was as good a place to den up as any, and lumbered over to a straw-filled corner to curl up for a nap.

When she woke, the sun shining at an angle in through the wrecked door; it was late afternoon. She made a good meal on a frozen goat, and lumbered out to the edge of the village. She ate snow to clear her nose and mouth and cleanse them of any other scent, then stood very, very still, breathing slow, deep breaths with her eyes closed.

There. Human. But fresher scent than the rest. She opened her eyes to discover her head had swung to the right. Still taking the scent in, she followed it until she found what she was looking for.

A human would never have seen it, not unless he was an expert tracker. Beneath the cover of new-fallen snow, the faintest of depressions. Footprints. She snuffled, and concluded with satisfaction that there were three different scents there. It could only be the men that she hunted.

She went back to where she had left her harness and pouch, and pawed and wriggled until she got the harness around her head and over her shoulders. Then she returned to where she had found the scent. With her head down, she began to track it.

She was, of course, not as good as a dog would be. But a Bear was not at all bad at following scent, and this was a Bear's nose with a human mind behind it.

She followed the trail, shuffling along with the Bear's clumsy, and deceptively slow-looking gait, past sunset, past moonrise and on into the night. She felt good—well-rested, with a full belly—and there was absolutely no reason to stop now. A Bear's eyes were not very good, so traveling at night was not exactly the problem it would have been for a creature that depended more upon sight. And as for the danger of at-tackers—there wasn't much that would be foolhardy enough to attack something as large and powerful as she was, not this early in the Winter. Later, perhaps, when wildlife began to starve, she would have been in danger from wolf packs. But not now, and not as long as there were frozen dead things back in that village. The only danger she was in would be from human hunters, and the only human hunters there would have been out here were all back in that village—dead.

Well, there was the possible danger from this Icehart, whatever it was...but so far, its chosen victims all seemed to be humans; the animals it had slain were simply the unfortunate creatures that shared space with its intended victims.

Or the intended victims of the Witch. Although it didn't make any sense—would the Witch have wiped out three full villages for no apparent reason?

It was a shame that the wretched North Wind had so poor a sense of direction, otherwise she could have gotten the location of the Witch's stronghold from him. But the Winds didn't really understand human concepts like maps. After all, the Winds went where they chose, and there wasn't much that could stop them, so what did they need with maps or directions?

On she lumbered. The scents got stronger under tree-canopy, but only because the trail wasn't hidden under snow. Whatever had happened to the missing men, they hadn't come back this way.

By the time the sun rose, even the Bear form's strength was beginning to flag. The scent actually was stronger, though, so at least it was more recent. She was tracking them across the side of a forest ridge now, and considered stopping and curling up for a nap, then decided to press on at least as far as the ridge ahead of her. So far she hadn't seen a good place to curl up anyway; there might be better cover ahead.

And then, just as the full sun hit the valley below, she crested the ridge—and stopped dead in her tracks.

Below her was a sight that was both stunningly beautiful and utterly horrible.

For as far as the eye could see, the sun reflected blindingly off the branches of a forest of trees of ice.

11

ANNUKKA STOOD WITH ONE ARM AROUND KAARI, COMFORTINGLY, as they stared at the wilderness ahead of them. Behind them was the village where Veikko had found his mentor, the Warrior-Mage Lemminkal; it was from here that he, Ilmari, and Ilmari's brother Lemminkal had departed. The villagers all agreed that they had gone to track down something called the Icehart, which was some sort of monstrous creature that had killed everyone in three separate villages. They had learned of this Icehart from a reindeer herdsman who had returned to his village to find everyone dead, frozen—and from all appearances, it had happened in a single moment in the middle of the night. He claimed that he had seen it, at a distance, moving away from a second village, to which he had gone for help. He had called it the Icehart because it looked like an enormous, ghostly stag, and wherever it went, it killed with cold.

And that was far more information than they had gotten before. At least now they knew to watch out for ghostly reindeer.

It was Lemminkal who had linked the Icehart with the Snow Queen, and according to those who had spoken to him before the three men left, he was determined to eliminate both the monster and its mistress.

Ilmari was more circumspect and rather less confident that they could take on the Snow Queen themselves.

Annukka and Kaari had decided to climb up from the valley where the village lay to have a look at what lay ahead of them as they followed the men. From this vantage, on the side of the mountain, what was before them was daunting, a patchwork of alpine forest and glacier, mountains already deep in snow. This was where the road had lost track of Veikko, because after this village, there was no road. And there was no use in calling up the North Wind again, because even if it would answer, which was dubious, the Winds were notoriously bad at being able to give good directions to humans. "Oh, over that mountain and to the east" was usually the best they could manage.

"Now what do we do?" Kaari asked, looking bleakly at the literally trackless wilderness in front of them.

"For one thing, we switch to sledges," Annukka replied. "Which means that we will be able to carry more supplies with us. That is no bad thing."

"But how are we going to find them?" Kaari wailed. "There's no road to follow, and any tracks they made are gone by now!"

Annukka hugged her shoulders harder. "Don't despair. I have an idea." She turned Kaari about, faced her toward the village and gave her a little shove. "You go get us sledges and supplies. And find out what, if anything, has been happening here since the men left. I will see if my idea will work."

Kaari got a firmer hold on herself, and nodded. She turned back to the village as Annukka walked down the slope to their camp, ducked under the flap of their cobbled-together tent and sat down on her bed to rummage through her pack. They had set up their tent here in the shelter of one of the reindeer sheds because this was a small village and had no inn. This was probably why the only witness to the appearance of the Icehart had taken his deer herd and moved on.

Which was a great pity, because Annukka would have liked to have been able to question him herself.

As for a way to track the three men into the wilderness, she had an idea, indeed. But it was nothing that she, nor anyone she knew, had ever tried. She had gotten this notion earlier today when one of the men of Ilmari's village had offered to sell them a lodestone, demonstrating for them how it always pointed to the North Star.

"But if it always points to the North Star, why would you need it?" Kaari had asked, shaking her head in puzzlement. "You can see the North Star!"

"You can't during the day," the man had said, with some impatience.

"But then you can see the sun," Kaari had replied, with the patience she used when speaking to particularly dense little boys. "The sun will tell you where North is."

"Well then, you can't see the North Star at night when it's cloudy!" the man responded, and Annukka got the impression that if it hadn't been Kaari he'd been talking to, he would have lost his temper.

"Why would I want to travel at night when it is cloudy?" Kaari asked, looking at him as if he was mad. "For that matter, why would I want to travel at night at all if there was no road to follow? It would be of much more use if it pointed to something other than the North Star—like the village you needed to go to." She looked at the lodestone indulgently, with the air of a girl who is looking at something that she considers to be a particularly foolish "boy's toy." Annukka had seen that look before, on the faces of most of the women she knew, when men came trotting up with some wonderful "new" thing that was allegedly better than any previous iteration of such a thing. Men never understood that look, and generally went off, aggrieved, to show the prize to another man, who certainly would understand why it was better, shinier and altogether superior to anything else that anyone had that was like it.

Now truth to tell, Annukka could certainly see a great deal of use for something like the lodestone. What if they had not had the road to follow when they were making their way through dense forest? You could see neither sun nor stars under trees like that and the only way of getting one's bearings would be to climb a tree at intervals. You could wander in circles forever in such a place, and people had. People had died under such circumstances.

So she had quietly traded for the lodestone herself from the fellow after soothing his wounded pride; a couple of copper coins from the bandit's loot, a handful of charms and one of the swords they clearly did not need. He had told her then that it came from a much larger piece of metal that had fallen from the sky, and showed her how it was also attracted to iron. Interesting, that, but not terribly useful. On the other hand, she could use that to make sure it didn't go astray, by storing it with the ax.

But what if such a thing could be made that pointed to other things? People, for instance? Kaari had been right; something that pointed to another object or person would be very, very useful. Especially now, when they didn't know where to begin looking for the three missing men.

If she could just work out a way to make a lodestone that pointed to Veikko... There should be a way to do so with magic. Loathe as she was to use it, nevertheless if ever there was a time to start, it was now.

But how to get it to point? She would have to have something of his, she thought. *If only I was home when I had thought of this. I have so much of his: his baby clothing, a lock of his baby hair...* When he had left, Kaari had given him a lock of hers, but he had not done the same. She supposed that was partly caution and partly a lack of sentiment.

After a thorough rummage through both her belongings and Kaari's, she had to give that idea up. Neither of them had so much as a hair from Veikko's head, nor any token from him that would have much magical attachment to him. But although disappointed, she was not discouraged. There should be a way to do this, and she would find it.

In the meantime, that lodestone would serve to guide them so that they did not go completely astray. They did know the general direction that the men went in when they were told about the strange creature that was killing whole villages. That would be the place to start.

Meanwhile, she would *find* a way to make this new sort of lodestone point to Veikko.

When Kaari returned, though, it was with the news that she could find only one sledge. Annukka was outside the tent again, looking to repack what they had to fit on sledges and trying to reckon what else could be traded for. They still had several swords, knives and bows that were fundamentally useless to them—but this village had been the home of a Mage-Smith, which meant that the weapons were somewhat devalued here.

On the other hand, with their resident magicians gone, some people were feeling anxious about magical protections. Her charms were unexpectedly welcome, it seemed.

But the droop of Kaari's shoulders as she approached warned of trouble. "I tried, Mother Anukka," she said, as soon as she was within hearing distance, "but they would only sell me one." She looked stricken, as if she felt she was personally to blame somehow.

That was an unwelcome development, but Annukka tried to put a good face on it. She shook her head, and patted Kaari's shoulder. "Never mind," she said, kindly. "We haven't got so much that we need more than one, and we'll be able to rest one deer while the other pulls."

Kaari bit her lip. "Well, there is another complication. I am not sure you would want this sledge, Mother Annukka," she said reluctantly. "I am told it belonged to Veikko's Master, the Warrior-Mage Lemminkal..."

And that was when it struck Annukka like a blow. They might not have anything that belonged to Veikko—but Kaari had just bought the sledge that had belonged to Veikko's Master! Now that was an unexpectedly good stroke of luck! A man spent a great deal of time with his sledge, and a surprising amount of emotional contamination rubbed off onto it. When it got stuck, or was reluctant to slide properly, anger seeped into it. When it was running smoothly and men were racing against each other, pleasure, excitement and other good things seeped into it. While not quite as "personal" as other effects might be, this was still as close as she was going to get without breaking into the Warrior-Mage's house.

And that...would be ill-advised. Not only was it possible he had left unpleasant surprises for anyone who tried such a thing—assuming he hadn't warded the place the way she had warded her house—but he would probably know just what they had done when they finally met up with him, and as a consequence they might well be marked as thieves and unfriendly from the beginning.

She jumped up and hugged Kaari, hard. "Want it?" she exclaimed. "This is the best thing you could have done! What does he want for it? Buy it! Hitch a deer to it and bring it here, quickly!"

She chuckled as a bewildered Kaari hurried back to whoever it was that was selling her the sledge. It was no bargain—two swords and two daggers, and a silver coin to boot—but Kaari's charms had worked on him as well.

Lodestone be damned. She was going to enchant the whole sledge. Besides all the emotional contamination, anything that had once belonged to a magician generally was alive with the residue of magic. It should be easy for her to use that.

This sledge was going to guide them to its Master!

Aleksia had thought that the frozen villages were a horror. Somehow this ice-coated forest was worse, because it was so beautiful. It was a deadly beauty, and had killed as surely as the Icehart had killed in the three villages.

It had been a birch forest, and birches were some of the first trees to lose their leaves in the Fall, so all of the trees were leafless at the point when this had happened to them. And normally in the Winter, birch forests like this were gorgeous, with white snow on the ground, and papery white trunks with their black markings rising out of the snow, the mist of white twigs softening the starkness. Somehow, even in the dead of Winter, birch trees managed to look alive. Maybe it was because of how supple they were, how they bent gracefully to the wind. Maybe it was because beneath that paper-white bark there was a creamy glow, a hint of warm color, too subtle to really point out to anyone, but there if you had eyes for it. For the Bear, at least, that was not the whole of it. Birches had a scent of life to them, even in the worst of the Winter, a subtle perfume that promised that when Spring came, the birches would be the first to awaken.

But not now.

The trees glittered, reflecting the cold light lifelessly, the trunks smooth, perfect and encased in at least an inch of ice. Every branch, every twig, every bit of undergrowth was sheathed in ice, perfectly preserved, and perfectly dead. There was no scent of life here, only the cold breath of the ice. Birch trees did not restrict much light, and beneath the canopy there had been a lively tangle of undergrowth—bushes, vines, weeds—exuberantly flourishing in the shelter of the birch branches. And now all that was frozen as hard and dead as a stone.

Aleksia stared. This was appalling. And this was where the men's trail had led.

Carefully, the Bear picked her way through the trees, digging her claws into the ice-crusted snow with every step, and the horror deepened as she worked her way inward. Here was a bird frozen in a bush, coated with ice…a rabbit with its eyes still wide open, coated with ice…a deer encased in ice like a statue, actually caught in midbrowse, a mouthful of grass pawed out of the snow, half-chewed, the individual stems poking out of its mouth also coated in ice.

Every hair on the Bear's body stood up, and not just because of the cold; she was afraid, instinctively afraid. Chills ran down her spine, and a coldness grew in her stomach as Aleksia fought against the rising discomfort that told her to flee, and won. For long moments, she stood there, shifting from paw to paw, with the ice-covered snow cracking beneath her weight.

I have no choice. I must find out what is in here. This is no village, and there is no obvious reason for the forest to have been frozen like this. There are thousands of acres of forest just like this one—so why freeze it? She forced herself to go deeper into the forest. The Icehart—for she was sure that was what had done all of this—must have had a compelling reason to freeze an entire forest. Even for a supernatural monster or a great Mage, this kind of act took too much power for it to be random. Just as she was certain that there was something in each of the frozen villages that the Icehart had wanted to stop, so she was certain that there was something here that had threatened it.

She had a fairly good idea what that something was.

And in a small clearing in the heart of the birches, she found them.

That is, she presumed they were the men she was looking for. There were two of them, in the midst of a tidy camp; both sitting, both as still as statues. One had a gray-blond beard and carried a kantele, his hands still on the strings as if he had been caught in the midst of playing it, the other was older, and had a sword strapped to his back. Both wore the clothing of the Sammi.

They sat beside the remains of a dead fire, one on either side of it, looking sightlessly at the coals. The older of the two of them had a forked stick with a gutted, skinned rabbit on it; presumably he had been holding it over the flames. The other had a flask down by his feet. There was a hide tent behind them, and a stack of wood beside it. Both were covered in an inch of ice, just like the trees. From the look of things, they had been taken completely by surprise.

These two were Ilmari and Lemminkal, and there was no sign of Veikko. She felt sickened, and if she had been a woman, she would have cried. She had never felt as close to anyone other than her Brownies as she had to these men. And now, to see them like this—it nearly broke her heart.

The Bear prowled around the campsite, snuffling, hunting for clues. There were three packs, three bedrolls in the tent, three rabbits to be cooked—two skinned and waiting the fate of the first—three of everything, in fact, except men. The village had been bad enough. These two men, staring into the long-dead fire, were enough to send a strong man screaming away, running as fast as he could. It took everything that Aleksia had to keep from doing just that.

A line of footprints led away from the camp; Aleksia followed them to where they ended.

There was no sign of a struggle, but there was a small hand-ax lying in the snow, under a layer of ice.

Aleksia nodded to herself. So, the third man, presumably Veikko, had been here, and had been abducted. If this was the work of the false Snow Queen, this only made sense. Veikko was young, handsome, and if the false Snow Queen was following Aleksia's pattern, she would be abducting young men. Both Ilmari and Lemminkal were too old to draw her interest.

So she had Veikko—or at least that was a good enough supposition to follow for now.

All right. The help I was hoping for in the shape of those men is gone. I am going to have to find the false Snow Queen's Palace, and learn what I can from it....

She sat down on her haunches to think, scarcely noticing that there was a little frozen bird cemented onto a branch beneath a coating of ice just under her nose. The ice prevented any scent from escaping, and she only caught sight of it because it was the wrong shape to be a stone or a last brown leaf.

Poor thing. This is just wanton and indiscriminate slaughter. Why is this creature doing these things? It doesn't make any sense. Why freeze an entire forest to get one man? Why kill an entire village?

She shook her massive head after a time, deciding that she was just too sane to be able to fathom the reasons this creature had for what it was doing.

Unless, of course, the false Snow Queen was trying to terrify the common folk, and eliminate any opposition. If she had decided that it was time to become a ruler and take over the land of the Sammi—

I should concentrate on finding the Icehart and figuring out a way to stop it, and worry about the false Snow Queen's motives later. While she thought, her warm breath puffed out over the little frozen bird.

All right. I'll try the most obvious. Let's see if I can detect her magic from here, or find the Icehart itself.

Aleksia turned her thoughts inward and went very, very still. Carefully, she "listened" first—some magic created a kind of resonance or hum that a magician could hear if he was in a quiet place…and certainly this was the quietest place she had ever been in.

But there was nothing.

With a sigh, she moved to the next possibility: scent. Magic often had an aroma to it, and not only could she as a Mage herself sniff it out, but the Bear form was particularly well suited for this sort of thing. She lifted her muzzle to the cool air and took in long, deep breaths; dropped it to the ground and tried finding the scent there.

But alas, again…nothing.

Finally she unfocused her eyes a moment, and looked for the faintest traces of power, particularly Traditional power. If there was another magician near here, that power would accrue to him, like water flowing down a slope. So if the power was moving at all, it would be moving in the direction of the magician.

She saw the magical energies as soon as she unfocused her eyes, like dust-motes in sunlight. And there was definitely a current to the movements....

Unfortunately, the center for those converging currents was—herself. *Bah.*

Right then, there was only one more possibility. Mirror-magic. And for this she wanted her own mirror, so she was going to have to go back to human form and get it out of the—

Chiurp!

The loud and cheerful sound, the first thing she had heard in this forest besides herself, would have been more than enough to make her jump with surprise and shock. Add to that the fact that it came from right below her nose, and was followed by a veritable explosion of brown feathers heading into the sky—well, that was enough to make her rear up, overbalance, and fall over sideways with the crash of shattering ice as she smashed into the ice-covered underbrush.

She lurched to her feet again; the bird was already gone. But there was no mistake about it—it had been that tiny frozen sparrow in the snow just below her nose.

She had thawed it by breathing on it. And it was still alive. If the bird was still alive—then this was an entirely different sort of spell than the one that had killed the villagers. Ilmari and Lemminkal were *not* dead! She could free them!

Heedless now, she reared up on her hindquarters and pivoted, crashing back to the campsite where she had left the two men. She skidded to a clumsy halt beside them, then closed her eyes and listened to them.

And to her shock, she heard what she had missed before.

Heartbeats. Very, very slow, but heartbeats all the same.

They were still alive! This wasn't merely ice, this was magical ice, magical cold, that preserved the victims rather than killing them.

She sat down on her haunches again, this time with a thud, and stared at the ice-bound figures.

They were alive.

So—now what should she do?

12

COULD ALEKSIA THAW THE MEN? THAT WAS THE MAIN question. She might not be able to do it alone. For that matter, she wasn't entirely sure how she had done it in the first place.

All right, she told herself. *Be calm. Think about this. They are safe enough as they are; this is clearly a special sort of spell that won't harm them for now. If you thaw them, they might attack you. They will certainly want to know where Veikko is, and you cannot answer that. Nor can you prove that you are not the one that did this to them. The answer, I think, is to leave them be for the moment.*

By way of experiment, however, she tried thawing other creatures, with mixed success. Sparrows and other small birds took some time, but she could release them simply by breathing on them. Slightly larger birds took more time. Rabbits, however, required that she curl up around them and breathe on them. This suggested that she was going to need to use magic to thaw the men, and if she did that—well, certainly, if she was wary and watching, the false Snow Queen would know what she was about and put a stop to it.

Caution was definitely the order of the day.

So was getting out of the birch forest.

Now that she knew the animals were still alive under their coats of ice, she felt terribly squeamish about eating them. It made no sense, of course, but...well, that was just how it was. And she was getting hungry again. Time for another transformation, and then to hunt for a place where she could safely become human.

The transition to bird—a Gyrfalcon this time—was much smoother and quicker, now that she had spent some time as the Swan. She wriggled back into the harness so that her little pack was safely on her back, and then forgot about it. Vision was so much keener than a human's it was almost painful. It was easier to get into the air as a Gyrfalcon, too; the body was smaller and a lot lighter than the Swan, and the wings were proportionally longer.

Of all the forms she knew how to take, the Falcon was one of her favorites; light, swift, incredibly maneuverable; the sheer flying ability had something to do with that. But there was one thing that appealed to her that she really rather would not have had anyone else know about...

A bird of prey was almost all hunting instinct. It had no conscience, no pity, and when hunting, was interested only in what it could catch and how fast it could catch and eat it. There was a certain freedom in such simplemindedness. And in order to hunt quickly and efficiently, she had to surrender to that simplemindedness.

After pumping her way up into the sky, Aleksia gave free rein to the bird. Immediately it began looking for prey, scanning the earth below for tiny hints of movement, for things that were not white, knowing instantly, long before the human mind would have puzzled it out, *rock, shadow, tree stump. Duck!*

Below her, an unwary duck was swimming as best it could in the small remaining bit of unfrozen pond. It had stayed too long. Now it would never leave.

The Falcon did a wingover, what in a human would have been something like a cartwheel; she folded her wings tight to her body, the protective membranes closing over her eyes, and plunged down toward the unwary duck, using the sun to mask her approach. Too late, the duck spotted her. It flapped hard, running across the water, and then across the ice, trying to gain height, or failing that, to gain the safety of cover.

Aleksia's heart sang with elation and bloodlust. The Bird was supreme and was doing what she did best. She was hunting. And she was about to kill.

Talons fisted, she plunged down toward the duck; she could see it laboring, see its chest heaving, see the desperate look in its eye as it glanced up and saw her too near, too near. Falcon instinct judged speed and height off the ground and made a split-second decision. Strike or bind?

Bind.

Her feet swung forward, talons extended, as she hit the duck where the neck met the back.

They tumbled out of the air together, the duck flapping desperately, flailing at her with its wings, as Aleksia beat her own wings hard to slow their descent. She was the bird of the foot, as the falconers said, and her feet were her weapons. A talon found the heart and pierced it. The duck shuddered, made one final spasm, and was still. They landed in the snow, duck beneath her, cushioning the last of her fall.

She did not hesitate. Half-mad with bloodlust now, she began ripping the feathers from her prize. In a moment, her beak would plunge into the bird's sweet breast meat, she would drink blood that was still hot and full of the taste of fear and desperation, and then she would settle down to feed.

When the Falcon was sated, Aleksia transformed back to the Bear and made short work of what was left of the duck. When even the last bit of bloodstained snow was licked up, she looked around, as best she could, and took long, deep sniffs of air.

And she scented what she had hoped to detect. Damp, chill—but not the chill and damp of snow and ice. This was cave-damp. A good place for her to become a human, and a good place for the Bear to sleep. She wished the last village was nearer, but it was not, and this was the best possible option for protection, from the elements, from wild creatures, and from the false Snow Queen and whatever she was using as her spies.

The Bear lumbered off, following its nose.

By a little past nightfall, it had found the cave. There was plenty of deadfall nearby and the Bear dragged in several large pieces, much larger than Aleksia could have handled. This was a good cave; it went back far enough that the bitter cold of Winter was held at bay, and the ceiling was high enough that smoke would pool up at the top. She could build her fire at the center of it.

The floor was littered with dead leaves, the bones of small animals and rocks. The musky scent told the Bear that a fox had used it for a den, and recently. Well, if it came back it was going to get a surprise; it wouldn't like the Bear or a human, but Annukka was inclined to leave it alone if it chose to just try and shelter here peacefully. As the Bear, she broke up the wood into fire-sized pieces; a simple enough trick for something of her weight and strength. The leaves and twigs that had blown in here would would supply plenty of tinder; there would be a good fire going here in no time.

But right now, she needed to be a human again in order to do that.

This form was, of course, the easiest of all, so long as she and not animal instinct, was in charge of her body. A moment of concentration, and there she was, gown and all—and she was quickly chilled and shivering without the Bear's thick coat. Hurriedly, she built herself a fire, and used the fire-starter rather than magic to get it ablaze.

Finally the fire was going well enough that she started to thaw; she held her hands to the dancing flames and basked in the warmth.

It occurred to her rather ruefully that she could have made a better clothing selection for this excursion before she had left. Breeches and boots, a warm knitted sweater and a tunic all under a heavy cloak would have been just as easy to transform to feathers as her gown.

But she was unused to wearing such things, and it might have been tricky to transform them back again.

Oh, bah. She fumbled out the hand-mirror. The first thing to do would be to see if there was anyone who had already magically caught "sight" of her presence and was spying on her.

None can hide who clear can see. I spy you as you spy me, she murmured in her mind, passing her hand over the surface of the glass. It clouded over a moment, and then cleared and showed—nothing. Nothing but her own reflection. She breathed a sigh of relief. So. She had gotten this far without being detected.

She passed her hand over the mirror again, and let a tiny trickle of magic tell the mirror-servant Jalmari back at the Palace of Ever-Winter that she was ready to talk. She would speak through him now, and let him—or whoever Elena found to replace her—be the ones using all the magic.

It was dangerous enough using the transformation magic. Anything more than that was adding another layer of hazard. She could not, dared not, do that. Not now. Not yet.

The face of her servant appeared briefly. "All is well, Godmother. What is it that you need?"

"I think I may be close enough for this mirror to see where the false Godmother is, if she is being incautious about her own magic use," Aleksia told him. "Do you think—"

Jalmari laughed. "To borrow a phrase from the Djinn, 'your wish is my command, Godmother.' If you will be patient a moment, I will see if there is anything *to* be seen."

The mirror clouded for a moment; she knew what he was doing, he was looking for currents of various sorts of magic, then seeing if they came from a single source. If there was one creature as good at mirror-magic as she was, it was her servant. And long before she might have gotten impatient, his face reappeared.

"This is truly remarkable!" Jalmari said without preamble. "If I had not seen this with my own—ah—well, since I don't precisely have eyes—"

"What did you see?" she asked, anxiously.

"Look for yourself, Godmother—" The mirror clouded again, and showed—

The Palace of Ever-Winter.

She frowned. "Is this a joke?" she asked. "If so, I find it rather—"

The view in the mirror receded, to reveal that at the end of the grounds, where the snow-garden ceased, there was a wall. A wall of huge bricks carved of ice, with a gate in it made not of iron or wood or even more ice, but of a shimmering curtain of power. And on the other side of that wall, was a village where the glacier should have been.

"That, Godmother," said the mirror-servant gravely, "is where your rival is."

It had taken the better part of a day, as well as most of her energy, for Annukka to put the spell on the sledge, but it had been worth every moment and every bit of strength to do so. When she and Kaari left the village, she attached a third and fourth very thin rein to each front corner of the sledge and attached those to the reindeer's halter. When the sledge was going the right way, both reins were slack. The farther off course the sledge got, the more it tried to turn, and the more it tugged on the deer's halter, steering it. All she and Kaari had to do was to ride next to the sledge and make sure that the reindeer didn't stop to browse. Usually a smart tap with a long willow-switch took care of that.

And now that they had guidance, Kaari was less anxious. Annukka, however, was seriously concerned. She had taken the loving-cup from Kaari and would not let her look at it anymore, having caught her taking it out and staring at it a dozen times a day. But there was no improvement in the situation there; the main body of the cup was just as black as ever, and there was still only a rim of bright silver remaining. Annukka only wished she could tell for certain whether or not there was any diminishing of the remaining silver.

But the going was slow, even with guidance. Travel on the road, even when it was scarcely more than a footpath, had been much easier. Annukka had never cared much for driving sledges, which was why she had put so much effort into breeding and training deer to ride. There were always hidden obstacles under the snow that the heavy sledge would get stuck on, or that would threaten to turn it over.

In fact, it seemed to her that by the time the sun was setting, they had made discouragingly little progress. From Kaari's long face as they set up camp, she felt the same.

"We haven't even reached the first stricken village yet," Kaari said quietly, as both of them stared into their little fire. "At this rate, it will be Spring before we get there."

Perhaps the sledge hadn't been as good an idea as she had thought, but what else were they to do? Whatever they were going to need had to be brought with them. The villages they were going to look at were all tiny in comparison to their home, and there was no way of knowing how much, if any, provisions were intact in the houses after animals got in. Which they would, it was inevitable. In general, this far to the North, so both of them learned, a village could be no more than four or five houses, and earned the name only because most of the people living there were not related to one another. Even if they actually encountered a village with people in it, though they were hospitable, most people in a village that small could not spare much for the traveler.

Ilmari's village had not been much larger than that, and with the early onset of Winter, they were looking at their stores with a worried eye. Coin did you little good if there was no food to buy with it. The deer could not carry all the supplies that they would need; the sledge could.

And there was the undisputed fact that the sledge was guiding them to the missing men. So the sledge was necessary, but it was slowing them down—and it might well be that time was running out for Veikko.

Help. Well, that was what they needed, wasn't it? With a sigh, Annukka got out her kantele.

She didn't want to worry Kaari more than she already was, so she opted for subtle magic rather than obvious. She didn't so much pick a tune as just let her fingers play something familiar. And rather than thinking the words to concentrate a spell, she simply held in the front of her mind the fact that they needed help. And all the while, to Kaari, she made it look as if she was strumming idly at the instrument. Kaari was busy mending the heavier clothing she had gotten at the village, and reinforcing seams; the wind was finding every single place it could leak in to chill them. Up until now, they had been sharing Annukka's clothing, but it was getting cold enough they would soon have to layer on every stitch they could. And even Annukka's spells of warmth woven into the cloaks wouldn't be enough to keep them comfortable.

Something coughed outside the circle of firelight.

Both of them froze. Was that just some animal? Annukka knew she hadn't heard anything creeping up on them. She peered into the darkness, but could make out nothing there.

It coughed again, whatever it was. And then what Annukka had thought was a huge snowdrift just at the very edge of visibility—moved. She felt as if someone had just dumped a barrel of icy water down her back. She wanted to scream, but nothing would come out. Kaari squeaked, and then was still.

Slowly, ponderously, the giant white Bear moved into the firelight, its head swinging a little from side to side as it walked.

Annukka's throat and mouth dried and her heart pounded so hard she thought it was going to break her ribs. She stared at the enormous creature, at the tiny black eyes, the wicked long claws on its forepaws. This Bear could disembowel a person with a single swat of that enormous paw and not even think twice about it. The White Bears of the North were known to be deadly and unpredictable, except in one thing. They never let anything get between them and food. And two lone humans—surprised—without weapons, probably looked a lot like food to it.

They were going to die....

"Mother Annukka?" Kaari said in a small, strangled voice. "It's wearing a pack."

The Bear nodded, and Annukka realized that what she had taken for shadow was the harness of the pack on his back.

Who put a pack on a Bear's back?

"You don't think there is anyone with it—him—do you?" Annukka whispered.

The Bear swung his head toward her, and slowly shook it.

She blinked. "You understand me?" she asked, in a slightly louder voice.

It nodded. She paused, and thought about what she had just done. Was it possible that her song-spell had had an effect so soon?

"Are—you here to help us?" she asked the Bear incredulously.

The Bear nodded. Then, with a sigh, it flopped down next to the fire and closed its eyes.

Annukka and Kaari stared at each other across the great bulk of the Bear, both their eyes wide with astonishment.

"How are we going to feed him?" Kaari whispered.

Annukka had to shrug. "I don't know," she replied, and shook her head "He's one of the White Bears. I suppose he can feed himself."

But all she could think of at this point was the cautionary that she should have kept in mind when she began the spell in the first place. *Be careful what you wish for. You might get it.*

Aleksia huddled close to the fire and cupped her hand-mirror close to her face. In the depths of the mirror, a disembodied blue head with a curiously cheerful expression hovered in what appeared to otherwise be a void. For all that she was an expert in mirror-magic, even she had no idea where the mirror-servants and mirror-slaves were, how they could look through so many mirrors simultaneously, where that void was, or if it was even a void to them. She also had no idea if the disembodied heads had bodies, or if their appearance was some sort of joke.

She had inherited Jalmari, along with the Great Mirror and the rest of the Palace. Veroushka had made much more use of the mirror-servant than Aleksia had, but rather than allow him to think she didn't need him, when she had nothing specific for him to do, she had given him the rather open-ended task of "keeping an eye on matters in Kingdoms with no Godmother and report back on trouble to Godmother Elena." Elena had never complained, so it seemed to suit everyone.

Now, whether he had always been self-reliant and able to act autonomously, or whether this had given him those abilities or strengthened the ones he already had, she had noted that increasingly he had been able to do mirror-magic all on his own. So now she was able to rely on him to do what she did not dare. The magical signature, if any, would be coming from the Palace of Ever-Winter, not from a cave in the frozen Northlands.

"So far as I can tell," Jalmari said, "this imposter does not use mirror-magic, and I do not believe she is aware that you do." He winked at her. He seemed terribly pleased with himself for his detection work.

Aleksia stared at him in disbelief. "How can she be a copy of me and not know mirror-magic?"

Jalmari pursed his lips. "Perhaps because she is not a copy of you. I have done a bit of spying on her, and other than the Palace, there is not much resemblance. She does have power over ice and snow, to a greater extent than you do, actually. Perhaps she got a name for being the Snow Queen and grew to like it while being unaware that there was another using that same title. Take that as a given, it is inevitable that when she came to build her Palace, The Tradition forced the design of *your* Palace into her mind."

Well, not knowing mirror-magic meant that Aleksia could be as bold as she pleased about ferreting out information. "That makes sense. What kind of a Sorceress is she? Is she cautious, or reckless? Do you know how easily she can tell when there is other magic about?"

"I do not think she is careless…but I think she has grown accustomed to never encountering any sort of opposition," he told her. "I know that I could slip in and around her Palace despite its barriers— for they are barriers to physical things and to attack, not to someone merely looking about."

"Then I should like to see what I can, if you will." Trying not to crow with glee, she asked Jalmari to find her a vantage point within the Palace itself.

The mirror clouded, then cleared, showing a room. The view shocked her. First, the interior of this place was…unfinished, as if it had been tunneled out of ice and snow, as if the exterior of the Palace had been created perfectly, but the inside left solid and the rooms cut in anyhow. And there was nothing warm or welcoming about this place; it looked better suited to hanging meat for storage than living in.

Then there were the servants. She had not expected to see Brownies running about, but she *had* expected to see human servants. Instead…

"What are those things?" she asked in a whisper. Jalmari's voice floated out of the mirror in much more normal tones. She stared. They looked like snowmen…well, snowmen made by a reasonable amateur artist. There was a human look about them, but like the walls, they also looked unfinished. No fingers, only shovel-like bits at the ends of their arms, with thumbs. Faces left mostly blank except for sketched-in features.

"Animated statues," the mirror-servant replied. "They are made of snow and ice." Aleksia watched the crude things wandering about with a sense of astonishment at how much magical energy it must take to keep them all going.

"Why use those instead of human servants?" she wondered aloud.

"Ah, that I have an answer for," Jalmari replied. "She hates people. Truly hates them. She won't have them near if she can help it. Those villages? She cleared them out because she decided that since she couldn't control them, she wanted them destroyed. At least, that is what things I have heard have led me to believe."

"But what about—" Aleksia began.

"I'll show you," Jalmari said, interrupting her. She nodded, and the view changed. This time the viewpoint was from somewhere near the top of the walls, looking down.

And there she was. The false Snow Queen. Sitting on a throne that looked to be carved from the same crystal as her own, this woman did not, however, look much like Aleksia. She had pale hair, rather washed out, done up in a very tight and severe style. Her gown was equally severe, and her eyes were a pale blue that was almost white. The throne looked nothing like Aleksia's, either; this one was extremely angular, more like slabs of ice stacked atop one another. The throne room looked like the interior of a glacier: rough walls, slick floor and no place to sit. Not that she needed any place to sit, since there was only one other person here, and that one was seated at her feet. Aleksia shuddered in sympathy; it looked as if he was sitting on ice.

He would have been exceedingly handsome, if his face had held any expression at all. Blond, like most Sammi, with brilliant blue eyes, chiseled features and a warrior's physique, he should have filled the room with vibrant warmth.

But instead, he looked no more animated than one of the snow-statue servants.

And she knew him. *Veikko*.

And being what she was, Aleksia knew exactly what had happened to him. While the legends about *her* often claimed that she put some sort of enchanted shards of ice in the hearts and souls of her victims to make them emotionless, it was quite clear to Aleksia that this was precisely what the false Snow Queen was doing in truth. It wouldn't be all that difficult for a reasonably adept Mage. And The Tradition would make it easy for her; that sort of thing was in stories all the time.

She was absently petting his hair as she sat there, her face very still, her brows knitted in thought. It seemed she must be planning something. Perhaps the retrieval of Ilmari and Lemminkal.

Aleksia shook her head. "This is bad," she said out loud.

"Without a doubt," Jalmari agreed. "My assessment is that the spell she put on this young man is literally killing him a bit at a time. Possibly the only thing that is saving him so far is that he is a Mage as well, and has some resistance to the magic."

Aleksia shivered, then considered her options. She needed to know about this Sorceress, everything she possibly could. And she didn't think it likely that the woman was going to simply babble what Aleksia needed to know. That sort of thing happened only in badly written stories.

That only left one option. Looking into the past.

"Jalmari," she said aloud, "I want to—"

"You want to mirror-scry into the past and find out what happened," Jalmari said smoothly. "Which means you want *me* to do it while you observe. Actually I agree with you entirely, Godmother. We need to find out what made her what she is, if we are going to find the key to taking her down again. If ever there was a situation with 'went to the bad' rather than 'born bad' written all over it, it is this one."

"What was your clue?" Aleksia asked, eager to hear more of what the mirror-servant had to say.

"The boy. If she was born bad, he would have been sucked dry by now." Jalmari's head bobbed, semitransparent, in front of the scene in the mirror. "That she keeps him alive tells me that she is trying to get some sort of comfort out of him, and if she needs comfort, something terrible happened to change her."

Aleksia sighed. "I also thought the rather unfinished state of her servants also indicated she didn't feel comfortable with cold and perfect simulacra of humanity. And that, too, tells me she wasn't born bad."

"Well, Godmother, you transform to the Bear, why don't you?" Jalmari suggested. "You look cold, and the Bear form will be more comfortable. You don't need to be human to stare into the mirror."

She felt rather foolish for not thinking of that. "Good notion, Jalmari," she said, and allowed herself, gratefully, to fall back into the warm furred form that did *not* find the pebble-strewn sand of the cave floor uncomfortable. She flopped herself down with the mirror between her paws and waited.

Brief scenes began to blink across the face of the mirror as Jalmari flicked through moments of the past that had been caught in reflective surfaces. Back they went. And back. And back. Until Aleksia finally realized that this false Snow Queen was a great deal older than she looked.

Much, much older, it seemed.

"Ha!" said Jalmari suddenly, and a scene formed and steadied. "This looks promising."

The scene steadied, and settled on a small stone tower situated near a village; the village was reasonably sized, and looked vaguely Sammi. A man and a woman were walking in the gardens around it—these were practical gardens, full of herbs rather than flowers. Aleksia identified them without hesitation as the gardens of a Witch or a Sorceress. He was perhaps in his midthirties, and dressed for travel, in sturdy boots, brown leather trews and a high necked tunic of sober dark brown wool. She was somewhat younger, and dressed rather carelessly, in a yellow skirt and a green and black tunic, as if she did not particularly care what garments she threw on so long as they kept her covered and warm. Her pale yellow hair showed the same disregard for her own appearance; it was bundled rather untidily into a net. Since Aleksia herself had, from time to time, looked exactly like that, she was in sympathy with the woman. There were times when she was so preoccupied that she just pulled on whatever was lying about. Sometimes there were things that were so important to take care of that even eating and drinking became somewhat secondary. It was a good thing she had the Brownies to keep track of her at times like that; they generally marched her back to her suite and dealt with the situation.

Even in this reflection of the past, Aleksia could see the woman's potential magic; from this little glimpse, it was not possible to say if The Tradition was putting pressure on her, but there was still plenty of magical energy ambient around her. She was definitely born a Sorceress; Aleksia was absolutely certain of that.

She and the man were too far away to hear their voices—past-scrying was limited by the physical limitations of whatever reflective surface was being used, so if the reflective object was too far for anyone to have heard voices where it was, well then you didn't hear speech. It was obvious, however, from the pack on his back and the belt full of pouches and implements, that he was going on a journey; she didn't want him to leave. But from the look of things, she was not pleading with him to stay, she was desperately asking that he hurry back. She wasn't weeping, but she wasn't far from it. She looked up into his face, searching it for something. Reassurance, perhaps.

He was a very comely man, with ageless, smooth features and bright blue eyes. Aleksia thought shrewdly that the woman was correct to be worried about losing him. She was no beauty, but he was a handsome devil.

He, in his turn, tilted her face up to his, kissed her, and sent her back into her tower, laughing. Then he strode off toward the village and the scene faded.

"Hmm," Aleksia said, thinking. "Well…as you said, this looks promising."

"Love and betrayal always are," Jalmari said cheerfully, and the scenes began again, flickering across the surface of the mirror. Then they steadied.

This time, the woman was certainly near enough to hear every word—not that this would be difficult, since she was in a towering rage, pacing back and forth across the room. She was cursing and not under her breath, either. Her hair had escaped from the net and billowed out around her shoulders like clouds boiling up before a storm. The vantage point must have been from a mirror on a wall. There was a window just within the field of vision; it was snowing heavily outside and nothing more could be seen. So the man was not back yet, and he had left in the Summer.

Someone dressed in a heavy cloak entered, shaking off snow. The woman whirled to face her. "Anything?" she demanded. The woman, who beneath the cloak was dressed as a servant, shook her head. The Sorceress's eyes blazed. "Not a word!" she raged. "Not a word, not a line, nothing! Faithless, worthless—" She broke down, hands clenched at her sides, sobbing aloud as tears poured along her red, streaked cheeks, painful, harsh sobs escaping that sounded as if each one physically hurt her.

It was a dreadful scene, and even though Aleksia knew it was in the

far, far past, it was still uncomfortable to watch. She wanted to find a
way to comfort the poor thing, even though, at the same time, she knew
that if she had actually been there, she would have been too clumsy and
awkward to actually manage to do that. This was not the sort of thing
that she was good at. Being cold and aloof, scathing and sarcastic—those
she was good at. Not at being comforting.

The scene shifted again, as Jalmari went hunting for more relevant
images. "Hmm. This seems typical," he said at last, as the mirror
steadied. It was a view of the same tower from the outside, somewhere
at a distance, but—what a difference! The gardens were dead, there was
a new wall about the place and the village looked deserted.

Ah, but it wasn't, not quite. There were some furtive movement in
the streets there—so there were still people in the village, but they did
not want to draw attention to themselves.

The point of view suddenly changed. To one of…the sky? And a
wooden wall of some sort. For a moment, Aleksia was puzzled, until
she realized that what she was seeing were the sides of a bucket from
the inside, and that Jalmari had moved the viewpoint here, not so that
they could see, but so that they could hear.

"Can she see us?" came a furtive whisper. Female.

A pause. "I don't think so. And I don't see any of her spies." A note
of desperation crept into the voice. "Aili, I have to see you more often!"

"No!" came the equally desperate reply. "You know what she will do
to us if she even guesses you think about me! Look what she did to all
the others! If she didn't outright murder them, she did horrible things
to them that made them hate each other! I couldn't bear it if she did
that to us!"

"Then come away with me!" the boy said. "You know she is only going
to get worse! She's forsworn love, and wants to destroy it—"

"And that is why we can't be together!" The girl sobbed.

"Yes, we can! She can't be everywhere! She might be a Sorceress, but she's not the only Sorceress in the world!" He dropped his voice again. "And look what she's been doing to her servants, Aili. They aren't even human anymore! They not only don't love, they don't even *feel!* That is what she will do to you, do to me, if she gets a chance. Do you want to end up like that?"

"I believe that will be enough there," Jalmari said smoothly. The image dissolved into Jalmari's face. "Now, just a little more forward in time...let us see what she has built for herself."

Now the scene was much more familiar—although the copy of the real Palace of Ever-Winter was not in place. The rest of it, however, was just as Aleksia had seen it in her first view of it. The ice wall. The magical barrier. The dark village outside the walls. And above all, the snow, the ice, the bleak impression that Winter had always been there and always would be there, camped at the gates of the tower like a guardian dog. Only the Sorceress's dwelling was different; it was still the stone keep. But around it, doing some sort of work, were the animated snow statues....

The scene again dissolved, darkened and became the void, with the mirror-servant in his usual spot. Jalmari bobbed thoughtfully in place while both of them considered what they had seen. "Well I am glad you urged me to that, Godmother. That answers a great many mysteries."

She nodded. "Now we know just where the false Snow Queen came from, and why she is doing what she does. She was betrayed, forswore love—" She grimaced. "You know, in a tale, that might seem a justifiable reason for going to the bad, but I have known any number of kindly folk who have done just that, and then dedicated themselves to God or good works instead. But she—"

"She declared war on love," Jalmari said, frowning. "With the results that we both saw. I suspect that the sheer misery she generates may be giving her a great deal of her power. The more misery, the more power. Whether she knows that or not, well, that would be the question, wouldn't it?"

Aleksia nosed the mirror, and shifted the Bear's weight. "That would be typical—although most of the dark magicians get their power through death rather than mere misery."

"But that would account for why she has been increasing her territory very slowly," Jalmari replied. Aleksia nodded.

"Can you show me something else?" she asked. "I would like to see why she took Veikko—and whether she has taken other young men in the past."

"Easily, Godmother," the being said, and the little hand-mirror misted over again.

Well, the second question was definitely answered right away...and it made her a little sick to watch it.

It was always the same. The Sorceress went through any number of young men; they tended not to last very long. It was always the same, she accosted a young man in some way, then bound him to her with a ritual spell. Once he was hers, he was as mindless as one of those snow statues, and she could do with him whatever she pleased. They became white-faced and expressionless, and day by day they faded a little until at last, they simply—stopped. The snow-servants would drag the bodies out and take them somewhere; Jalmari did not bother to find out where. And another question was answered, one that Aleksia had not actually asked out loud.

For Jalmari showed her the taking of Veikko.

The question was: what was the spell she used to make certain of these young men? Everything pointed to a peculiar enchantment that only those magicians whose power was linked to ice and snow ever used. It was very effective, but far, far rarer than all of the tales that were told about such things ever indicated. It was difficult. Only the most skilled and powerful of magicians ever mastered it.

So they watched carefully as she surprised Veikko at his wood-gathering, as she bound him in place so he could not move. And then as she did, indeed, in a rather horrifying ritual, stab an enchanted sliver of ice into his heart.

Now that she could see it happen, she could analyze the magic. And it didn't merely look horrifying, it *was* horrifying. It ate at people, devouring them slowly from within. That was why the young men she took for herself didn't last very long.

But the oddest thing was, Aleksia was also certain that the false Snow Queen didn't know this. As Jalmari replayed what he could to confirm this, they realized something else. She also never saw them die. She had no idea that at some point, each of them would wander out into the snow at night and just walk northwards until they stopped. All she knew was that they disappeared, which was an inconvenience to her, but nothing more. This was unexpected.

"Is there a mirror in her room of magic-working?" she asked, finally.

"There should be," the mirror-servant said. "Why?"

"Go as far back as you can—you don't need to show it to me, but tell me if she ever had a mentor or if she has done all of her learning out of books."

While Jalmari searched, the Bear dozed with the mirror between her forepaws, and her back to the fire. The Bear form was good for that; dropping into a half-sleep that was as refreshing as a human's full sleep. A cough from between her paws made her open her eyes again.

"She inherited the tower and its contents from her grandfather," Jalmari said flatly. "She never had a mentor."

"Then that explains a great deal."

The mirror-spirit nodded. "She looks up what she wishes to do in a book, she masters the spell and she looks no further than that. She would not be able to do this if she was not as powerful as she is—and that is the problem. She does not know to research what she wishes to do further. She thinks it is like a cooking book—you look up the dish that you want and you make it, and there are no other considerations other than eating it."

Aleksia nodded. "Like the young apprentice who tried to create a servant to do his chores for him but did not look further to discover that it would continue to work until it wore out. She has set in motion things of which she has no idea. And now we must be the ones to set them to rest."

The mirror-servant sighed. "Better in your hands than mine, God-mother," he said. "Is there anything more?"

"Not now," she replied, and the mirror went blank.

She pondered the situation that faced her for a long time, occasionally getting up to grasp another few pieces of wood in her teeth and drop them on the fire. She was faced with a Sorceress powerful enough to have learned her magic solely out of books. She must not have had much of a childhood and adolescence. And perhaps she had been one of those souls who, solitary by nature, preferred being left alone. But one day, long after most women had had their first love and either gotten over him or married him, she encountered a man that captured her. And she must have given him all the passion she had pent up for—perhaps—years.

Now Aleksia had no idea why the man had not returned. But this Sorceress had been convinced that he had abandoned her, and passionate love turned to passionate anger. At that point, she had forsworn love, went out of her way to destroy lovers and had placed a barrier around her stronghold. Nothing could pass that barrier, and probably she was the only one that could open it.

In keeping with the state of her emotions, she had locked her land in eternal Winter. Then—

Well, all Aleksia could think was that she had become incredibly lonely. Why else would she have started to kidnap young men? But she couldn't chance them abandoning her like her love had, nor did she want them to love her. She wanted them as objects, and that was when she had looked up and found the ice-shard spell. And she went no further than to find how to control them, not what the shard would do to them.

Veikko, however, might last a bit longer due to being a Warrior and a Mage.

Aleksia brooded over what she had seen in the mirror. The Imposter, it seemed, used to hate living things; but now she had lived so long that she had even worn out hatred. She seemed weary, more than anything. But the one thing that seemed to keep her going is the will to make others suffer as she did, when her false-true-love abandoned her.

What an utterly miserable life.

13

ALEKSIA DROPPED THE LAST OF THE WOOD ON THE FIRE
and dozed off in Bear form. By the standards of the Bear, the cave was pleas-
antly warm at this point. By spending a few moments shoving rocks into
a ring around the fire, she was fairly certain that the cave would remain
that way as long as she was asleep. There was something to be said for being
in this form, besides the obvious. The Bear did not have nightmares. In fact,
she rarely remembered the Bear's dreams at all, and mostly they seemed
to feature food. This night was no exception; she dreamed of feasting on
honey, berries and fat, rich salmon. By the time she woke, the fire was down
to coals and she had a better idea of what she was going to do.

It was time to get help. She had been fairly sure she was going to need
it when she started this—it had all the earmarks of the start of a quest,
and The Tradition had very firm paths for quests. Even if you began one
alone, even if you would say to your friends, over and over, "You can't
come with me," at least one and probably more would find a way to
follow you or otherwise get involved. She already had the Godmothers looking out for her at a distance, which *might* satisfy the need for
questing partners, except that there were people out here already on

the same quest. So she might as well give in to it and round them all up. At least that way they wouldn't be stumbling over each other and interfering with each other's plans.

Now, knowing that the Sorceress in question did not know mirror-magic, made things a little more straightforward. At least Aleksia knew that she and her allies would not be spied on by means of reflective surfaces, so that meant they need only beware of the usual sorts of spying, and perhaps not so many of those. Most of the other ways she knew to spy magically were through agents, either animals or human, and she had seen no evidence of either. The Sorceress's abilities seemed oddly patchy.

Still, Aleksia was going to be vigilant. She would, either herself or through one of the others, keep one eye out for birds that never seemed to leave their trail, animals acting oddly and humans in general. Given the situation, any human out here had to be viewed with suspicion.

But, yes, it was time to gather up the bits and pieces of this incipient quest-party and put together a united front.

So, the first thing to do was to see where the two Sammi women were. After some hunting in the litter of the cave floor, she found where she had nudged the mirror aside in her sleep and invoked just a tiny trickle of magic to tell her where they were. Since they couldn't be far from where she was now, it wouldn't take that much magic.

The source of reflection was—as might be expected—more ice, this time the frozen surface of a stream, which made a good road. Mentally she applauded their resourcefulness, since she was fairly certain that neither of them had ever spent this much time in the wilderness before. They appeared to be handling themselves well. But the women were not alone. In fact, they were accompanied by Urho the Great Bear, who was hitched to their sledge and pulling it along at a good rate.

Well, that was a surprise. A pleasant one, but a surprise. She had not expected him to seek them out, even though he had known they were out there. Nor would she have asked him to; he was doing her a great enough favor by bringing supplies to her. *I see you are working for your keep,* she sent into his mind.

Huh. I am feeding them, I will have you know! Urho replied with much amusement. Aleksia watched for any reaction from the Sammi but neither woman gave any indication that they "heard" this silent conversation. Good. At the moment she had rather they did not know that Urho could "talk." *Can you see where we are?* he asked.

With care, and one eye out for trouble, Aleksia moved her focus out and out, finally finding a bit of ice at the top of a tree, until she had a good idea where the trio was. Swiftly she moved back to another viewpoint of a bit of brass on Urho's harness. *I found the older men, but not the younger one. The older men are both spellbound, and although I think I know how to free them, I would rather have some help along before I try. If you keep going straight on your current course, I can intercept you before you reach them.*

Then I will do that, Urho replied. *Now you must be silent. Too much talk, too much magic, is dangerous. Be careful, Godmother.* That warning came just as Aleksia detected a faint stirring that indicated something might have noticed her use of magic. Quickly, she severed the connection between them and went very quiet, magically speaking. She put her head down and thought Bearish thoughts; mostly about the dream she'd had that night, concentrating on how good the dream-food had been, licking the sticky honey from her paws, feeling the sweet juice slipping down her throat.

The uneasy feeling passed. She waited for some time longer, just to be sure. Now was not the time to ruin everything by being impatient. Instead, she used the time to think, to analyze everything she knew about Traditional tales, to try to passively sense what was going on in the currents of Traditional power.

The first thing that came to mind was this: there was no Traditional path for what was happening now. No one had ever impersonated a God-mother before. There *were* tales of beautiful, cold, seductive Sorceresses, of course. The Tradition was probably reinforcing everything about this woman that followed that path. But as for the rest…Aleksia herself was only following bits and pieces. Godmothers did not openly lead the op-position. Godmothers always worked behind the scenes. It was up to the Heroes and Heroines, the Knights, the Champions, the Wise Fools and the Brave Goosegirls and the like to be the ones to bring the Villains down.

Yet, that was exactly what could not happen here. There was no time to bring a Champion this far North, and even if one could be brought, it would *not* be someone perfectly suited to the job and the enemy. And Aleksia knew very well what The Tradition did to "any old" would-be Hero or Champion that turned up under circumstances like those.

The Tradition destroyed them. Or, more to the point, The Tradition strengthened the Villain so that he or she could do the destruction.

No, the one thing that Aleksia *could* see was that the perfect Hero to oppose this Villain was—herself. The trick would be to get The Tra-dition to steer that course as well.

Meanwhile, Traditional magic was eddying around the situation in a state of partial chaos, "looking" for patterns it "recognized," and not finding them.

All the more reason to put together a Questing Party. The Tradition recognized that. The more she could get The Tradition to recognize, the better off they all would be.

Finally, it felt like enough time had passed since that tentative probe to be safe. She stood up on her hind legs, and willed herself back into human form just long enough to put the mirror away and loosely buckle on her pack. Then she transformed back to the Swan for the sake of speed and endurance and waddled out into the snow again, leaving behind the last embers of the fire to warm the cave for whatever else might seek its shelter.

The air was as clear as crystal, the sun shining down out of a sky marked only by the thinnest wisps of cloud. The cold air struck her like a blow. Whatever else was afoot, the false Snow Queen was indeed extending her reach. By the sun, Winter had only just begun, but by the weather it was as cold as the day after the MidWinter Solstice.

It was possible she was being strengthened by drawing on Veikko's magic, either inadvertently or by deliberate draining. As Aleksia ran clumsily across the snow, wings pumping hard to get airborne, she considered that possibility, and decided rather grimly that things were progressing faster than she liked. She needed to meet with the Sammi women, win their confidence and formulate a plan, and she had to do so very soon. She could only hope that the women were as open to getting help from her.

She actually passed over the trio laboring across the face of a slope below her as her powerful wings drove her forward; the four brown reindeer, the dark brown sledge laden with bundles, and the huge white Bear straining against the harness. They didn't look up as she passed over their heads, but she sensed Urho's attention. The Great Bear had his own mysterious powers, and they brushed against her magics like a friendly hand.

She drove on, looking for two things: a place where she could get something to eat, and a good place to meet with Urho and the two women. Those would probably be exclusive, since she intended to eat as the Bear, and that was...messy. Not that Aleksia thought either woman was squeamish, but she also did not want them to think they might be on the menu.

She found the first far sooner than she had expected.

Something had brought down a deer and left it to die in the snow and Ravens were feasting on it. Aleksia was not at all averse to some opportunistic scavenging, and proceeded to land nearby, again making the transformation into the Bear form. Once in that familiar shape, she left her little pack lying in the snow and lumbered toward the carcass.

The Ravens were loathe to surrender their prize, but there were only three of them, and Aleksia was willing to share. With the Bear's massive claws she made short work of some crude butchery, and shortly she was feasting on the hindquarters that she had dragged some little distance off, while they were back to enjoying the rest of the deer.

She tried not to think about what she was doing when the Bear ate, because to be honest, it was pretty horrific, even when it was something like a fish. When it was something like this—well, it was better to take a little absence from reality. She just sat back and thought about other things while the Bear instinct took over the body. When her stomach was full, she cleaned herself off in the snow, put her head down and headed off at the Bear's best pace to find the place she had seen from the air where she would intercept Urho and the two women. It was a stroke of luck that it was only a few furlongs away; she could easily reach it before they did.

This would have to be set up carefully, because although she knew that the two Sammi women needed her as much as she needed them, all that *they* would know, when they first saw her, was that here was a woman appearing in the middle of the wilderness—when, in fact, the North Wind had told them that the terrible creature that had stolen their son and beloved was a powerful Sorceress—who could, of course, appear out of nowhere in the middle of the wilderness. Even her appearance would tell against her; at this point she looked every inch the Snow Queen, and so...

She would have to set things up so that there was enough doubt for her to convince them that *she* was not the enemy. With luck all The Traditional forces now moving sluggishly in favor of her putting together a Questing Party would work to keep the women from rejecting her and her overtures outright.

She arrived at the site not even winded. Really she was fortunate in the lay of the land here. It was perhaps the most perfect place for a secluded campsite; another cave, where they would be able to get away from possible watchers. This one was more than big enough to hold all of them and the reindeer. Once again, she used the Bear's enormous strength to drag some wood inside, and break it apart. She transformed to human again to clean out the rubbish, make a fire pit in the middle of the sandy floor and start the fire. Unfortunately, she had nothing with her to make things more inviting than that—not without using magic, and that, she was not going to do. Not only might that draw attention from the false Snow Queen, it might well make the women more wary. She needed to appear as ordinary as possible until they were convinced. When she was certain she could do all that was possible with the little that she had, she took out her mirror to watch for the trio to approach. And then she waited. This was going to be very interesting.

Annukka could scarcely believe the difference that having the Bear with them made in their journey. They had crossed more land in the course of a morning than they had in two days with just the reindeer pulling. The White Bear's great strength meant that there was nothing that would hang the sledge up for very long. And rather than having to feed him out of their stores, they found that the shoe was on the other foot. By evening of the first day after he joined them, he was feeding them with his hunting. He could easily dig a hare out of its burrow, or find both ends and dig at one end while the women waited with a net-snare at the other. Annukka had the feeling that if he chose to, he could pull down a deer.

Of course, when they came to the first dead village, that all became moot.

When they had heard about the three villages, it had not really come home to Annukka, nor to Kaari, just what that meant.

It meant a silent cluster of houses, with nothing moving. It meant dead animals and birds everywhere—not just the livestock, but the wild birds dropped out of the eaves, frozen in the bushes. It meant a quiet that was so nerve-racking that you wanted to do anything to break it.

Still, with the entire village dead, that meant that everything here was pretty much at their disposal. She and Kaari didn't exactly talk about it— but it looked as if the men had already done something of the sort, helping themselves to some gear and supplies, and that made it easier to go ahead and follow their example. It did give Annukka a bit of an odd feeling, as she and Kaari went meticulously through peoples' belongings....

But these weren't people she had known. They were strangers whose faces she didn't have to remember. She could only tell herself that surely the former owners approved. After all, she and Kaari were here to do something about the thing that had killed them. Surely that would be what they would want; surely they would be happy to see their things going to serve that purpose.

Both of them needed more warm clothing. It was bitterly, bitterly cold, and it was not going to get better. If they did not help themselves to clothing and bedding, they might freeze.

They picked one house and completely rearranged it, got it warmed and set things up to their liking. They slept the night in that house with a fire and in real beds and with the Bear sleeping like a mound of fur across the door, just in case. They cooked real food—and in fact, they decided to stay over a second day in order to bake bread and cook meats to add to their provisions. The one thing they didn't have to worry about now that they were in weather suited to the heart of Winter was that anything would spoil. Not in this cold, packed on the sledge.

The deer appreciated the extra day, too, and dozed in the sunlight and ate the grain that Kaari spilled out on the snow for them. The Bear dragged the frozen carcasses that had been in the paddock away so they would not be disturbed by their presence. Annukka did not go to look to see what the Bear did with them; she presumed he was eating them. Frankly, frozen hard as they were, it was too much trouble to try to butcher them. Better to make use of the smoked meats already in storage.

Annukka had made a decision during that day, and as they finally left the village, they left behind them a growing plume of smoke. She and Kaari had packed the house that held all the dead bodies of the villagers with oil-soaked hay, had made the prayers for the dead, and set fire to it as they left. They didn't know when, or even if, anyone would be back here, and something needed to be done. Annukka couldn't bear to leave the sad corpses to the vermin, the scavengers, and sooner or later, that was exactly what would happen to them. Since Annukka was a Wise Woman, she had the right to make that decision and to see the dead off with the proper rites. Neither of them looked back.

Later, they came to the second village, where they did essentially the same thing. The Bear seemed to approve. He was no ordinary beast, that was certain. Annukka was pretty sure he was one of the Great Beasts, the creatures able to think like humans, and sometimes talk like them. So far, he hadn't actually spoken to either of them, but that might just be a matter of time.

It was at the third village that they found some very odd signs of depredation. There were a few doors broken in, with the same signs as if a Bear had done the work, and yet if it *was* a Bear, it was an oddly intelligent one, and it had not done the kind of destruction she would have expected from a wild creature.

Which might just mean it was not a wild creature at all....

Their Bear snuffled at the tracks, but did not look agitated. That was peculiar, too—unless, of course, this was another of the Great Beasts and he recognized the scent.

They left the same burning building behind them as they left the third village, but this time, as they left, the Bear began to pull the sledge with perceptibly more speed, as if he was trying to get somewhere as quickly as he could. Now Annukka was certain there was something more going on than she had been able to puzzle out. But her instincts told her that the Bear could be trusted, although she hardly knew why.

But it was when they saw a thin plume of smoke in the distance, a plume of smoke toward which they were heading, that she was sure that there was a great deal more going on here than she could ever have guessed.

They left the stream that they had been using as a road, crossed what must have been a meadow, and which now was a blessedly flat stretch of snow, approaching a mountainside and the start of a forest. The smoke rose above the trees in a thin, white stream. She wasn't at all surprised to see that there was a human-shaped figure waiting for them—but what did surprise her, and send a jolt of fear down her spine, was when she realized that the person beneath the long, white, fur cloak was a woman.

All she could think of was—this was the Snow Queen! The terrible creature that the North Wind had told them about, the thing that had stolen Veikko from them, had somehow found them. The Witch had tracked them down and the Bear was *her* creature, sent to bring them straight into her trap.

Kaari realized it at the same time, and both of them pulled their deer to a halt and fumbled for their bows.

"Peace!" called a clear, low-pitched voice, as their Bear put on a burst of speed and interposed his body between them and the woman—*was she the Snow Queen after all?*—so that they could not shoot her without shooting him.

Peace indeed, came a rumbling voice in Annukka's mind, startling her

so much that she fumbled the arrow she was trying to notch to the bow-
string, dropping it entirely. *This is the Snow Queen, yes, but not the one you want.*

As Annukka sat on the back of her deer like an old sack of grain, the
woman spoke again. "I am Godmother Aleksia, the Ice Fairy, also known
as the Snow Queen," came the voice from the other side of the bulk of
the Bear. The woman stepped out into the open, with one hand on the
Bear's shoulder. "And I am not the one who stole your son and betrothed,
Annukka and Kaari. Nor am I the one who slew helpless people of three
villages." Her eyes flicked from Annukka to Kaari and back again. "Still,
I know who did. And I mean to stop her. But I need your help."

She was one of the most striking women that Annukka had ever seen.
It began with her hair, arranged in braids coiled about her head, as white
as the snow around her, yet it was clear from her smooth face that she
was no ancient. And that face itself was remarkable; strong and full of
character, with a delicate, but square chin, high cheekbones and penetrating eyes of a piercing blue. She held herself as upright as a spear,
and there was a sense that there was nothing she would not face if she
had to. Annukka judged her age to be near her own or, remarkably,
perhaps a bit younger.

She wore garments as white as her hair; white boots, white trews
beneath a short gown, a white fur coat, held close to her body by a belt
of silver plaques.

You have trusted me. This is my good and wise friend, added the deep
voice in her mind, that Annukka assumed must belong to the Bear. *Will
you trust her?*

The silence lingered. The sun shone down on them all, and there was
no sound but the sighing of the wind in the bare branches. Kaari was
the first to put up her bow, stowing it in the sheath at the side of her
saddle. "Mother Annukka, if this woman had wanted us dead, she could
have had the Bear slay us days ago," the girl pointed out. "How hard

would that have been? And what could she gain by bringing us here to kill us? If she meant to capture us, for what purpose? We are of no use to her. She knows our names, she knows about Veikko. I have heard of the Godmothers, though our land has never seen one. They are said to be able to hold the fates of entire lands in their hands. We would be foolish not to trust her."

Annukka did not bother to point out that an enemy would also be able to know their names and their intentions. Because Kaari was right—if this "Godmother" had wanted them dead, the Bear could have finished them off long ago. She and Kaari would make poor slaves, and if they had been meant as sacrifices—well, there were easier wasy to have sacrificed them. She put down her bow. But unlike Kaari, she did not stow it away, instead, she kept it on her lap, with one hand on the quiver full of arrows.

"All right," she replied cautiously. "I am willing to listen."

"Then come into this cave and out of the bitter cold," the woman said, with a glance at the setting sun. "There is room for deer and all there, and I have started a fire. These things are better discussed over heat and food and drink. We have a hard task ahead of us—and one that will require much planning."

The woman had cleared the cave and the fire she had built was burning bright, showing the rough stone walls around them. The sledge they left outside, disguised with brush and snow, but the contents were all brought into the cave, as were the deer. And, of course, the Bear, who was indeed one of the Great Beasts and who was called, so the woman said, Urho. The pack on Urho's back proved to belong to the woman, and held clothing, a sleeping roll and most of the same things that Annukka and Kaari had with them. That, strangely enough, was reassuring. This was not some strange monstrous thing in the shape of a woman, nor a ghost nor vengeful spirit, nor one of the creatures like the forest spirits. This was a woman who needed clothing, needed a comb and hair pins, needed blankets to sleep in. If she was some sort of powerful Witch or Sorceress, she was not making profligate use of magic, and that was reassuring.

And the more she spoke, the better Annukka liked her.

She begged their hospitality, as she had no provisions of her own. "There are means I can take later to help our supplies," she said, spreading her hands wide, "But not at the moment."

"We have enough to spare," Annukka replied after she and Kaari exchanged a long look. "As you have welcomed us to your shelter, we welcome you to share what we have."

It was clear that the woman did not know how to cook, but Annukka would hardly have expected that of her kind. They were used to servants and being tended to, not doing the tending. Nevertheless she was willing to put her hand to whatever was needed, and for that, Annukka had to give her full credit.

It was a long night around the fire in the cave. Wariness slowly gave way to agreement, and agreement to trust. Odd as that seemed. Perhaps it was because of the way that the woman spoke to them—as equals, not as inferiors, asking rather than dictating what would be done.

Annukka began to believe that they had—as had been predicted— an ally in an unexpected place.

Aleksia was actually relieved; she had anticipated a great deal more trouble convincing the two women that she meant no harm to them. After all, if she had been in their place, *she* would not have trusted her! Here she was, intercepting them by means of—presumably—magic, getting a Great Bear to bring them here in the first place....

And she had no provisions to add to their stores, which should have made her unwelcome.

But as they spoke over cups of herbal tea, and shared out some of the food the women had wisely brought from the destroyed villages, a strange bond began to form among the three women. Logically, she could not account for it.

Then again, she could see and sense The Traditional magic swirling around all of them in a kind of state of agitation, so that might have had something to do with the way they readily fell in with her and her suggestions. As she had guessed, The Tradition did not have a clear path to follow, and it wanted one. The best it could manage was to induce them all to form a Questing Party. After that, it was lost, and it did not "like" that. It wanted direction.

They were going to have to give it a direction. That much was clear.

Aleksia began by telling them what she knew.

When Aleksia had finally finished describing everything she had found or seen until now, the girl Kaari was pale, but looked determined and the older woman, Annukka, looked very thoughtful.

"Veikko is still alive, then?" was the first thing she asked.

"When last I saw him, yes, and I think he is not likely to fade too much for some several weeks or moons more," Aleksia replied firmly. "I would show him to you in my mirror, but I do not know if you could see him in there, and I am loathe to use enough magic to enable you to do so—"

"Nor would I ask you," Annukka replied with a shudder. "Let us not, by all means, set aflame a bonfire that all may see where we are and what we are made of. No, the less magic, the better, unless it is something we truly, truly need." On that, it was clear, they were in complete agreement.

I concur, said the Bear, Urho. *Just because Godmother Aleksia and her servant did not see this Sorceress looking for mirror-magic, it does not follow that she does not have things to alert her if other magic is used.*

"Actually," Aleksia confessed, reluctantly, "I thought I sensed her hunting for me at one point. It was not because of mirror-magic, but it might have been because she sensed some of my other abilities."

Even though Kaari bit her lip and looked unhappy, Annukka nodded. "You have told us that Veikko is alive, if not well, and is like to stay that way for now. That is enough for me. Now about the others, Ilmari and Lemminkal—you think they can be revived?"

Aleksia hesitated. "I know that the bird was. I also know that the larger the creature, the harder it was to revive. I never tried anything larger than a hare. So I cannot be sure that they can be brought back to life, but...I think, working together, we may well be able to find a way to do so."

Annukka rubbed her thumb back and forth over the surface of a little bone toggle holding her sleeves closed at her wrist. "Even if it wasn't a terrible and cruel thing to leave them to die," she said, finally, "I think there is no doubt that we need them. They are, after all, great magicians." She could easily see where it might take more than one magician to defeat this other woman. In fact, she could easily see where it might require an army.

And all they had were themselves.

"How great can they be if they were caught so easily?" Kaari demanded, her voice cracking a little with pent-up nerve. "Look, they froze solid just sitting there while Veikko was fighting for his life!"

"We don't know that—he could have been surprised as readily as the others. No sign does not mean no struggle. And these two were frozen in the midst of their camp," Aleksia felt impelled to point out. "And these men are very great Mages indeed. When one has been virtually unopposed for a long time, it is easy to become complacent. No, do not fault them for this. It is no measure of their power. Even a dragon can be caught while asleep."

The girl nodded, as did Annukka, the girl with reluctance, the older woman with understanding.

"Then on the morrow we will try to revive the magicians," Aleksia said. "And if we can, we will then see what they have to say." She stood up and stretched. "And since I have an acute dislike for sleeping vulnerable—you will forgive me, but I am going to shift my shape, as I described to you."

Aleksia had decided that rather than trying to hide the fact that she was shifting, she would let both women know she could do it, and see her do it *now,* under circumstances that were relatively controlled, rather than shock them at a time when none of them could afford to be shocked. If she had to hide herself every time she needed to shift, and hide the fact she was the one that was the helpful Bear, Swan, Falcon and so forth, making up excuses for her disappearances, she would grow mad. And worse, when the women did find out about it, they would no longer trust her. So as she continued her stretch, she let herself slide into the Bear form, feeling herself growing taller and bulkier, feeling her weight and center of balance shift, until at last it was a Bear that stood there on its hind legs, looking down at them benignly.

It was somewhat amusing to see the girl's eyes widen, see her shrink involuntarily back, as Aleksia dropped to all fours. Her muzzle was somewhat distorted compared to Urho's—she had kept enough of the human shape to it to be able to make understandable words. Urho could speak mind-to-mind with other creatures naturally. She could not.

"It is a great deal safer to have two Bears and two women sleeping in this cave, than three women and a single Bear," she pointed out, her voice low and a combination of human speech and ursine growl. She tilted her head to the side, watching the fear and startlement fade from the younger woman's eyes.

The older woman laughed. After the initial moment of shock she had looked approving rather than frightened. Aleksia liked her more with every moment that passed. This was a sensible woman, much after her own heart. "I have heard of such magic as this, but never seen it," Annukka said. "Can it be learned?"

"I would say 'perhaps,'" Aleksia replied, as Urho chuckled deep in his chest. "I am not as adept at it as my mentor was."

"Since I see you doing this now, when you have warned against the use of much magic, I assume it does not shout one's presence as much as other spells?" Annukka continued, as Kaari slowly recovered from watching Aleksia shift.

"You assume correctly." Aleksia coughed. "And it is unfamiliar to most magicians, so they do not think to look for it. Also—the creatures that have magic, like some of the things that dwell in deep forest, also use this same magic. Someone who knows to look for it not might think that it is a human that is using it."

"And are you a human?" came the forthright question. Annukka stared directly into Aleksia's Bearish eyes. "Truly?"

"Human and as mortal as you," Aleksia replied. "In time I will take an apprentice to replace me. I am no Fae."

Annukka let out her breath with a sigh. "Well then. I would be interested to see if I can learn this shifting magic."

"I would be willing to teach you. And I am sure you understand there are risks—"

"There are risks in all magic, and I am not so foolish as to want to venture it here and now," Annukka told her firmly. "But someday, when this is over and we are the unrecognizable beings in a tale. Meanwhile there is another advantage to this shape of yours. We will *all* certainly sleep warm." She grinned at Aleksia. "One Bear was a fine thing to sleep up against. To sleep between two will be a grand luxury."

Aleksia had to chuckle a bit herself.

They all slept soundly, with no dreams that Aleksia could recall. At dawn she and Urho went a-hunting as the two women prepared a more traditional meal for themselves. Aleksia did not want to stretch their supplies any more than was strictly necessary. Once they were all fed, they were off to the ice-forest as fast as they could manage with the sledge, with Aleksia scouting ahead in Hawk form. She saw nothing whatsoever to be worried about, but that did not stop her from being as wary as if she had spotted a potential ambush. Now was a vulnerable time for a Questing Party; The Tradition had not yet fully recognized them as such, and it would be very easy for it to turn its magics against them.

But there was nothing untoward. She landed beside the two frozen magicians, transformed into her human shape, and waited.

She did not have to wait for very long. Urho and the women had made excellent progress; she heard them arrive, then heard the sounds of footsteps crunching through the ice-covered snow until they entered the clearing, each leading her riding deer.

Annukka was first, with Kaari close behind her. They opened their mouths to greet Aleksia, but the greeting turned to a gasp as they caught sight of the two frozen Mages. And it was not that she had not described the bizarre sight—it was because no one could look on that and not gasp in shock.

For a moment there was nothing but the faint tinkle of ice as a breeze stirred the branches and bits broke from the birch twigs and fell.

Annukka was the first of the two to step forward to examine the two "patients," and she hummed and peered at them as Kaari waited nervously.

"Now...I have to wonder," Annukka said, looking sideways at Aleksia. "Do you know much about Sammi magic?"

"Not much," Aleksia replied honestly. "Mostly that the most powerful is done through music."

"And as such it tends to be compatible with just about every other form of magic," the Wise Woman replied. "And it is in my mind that if you and I added our magic together, the whole is likely to be more powerful than the two used separately."

Aleksia had to nod at that. "What did you have in mind?"

"That I will sing, and you see how you can fit one of your magics into the song." The older woman was already rummaging through the saddlebag on the side of her deer. She brought out an object wrapped in soft hide that proved to be a kantele when unwrapped.

She tuned it deftly and looked to Aleksia, who nodded. And with no more preamble than that, she began to play and sing.

She had a lovely, warm voice, low rather than the high-pitched tones most older women developed. The pitch was true, the tone was strong. It would have been a pleasure to listen to even if it had not been bearing great magic. As it was, the power in the magic made the music that much richer.

Aleksia listened, rather than acting at once, waiting to *feel* the song, and the flow of the magic, before she interfered. This would be a very delicate operation—not that she hadn't blended her magic with that of someone else before, but it was always tricky to accomplish, and it was seldom obvious how best to make the two fit together.

After a moment, she recognized the song; it was one that the Sammi sang at MidWinter, when the world was dark and cold, before the sun came up. The lyrics were very, very old, in a form of the language that was archaic even by Sammi standards. And yet, it was possible to sense what the song was about even without being able to understand the language. It spoke of hope and renewal, of pushing back the dark, of new birth and new life and the warmth of Spring even in the darkest hours of Winter.

When she came to the second verse, Aleksia began to fit in her own magics along with that of the song; she used images, rather than words. Annukka was clearly her superior in the area of words and music—if she were to make a judgment, she would have to reckon Annukka among the greatest of Bardic musicians. She wondered, in the back of her mind, how such a talent had remained overlooked in the vast hinterland that was the Kingdom of the Sammi.

Or had she been? Perhaps the talent had never blossomed until now, either because it had never been needed, or because it had not been wanted. Power was a blessing *and* a curse, and there were those who were willing, more than willing, to do without the blessing in order to avoid the curse. She saw that often enough as a Godmother—people caught up in Traditional paths who only wanted normal lives, no matter what they had to give up to get them.

She turned her attention back to the task at hand, and loaded each trickle of power with memories of warm Spring days, of the sun shining on the wakening earth, of seedlings pushing their way through the warm earth, of buds unfolding, of flowers blooming. She remembered her own childhood and how magical even the most ordinary of Spring days had seemed. She remembered baby things—lambs, kittens, rabbits, chicks. No matter that later those baby things grew up to become dinner; in the Spring, all babies were precious and life-affirming. She reached out to add those memories to the mix. Kaari closed her eyes and began to hum, her face flushed and her lips growing a little redder, as if the sun—or something else—had kissed them. From Kaari came other sorts of memories and images, also life-affirming. How it felt to be in love on a warm Spring day. The touch of a lover's hand, the sweetness of a kiss. The stirring within, when life demanded to be created and re-created again. The sensual joy of skin on skin.

Aleksia felt The Traditional magic eddying formlessly around them seize on the song, and the images—and suddenly, completely out of the blue, she had a *lot* more power on her hands! The Tradition itself was answering the age-old call of Spring and new life, even now, in the midst of Winter.

She looked up to see if either of the other women had noticed. A glance at the Sammi woman told Aleksia that Annukka was thoroughly wrapped up in her song-spell now, and an erupting volcano couldn't shake her. Kaari was the same. Both were lost to the music and the magic, weaving it into a web of life-affirming and life-giving power tied to the very earth itself.

Aleksia opened her mind and let The Traditional power flow through her, like a warm golden river. This was the moment that made all the hard work of being a Godmother worthwhile, when the power answered you at last, when you coaxed it into the shape you wanted, and you knew there was going to be a happy ending. Even if she only shared in that ending vicariously, the power sang in her veins now, and brought everything about her to life.

The power flooded through her. And through her, into Annukka, and into Annukka's song.

Suddenly, the clearing filled with the scent of blooming flowers and new grass. A thousand wonderful scents filled the air, of new rain, and freshly turned earth, of young herbs and linen drying in the sun, of honey in the comb and grapes ripening on the vine.

A warm breeze circled the place, banishing the icy cold for a moment; the sun acquired new warmth as it touched them, and somewhere in the distance a bird broke into song.

A brilliant ray of sunshine broke through the clouds, penetrating the bare branches of the birch grove, and gilding everything with warm, golden light. Everything felt suddenly more vivid, more real, more alive. Aleksia felt the sudden urge to run and dance, as the snow in the clearing began to melt. Never had she ever seen snow melt this quickly. She spread out her arms to the warmth of the sun, basking in it. Both Annukka and

Kaari had their faces tilted up to the sunlight, eyes still closed. Aleksia continued to weave her magic into Annukka's, and watched, eyes narrowed, as the ice encasing the two Mages began to melt.

It was the elder of the two, Lemminkal, who thawed first, dropping out of his frigid position with a huge gasp, to half-lie, panting for breath, on the thin brown grass revealed by the melting snow and ice. Then Ilmari followed, and as the Sammi magician reached the final verse of the song and took a deep breath to begin another iteration, Aleksia tapped on Annukka's shoulder to tell her to stop.

She strummed a few final chords and let the music die away. The golden light faded first, returning to the dull gray of a deep-Winter afternoon. After that, the cold returned, and the clearing began to freeze over again. The snow was gone, but the ground turned hard in moments, and any moisture that remained became ice again. The scents vanished altogether, leaving not a hint behind—if indeed they had ever been there at all, and had not been figments of their imaginations. And the birdsong stilled, bringing back the frozen silence of this forest of ice. It all returned to the state it had been when they first entered the clearing. Aleksia watched this with regret. The hint of Summer in the midst of all this cold, of life in all of this death—it had been a moment of relief, as well as a reminder of why she was here in the first place.

But at least the men were still thawed, slowly helping each other up off the ground, looking dazed and a little confused. Aleksia surveyed them without betraying that she already knew them. That would only excite their suspicion. And despite her familiarity with them, she had to wonder how much of what she had listened to was boast and how much was reality. They had great reputations, they had tales enough, and they looked the part of Heroes, but would they measure up? She found herself praying that they would and not just because they would double the strength of this party.

Because she wanted to listen to Ilmari again. And this time, have it not be something of a sham.

Annukka looked around in something of a daze herself. "What happened?" she asked, shaking her head. "I remember that I meant to do a spell-song to help Aleksia free Ilmari and Lemminkal, but I do not remember anything past the first few bars. This is most peculiar. I have never done anything like that before."

"You brought the Spring, Mother Annukka," Kaari said, her eyes vague and a little unfocused, as if she was still a little lost in her own vision of Spring. Well that was as good an explanation as any for now.

"And...you saved us...Wise One," Ilmari managed to get out, struggling to stand. "I do not know how, but I do not doubt the result."

"Yes," Lemminkal confirmed, then his gaze sharpened and his hand went to the hilt of his sword. "You saved us indeed. But that brings up a very good question. Who are you? Where do you come from? How did you find us? And why did you save us?"

"Yes, and who sent you? And how did you get here?" Ilmari added. "The last three villages we came through are dead and we nearly fell prey to the same thing that destroyed them. Why aren't we dead as well? Why aren't you?"

And the two magicians turned identical expression of wariness on the women and their companion.

14

BOTH MEN DREW THEIR SWORDS, OR DID SO AS BEST THEY could, and tried to look defiant and strong. Which was—less than awe-inspiring. They were still rather unsteady, and their hands had a perceptible tremble.

But as they asked their questions, they were looking straight at Aleksia, who shook her head sadly, as much to herself as anything else. She knew exactly what was coming next.

Nor was she incorrect.

"The Snow Witch!" Ilmari spat, his gaze filled with anger. "Beware my steel, foul hag! We know your intentions, and we know your plans! What have you done with Veikko?"

"*I* have done nothing with Veikko," Aleksia said crossly, feeling very much put-upon and getting altogether weary of being blamed for what the false Snow Queen had done. "I might just as well ask you the same, and to as much purpose. You had the stripling, and you were responsible for him. You seem to have misplaced him. What did *you* do with him?" She looked the two men up and down; they were still wobbly on their feet, and she had the strong feeling that even she, untutored as she was in the art of bladework, could slap their swords aside without a great deal of difficulty.

Now, at last, she could get her first truly good look at both of them. They were rather fine specimens of Sammi manhood, with similar, surprisingly youthful round faces with prominent cheekbones and startling blue eyes. Lemminkal Heikkinen boasted long gray-blond hair with two side-braids, and a beard that reached to the middle of his chest. He wore beautifully worked chain mail over thick brown woolen trousers and a black Sammi tunic decorated with embroidered bands, well-worn leather boots, with a heavy brown woolen cloak thrown back over his shoulders and clasped with a bronze pennanular brooch. Discarded on the ground beside him was a staff made from a gnarled sapling. Belted over the chain mail was the scabbard to the sword now in his hand.

Ilmari Heikkinen, the younger brother of Lemminkal, was blonder, as his hair was not yet graying. He wore both his hair and beard shorter than Lemminkal, his hair reaching only to his shoulders and his beard close-cropped around his chin. According to everything that Aleksia had learned, he was a Wonder-smith, who created enchanted items like swords and knives. He wore a similar outfit to his brother, and at the moment there was a forge hammer stuck through his belt and a sword of his own making was in his hands.

Both those sets of blue eyes were leveled at her. "I am also *not* the Snow Witch, or whatever you choose to call her," Aleksia persisted. "In fact, I have never been here before. Until recently, this was an unregulated part of the world that was only loosely under my supervision. This—creature—that you call the Icehart or Snow Witch changed all that." She drew herself up to her full height. "I am Godmother Aleksia, the Snow Queen, the Ice Fairy. My stronghold is the Palace of Ever-Winter, which I *assure* you is *not* in that direction!" She pointed to the north and west. "That way lies the dwelling of the one you seek to bring to justice. I seek retribution as much as you do, if not more. This creature is a murderer and a thief. She has stolen my identity, crudely copied my Palace and is ruining your countryside and decimating your villages, and I am here to put a stop to her!"

It was a lovely speech, rather marred by the fact that she was wearing clothing she had slept in, stray hairs were escaping from her braids, and she had no visible support except for a rather bemused Bear and two women.

"Brave words, *carlin,* but what reason have we to trust you?" Ilmari sneered. "And even if we did trust you, even if we did believe you, what army did you bring with you to oppose the Snow Witch, hmm?"

She bristled. *Carlin? I am no older than he!* She was about to retort when Lemminkal said, dazedly, "Wait, what?" He rubbed his head and the tip of his sword dropped. He still looked stunned. Aleksia began to wonder if that was his perpetual expression.

Oh, grand. This is Veikko's mentor, the Warrior-Mage Lemminkal, who has about the same intelligence as his sword…or perhaps the sword is the smarter of the two. And on top of that, it looks as if he is going to fall on his nose in the next moment.

But Lemminkal was shaking his head, and not as if he did not believe Aleksia, more as if he was disagreeing with what she was saying. "No, no, the Snow Witch and the Icehart are not the same thing! I am not even sure they are connected in any way—" At least some vague impression of intelligence was creeping back into his eyes; which effect was then marred by the fact that he turned as suspicious as his brother. "But why should we trust that you are what you say you are?"

She graced both of them with a look of disdain. She was trying to make allowances for their heads being frozen, but really, of all of the Heroes and Champions she had ever worked with, these two were the *dimmest* creatures she had ever set eyes on! What had happened to the clever men she had listened to at their own hearth fire? "You should trust what I say because if I were not, I would not have bothered to bring the Wise Woman here and thaw you out."

The men exchanged silent glances. She was about to elaborate, when Lemminkal shook his head again. "The Icehart—" he began, and looked alarmed. "The time!"

Ilmari cursed, and looked at the sun, now visible as it dropped below the level of the clouds and shone straight into the birch forest. Somewhat to her shock and dismay, Aleksia realized that it was setting. It had been scarcely midday when they all converged here and Annukka had begun her singing. It had seemed like no more than a moment had passed—yet clearly several hours had gone by.

But why should this be a cause for alarm?

"We are in great danger!" Ilmari said, all animosity momentarily forgotten. "This is the place from which the Icehart manifests! It was not the Snow Witch that froze us, it was the Icehart, and it is nothing like a mortal creature at all—"

"It is a ghost of some kind," Lemminkal interrupted, his face blanching. His eyes searched the clearing, as if looking for something. "A vengeful spirit. We faced it here. We think that it was awakened not long ago, and it has been looking for something ever since. When it does not find what it is looking for, it shows its displeasure and moves on."

"And in its wake, it leaves death," Ilmari said grimly. "As you saw."

"But why were you not dead?" Annukka asked. She tucked her kantele away in the saddlebags, and turned back to face them.

That is a good question, Urho rumbled. *In fact, I can think of no reason why you should be alive.*

The brothers exchanged looks again. "Perhaps because we are Mages?" Lemminkal said weakly. "Perhaps the fact that we have magic all about us shielded us from the worst that the Icehart could do—"

"But this place is very different from the villages. I was able to free birds and animals from the ice, and they lived," Aleksia pointed out. "In the villages, everything was already dead and frozen that way, not sleeping under the ice."

"Then perhaps the Snow Witch's spreading power and the Icehart's magic clashed in some way—and it matters not!" Ilmari interjected, looking panicked. "This is the place from which the Icehart manifests! It appears at sundown and we must be gone before it returns!"

"Ah...brother..." The last rays of the sun pierced gaps between the white trunks of the birch forest, lancing through the maze of trees like so many golden spears. And as swiftly as the light had come, it faded. Night descended as suddenly as a dropping curtain; they went without warning from golden light to a dim blue dusk, and the air abruptly became burningly cold.

"I think we are too late..."

The reindeer started; with their eyes rolling, they huddled together, shivering so hard they looked as if they were having fits. Something white and glowing softly ghosted through the tree trunks at the limit of vision. Obscured, revealed, only to be obscured again, it was drawing closer, but not in any direct fashion. Instinctively they all drew together, even the Bear and the reindeer. Then the deer froze, eyes staring fixedly, refusing to move.

"Urho?" Aleksia whispered, hoping that the Bear's senses would tell her something she did not know.

It is a ghost. More than that, I cannot tell.

So it was not some new manifestation of a Great Beast. Aleksia shivered. Life would have been much easier if it had been. She seldom had anything to do with ghosts. That was just not something she was an expert in. Godmothers rarely had to deal with such spirits. Godmothers tended to deal with the living, not the dead.

Yes, but now you are part of the story, and you are subject to new rules, aren't you? She was beginning to dislike that little voice in her head.

By now, the poor deer were as rigid as statues. The temperature in the clearing was dropping more with every moment that passed, and a feeling of terrible menace increased proportionally. They watched in growing fear as the pale, glowing thing slowly drifted in their direction. She couldn't make out anything of the creature except for the dim, blue-white glow of it as it advanced through the trees.

Although "advanced" was a misnomer. It did not approach them directly. It was spiraling in toward them, slowly, a tactic that only made the tension mount as it sidled through the trunks. Aleksia's body was rigid with the tension, and she shivered uncontrollably. And in the back of her mind, a little voice kept asking, in an increasingly hysterical tone, why she had ever considered facing this menace herself. *What did I let myself in for?* And, of course, the only answer was that she had taken herself out of the protected realm of the Godmother and placed herself right alongside of the true players in the situation.

The pale form paused for a moment. Aleksia got the feeling that it was surveying them coolly. Then, suddenly, it disappeared. Or rather, the glow of it vanished among the trees.

Aleksia held her breath. The others went very stiff, all of them listening as hard as ever they could. In the little clearing the silence was so profound that it weighed like lead on all of them.

The only sound was that of their breathing. There was not even the sound of an ice fragment falling from one of the branches around them. It grew darker still, and the silence took on a menacing life of its own.

The darkness pressed in on them, and the cold deepened. There was no moon, and the only thing that Aleksia could make out, peering as hard as she could into the darkness, was the vague pale shapes of the nearest birch trunks. Something had to be done. They could not bear this for much longer.

Ilmari swore under his breath.

Aleksia tried to speak; nothing came out. She swallowed, licked her lips and tried again. There was something she could do, now this moment, if only she could manage to offer it. Her stomach was knotted into an icy ball; she felt her hand shaking; and it was all she could do to keep her teeth from chattering. This was so different from being on the other side of the mirror, watching the conflict about to take place, poised to interfere if she needed to—

Oh, this was horribly unlike that.

"Should I make a light?" she whispered.

"Yes!" Ilmari barked, sounding relieved and frantic at the same time. Aleksia shivered, wondering what was going on in his mind. "Anything but this damned darkness! This is how it happened the last time—"

Before he could finish the sentence, Aleksia had gathered personal power, called up the light spell in her mind, and with a little flinging motion, tossed an invisible bit of magical energy straight up. "Stay there," she whispered to it. Then she gave the spell a little twist to activate it. The "ball" of power became a ball of light over their heads.

The clearing was revealed with pitiless clarity. Kaari screamed. Annukka and Aleksia yipped and started back. The two men swore.

The Icehart stood looming above them, not ten feet away.

It could have been a sculpture made of the clearest ice, beautifully carved, exquisitely detailed, perfect down to the last hair, of a roe deer in the prime of life. Only this deer was twice the size of the largest reindeer that Aleksia had ever seen; it had a rack of antlers whose points glittered wickedly in the blue Mage-light, and she had no doubt that each point was sharper than a spear. It regarded them from clouded white eyes, the only part of it that was not utterly transparent. It exuded cold in waves, and as they stared at it, it finally moved.

It opened its mouth and began to take a deep breath, its sides expanding as what passed for lungs filled. She could hear the hiss of its breath as it inhaled. She was terrified and puzzled all at the same time. What was this thing doing?

Ilmari cursed frantically. *"Brother!"* he shouted. And as if that had been a signal, Aleksia found herself seized around the waist by a pair of the strongest arms she had ever felt. Ilmari lunged for the right, taking her with him. Lemminkal was doing the same with Annukka to the left, and Urho grabbed Kaari's collar in his teeth and heaved her after the other Sammi woman before following Ilmari to the right. The Icehart continued to inhale, oblivious of them.

Then the thing exhaled, as if letting go of an enormous sigh.

They got out of the way just as the Icehart let out its breath, and where its breath passed, everything was instantly coated in ice. Despite her terror, Aleksia found herself gawking. This was the strangest magic she had ever seen. She could sense the power around them, and everything she knew told her it should feel evil and dark—and all it felt was alien. It was not even hostile. It was as if even emotion was chilled and numbed by the terrible cold.

Everything that had thawed out was frozen again, and as Aleksia tried to get up, she felt her cloak tugging at her throat and shoulders. She grabbed a handful of fur and fabric and yanked hard. A shower of ice crystals followed as she pulled a corner of her cloak loose from the ground where it had been frozen into place.

Just one touch of that breath and she would be as frozen as the brothers had been. And if Annukka was frozen, too—

She whimpered a little in her throat.

The men, however, were not waiting about for the Icehart to deliver another deadly breath.

Moving as one, as if they had done this a thousand times, they attacked it, one to either side, while Urho roared and leveled a blow with a massive paw to its muzzle.

The Icehart did not seem to move, yet somehow it evaded the Bear's smashing blow, and fended off both the men with its antlers. One moment it was standing there; the next, it had ducked under Urho's paw, then with a flick of its antlers, knocked both swords to the side.

Then it reared, and one of its forehooves came crashing on Urho's skull. The Bear went down as if it had been felled by a tree trunk, to lie semiconscious and groaning on the ground. Aleksia gasped and started to run to the Bear's side; Annuka grabbed her by the elbow in a crushing grip and prevented her from doing so. Just as well, as the Icehart reared and spun again, and had she been beside the Bear, she would surely have been felled by those deadly hooves.

The Icehart turned its attention to Ilmari. Moving its head in tiny circles, threatening him with its antlers, it lunged at him again and again. He darted out of the way, only to find that the Icehart had managed to drive him together with his brother, so that it only had to face one front, not two. The Icehart had them right where it wanted them. Now it could hunt them around the clearing until it could ready one of those terrible breaths to freeze them both where they stood.

Aleksia sought through her memory for any sort of spell that would help in this situation, and cursed under her breath as she realized how woefully inadequate she was at combat. Fireballs? No, she had only seen those, never made them herself. Levin bolts? The same. A magical weapon, sword, lance, shield? No, no and no—they all took too long to create. Lightning? Nothing to call it down from.

Light! she thought, finally, and with a cantrip of three words, caused another ball of Mage-light energy to appear in front of the Icehart's nose. Only this time, instead of letting it build to a steady glow, she made it explode in a wash of brilliance.

The Icehart started back, but Ilmari and Lemminkal also stumbled backward with profane exclamations of pain. "Curse it, you fool woman!" Lemminkal spat. "I can't see!"

Hastily she summoned a spell for clearing the perceptions and graced both of them with it—and just in time. The Icehart shook off the effects of the light and lunged for them, taking care to come at them obliquely so that they could not separate again. They scrambled out of the way, as Aleksia pummeled her brain for something else that might work.

So much of her magic had to do with ice and snow, and she was sure the Icehart was immune to the effects of both of these! A blizzard? No, that would handicap the men more than the Icehart. Ice underfoot? Same. Cold? It was already cold enough to burn, and the Icehart did not even notice it.

She tried a spell of warmth, such as the ones that let her stay comfortable when her throne room was set to discourage Kay, setting it on the spirit in hopes of making it uncomfortable.

The Icehart didn't seem to notice, and the clearing became no warmer.

She saw its flanks heave as it inhaled again, and shouted a warning; both men flung themselves to the side as it breathed out deathly cold for the second time.

This time was worse. This time it wasn't just a coating of ice it left behind; everything in the path of that breath was frozen.

The men hadn't yet gotten to their feet, and she saw it take another deep breath. They would not escape this breath. Desperately, she did the only thing she could think of. With an outflung hand she created a mirror of ice between the Icehart and the two men.

The outrushing breath hit the mirror and—somehow reflected back. The mirror, ice already, became coated in the stuff, but it also sent the breath back to hit the Icehart full in the face. And the Icehart danced away awkwardly, shaking its massive head from side to side as it tried to free face, muzzle and antlers from the sudden overburden of ice coating it. From the way it blundered and slipped as it moved, Aleksia wondered if it had been temporarily blinded by its own power.

But it had not been so blinded that it could not continue to fight back. Even as the men closed in, swords swinging in deadly arcs, it swept its massive antlers at them and nearly knocked the swords from their hands. A shake of the head, and showers of ice exploded in every direction from it, like a thousand tiny knives. It lunged at the men, but this time they managed to split and attack it from the side.

Ilmari missed, Lemminkal hit, but his blade clanged and skidded on the beast's flank without so much as scratching it, and it reared and whirled on its hind hooves and lashed at him with its forehooves. He stumbled backward and it began another of those long inhalations, preparatory to one of its icy blasts.

Urho slammed into it from the side. Both of them tumbled to the ground. The Icehart got up first, but it had lost its breath, and the Bear managed to roll out of the way of its hooves.

The Icehart was now at the far end of the clearing. The Bear shuffled back to the women, standing at their side, head down, a splotch of red blood making an ugly mess of the white fur of the top of his head.

Ilmari and Lemminkal crouched at the side of the clearing about halfway between the Icehart and the women. They were not making a protective stance to shield the women. They were pressed back against the tree trunks, panting, faces cut by the close passage of antler tips and flying shards of ice. They were half ice as well; beards and hair crusted with it, and ice glazing their chain mail. To Aleksia's eyes, their movements were slowed. They had not completely escaped the Icehart's breath, and they were showing the effects.

Her heart was in her mouth. They were all the worse for wear, and the spirit did not even look winded.

The Icehart stood very still. It was impossible to say who it was looking at, given those strange, clouded eyes, but it was not moving, and it was certainly looking at something—or someone.

Annukka was fumbling with the pack on her terrified deer, and in a moment had brought something out. Aleksia was going to caution her against using her bow, unless somewhere in there she had managed to get hold of arrows capable of destroying a spirit, but it was not a weapon that she brought out.

It was her kantele.

Before Aleksia could say or do anything, Annukka had struck the first chords, and with a look of fierce determination on her face, began to sing.

With the sound of the first bars, the two men roused themselves with difficulty and brought up their weapons, moving sluggishly.

She is going to sing a war song to strengthen them, but will that be enough? Aleksia wondered. She searched for the energies of The Tradition; they were here, but unfocused, and all but useless. So, anything she put into Annukka's song would have to come from her own reserves, which meant she would somehow have to do that *and* create another ice-mirror shield if it came to that.

But with the first words, it was evident that both Aleksia and the men had been mistaken in Annukka's intentions. This was not a war song.

It was a love song.

Or rather, it was a song of love lost, gone beyond all regaining.

As Annukka sang, a great lump came into Aleksia's throat, and tears unbidden sprang into her eyes. She was not familiar with this particular ballad, but the subject was common enough. This was the lament of a woman left behind, her beloved gone—though this song made no reference to the circumstances, only the bereavement, the agony, the loss and the loneliness. The words hung in the clearing, sweet and mournful, bringing an ache to the chest and waking up the memory of every loss ever suffered in one's life. Aleksia remembered her sister's husband and she felt again the bitter agony of knowing that he and she were perfect for each other and yet she would never, ever have him. Was there ever any sadder situation than "I love you, but you will never love me"?

There is an empty space where you should be, the song said. *It is a mortal wound that I will never recover from. Where are you? I would give all that I have to join you. Without you, the sunlight is dim. Without you, food is tasteless, flowers have lost their scent, birdsong has no melody. Without you, why is there Spring? Without you, life has no meaning. My friends try to comfort me, but there is no comfort to be had. I am alone in the darkness and cold of my own soul, and there is nothing good in the world without you.*

Perhaps Annukka thought that, being a spirit, the Icehart might take pause at this song, and turn aside. After all, if this was a vengeful ghost there were generally only two things to be revenged to this extent— the loss of love or the loss of honor, and Annukka had a fifty percent chance that it was a loss of love.

But she surely did not expect the reaction that she got.

The Icehart itself froze.

The air around it chilled further, calling a flurry of ice flakes out of the air itself. A coat of frost formed instantly all over it, rendering it translucent. That bereavement in the song was amplified past all bearing, as if something in the Icehart resonated to it and sent it back out again. Aleksia wanted to fling herself to the ground and weep until there were no more tears left. Nor was she the only one; the men were weeping, Lemminkal silently, and Ilmari sobbing openly. Kaari's face was wet with tears.

It turned its frosted eyes toward Annukka, eyes that glowed for a moment. Aleksia took an abortive step forward to put herself between the Sammi woman and the creature, fearing an attack.

But no attack came.

The Icehart suddenly raised its muzzle to the sky. It opened its mouth, but what came out was not its deadly cold breath, but a long, heartbroken cry, a moan that cut Aleksia to the soul and called a pain-filled sob out of her throat as well.

That note of agony hung in the air for a terrible, timeless moment. And then, with a flash of blue-white light, the Icehart was gone.

Annukka ceased her song immediately, but the sorrow of it held them all captive, paralyzed with grief. Finally, Annukka strummed a few more notes out of her kantele—but this time, it was a child's song.

Slowly, as she played, the sorrow ebbed, faded. Kaari dried her eyes, the men turned away, stiffly; there was a flash of heat and light, and then they were free of the overburden of ice and moving easily again.

"Well played, Wise Woman," Ilmari said, gruffly. "Clever."

Something gleamed on the snow where the Icehart had stood. Slowly, Aleksia walked to the place and looked down.

Nestled in the snow, gleaming in the blue-white light of the Mage-light, was half of a crystal heart.

Aleksia picked it up. It was cool, but not cold, to the touch. It did not seem to be made of ice—but what could it be? What could it signify?

She brought it back to Annukka and Kaari; the Wise Woman handled it carefully, then shrugged. "I have no more notion than you," she admitted, then rubbed her temple a little. "But I know this. If I do not rest soon, my nose will be hitting the snow in no graceful fashion."

Aleksia looked to Ilmari, after slipping the crystal into her pocket. "Are we safe for the night, do you think?" she asked the Mage-Smith in a low voice. He regarded her thoughtfully.

"I think," he replied, in tones of surprising courtesy, "that between you women, you have frightened it, made it grieve as it never has. I think it will not touch us now." He regarded both her and Annukka with a new respect. "One Mage to another, lady, whether you are a God-mother as you say or not, you made good use of your powers this day."

"Powers!" She came to herself with a start. "Urho!"

She searched for the pack that Urho had brought with him, found it and unpacked it until she found the carefully wrapped vial that she was looking for, and the pot of salve with it. She took both to where the Bear was sitting next to Kaari as she started a fire.

Aleksia looked down at the girl, who was doing a good job of getting it going. "Kaari, do you feel equal to some wood gathering?" She glanced around the clearing, particularly at the two men, who looked very much as if they wanted to find a flat place to lie down.

The young woman looked up, with a serious expression on her face. "Actually, I think we should move back to where we left the sledge and set up camp there. This is just to give people a place to warm their hands."

Aleksia nodded approval. "You are wiser. Let me treat Urho, and then we can do just that."

The Bear raised his head with a little difficulty. *I am seeing double.*

She patted his massive shoulder reassuringly. "I am not surprised. But you carried your own cure on your back the entire way here. Open."

The Bear opened his mouth obediently, and she measured exactly three drops of the cordial onto his tongue. He closed his mouth, and suddenly his eyes, which had been scrunched up in pain, relaxed.

She cleaned the blood from the fur of his head as best she could, then carefully applied tiny dabs of the salve to the gash there. It began to close almost immediately, and by the time she was done, it was half healed.

The cordial and the salve were of true Fae make, from the Elves themselves. Every Godmother had a supply; tales did not always go well, and sometimes it was necessary to patch up Heroes and Champions as well as guide them. But these things were to be used sparingly. She had only one vial and one pot, and when they were gone, the only place to get more was from the Elves themselves.

She helped Urho heave himself onto his feet, and the entire group wearily staggered to where they had left the sledge and the other two reindeer. The deer were unmolested, greedily grazing on the sweet tips of young birch saplings. Urho volunteered to drag in wood, and since he was clearly feeling a bit better, Aleksia allowed him to do so. After all, he could bring in far more than they could, with far less effort.

Meanwhile the three who had put the most effort out in the fight, Ilmari, Annukka and Lemminkal, were made to sit on the sledge while she and Kaari made camp.

It was a very crude camp, and it was a good thing that no storms were threatening, because Aleksia very much doubted that the camp would have stood up to a storm. Neither of them could manage to get the hide tents up. But there was another reason why Aleksia wanted the others to allow her and Kaari to deal with making camp. She was, after all, a Godmother. And there was potential here for trouble...and potential for something other than trouble. So long as she set things up carefully.

So, she kept Kaari away from the men...and made sure that Lemminkal talked to Annukka. By the time they all rolled into their blankets, with the fire on one side, and the huge bulk of Urho providing warmth on the other, things were progressing to Aleksia's satisfaction.

15

IN THE MORNING, EVERYTHING LOOKED BETTER. THE SUN
was shining, and although the frozen forest was still encased in ice, it
was beautiful. The air, while still bitterly cold, was not laden with the
deathly chill of the Icehart's presence. Urho had been wonderful to sleep
up against.

On the other hand, as soon as Aleksia moved, she wished she had not.
The exposed skin on her face hurt. She had bruises where she would
rather not think about. If this was being a Hero, she envied the stamina
of those who did it all the time.

On the other hand, they had slept the night through undisturbed;
Urho went out as soon as all the humans were awake and came back
with four fish from a frozen stream. Aleksia would have felt very guilty
had he returned with a rabbit or some other animal, knowing that it
was still alive under that ice, and had been totally helpless, but she felt
no sympathy for fish. Although she could not help with the cooking—
the honest truth was that she was totally helpless when it came to that
skill—she was at least able to create a subtle warming spell to make
them all comfortable in the cold until the fire built up again. While the

fish were grilling over the fire, Annukka declared that they were all going to be looked over and tended to.

It turned out they were all injured in some way or other. For one thing, all of them were frost-burned—like a sunburn, but caused by the Icehart's freezing breath. The skin on their faces was sensitive at the least, painful at worst. In fact, the two men were lucky that they had escaped frostbite. Had it not been for their thick hair and beards, both Lemminkal and Ilmari might well have lost the tips of their ears. And in fact, Lemminkal did lose the bottom half of his long beard, for the hair had been frozen so stiff it had, to his chagrin, actually snapped off in the cold.

As it was, Annukka treated them all with salves to their tender faces, and warned them that the burned skin would slough off in a few days, and that they must be careful about further burns. Aleksia's tender forehead and nose gave her problems every time she did something that moved the skin, although she knew from past experience that once she shifted forms a time or two, that would mend itself. That was another benefit of shifting; by doing so, one could heal oneself.

Urho, of course, had his head wound, which Annukka cleaned and treated again, this time getting most of the blood out of his fur and putting an herbal plaster over the gash. Both men had dozens of small cuts on face and neck from flying shards of ice, and both moved in a way that suggested they had more than a few bruises, and that they were a lot more painful than Aleksia's. Honestly, they were all lucky that no one had broken bones, something that could be attributed only to the men's skill as fighters. Annukka set up the hide tent and ordered them in, one at a time, with a bottle. Both came out smelling like pine-sap liniment.

By then, the fish was grilled, and they divided the fillets up, with the lion's share going to the men, and Aleksia taking only as much as would satisfy her immediate hunger. She had ways of feeding herself that the others obviously didn't. As they all picked the last bits of fish from the bones and surveyed the chaos of their camp, Aleksia finally spoke up, and began explaining herself.

"Well," she said, dryly, looking about at all four of them. "You have probably gathered that I am not the ordinary sort of traveler."

Ilmari snorted. "We are waiting patiently to hear just what sort of traveler you are."

She nodded, and launched into her part of this tale. Or rather, she explained as much of herself as she felt comfortable revealing. The Sammi did not have Godmothers; Ilmari and Lemminkal might have heard of them, Annukka and Kari probably had not. She had announced herself as "Godmother Aleksia" and gotten no recognition from any of them, so she elected to leave that out. Knowledge of The Tradition, Traditional magic and Traditional paths was anything but common, and it was acknowledged among the Godmothers that it was probably best not to spread that sort of information too widely. Aleksia didn't see any reason why this should change. Such information would do them no good, and might cause them to second-guess themselves at a moment when that was the last thing they all needed. So she glossed over the business of being a Godmother, leaving it as vague as she possibly could. And if she left them with the impression that she was merely a sort of sentry mounting a simple watch over the North, that was just fine. They gathered that she was considered a powerful and important Sorceress among her own folk, and that would certainly do.

"And you keep watch, why?" Lemminkal asked.

"To report troubles to those better able to deal with them," she said easily, because that was certainly true. "Various Orders of Champions, for instance." That was also true. "I supply them with information they cannot otherwise obtain." She didn't want the Sammi to get the impression that she was some sort of guardian who could be counted on to come to the rescue if any little thing went wrong. That was not what Godmothers did. And it wasn't as if she didn't have quite enough on her plate as it was without starting that. Fixing things was the job of Champions and Heroes. Trying to make sure they wouldn't need fixing—that was for the Godmothers.

"Bah. Champions." Lemminkal snorted, but his eyes were twinkling. "Everyone knows that a true Hero goes up against incredible odds all on his own!"

"Perhaps that is true for the Sammi, but it is not so elsewhere," she temporized, and went on.

However, when it got to specifics—well, she was quite willing to be specific.

"Mirror-magic," she told them. "That is my specialty, really. I can watch through mirrors, or any reflective surface. I can talk to people at a distance that way, if they are magicians or have a magic mirror, and sometimes I can work other magic through the mirrors. That was how I learned about the one you are calling the Snow Witch, how she had taken my name and even the look of my Palace. The harm she was causing! That was when I knew I must become involved."

She was adept at reading body language, and when it came down to it, the two men were surprisingly simple souls. They trusted her now, and would continue to do so unless she betrayed them—the fatal Traditional flaw and strength of most Heroes. In that, The Tradition was working for her. Ilmari nodded. "Being able to do things at a distance— that is most useful."

Kaari also trusted her, probably because Kaari's nature was constructed on trust. Annukka was the only one more reserved, and for someone like Annukka, only time would help. That was fine. She suspected that they thoroughly understood each other. "The Snow Witch, at least, does not seem to use mirror-magic, so despite having my name, she does not seem to be using powers like mine. This means I can probably continue to watch her." She hesitated, then added, "From all that I can see, she has learned all she knows from books, and has never ventured outside the magics associated with ice, snow and cold." There. For a Wise Woman, a Wonder-smith and a Warrior-Mage, she had just delivered an enormously important piece of information. "I am not sure she can detect magic if it is not associated with those things. And I am also not sure she is looking very hard for magical opposition. She seems very..." she hesitated "...*tired,* is the only word I have for this. As if she has been doing this for too long."

Ilmari pursed his lips. "Still, it does not do to take risks—"

"No," she agreed. "It does not. I do not use magic if I do not have to. And I am not going to underestimate this foe. I know that I have not sensed anyone searching for magic since we fought the Icehart—"

"Nor have I," Ilmari was quick to say, as Lemminkal and Annukka both shook their heads. "But in that we may simply have had great good luck that we cannot count on. Any magic that we use from now on, should be small and personal, and as far from ice, snow and cold as can be. There is no point in shouting our presence for all the world to hear."

Relieved, Aleksia nodded, and was going to leave it at that.

But Annukka added, rather too casually, "But Aleksia can shape-shift, too."

Bother. I was hoping to surprise them. She sensed that her mirror-magic did not much impress Ilmari with its practical application to their current problems, and she did not seem to have much that was useful in *fighting* the Snow Witch. She had been thinking she might be able to set him off balance by transforming in front of them.

Ilmari raised a bushy eyebrow, and winced a little as the skin of his forehead wrinkled. "And you intended to tell us of this, when?"

"Soon enough," she replied crossly. "Since I was going to shift to a bird to scout ahead when we leave." She was rather put out, actually. She had been hoping to astonish the men at least a little.

"Speaking of leaving…" Annuka glanced over the camp meaningfully. "It really is time we were going."

"Then I will hunt and scout a little ahead," Aleksia told them, eager enough to get out of the packing up and cleaning up. "I will bring back some game to add to our stores. You will be a while organizing things."

"More than a while," Ilmari grumbled a little. "Let me pack the sledge, if you please. It is a wonder you didn't turn over a dozen times, top-heavy as it is—"

Annuka threw up her hands. "By all means—since you are so much more expert at such things!"

They eyed each other with the resentment only two strong personalities looking for ascendancy could show. Before the exchange got heated, Aleksia made the transformation and flung herself into the sky.

She had chosen the Gyrfalcon this time, because among other things, she wanted to hunt. Urho was a good fellow, but there were five of them now, and he would be hard-pressed to feed them all. With the Gyrfalcon form she was able to get very high indeed, and the bird's keen sight enabled her to see things very, very far beneath her. While she could not take down a deer—well, she *could,* if she was very lucky and very clever, but it was unlikely—there were plenty of things she could kill.

Finally she found what she had hoped for: a flock of geese fitfully dozing on the surface of a completely frozen lake. She studied them from above. She was white, against a blue sky swirled with plumes of cloud. She was much harder to see than, say, an eagle. They were not aware of her.

This would have to be carefully done. She would have to do the work of a full cast of Falcons, but if all went well, she would be able to take down two geese at least, and possibly four. One would feed all of them dinner—except Urho, and he could and would hunt for himself.

Now one of the pastimes that she *had* enjoyed with the Court in the days when she was Princess Aleksia had been falconry. Well, not precisely with the Court—she had preferred to go out with the serious hunters, her father's chief falconer and his men and the few—mostly older—men and women who took the sport with great gravitas. Now everything she had learned from that good man would stand her in good stead.

But this would take care, planning and exquisite timing.

She could do this.

She set herself up carefully, choosing her first target, one of the birds with its head under its wing. This goose would have to wake up, and then get her direction, before she could even begin to try to escape. And a Falcon's attack was all about fractions of moments. If Aleksia did this right, there would be no time for the goose to do more than awaken, and her next target would still be scrambling to escape when she hit it.

When she thought she had everything thought through as perfect as could be, she took a long, deep breath, folded her wings and dove.

She had set herself up so that she dove out of the sun, taloned feet tucked tight to her body, wings clamped down hard. The geese literally did not see her until she was practically on them. Then with a chorus of panicked honks, and an explosion of pinions, they tried to make their escape. She kept her focus on the one chosen as her target. It had thrown up its head, eyes still a little sleep-dazed, and was looking for where the attacker was. She was practically atop it. At that last minute her feet shot out—

But she did not have those talons extended. Instead, they were curled into small, hard fists, and as she closed with her quarry, she lashed out with those fists. She felt the shock as her feet impacted the back of the goose's head, felt the transmitted shock in her legs as she broke its neck and shattered the back half of her quarry's head. The goose flopped to

the snow; she used the momentum of the impact to bounce up, and
snapped her wings open to claw for height again. The Raptor's wonderful eyes scanned the panicking geese below. More than half of them
still did not know what was wrong. One simply stood there, craning his
neck, still trying to see where the attacker was—

She did a wingover and dove again, aiming for that bird. There was
not as much force to this blow, but it was still enough to break the
second bird's neck. She bounced up again, and drove herself into the
sky with the most powerful wing-beats she could manage. She needed
more height. If she was about to tail-chase, she needed speed, and
plenty of it.

She folded her wings and dropped again, her eyes fixed on a bird that
was only now beginning the labored effort to escape. Its goal, of course,
was to get enough speed to flee. Hers was to hit it before it could.

Time slowed to a crawl. She watched the wings of her target pump
with agonizing slowness, watched the goose's neck stretch out, caught
the frantic roll of its eye as it looked behind it and saw her coming, saw
the sudden, desperate effort, the last pump of wings—

And she hit it, as she had the others, sending it crashing into the ice of
the lake. And ahead of her, a fourth bird was on the same path and if she
tried, if she put impossible effort into it, she might be able to catch it.

She opened her wings and drove toward it. It glanced back at her and
redoubled its efforts. She did the same. She was closing on it. She was nearly
there. She swung her feet forward, talons extended, reaching, reaching—

The goose shuddered once, and was still as they hit the ground.

She rested there a moment, panting, fighting the Falcon instinct that
screamed at her to feed even though her stomach was still comfortably
full. Then she shoved herself into the air again, to make certain of the
other four birds, while the rest of the flock, honking their fear and
distress, arrowed away toward the south.

* * *

She had gone human and strung the geese together at the neck then changed to Bear form to come galumphing back with the geese draped over her neck and shoulders. One bird had been gutted—that had been her true breakfast, a feast for a bird of prey, and it wasn't as if the others would miss goose-innards. Her father's master falconer would have been astonished—and pleased. She had used everything she had ever learned about hunting with birds, and applied it to bring down four quarry. Four! It was unheard of for a single Falcon to do that in so short a period of time! Of course, this was a Falcon with a human's mind, but still it was unusual even for a full cast of Falcons to bring down that many quarry at once.

And four geese meant that they could eat for four days without dipping into their precious stores or hoping that she and Urho would find something. Goose would be a nice change from hare and rabbit and dried meat, too.

All this was in her mind as she closed on the camp, looking forward to the astonishment and pleasure that she would see in the faces of the others at her prizes.

But instead, she saw them all huddled together, and heard the sound of sobbing.

She increased her trot to a gallop, and transformed from Bear to human on the run, the geese flopping awkwardly against her as she ran. Kaari was weeping, with Annukka trying to comfort her, Lemminkal standing by awkwardly and Ilmari a bit apart, looking—guilty.

She flung her grotesque necklace of heavy geese aside on the sledge as she reached them, seizing Ilmari's arm and hissing, *"What did you do?"*

"She showed us the loving-cup," he said, hunching his shoulders. "And I told her that since Veikko could be at no great distance, and since I had some of his things still with us, I could probably scry for him using very little power. And that would at least serve to show us if he was still well—"

He gestured awkwardly at a tiny forge fire lying between him and Kaari, that had his forge hammer lying beside it. And there in the flames—

Was a scene that she herself had seen not all that long ago. The crude throne room. The Snow Witch on her throne. The shambling, clumsy snow-servants.

And Veikko, in a pose of great intimacy, sitting at the Snow Witch's feet and leaning against her leg.

No wonder Kaari was crying.

Aleksia was furious, both at Ilmari and herself. She should have known that something like this would happen. Someone like Ilmari could not resist someone like Kaari. Never mind that the girl was the betrothed of his brother's apprentice. The relationship of Master and apprentice had kept Lemminkal from even considering pursuing Kaari for himself—but not Ilmari.

Stupid, stupid man!

She seized Ilmari's arm and dragged him away. "Do you think I am so stupid that I do not know what you are about, *old man?*" she spat. "Old *fool* is more like! You knew very well the sort of state you were likely to find Veikko in! Yes, and you were looking forward to showing Kaari, too, so you could comfort her and win her for yourself! Idiot! You know what her Wyrd is like. And even if it were not, do you think for one moment *she* would look favorably on the advances of a man old enough to be her father? Even if she should give up on Veikko, there are dozens of handsome young men who would be glad to comfort her in her bereavement in her village, and dozens more who have yet to meet her!"

For one moment, Ilmari glared at her, his eyes flashing with rage. He opened his mouth, doubtlessly to give her a scathing piece of his own mind—

And then he stopped, flushed, and hung his head. "You are right," he sighed. "Curse it, you are right. I have been down this road before, and there is no good ending to it."

It was Aleksia's turn to open her mouth to deliver another few choice words—then she stopped. She had said enough. More scolding and nothing would be accomplished, because she would drive this man into the opposite direction, determined to prove her wrong. She must appeal to his better nature.

"Then come and help me show her the truth," she said instead, letting go of his arm. Ilmari nodded, and they both turned toward Kaari.

"Kaari!" she said, sharply enough to make the girl's head come up. Her eyes brimmed with crystal tears that rolled down her cheeks like lovely raindrops. *Curse the girl and her runes,* Aleksia thought, half in annoyance and half in exasperation. *Can she not even cry like a normal woman? Where are the red eyes, the blotched cheeks, the running nose?*

But she could not remain annoyed with Kaari for long, and after all, it was hardly her fault that she was so perfect. She had been outstandingly brave and helpful through all of this, coming into as she did, with no experience and only her own courage and her love for Veikko to sustain her.

"Kaari," she said, in a more kindly tone. "Listen to me. I knew all about this. I saw it all in my mirrors long before I came here. And I did not tell you, because you already knew all that mattered, that Veikko was in peril, and that we must all work to save him." She gestured at the image. "This is all false. This is what the Snow Witch does. Veikko is under a spell, an enchantment, and somewhere under all of that, Veikko is screaming in horror at what he is being made to do." She turned toward Ilmari. "Am I not right?" she asked sharply.

The Wonder-smith shrugged. "The tales are all about how she takes handsome young men and makes them betray everything to follow her.

I have heard of such. I suppose she must have somehow seen Veikko, and decided to take him for herself. I know he would not have gone to her willingly," he said, and added reluctantly, "I cannot imagine Veikko to ever betray the trust of Kaari."

"You see?" Aleksia went on one knee beside the girl, whose eyes were finally starting to reflect hope. "I have *seen* her do this, time and time and time again. I have looked into the past in my mirror. She abducts handsome young men, she puts their hearts, souls and minds under enchantment, and she uses them as she pleases. Veikko is not the first, though with our company, we can ensure he is the last and make her answer for her crimes." She put conviction she in nowise felt into her words, and hoped that Kaari would respond.

She did; it was Kaari's nature always to respond to the promise of hope. That was *her* great weakness—and strength. "We can free him? And he will be the same again?" Her face was alight again.

"That is what I came here to do," she replied. "But you—there is something that *you* must do for him. And only you."

"There is?" For the first time, she had been told that she personally could do something to help her beloved, and it transformed her. Kaari's expression would have melted a harder heart than Aleksia's. Ilmari gulped with guilt, and looked away. Now Aleksia was glad she had not scolded him further. His own sense of guilt would punish him more than any words of hers could.

"Of course there is." She put an awkward hand on the girl's shoulder. "Listen to me. You must keep love in your heart for him. You must concentrate on it, and love him with all your heart. As long as you remain brave and keep that love for him, the Snow Witch can never win, and you strengthen him." She looked up at Ilmari. "Am I correct?"

She could see the struggle in his eyes, but honesty and his better nature won out. "Yes," he said. "Love has an energy, and a magic all of its own. Veikko is a Mage, and that energy will surely reach him and make him stronger. There are tales and tales and tales of such a thing, and I believe them."

In that moment, Aleksia looked up and caught his gaze, and saw something in the man that she had not seen before. He had realized something profound about himself, and in a single moment his soul had—well, grown. There was no other way to put it. She smiled at him, encouragingly. He looked surprised, then smiled back and there was a shyness in that smile that was both odd in one with his years, and strangely endearing.

She stood up. "I will go back into the sky," she said. "For one thing, there are only four deer, and although I could ride Urho while he pulls the sledge, I am of more use where I can see any possible ambushes. I just did some hunting—" She noticed more frozen fish, neatly wrapped in a bit of leather, tied onto the top of the sledge, and smiled. "And with that and what Urho has got for us, we are well-provisioned. Now, let me do some real scouting, and I will come back to you with word."

Without waiting for an answer, she transformed into the Gyrfalcon again—

But before she could labor into the air, Ilmari unexpectedly bent and offered his arm. "Lady?" he said, and smiled. "I am no stranger to falconry, though I have not got a bird at present."

After a moment of surprise, she jumped onto his arm, taking care not to put her talons through his coat and into his arm. He launched her expertly into the sky with a hard shove of his arm upwards, and she labored skyward.

This time she was looking at the horizon, rather than below her— and as a consequence, got a bit of a surprise.

On that horizon was a shape that she recognized from hours and hours of scrying.

The original tower of the Snow Witch was in a valley with a mountain behind it. Now, this was not the most distinctive mountain that Aleksia had ever seen, but after looking at it for so long, she knew she was seeing its shape again.

And that meant that they were not as far from their goal as they had thought. Two or three days at most would bring them to the village outside the gates.

Movement below caught her eye, and she glanced down. It was the rest of the group, finally on the move again. All four deer were being ridden now, as Urho was making light work of the sledge.

I shall have to make sure I stay in some form other than human when we are on the move, Aleksia thought to herself. Bird by preference, really: she could continue to hunt and feed herself easily enough, and coming to earth by night should keep the Falcon from taking over.

She was about to go on ahead when more movement on the trail caught her attention, and she kited back a little.

And that was when she nearly sideslipped out of the sky, she was so startled.

Because following them, and staying just out of sight, was the Icehart. Moving in broad daylight, surrounded by an obscuring mist of ice-fog, passing like a ghost on the face of the snow.

Two days later Aleksia and Ilmari stood quietly just beyond the edge of the firelight, staring at the Icehart. It was doing nothing, except staring back at them. She could sense nothing from it by ordinary means and she hesitated to do anything to it with magic. For now, it was just following them, and given the results of their last confrontation, she did not want to goad it into battle.

"Do you still have the crystal?" Ilmari asked in an undertone. "It might want that…"

"But you don't think so," she stated, staring at the ghostly stag. Moon-light glittered on the points of its antlers, and the misty eyes seemed to be looking right through them.

"You don't, either." Nervously, he rubbed his neck.

"No, I don't," she admitted. "But I also have no idea what it *does* want."

She stared at the strange beast. This was the third night it had come to stand at the edge of their camp and...do nothing. She felt for the crystal in her pocket. It was still there. She weighed all the considerations, and finally decided that, since two nights had gone by without it attacking, it was worth taking a risk.

"I am going to approach it," she told Ilmari. She expected him to object, but instead, he nodded.

"I will go with you," he said instead. It didn't sound like a request, but at this point her nerves were feeling so rattled she decided that not going alone was a very good idea. "Don't worry, I won't attack unless we are attacked first. But I would rather you did not go alone, Aleksia. It took all four of us the last time to defeat it. I would rather you had someone to guard your back."

She nodded. And felt oddly touched. Because he had not blustered that she was merely a woman and could not face this thing—he had given her the courtesy of assuming she was his equal.

The two of them approached the strange deer, their feet making crunch-ing sounds on the snow as they broke through the ice-crust atop it. Tonight there was just enough moonlight to be able to see the Icehart clearly.

It seemed to Aleksia that there was something odd going on with the Icehart's face. The eyes....around the eyes...there was movement.

Then as the Icehart looked away from her for a moment and at Ilmari instead, she realized what it was. She saw shining bits of ice dropping from its cheeks. She had seen that before—when Kaari had wept for the forest-spirits.

"It's *weeping,*" she said, so shocked that she was not sure she was really seeing what she thought she was. "Why would this thing be weeping?"

There was a silence from Ilmari, then the Wonder-smith sighed. "You may think me mad," he said, slowly, "but I believe that it is weeping because it has a broken heart."

She shook her head. None of this was making any sense. First the thing attacked them. Now it followed them, crying. It was clearly intelligent, yet it was not telling them what, if anything, it wanted.

She *knew* it was responsible, in part at least, for the deaths of dozens of people, and yet her heart went out to it.

"How can a spirit have a broken heart?" she asked, falteringly.

Ilmari sighed. "I do not know," he replied, as the Icehart slowly stalked away, leaving them with nothing but questions. "Perhaps it, too, is a victim of the Snow Witch. Perhaps it has lost all it ever cared about to her. All that I know is that not even a Wonder-smith can mend a heart when it is broken."

16

THE VILLAGE WAS NAMED KURJALA, AND ALEKSIA SUSPECTED
this was an attempt at sarcasm, since the word meant "misery." Certainly
it lived up to—or down to—the name. The area seemed to be under
a perpetual overcast. The houses were dark, and poorly repaired, and
the people in them shabby and unsocial. Even the ice and snow in the
streets was filthy. When they first approached the place, she had not at
all been sure there was anyone living there. Only when they actually
entered it did they see the occasional surly or furtive figure crossing a
street ahead of or behind them, although doors were always firmly
closed by the time they reached the spot where the figure had been seen.

Only after they came to what passed for a village market did they
find anyone willing to speak to them. Once they showed their coin,
though, people did come out. Money, it seemed, overcame just about
every other consideration.

The barrier across the Palace gate that Aleksia had seen in her mirror
visions had become a barrier around the entire Palace. There was literally no way to get past it.

The group was now camped outside the wall around the Palace, a good distance from the village at the front gate. They had originally thought to stay within the village, rather than camping, but a quick look through the place had convinced all five of the humans that this was absolutely the last thing they wanted to do. Urho, who must have had some way of telling what lay ahead of them here, had already been convinced that they should not chance the village.

It was full of the most repellant individuals that Aleksia had ever seen.

She remembered the fragment of conversation that she had heard in her mirror-visions. She had assumed that the speakers had meant that the people of this place were being killed by the Snow Witch if they showed any sign of human feeling.

The truth was far worse.

Once they were outside Kurjala and safe from observation, Aleksia took out her hand-mirror and did a touch of scrying. What she saw behind those closed doors shocked and dismayed her, and finally made her put the mirror away, feeling sick. There was no hope here, no love—no kind of human feeling or kindness at all. Even the children were heartless, competing grimly with siblings, if need be, and parents used them as virtual slave labor. But how was that surprising for children born to mothers who gave their bodies to men out of desperation, men who took them with no thought for anything past the fleeting pleasure of the night? There were no marriages here, only temporary alliances for purely material reasons. No real market, no inn, no places of worship or gathering; no beauty, no music, nothing that was not strictly utilitarian. There was, literally, nothing to lift the heart, or even touch it.

In villages this far north, villages that got so few visitors, newcomers were often greeted with enthusiasm and welcome and, if there was no inn, offered a bed with some prominent person of the village.

But here—that was, to put it mildly, not the case. One and all, the villagers turned the travelers away coldly, until Lemminkal offered them money from the bandit store, but even that only bought them fodder for the deer, supplies for themselves and permission to camp outside the wall, not house-room.

They huddled around their fire, looking at the dim lights of the village houses, feeling a depression of spirits so great that it was hard to muster the energy to do anything more than make camp, fix a meal and stare at the fire or into the night.

"Is this us?" Kaari asked, suddenly. "Or is it this place?"

That aroused Lemminkal. "It is the place," the soft-spoken warrior said, with difficulty. "Which must be the work of the Snow Witch…"

"It's what she wants," Aleksia managed. "The more misery, the better."

They had not seen the Icehart since camping here, and Aleksia was not at all surprised. If the creature wept because it had a broken heart now, setting foot in this place would drive it to fling itself off a cliff. She was not all that far from doing the same thing herself. "Whatever made them like this is foul," she said, finally. "Just foul. These folk are worse off than animals. Even animals have joy."

"It is the ice in their hearts," Lemminkal said, unexpectedly.

"What?" Aleksia turned to face him. She could have sworn she had said nothing about how Veikko had been changed.

"I…feel it," the big man said, scratching his head in puzzlement. "It is a part of my magic to feel things. It lets me know what my foe is going to do, and it lets me know what his heart is like. There is ice in their hearts, a tiny grain of it, and it is the ice that has frozen them and made them cold and cruel." He shook his head, showing his grief. "I cannot help them."

"Only defeating the Snow Witch will help them," Annukka responded, lifting her head as if it felt very heavy. Then she patted Lemminkal's hand comfortingly, and the big man put one of his massive paws over hers and held it as if it sustained him. "But how are we to do that if we cannot even get inside?"

Aleksia racked her brains. "We cannot fight her, we cannot force our way in—we have to trick her." She went over the scenes of the Snow Witch in her mind, trying to think of a way to get past the barrier, past the snow-servants and into the Palace. "We have to get her to let us inside, or at least to let us get to Veikko. One of us at any rate."

"You know, she's not an idiot," Ilmari said crossly. "She knows we're here now, if she didn't before. She has probably figured out that we are here for Veikko. Just what do you propose to do about this? Make her forget all that and invite us in for a welcome feast?" As soon as the words were out of his mouth, he flushed. "Forgive me. You did not deserve that. It is this place…"

She had felt a flash of anger, but suppressed it, because he was right. It *was* this place. "No…" Aleksia said, slowly. "But I think I have an idea. What we need to do is make her think that we are weaker than we actually are. Contemptible. She will want to laugh at us, taunt us, and that will bring her to the gate. But we also need something to bargain with. Turn out your packs!" she demanded. "We need the sort of pretty things that women crave! She likes beautiful, rare things that no one else has. She collects them, as she collects beautiful, rare boys."

They all went through their belongings, though in the end they had only two things that Aleksia thought would pass muster; a mother-of-pearl comb that was in Annukka's pack, a beautiful thing carved with seaweed and waves, and a nearly finished kantele, inlaid with so many tiny bits of metal and wire that scarcely anything of the wood could be seen, that had been among Ilmari's things.

"This is stunning," Aleksia said, touching the silk-smooth mosaic with a wondering finger. "I have never seen the like. You are an artist, Ilmari."

"I work on this in my spare time," the Wonder-smith said sheepishly, looking pleased. "I started it for myself, but I never liked it—I thought one day I could give it to someone I wanted to impress." He looked up at her for a moment, and she was flattered to see frank admiration in his eyes. "Perhaps one day I can make one for you."

She felt herself blushing, and quickly went back to the subject. "Can you work some kind of spell on them, so that they become unique as well as beautiful?" Aleksia asked anxiously.

Ilmari looked at both pieces. "Well, this is easy," he said, finally, pointing at his kantele. "I simply work a bit of magic into it so that it plays itself. But this—" He held the comb in his hand for a moment, muttering over it. "I cannot think what one could do with a comb—"

"What if it were to comb hair by itself, and magically untangle all knots?" Aleksia asked, thinking back to hours of misery as a child as her nurses would, none too gently, pull and tug on her hair and her sister to get them both presentable. The Snow Witch had only the crudest of servants, and surely they were about as gentle as Aleksia's nursemaids had been. Perhaps when the Witch had young men, they would do the office, but she did not always have them.

Ilmari turned the comb over and over in his hands, considering it. "Yes," he said, finally. "I can do that. Should I do so tonight?"

"Please. I do not want to linger here any longer than we have to." Aleksia looked at the village and shivered. "I think their heartlessness may be catching."

"All right then, I will prepare my forge," the Wonder-smith said, and then smiled a little. "And do not be alarmed at what I do. I shall not harm these things, though you would not know it to watch me at work."

Indeed, they shook off some of their own low spirits as they watched him prepare the tiny forge. He built it painstakingly from flat rocks culled from the rubble at the base of the wall. When it was done, he shoveled coals from the fire into it, and began to alternately blow on it and chant over it. Aleksia could not hear what he was chanting, and truth to tell, she did not even really try. Every Mage had his or her secrets, and deserved to be able to keep them.

As he chanted and blew, the coals glowed, brighter and hotter, until at last they were white-hot. That was when he took a small pair of tongs from his pack, the forge hammer from his belt, picked up the comb in the tongs and placed it in the fire.

It should have crumbled, or burned up, or otherwise gone to bits. It did nothing of the sort. It, too, began to glow, until it was as white as the coals. He pulled the comb out with the tongs, placed it in a flat rock, and began to hammer on it, chanting in time to his blows.

It was not just random hammer strokes, either. A tap here, a tap there, a heavy overhanded blow, all in time to the chanting—there was a pattern there, but Aleksia could not discern it.

It all blended into a rhythmical whole, though, not unlike Annukka's singing.

"Annukka—do you know any songs that talk of the beauty of a girl's hair?" Lemminkal asked quietly. "If you could sing them to the beat of the hammer—"

Annukka nodded, and blended her own music with that of the forge-song.

Ilmari raised an eyebrow at her and caught her eye. He nodded and Aleksia felt the two songs blend into one, with an unspoken communication between the two Sammi. The spell-singing built to a crescendo, and both ended on the same note, as Ilmari seized the white-hot comb and thrust it into the snow.

Steam rose in clouds around it, filling the camp for a moment, and silence rang hollowly in the absence of the spell-song.

When steam stopped rising in billow from the snowdrift, Ilmari reached gingerly into it and came out with the comb. It would not be fair to say that it was untouched—somehow, it had become more sensual to look at, shining like the light of the moon in his hand. He gave it to Kaari, who, as a maiden, wore her hair unbound—and at the moment, it was rather tangled and tousled from travel.

"Let's see if I'm still good at improvising." The Wonder-smith chuckled. "Try it, Kaari."

Kaari pulled off her hat and headband, and gingerly touched the comb to her hair.

The thing leapt from her hand as if some invisible servant had taken it, and began gliding through the knots and tangles, leaving Kaari's tresses clean, smooth and shining, like a golden waterfall. And when she put her hand up to it, it obligingly left her hair, and lay quietly in her hand.

"Well, there is our first wonder," Ilmari said, with a significant look at Aleksia. "From the look of you, lady, you have a cunning plan."

"I do, and if it works, we won't need a third wonder," the Godmother replied, looking around the fire at her companions. "Nor do I intend to keep you in the dark on this. I want you to think out your parts as you go to sleep. And here they are.

"Kaari," she said, turning to the girl, "yours will be the hardest. My plan is that the three of you who know and love Veikko are to try to get him to recognize you, to crack the shell of magic the Witch has cast about him and get him awakened so that he had fight from within as we fight from without. I intend to use you last of all, but that means that tomorrow, and perhaps the next day, you must stay here in camp and do nothing more than to concentrate with all your heart on Veikko. You must not come down to the gate, and you must not stop thinking about him and how he used to be until we come and tell you otherwise. You remember how Ilmari told you that love has a magic all its own. Can you do that?"

Slowly, Kaari nodded.

"Let me explain this. I will use the three people with whom Veikko has the strongest bonds to try to win him free. First, you, Annukka, his mother. If you fail, on the morrow, Lemminkal will take your place with the kantele—his bond being that not only of mentor and master, but of trusted friend." She smiled as Lemminkal flushed with pleasure. She had not mistaken it, then. She would not further embarrass the old warrior with "father-figure," but she was certain that Lemminkal also filled that role.

"Once again, Kaari, I will ask you to remain here and bend your mind on Veikko." She paused and pursed her lips, thinking. "Now, listen to me carefully. Even if this appears not to work, I swear to you, you will be eroding some of those walls about his heart and mind. As a tree's root slowly cracks a stone, the result might not be visible until it shatters. Do you understand me?"

Kaari nodded.

Aleksia could feel magic, Traditional and otherwise, slowly gathering about them. Even though she did not have a tale to follow, all this had the same *sure and right* feeling that came when a Traditional tale was coming to an end. The trouble was, being inside it, rather than outside it, she could not tell for sure if the ending was going to be a happy one.

"Now you, Kaari, we will save for the third day." She nodded, as the young woman's cheeks flushed. "The Witch will probably think us fools by then. She will underestimate you. She does not know the strength that lies in the heart of a woman that truly loves and is loved."

Like the strength in Gerda's heart, as she held to Kay through all his transformations, or the strength in Annukka's, who has raised her son all alone for the sake of the man who made her his wife. Urho's thoughts rumbled through them all, and Annukka flushed, and her eyes grew very bright. The Bear's words rang true for all of them, even though only Aleksia knew who Kay and Gerda were.

"So, you will be our most potent weapon, Kaari. We will use you when she underestimates us most. It is a good combination." Again she looked around the fire and was pleased to see both men nod in agreement.

"But what will we use for a wonder?" Kaari asked.

At that, Aleksia frowned. "I am not sure yet," she admitted. "But I will think of something. The four of us are skilled workers in many crafts, and Ilmari could probably forge an enchanting brooch from an old buckle and a bit of glass. Now, do we all know our parts?"

All of them nodded.

"Very well, then," she said. "Sleep and rest, and strengthen yourself for tomorrow."

She went immediately to her bedroll to set a good example, although she secretly thought there was a strong likelihood that she would stare at the inside of her eyes for a very long time. To her surprise, as Urho took up his usual position to warm all of them, she felt herself drifting off.

And drifted straight into a dream.

A dream in which the Icehart came, and stood at the barricaded gate, and wept and wept and wept.

Kaari did not try to sleep. Instead, she filled her mind with every memory of Veikko she had—how as a child he had not brought her gifts as the others did, he brought her *to* things—taught her not to fear, by showing her that the things she feared, like climbing trees and learning to swim, were challenges, not obstacles. How he had patiently waited while the other young men made their pleas to her and were rejected, and had never failed to be kind, not only to her, but to the other young men. How she had somehow known that if she *had* fallen in love with one of them, he would have accepted it although his own heart would have been broken, because it was what she wanted. How even when they quarreled, it was because they both wanted what was right, and they just hadn't worked out what that right thing was. How his eyes crinkled at the corners when he laughed, which was often. How he never laughed *at* someone, only *with* the other. How his hand felt, holding hers, strong and sure.

Most of all, how much more alive she and the world felt, just knowing he was in it, and how there was nothing more precious to know that she was loved by, and loved, him.

And with her mind still full to bursting with all of this, she finally fell asleep.

"Are you ready?" Aleksia asked.

Annukka nodded. The villagers had followed them, radiating mingled curiosity and hostility, as far as the short road to the gate. There, they hastily turned back and closed themselves in their houses. Aleksia sensed eyes peering at them from behind the shutters, but the villagers were not about to show themselves if there was going to be a challenge at the Witch's gate.

Annukka was dressed in Aleksia's fine white clothing, while Aleksia had donned Annukka's things. It would do no harm for the Snow Witch to think—if she even knew about Godmothers and the Ice Fairy—that it was Annukka who was the Snow Queen and was the person whose name and reputation she was ruining. That might give Annukka a measure of protection she would not otherwise have, as the Witch might hesitate to attack someone that powerful.

Lemminkal put down the piece of stump he had been carrying for Annukka to sit on. Annukka took her seat gravely, with Lemminkal holding her hand for a long moment as she did so. Then he and the others withdrew—close enough to spring to her defense, but far enough to, hopefully, not look like a threat. Annukka took down her braids and undid them, took out the comb and touched it to her hair, and sat with her hands in her lap, waiting, the very personification of patience as the comb worked its magic. Lemminkal did not take his eyes off her, his very stillness betraying his intense anxiety.

Eventually one of the snow servants came to the Barrier. A hole formed in its head where a mouth would have been. "Who are you?" it said, in a voice like the cold echo from the back of an ice-cave. "What do you want?"

Annukka did not answer for a moment. Then, "That is for your mistress's ears alone," she replied, with great dignity.

The thing repeated its questions twice more, but Annukka did not answer. The comb moved through her hair, gleaming, the brightest thing in that dead landscape. Annukka remained, unmoving and unmoved. Eventually the snow-servant went away.

There was a commotion at the door of the Palace on the other side of the Barrier. Something was coming toward the gate.

It quickly resolved into a sleigh drawn by two horses—but the horses, like the servants, were crude snow statues barely recognizable as horses, and the sleigh seemed to be made of ice. The entire rig pulled up beside the gate, and from the other side of the Barrier, the Snow Witch glared at them from her seat in the sleigh.

And the driver, seemingly indifferent to everything around him, was Veikko.

Annukka let the comb continue to do its work for a moment longer, then put her hand up to it. It stopped, and fell into her hand.

She held it, and simply looked at the Snow Witch, neither showing subservience nor fear.

The Witch looked possessively at the gleaming comb in her hand. "Your comb," she said abruptly. "I want it."

"I can well imagine," Annukka replied, neutrally. "There is not another like it in the world."

The Witch's eyes practically lit up with greed. "I will give you a diamond the size of my hand," she said.

Annukka shook her head. "I do not want diamonds. I want an hour with that man—" and she pointed at Veikko.

The Witch barked a startled laugh. "With my *leman?* Why? It will do you no good. He is mine, heart and mind and soul, and even if he were not, *you* are old enough to be his mother!"

Aleksia held her breath. *Tell only the truth,* she silently urged Annukka. Only the truth would serve them here. Every lie would make the Witch's power stronger.

"As it happens, I *am* his mother," said Annukka, mildly. The Witch started, and laughed. Annukka held out the comb. "One hour, alone with him, and this is yours."

"You may not take him by force," the Witch said sharply. "He will come no farther than the gate. And you may not have those companions I see lurking there anywhere near him."

"Done," said Annukka, and the Barrier came briefly down, the gate swung open and Veikko came down stiffly from the driver's seat of the sleigh and walked across to his mother. The Barrier went up again, in a flash of blue, looking like the Northern Lights.

"Give the comb to him," said the Witch from her sleigh.

Annukka did so. Veikko pocketed the comb with no sign of recognition, and stood beside the gate, indifferently.

Then began what Aleksia was sure was possibly the most painful hour of Annukka's life, except perhaps when her husband had died. As Veikko stood there with about the same amount of expression as the gateposts, she begged him to recognize her. A cruel smile fixed itself on the Witch's face as she watched Annukka and listened to her pleading. Annukka used every ploy she could think of, telling Veikko stories out of his own childhood, reminding him of past joys and sorrows, scolding him, praising him, weeping over him. She sang him lullabies, described the cloak she was making for him. All to no avail. And when she had talked, wept, begged herself hoarse, the last moments of the hour trickled away, the Barrier dropped, Veikko turned on his heel and left her, and the gates closed and the Barrier came up again. As they all watched, Veikko took his seat as the driver of the sleigh again, handed the Witch her comb, took up the reins and turned the horses. With a final triumphant smile, the Witch was driven back to her mockery of a Palace.

Lemminkal sprinted for the gate, gathered Annukka in his arms and led her away to the rest. When the pair reached Ilmari, Aleksia and Urho, they could all see that she was sobbing silently. Once among friends, Lemminkal folded his arms around her and let her sob into his chest, silently stroking her hair.

There was silence for a long time, as Annukka cried herself out.

Lemminkal cleared his throat, breaking the silence.

"Well," he said, carefully. "Tomorrow, we will have to work even harder."

Lemminkal sat at the gates of the Witch's Palace, on the stump they had put there yesterday. He was not dressed in finery; instead, he was wearing his shabbiest and most ill-used clothing. They had the Witch's attention, after all, and now she knew how the game was to be played. So Lemminkal was playing the feeble, absentminded old man, and providing a contrast, given his dilapidated condition, to the kantele on his lap. The last thing they wanted the Witch to know was that he was a Warrior-Mage.

Ilmari and Aleksia had debated over the presentation for some time last night. The truth was, the men didn't have anything that was the equal of Aleksia's outfit, and they didn't have time nor the energy to spare to conjure one up—not even if they used one of his two existing sets of clothing to build from. Granted, they could put an illusion over Lemminkal, but the Witch could probably see through illusion, and she would laugh at them.

So Ilmari's reasoning had gone, and eventually Aleksia had agreed with him.

Lemminkal carefully unwrapped the kantele from the hide it had been stored in, and put it into position on his knees. He plucked three of the strings, then took his hands away, and the kantele began to play by itself.

This time, there was no snow-servant to ask what it was that they wanted. The Witch drove down from the Palace with Veikko, and sat in her sleigh, staring with lust at the kantele.

"I have not heard music in a very long time," she said, in hushed tones. "And even then—it was never music like this! Will it play for anyone, as the comb works for anyone?"

"Yes," Lemminkal said, simply.

"And what do you want for it?" the Witch asked breathlessly, her eyes fixed on the strings. "I will give you all the gold you can carry away."

"There is not another like it in the world," Lemminkal replied. "And we want the same as yesterday. One hour, with him."

The Witch barked a startled laugh. "I could make you as rich as a king!" she scoffed. "I could give you near-immortality! I could give you an army of snow creatures so that you could go out and seize power wherever you choose! What kind of fool are you?"

Lemminkal just smiled. "Give me an hour and find out."

With a shrug, the Witch brought down the Barrier, and once again, Veikko crossed, to stand indifferently in the face of everything that Lemminkal could think of to bring to bear on him.

At the end of the hour, the result was the same. Veikko crossed back to the carriage. The Witch watched him, with an odd glance cast at Lemminkal, and again, they returned to her Palace.

When Lemminkal, Annukka, Aleksia and Ilmari returned to camp, they found Kaari in what could only be described as a state. She was not hysterical, not yet, but it was very clear that with a small push, she could be.

"I tried and tried!" she said frantically, her fists balled up in Urho's fur. The Bear winced, but said nothing and did not try to pull away. "There wasn't even a glimmer! There was nothing! And we have no more treasures to offer! What are we to do?"

"Stop." Aleksia held up a hand. She had just felt a now-familiar chill on the back of her neck, and out of the corner of her eye, she caught a glimpse of something pale....

She grasped Kaari by the shoulders and turned her to face in that direction.

Slowly, the Icehart stepped forward, toward them. As the firelight touched its face, they could see it was weeping. It bowed its head to Aleksia—or was it to Kaari?—and uttered a low moan.

Then it faded out and was gone. And Aleksia knew, in that moment, what Kaari was to offer the Witch.

"I do not think it is an accident that the Icehart followed us here," Aleksia said, in a low voice. "I do not think that it is an accident that it left that crystal with us. It wants us to put that stone in her hands. And when that happens—I think the Icehart holds the key to defeating her. Now. This is what you will do tomorrow. You will go to the gate and you will sit, without any treasure in your hands. The Witch will not think that she has anything to fear from a pretty, helpless-looking girl like you." Aleksia's chin firmed. "But she will be wrong."

Kaari sat quietly at the gate to the Snow Witch's Palace, hands folded in her lap, doing nothing. Aleksia and the others stood by, as they had for the past two days. The tension in the air was so palpable that even some of the villagers had ventured out of their houses to stand beside their doors and watch. Poor Kaari was as pale as the snow around her, but her hands had not trembled and her voice had been firm as she had rehearsed what she was to say.

It took longer for the Witch to emerge this time, perhaps because

Kaari had nothing obvious to attract her attention. But curiosity got the better even of her, and eventually, out she came.

Annukka wondered if Kaari would break when she got her first glimpse of Veikko. Fiercely, she willed the girl to hold—and aside from a single strangled sob when Veikko did not even look at her, hold she did.

"Well?" the Witch called, when Kaari said, and displayed, nothing. "What do *you* want?"

"I have something better than either of the first gifts," Kaari replied, her voice sounding breathless, but not shaky. "But it is so precious that I think it should be put directly in your hands so that you can see it for yourself." She gulped. "You must open the Barrier at the gate for me, and let me inside."

"Your friends may not pass," the Witch countered, with a faint sneer in their direction. "They had their chance and failed, and I don't trust them not to try to—renegotiate our bargain. But you don't look as if you have the courage to frighten a rabbit." She looked down her nose at Kaari. "Very well. You may come inside."

She gestured, and the Barrier dropped. Kaari got up and walked unsteadily across the place where it had been.

"Well?" the Witch said sharply.

Wordlessly, Kaari reached into the pocket of her coat and offered the Witch the strange blue crystal, shaped like half a heart, that Aleksia had given to her.

To her obvious surprise, and Aleksia's fierce joy, the Witch's face— changed. She lost the sneer and the superior attitude. In fact, had any of them put a name to that expression at that moment, it would probably have been "shock."

The Witch, face gone paper-white, reached out and carefully took the crystal. Cradling it in both hands, she stood there staring at it.

Kaari ran to Veikko.

But Veikko was paying no attention to her, or to anyone else. He was indifferent to the Witch's state, and he didn't recognize Kaari. As she flung her arms about him, he looked down at her with a puzzled expression, as if he was trying to think, not of who she was, but how to get rid of this unwanted encumbrance.

Behind Aleksia there was a sound of wind in lonely valleys, and the unsettling sensation that suddenly she was alone on an empty glacier—utterly alone. And always had been. And always would be. Forever, living—and dying—alone.

She shuddered, and a little moan escaped her. And it was at that moment that she felt someone's hand fumble for hers.

Ilmari—

Warmth spread from his hand to hers, even through their fur gloves. And warmth from hers to his. Suddenly the loneliness receded, as snow does from a fire. It was still out there—but it could not touch her anymore.

From behind came a breath of bitter cold, the tinkle of shattering ice—

And the Icehart shouldered them all gently aside as it pushed its way through and past them, and walked with slow, deliberate footsteps toward the gate, toward the heart and toward the one holding the heart.

Aleksia smothered an exclamation. Ilmari's hand clamped on her hand with excitement. "Now she's done it!" he muttered. "Now she's let the enemy in! Now she is going to pay, and pay, and pay—"

They waited, breathlessly, for the Icehart to attack.

It did nothing of the sort.

It simply stood there, staring at the Witch. The Witch stared into the crystal, then slowly turned her head to look at the Icehart without any sign of recognition.

But now Aleksia could see the form of a man faintly over that of the deer.

Her eyes widened as enlightenment dawned. "Ilmari! Annukka!" she hissed. "Help me! I must spellcast *now!*"

Bringing her free hand up in a beckoning gesture, she suddenly felt a tidal wave of Traditional magic engulf her. She gathered it up, spun it around her, building it into the one spell, the first spell that every God-mother learned when she first was allowed to do the truly Kingdom-shattering magics—

The Spell of Restoration.

You learned to do it—that did not mean you ever would. You might never see that much power in your lifetime. The Spell of Restoration had one purpose—it *restored*. It put things back the way they should be. It was possible, it was said, for it to raise the dead with enough power. That would be the power of a god—and so far as Aleksia knew, no one had ever done that. But with enough power behind it, the kind that a Godmother might see in her lifetime, it could *make everything right again*.

She felt Ilmari steady her, heard Annukka humming to help her hold the form of the spell in the dizzying rush of power. She felt the words forming in her mind. Simple words, for the strongest spells were the simplest. She was the center of a hurricane of power, but within it, she could feel the others, steadying her, feeding her. Kaari, burning hot with love and devotion. Annukka and Lemminkal, pillars of steadfast affec-tion. Urho, a mountain of loyalty. Ilmari, holding firm, decent and honorable, scarred with harsh lessons, but the stronger for all that. And all of them holding the same vision to make it right for everyone.

All will be well—naught shall go ill. Let joy return again—so this I will!

The Spell completed, it exploded like a firework only she and her helpers could see. She felt it spread all across this part of the world, felt the power wash over the villagers and instantly melt the ice that had bound their souls in fetters harder than iron, felt the moment that they became human again.

But what was immediately in front of her was that the Icehart, the great spirit stag, transformed in an instant to the fairly tangible spirit of a man, and speechlessly held out his arms to the Snow Witch.

The Witch stared at him, dumbfounded, too overcome by shock to show the joy that was about to erupt inside her. But it was there. It was there—the heart was thawing, and in a moment, it would all burst out.

And then it did. Tears sprung into her eyes, and her voice was fraught with mingled anguish and love. "I thought you lost! I swore I would never love again, nor let any other love exist!"

The spirit sighed and in his voice was the sound of wind in all the mournful places of the world. "An enemy caught me far away, all unaware and alone and bound me to the form of the Icehart. I swore I would walk the world until I found you again, but the magic you held against love kept me out, until these helped me in."

There was a trembling in the air, as something in the Snow Witch's power weakened and broke. Veikko made a small sound, and dropped to his knees, staring at the Witch.

The Witch and the spirit rushed to each other and fell into each others' arms.

Kaari, who had been crying silently, bent to embrace Veikko protectively. Her tears fell on his face.

There was another sensation of trembling, then of cracking. The light suddenly came back into his eyes, and he recognized her.

"Kaari?" he said incredulously. She uttered a wordless cry of relief and love and joy.

With a sound like thunder, the snow-servants burst apart, the Barrier evaporated and the Palace cracked in half and began to cave in on itself, as the wall around the palace shook. The man who had been the Icehart, and the woman who had been the Snow Witch, paid no heed, blissfully lost in each other's arms.

Ilmari uttered an oath and ran into the gate, with Lemminkal close behind. They seized Kaari and Veikko and fled with them just as the earth shook, cracked, ice-fog erupted from the cracks obscuring the pair still clasped in an unbreakable embrace and the wall began to tumble down.

Epilogue

"SO...THIS IS ALL THAT IS LEFT OF THEM?"

Aleksia shrugged. "I have no idea," she replied to Ilmari. "But those trees weren't there before."

There was no sign, now, that anything had ever been here. Palace, walls, servants, even the original stone tower, were all gone. All that was left was an expanse of ice and snow that would probably be a fine meadow in the Spring, with two trees in the midst of it. One was an ash, one a linden, and they were twined so closely about each other that there was no telling where one ended and the next began. They were leafless now, but Aleksia sensed a vitality in them that meant that when Spring came, they would make a glorious show.

Behind them, the village once called "Misery" was now looking a great deal less dour. People spoke to each other in the streets, houses were being repaired, children played. Lemminkal and Annukka had performed six marriages already, and there was talk of building a church and finding a priest.

No one wanted to talk about the way things had been. Aleksia did not blame them. She actually hoped that the Spell of Restoration had cleansed some of that from their minds, and replaced it with dimmed memories. No one deserved to have the memory of that kind of inhumanity on his shoulders.

Kaari and Veikko had already been sent home with Urho pulling their sledge. They would be living in Annukka's house for now....

And now the four who were left were waiting for the Godmother's sleigh that Rosemary had sent, and surveying the changed landscape.

"Spring will be beautiful here," murmured Annukka, at Aleksia's left. "And if ever there was a place in need of a Wise One...there are vacant homes in plenty here, sad to say, and if I were to remain, Veikko and Kaari would not need to build a place of their own." She smiled a little crookedly. "Kaari will make a good Wise One, I think."

"I am too old to be a warrior anymore, Autumn Flower," Lemminkal murmured. "But it occurs to me that it might be in me to be a good leader of such a place. Of course, if you would have me—"

Annukka's enthusiastic embrace would have confirmed her thoughts on that subject to the most skeptical of men—which, of course, Lemminkal was not.

"It is time for me to go back to my place." Aleksia sighed. "I will be glad to sleep in a bed...and have someone cook for me...and, yes, even to steer the lives of feckless children who are not careful of what they wish for." But she felt a pang as she said it. She was going to miss having adventures.

And she was going to miss the company of others. Ilmari, especially....

He cleared his throat. "As to that," he said cautiously. "Would you be averse to a neighbor? There is much I can learn from you. And perhaps I can give you a little help with those feckless children."

She smiled, broadly, feeling warm inside. "A neighbor would be very welcome," she replied. "And a little help would be useful."

He coughed, and looked down at his feet a moment, then up into her eyes, as he flushed. "And more than that?" he asked hopefully.

She smiled, as unaccustomed warmth filled her heart. "One never knows," she said. "We'll.....see."

TE DUE / DATE DE RETOUR

JUL 1 0 2008		
2 4 2008		
A 2008		
AU 008		
A 8		
N		
J		
MAY		
CARR		

38-297